The
TIDE OF WAR

SETH HUNTER

headline
review

First published in 2009 by HEADLINE REVIEW
An imprint of HEADLINE PUBLISHING GROUP

First published in paperback in 2010 by HEADLINE REVIEW
An imprint of HEADLINE PUBLISHING GROUP

1

Cataloguing in Publication Data is available from the British Library

ISBN 978 0 7553 5761 1 (B Format)
ISBN 978 0 7553 4310 2 (A Format)

Typeset in Sabon by Avon DataSet Ltd,
Bidford-on-Avon, Warwickshire

Printed and bound in the UK by CPI Mackays, Chatham ME5 8TD

Headline's policy is to use papers that are natural, renewable and
recyclable products and made from wood grown in sustainable forests.
The logging and manufacturing processes are expected to conform
to the environmental regulations of the country of origin.

HEADLINE PUBLISHING GROUP
An Hachette UK Company
338 Euston Road
London NW1 3BH

www.headline.co.uk
www.hachette.co.uk

For Pat

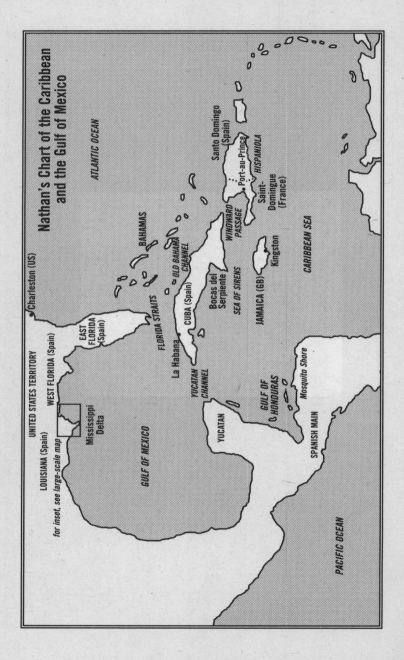

Nathan's Chart of the Caribbean and the Gulf of Mexico

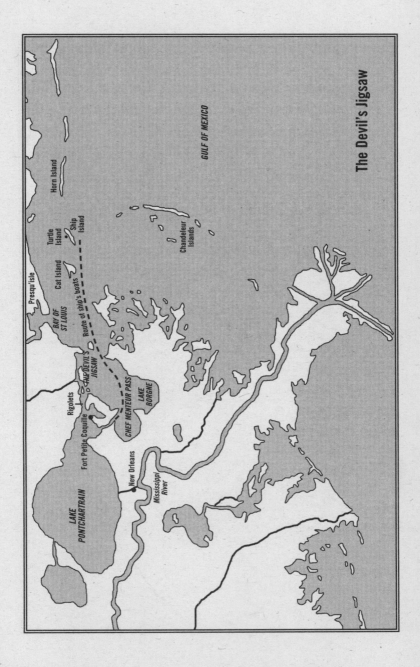

The Devil's Jigsaw

New Orleans, 1794

The body had been brought up from the coast in a hogshead of rum, and at the governor's request they fished it out for him and laid it on a tarp, the head lolling horribly in the glare of the new oil lamps from Philadelphia. Several of the spectators crossed themselves and the governor turned his head and held a lace handkerchief to his patrician nostrils.

Another problem. As if he did not have enough with the French and the Americans. And the Indians and the bandits and the Negroes and the spies and all the other little pleasantries that New Orleans had to offer.

He observed the young officer with dislike. Why did you not bury it, he thought, or throw it back in the sea? But oh no, he had to pollute a perfectly good barrel of rum and take it on a three-day journey through the swamps and bayous of the Mississippi Delta just to add to the miseries of a colonial governor in the service of His Most Catholic Majesty the King of Spain.

'I have brought something I think you will want to see, Excellency.'

Wrong, *Teniente*, you smirking son of a Havana whore, this is not something I want to see. What I want to see is the snow falling on a frozen lake in Flanders or the dew rising from a field of poppies on a September morning. What I want to see is a neat, ordered landscape: a vista of windmills and canals and ploughed fields and gentle rivers of clear water and silver fish – rivers that know their place and stick to that place and do not constantly move about like the murky creeks of Louisiana; and good, honest peasants who know *their* place and are content to abide there without complaint and are not forever promising to split your skull with a cutlass or a tomahawk or whatever other vile piece of weaponry comes to hand in this armpit of the Spanish Empire.

Baron Francisco Luis Hector de Carondelet, Knight of Malta, Governor-General of Louisiana and West Florida, Native of Flanders . . .

Who Died Far from his Home in the Service of the King of Spain . . .

Whenever he signs his name of late he sees the inscription on his tomb. If he should be so fortunate as to possess such a luxury.

'Did I not do the right thing, Excellency?' A frown of concern on the officer's bovine countenance as it dawned on him that his initiative might not be appreciated in this instance, might not provide a secure route to promotion.

Carondelet gazed over the capital of his province, easily visible from the levee now that the new street lamps had been installed. Eighty of them: his latest innovation, purchased and maintained by a chimney tax in the teeth of fierce opposition from the Cabildo, the colonial seat of government, God rot them. Already murders were down by half for the time of year. He could have wished, of course, that the streets they illuminated had been more elegant, the population more deserving, but New Orleans was a frontier town: a sanctuary for the riff-raff and renegades of the Americas, the repository of 5,000 souls long since sold to the Devil.

And now this.

The governor sighed. 'Where did you find it?'

'It was found floating near the shore, Excellency, near the mouth of the Rigolets.'

The Rigolets. The Gutter. A winding channel from the Gulf of Mexico to Lake Pontchartrain: the back door to New Orleans. There was a possibility that the body had been washed up from way out to sea – and the death blamed on pirates or the French – but only a faint one, given the predators native to these waters.

From over to his right, among the taverns of the waterfront under the black bulk of the eastern redoubt, came a raucous blast somewhat between a bellow and a roar of fiendish laughter which the governor identified as the sound of a conch, known locally as *boca del diablo*, the mouth of the devil, and normally used by the crew of a small riverboat – *caboteur* or *goelette* – to announce their arrival in this city of sin and the certain prospect of custom for the innkeepers and whores who infested it. In its wake came an even more hellish sound, at least to the governor's ears: a strident verse of the 'Marseillaise', the anthem of the French revolutionists, which he had succeeded in banning from the streets and the theatres but not – alas – from the taverns. Not yet.

Only last night, he had written to the Duke of Alcudia, Secretary of State in Madrid, assuring him that the recent report conveyed by one of his agents was misleading and alarmist. He recalled his exact words:

By extreme vigilance and sleepless nights, by scaring some and punishing others, by banishing those who were debauching the people with their Republican teaching, by intercepting letters and documents suspected of being incendiary, I have done better than I expected and the Province is now quite orderly and quiet.

Another blast from the devil's mouth, mocking his illusions.

'You do not think I have seen enough corpses in my time here?' he enquired sardonically of his anxious subordinate. 'You think perhaps I am desirous of adding to the collection?'

'Yes, Excellency. I mean, no, Excellency. But this one . . . I thought . . .' He made a gesture at the object at his feet. 'I thought exceptional.'

He was right, of course, for all the inconvenience it would cause.

Exceptional it most certainly was.

For it wore the uniform of a captain in His Britannic

Majesty's Navy, and despite the post-mortem attentions of beak and claw, it was apparent that the original cause of its discomfort was the livid gash in the throat that came close to separating the head from the body – a wound that had almost certainly been made by a knife or some such other sharp-edged instrument of human devising, making any subsequent violations entirely superfluous.

Chapter One

On the Beach

———◆———

Commander Nathan Peake of His Britannic Majesty's Navy stood up to his knees in water, bearded, browned by the sun, his canvas ducks rolled to the thigh and a straw hat upon his head: the very Neptune of his domain, save that instead of the traditional trident he carried a large net, this being considered a more suitable implement on the south coast of England for the hunting of that native delicacy, the prawn.

A movement in the mud at his feet, the merest clouding of the pristine waters and he had it. A slender crustacean about the size and colouring of a grasshopper but by no means as pert, with twitching antennae as long as its body and thin scuttling legs. They scuttled in vain. Into the bucket it went, to join its five brothers – or sisters. All as one in the pot.

'*Encore! Et encore une fois!*'

Looking up, Nathan beheld the figure of a small boy

who had scrambled to the top of a neighbouring rock with a large bucket clutched in both hands.

'*Vingt crevettes. J'ai gagné. Je suis le vainqueur, n'est-ce pas?*'

He looked so happy Nathan did not have the heart to remind him to speak English, though the lapse into a foreign tongue – the tongue of their past and present enemy – would have called for a sharp rebuke in certain quarters not so very far from here.

'Well done,' Nathan replied in the King's English. 'Yes, you are the victor, Alex – for I have but six.'

'*Ça suffit, monsieur?*'

'Yes. It is enough. We will have a rare feast. Do you want to go home now?'

The boy looked at him uncertainly and Nathan knew he was trying to guess what Nathan wanted to do. Or more to the point, what Nathan wanted *him* to do: to carry on splashing in the rock pools in the warm September sunshine, or return to the dubious sanctuary of Windover House and the English lesson that was scheduled to start at five o'clock precisely.

'If you wish it, sir,' said the boy, in a diplomatic, if heavily accented English, and with an expression that pulled on Nathan's heartstrings.

They clambered over the rocks together and dropped down on to the thin strip of sand exposed by the retreating tide. Over to the east, beyond the meagre outlet of the Cuckmere River, were the chalk-white cliffs of the Seven Sisters, curving away toward Beachy Head, almost lost in the distant haze. The sun bounced off their pale faces and shattered into a billion gold pieces on the flat-iron surface of the shimmering sea: as empty as on the third day of Creation. But no, as Nathan shielded his eyes against the glare he could make out something of a later construct: a pair of triangular red sails about halfway between Beachy Head and the Cuckmere. It stirred a distant memory and for a moment he imagined she was his old adversary, the *Fortune*, a big, heavily armed lugger owned by Mr Williams of Shoreham, a notorious smuggler who had plagued the Revenue officers along the south coast for a decade or more. But this was not the *Fortune*. The haze had misled him. She was a smaller vessel, a fishing boat or coaster. But the sight brought a flood of memories and he stayed a while gazing out to sea while his mind wandered to other places, other adversaries . . .

It was an encounter with the *Fortune* one dark night off the Cuckmere that had first sent him to France on his chequered career as a blockade runner and secret agent in the service of the King's chief minister William Pitt. He glanced down at the scars on his legs, stripes almost, like the markings on a tiger, save that they were a shameful red. There were more on his chest and back and buttocks from the flaying he had received in the House of Arrest in Paris. They would heal in time, he had been assured, and indeed they were much faded already. But there were other scars that would take longer, if they healed at all.

'*Monsieur*? Nathan?' Alex tugged at his sleeve but even the voice, the accent and the way he pronounced it – *Nat-Ann* – reminded him of Sara . . .

Sara, Countess of Turenne: Nathan's lover and Alex's mother who had died on the guillotine.

Nathan had played his part in the coup that had consigned Sara's killers to the same fate and had promised an end to the dark days of what the French called the Terror. But the war continued and Nathan knew he should be a part of it: *needed* to be a part of it. He was still officially the master and commander of the *Speedwell*, an American barque in the King's service, but he had been promised a captaincy and the command of a frigate by no less a personage than the Earl of Chatham, First Lord of the Admiralty. But the promise had yet to materialise and Nathan had no spirit to remind him of it. He knew this was a part of his grieving for Sara, and that the only cure for this affliction was action. But he was seized by a dreadful lethargy, a sense that nothing mattered and that in any case he could make little difference one way or another.

And so he played nursemaid to Sara's son. And fished in rock pools. And rode the Downs for long hours alone or walked beside the meandering Cuckmere and the indifferent but curiously healing sea, comforted by the rhythms of the waves. Or at least drugged: numbed as if by some slow-acting opiate or belladonna released into his mind, calming his destructive rages.

Perhaps in time he would become as indifferent as the sea.

They walked on, up the sloping shingle to the little cluster of fishing huts and upturned boats and net-drying sheds where the beach ended and the marshes began and where they had left their pony to graze while they scavenged among the rock pools. Now Nathan called her to them and harnessed her to the little trap, and they climbed in with their buckets at their feet and followed the raised track beside the Cuckmere, inland toward home.

Nathan's home, if not the boy's. Not yet.

But it was his fond hope that Alex, orphaned and in a strange land, would learn to love it as he did, or at least to make the best of it.

Nathan had been much the same age when he had first come here – from America with his mother – and had spent the happiest days of his life here, running wild with a pack of lads and dogs as reckless and as reprobate as himself. He knew it as no other place on earth, and more of its secrets – and its villainies – than his father and his tutors would have wished.

But for the moment he was content to show the boy its gentler nature, instructing him in the English names of the plants and wild flowers as they plodded up from the beach.

'Sea Aster,' pointing at a clump of mauve and yellow flowers that grew close by the shore, 'and see there, that yellow plant, like a flame? We call it Toadflax. Toad. *Crapaud.* Because it is a weed – useless. Like Johnny Crapaud, that we call the French.'

He grinned to soften the insult. The boy looked puzzled; the English sense of humour was still something of a mystery to him.

'I am sorry, I must not tease you. Now here is another

you should know, much more useful.' Nathan pointed to the dark green plant growing by the river, a little browned here and there by the sun. 'That is samphire, one of my favourites because you can eat it. *L'herbe de Saint Pierre* in French. I don't know what you use it for, but we eat it with fish. It's very salty but it will go very well *avec nos crevettes*.' He stopped the pony, jumped down and leaped along by the side of the river, plucking up a great handful of samphire and bringing it back to drop in the bucket with the sad-looking prawns.

They plodded on, up through the marshland beside the placid river, past the indifferent herons stalking the shallows, and once they saw the flashing blue of a kingfisher. Up into the meadows below the deserted village of Exceat, wiped out by the Black Death 400 years ago, its stone ruins hiding beneath fields of golden celandine and great white dishes of cow parsley and other plants of God's creation – or the Devil's.

'See that?' Nathan pointed with his whip at a feathery plant with flat white flowers that grew in great profusion among the grasses on the riverbank. 'Its real name is yarrow but the locals call it Old Man's Mustard – the Old Man being the Devil, do you see?'

The poor boy's frown suggested otherwise but Nathan continued regardless.

'They say he uses it in his spells when he wants to harm someone. When I was younger and got in a scrap I'd use it to stop a nosebleed, but of course the folk around here, they always see the Devil in things.'

Nathan had learned his botany, and much besides,

from Old Abe Eldridge, his father's head shepherd, highly spiced with legend and superstition.

They crossed the river by the little stone bridge beyond Exceat and began to climb up into the Downs towards Littlington through clouds of gossamer seeds floating in the still air and hordes of Daddy Long Legs bowling through the sun-bleached grass as if they were off to a ball.

'*Beaucoup de papillons,*' the boy pointed out. Then, struggling to correct himself: 'So many butter-flea . . .' Indeed, the hillside seemed to be alive with them, an ephemeral lilac-blue haze floating above the grass but almost certainly the effect of the field scabious that grew here, or vervain – or a mixture of the two.

'Both plants are used in healing,' Nathan explained. 'Scabious for the scabies or dandruff. Dandruff. *Pour la tête.*' Scratching the boy's head for his better understanding. 'And vervain for almost anything – from itchy heads to sore bums. Because it was believed to grow on Calvary, do you see, and they used it to staunch Christ's wounds when He was taken down from the Cross, though as I explained to Old Abe, the ignoramus, "The dead don't bleed", I said. And he said that was blasphemous and he would tell on me to the vicar and I would be publicly denounced from the pulpit and get a beating from my tutor. But he didn't, in case I was in the right of it and he was wrong, ha ha.'

On they climbed up through the woods, past a few lingering foxgloves – Dead Man's Fingers in Abe's grim lexicon – and out again, stopping once more for Nathan to point out a plant with a purple flower that was called the Carline Thistle: 'Named after a King of France, Charlemagne, who prayed to God for help when his army was hit by the plague. Upon which an angel appeared and told him to shoot an arrow into the air and the plant it landed beside would provide the cure.'

'The King of France.' The boy nodded sagely, grasping at what little he had understood of this helpful anecdote.

'Charlemagne,' Nathan repeated. 'But the people here could not pronounce it as well as we scholars, so they called it Carline. The Carline Thistle, wearing the purple of the King, do you see, or an Emperor.'

'Is it he that is call Louis Capet,' enquired the boy, 'that is make to die at the *guillotine*?'

'No,' said Nathan quietly. 'No, not that one.'

The guillotine and the memory of another who had died upon it cast a shadow over their journey, and they were quiet as the pony plodded on through Littlington and out again into the high Downland, with Windover Hill rising steeply to their right, powdered with his father's flocks.

Could the boy ever be at home here? It seemed impossible now to Nathan, in this black mood, that Alex should enjoy the same careless childhood as had he. He could not run wild with the local youth, not with that accent. They would tear him limb from limb. He was doomed to be a stranger in a foreign land. The land of the enemy.

Nathan began to consider other problems of bringing

the boy up in England. Alex had been christened a
Catholic and appeared to have absorbed at least some of
its teaching. How – in Revolutionary France? Nathan did
not care to ask. But should it be continued? Would Sara
want him to be brought up a Catholic? Was she a – what
did you call it – a *communiant*? Nathan did not know. It
was not something they had discussed. They'd had so
little time together. But her family had been Catholic. Her
father had been a Scottish soldier of fortune, a supporter
of the Catholic Stuarts who had fled to France after the
Rising of '45. And her husband had been a member of one
of the great Catholic families of France. Alex had
inherited his title – at least as far as the royalists were
concerned. He was Charles Louis Alexandre Tour de
l'Auvergne, Vicomte de Turenne. He should at least be
given the choice of a Catholic upbringing.

It was easier now in England since the Catholic Relief
Act. Priests were now permitted to say the Mass in public,
and there were no longer penalties for hearing it said.
Catholics could even build churches – provided they did
not have a steeple or a bell and did not lock the door
during the ceremony so that they might plot treason. They
could open schools, too.

But where to find them? Nathan did not know of any.
And his father would surely be opposed to any such
scheme, for he was an upstanding member of the Church
of England and a Tory. He could not abide Papists.
Nathan had often heard him say so.

So many problems.

'So many sheeps,' said the boy, making an effort to

resume their converse which, for all its difficulties, was better than silent contemplation.

'Sheep,' Nathan corrected him absently. 'Yes. It is the great woolsack of England. They reckon there are two hundred thousand ewes in the thirty miles between Eastbourne and Steyning. *Deux cents milles moutons*,' he repeated, to make sure the boy had understood. It was the kind of fact that, if absorbed, would impress his father.

The boy shook his head wonderingly. 'Is many, many sheeps.' But something seemed to be troubling him. 'How you know this?' he demanded suddenly.

'How do I know? Because I have counted them.'

'You count zem – all of zem?'

'All of zem. Them.'

'How long it take you?' With suspicion.

'Oh, all night sometimes.'

'You count zem at night?'

'Yes. It is the only way. They stand out, you see, with the white coats, in the moonlight. And they do not move around so much at night.'

The boy brooded on this for a while as they began to climb towards the farm, passing small flocks coming down from the high Downs, driven by the shepherds and their dogs, to feed on the clover and the mustard in the leys.

They approached the farm along a broad chalk track lined with dusty hedgerows, passing labourers walking back from the fields with their scythes and their hoes; past a team of oxen swinging their great heads and blowing gently through moist nostrils, the drover touching the whip to his straw hat and Nathan touching his in response. On through the farmyard, scattering frantic hens and indignant geese, past a row of farm cottages where those too old or young for gainful employment sat or played in the late-afternoon sun. Round by the noxious pond and up the slight rise between stately elms and the ancient stone gateposts – one lion, one unicorn, no gate – to the house.

Windover House. Nathan's home.

There had been a house at Windover before the Conquest, its last Saxon thane slain with the last Saxon king, it was said, on the bloody field at Senlac and the manor given to the pro-Norman Church. In whose custody it had remained until the Reformation, when the monks were given their marching orders and the long reign of the squires began.

The Tudor house of those days with its half-timbered frame and mullioned windows still remained, now a mere wing facing the farm, but a latter and more prosperous generation had built a grander house of brick and local flint, its tall windows looking out over the valley with the silver ribbon of the Cuckmere like a snail's trail far below and the steeple of Alfriston Church just visible above the ridge that concealed the village. A stable block had been added with a clock tower. And some more sensitive soul had incorporated a sunken garden into the complex with an ornamental pool and a fountain and a wall to protect the less robust species of plant from the salt-laden wind. And then Nathan's father had come along with his contribution – a pair of bronze cannon, taken from a

French third-rate at the Battle of the Saints – and had planted them in the herbaceous border below the terrace, pointing directly at the Long Man of Wilmington, etched in chalk halfway up Windover Hill, marching down on them with his two staves and his war helmet like a giant warrior hero of old.

It was one of the finest manors in the county but far too much of a mish-mash to be called grand. And Nathan loved it. Loved coming back to it from his travels. Loved its tall beckoning chimneys and its fungus-coated walls and its rust-coloured roof and its whims and follies, and the play of light on the warm brick and the sharp-edged flint, and the way it seemed to settle into the hillside as if its myriad parts had rolled down there and subsided with a sigh, fitting their inelegant limbs and awkward angles into the folds of a worn and comfortable sofa.

They drove into the stableyard. Two great hounds loped out to meet them – Hector and Agamemnon, known as Gammon, and a small yapping terrier with an eye-patch called Pirate. After giving them their due attention, Nathan and Alex left the pony with one of the stable boys and made their way up through the garden carrying their now noisome buckets and in through the scullery door to the kitchens. Here was the cook Mrs Madley, whom everyone called Maddie or Ma, just settling down by the range with her pipe and a mug of ale while the kitchen maids scoured the pans from dinner. She had fixed them a substantial picnic before they left and grumbled now that she supposed they would be after the leftovers from dinner and were out of luck, for 'there ben't none', but when Nathan stated his intention of boiling up a pan of water for the prawns she levered herself out of her chair and insisted on doing it herself for all that they were a plague to her and a curse on her old age.

Maddie was an odd shape for a cook: tall and gaunt with sharp angular features flinty as the house walls and a tongue that could strike sparks, but she had a soft heart and a great fondness for Nathan, treating him with the same rough affection and scandalised censure as did all the older servants, as if he was the same small savage who had arrived from the Americas twenty years ago. So she made them scrub their grubby hands at the kitchen sink and sat them at the kitchen table with a mug of ale for Nathan and of lemonade for Alex whom she referred to privately – inasmuch as there was such a thing as privacy at Windover House – as 'the Frenchie'.

Nathan was more at home in the kitchen than in any other part of the house. Indeed, he had practically been raised here, playing with his toys on the stone floor when it was too cold or wet to play outside, manoeuvring his leaden armies and wheeling his wooden horses into the heart of Maddie's Troy, eating scraps and leftovers at the kitchen table (for he kept no regular mealtimes) and in later years warming himself by the kitchen fire when he came home soaked from woods, shore or riverbank where he had been up to mischief with the local banditry.

'Why thankee kindly, Ma,' he said, as she set bowls of steaming prawns and samphire before them with a loaf of fresh-baked bread and a dish of melted butter. 'Here is a rare treat, eh, Alex? And a sight better than they looked in the pool.'

They ate in a convivial silence, snapping off heads and eating the rest whole with great hunks of bread to make up for the deficiency in bulk, and Nathan was about to pour himself another mug of ale when the morose figure of Gilbert Gabriel appeared at the kitchen door.

Gabriel was Nathan's steward when he was at sea but he had served Nathan's father in a similar capacity for many years before, and Nathan still thought of him as his father's man. Certainly, whenever they were at Windover House he reverted to this role and treated Nathan more as a junior officer in the admiral's service rather than a Commander in his own right. Gabriel had been a highwayman in his younger days – Nathan's father had saved him from the gallows – and there was in his steely countenance, his abrupt appearances and his cursory address a strong suggestion of this former occupation, as if he had just ridden out from behind a bush and demanded money with menaces. Nathan's crew had called him the Angel Gabriel, almost certainly in a spirit of irony. But he was devoted to Nathan's father and possibly even to Nathan, though it was hard to believe it at times.

'The admiral's compliments,' he now intoned in the voice that had once stopped the Royal Mail, 'and would be pleased to see the commander in his study whenever he is at leisure.'

'My duty to the admiral,' Nathan responded formally, 'and will be with him shortly.'

Though Windover House could not be managed with

the same brisk efficiency as a man-of-war, it did its best to maintain the naval tradition while remaining firmly grounded in the South Downs.

'Whenever he is at leisure' meant upon the instant, but not necessarily at the double. So Nathan finished his beer, packed Alex off to his tutor, then set off for his father's study in the Tudor wing, wondering a little at the nature of the summons for he met his father often enough at mealtimes for the exchange of whatever information was considered necessary for their continuing amiable relations. He was inclined to think it concerned Alex, and was braced for a debate in which the subjects of Papists, discipline and the Protestant religion would be fully aired.

In the event, this would have been a relief compared to the subject that was uppermost in his father's mind.

'Ah, Nathaniel. Good day?' Sir Michael turned from the apparent contemplation of a row of books upon his shelves, though they had been there to Nathan's knowledge for some twenty years without evoking his father's even passing interest. He was clearly nervous. But why?

'Excellent, thank you, sir. We caught twenty-six prawn.' Cursing this betrayal of his own nervousness and the occasional tendency to behave in his father's presence as if he were five years old and not twenty-five.

'Really? And you took the boy?' Raising his bushy brows a trifle as if Nathan had exposed young Alex to unnecessary danger.

'I did.' Restraining an impulse to add that he seemed ready for it.

'Very good, very good.' The admiral waved Nathan to a chair and eased himself into the one opposite, from whence they continued to steer their conversation as clumsily as two rudderless hulks in a flat calm.

Father and son were rarely relaxed in each other's presence. They shared little in common beyond a career in the Navy, though that was enough to unite the majority of those in His Majesty's Service. Nathan's father was a burly, handsome, ruddy-faced country gentleman of fifty-six years with a commanding presence and a decisive manner. Nathan was darker, slimmer and taller, and said to take after his mother in both appearance and character, an opinion which he found alarming. Possibly it alarmed his father, also. Sir Michael had enjoyed a distinguished career and retired from the sea with the rank of rear-admiral, having served his King and country for forty-four years and through two major wars. Surprisingly, instead of retiring to his country estate and indulging in the leisurely pursuits of other country gentlemen, he had become actively involved in its management, joining with several like-minded neighbours in the development of a new breed of sheep: the Southdown, which was considered superior to anything else in that line of creation.

Of late, as Nathan knew, there had been problems. His father had invested heavily in the breed – and in other improvements to the farm – and the returns were not as great as he had hoped. The traditional overseas markets for English wool had suffered from the war and prices had dropped considerably. From the way the conversation was going, Nathan feared the worst. Their debts had been called in, the estate was to be sold, penury beckoned. At length, however, Sir Michael came to the point.

'Well then, the fact is that I have something I wanted to tell you. Yes. Something, that I expect you will find extraordinary. So, not to beat about the bush, what would you say if I told you I was considering the prospect . . . well, had committed myself to the prospect . . . of matrimony?'

'Matrimony?' Nathan repeated, startled – and indeed, as perplexed as his ward had been by such wonders as Toadflax and Old Man's Mustard and such other curiosities as they had encountered on the road from Cuckmere.

'Marriage,' his father translated for him, helpfully. '*My* marriage.'

'But . . .' Nathan struggled for a way of putting it more diplomatically, but there was none. 'But, Father, you are already married. To my mother.'

Sir Michael frowned. A frost formed in the small space between them.

'I am not yet so addled in my wits as to forget *that* circumstance.' The word 'unfortunate', though missing from the body of this sentence, was present in spirit. 'However, I believe you are not unaware of the situation between your mother and myself,' he added wearily.

Nathan's parents had not seen eye to eye for many years, nor indeed shared the same house. Not since Sir Michael's decision to retire from the Navy and devote himself to sheep.

'You know I cannot be doing with sheep,' Lady

Catherine had informed Nathan subsequently, the nearest he had ever come to receiving an explanation of the rift from either parent. But although sheep had undoubtedly played a part in the breakdown of their marriage, the real reason was politics.

Nathan's father and mother had met in New York when it was still a British colony. He was a young naval officer, she the daughter of wealthy merchants – the descendants of French Huguenots. This proved no impediment to their romance, however, and the young naval officer found himself married into one of the wealthiest families in the colony. Nathan was born in New York and spent the first five years of his life there, but throughout this period tensions were rising between the American colonists and their British governors, and his mother showed a disturbing tendency to side with the former. Such was her enthusiasm for these miscreants that her husband elected to remove her and their young son to the mother country where she might learn to keep her opinions to herself – or have none, like all good Englishwomen.

Although his wife submitted to his plans – being secretly desirous of living in London – as soon as she arrived there she began to associate with even worse villains than those in the colonies. Among the regular visitors to her home in St James's were Mr Fox and Mr Wilkes and other dangerous radicals, men who supported the rebel cause in America even while her husband was engaged in its suppression.

Captain Peake, as he now was, served with the British

fleet that descended upon New York in the summer of
1776 and landed a large army of Redcoats and German
mercenaries on the island of Manhattan. Two of Kitty's
brothers fought against them and one, the youngest, died
on the Heights of Harlem.

The marriage endured but the wounds did not heal.
Nathan's father remained in the Americas for the duration
of the war while his mother gave comfort to the King's
enemies in London. Meanwhile, Nathan ran wild on the
family estate in Sussex, his mother's only stricture to his
tutors being to ensure that he continued to improve his
French.

When the war ended, Nathan's father and mother
found it as hard to be reconciled as did Britain and her
former colonies, now the United States of America.
Indeed, Nathan's mother made her own Declaration of
Independence. Henceforth she would remain in London
and her husband, when he was not at sea, would make his
home in Sussex.

Nathan was not unduly troubled by this arrangement.
It was not uncommon among couples of a certain class,
and even those who shared the same roof were often as
divided. He loved both his parents and declined to take
sides in their conflicts – though if he stayed for much
above an hour in the company of either one he was very
much inclined to see the point of view of the other.

But he had not considered the possibility of either
parent seeking to remarry. And, indeed, there were
considerable obstacles to such a course.

'But that would mean divorce,' Nathan pointed out.

'So I am led to believe,' agreed his father, 'if I am to avoid the charge of bigamy. Or turn Mohammedan.'

'I am sorry, Father, but you have quite taken me aback.'

'I am advised that I must bring a case before the ecclesiastical courts. And as a man cannot be divorced for adultery, according to canon law, I fear the blame must be placed at your mother's door.'

'You would accuse my mother of adultery?' There would be no shortage of candidates. But this was scarcely the point.

'It is very regrettable,' his father agreed, 'but I see no alternative at present. And, well . . . I doubt it would ruin her reputation.'

'But – it will be a great scandal.'

'Will it? I wonder.' An uneasy silence. Each lost in thought. It was Sir Michael who broke it, smiling a little. 'You have not asked me who it is I wish to marry.'

This seemed a minor consideration. 'I'm sorry, Father, I . . .' Nathan shook his head. 'Who is the lady?'

'Her name is Frances Wyndham. I believe you have met. She has hunted here once or twice.'

'Fanny Wyndham! My God!'

'Is that so shocking? You have gone quite pale.'

This was perfectly possible, for Fanny Wyndham was indeed known to him. A boisterous girl, rather too horsy to be considered handsome but with a fine seat. And an outstanding bosom. Once, while the rest of the hunt was otherwise engaged, they had enjoyed what was described in hunting terms as a 'tussle' in Windover Wood. The memory of it brought the colour rushing back to Nathan's face.

Fanny was the eldest child of George Wyndham, Earl of Egremont, one of the greatest landowners in Sussex, in fact in all England. Though his estate at Petworth was on the far side of the county, he often visited with the Gages at Firle or Mr Ellman of Glynde, who shared his enthusiasm for agricultural improvement. And Sir Michael, Nathan now recalled, had often visited Petworth, ostensibly to discuss the perfection of the Southdown sheep.

'Maternal loyalties aside, you have some objection to the lady?'

The 'tussle' in Windover Wood could not be raised as a legitimate concern – but there were others.

'She is very young,' Nathan commented.

'She is twenty-three. Past the first flush of youth, I believe.'

'Well, yes, but . . .' Should he point out that his father was fifty-six: a good ten years older than the girl's father? Perhaps not. 'But . . . is it fair to put her through such an ordeal?'

'As marriage to myself?' Sir Michael queried mildly.

'I was thinking more of the divorce from my mother.' Another objection occurred to Nathan. 'Is it permitted to marry again – if one has been divorced?'

His father sighed. 'It is not impossible. There are precedents – though it requires an Act of Parliament in each case.'

'You would put it to Parliament?'

'My lord Egremont has agreed to ease the way, as it were. He is not without influence in that realm.'

Indeed, thought Nathan, he must own at least half-a-dozen boroughs, if not more. But why would he wish to marry his daughter to a man ten years older than himself: even a man with 3,000 acres of Sussex Downland?

Egremont, Nathan recalled, had been something of a womaniser in his youth. Still was, by some accounts. And he was still unmarried. Of course. Frances – and her two brothers – were illegitimate. Nathan would never have raised this as an objection to the marriage, but he wondered if it had some bearing on his lordship's lack of opposition.

'Egremont has offered a very generous settlement,' his father explained. 'And I will not conceal from you that Windover is very much encumbered. Indeed, I fear that if matters continue as they are now, I might have to sell up or at least increase the mortgage to a point where it would be very difficult to carry on.'

So there he had it. It was not just Fanny Wyndham's proportions that Sir Michael admired.

'Do not look so dismayed,' his father rebuked him gently. 'The estate is entailed. Your inheritance is secure. Indeed, I trust it will come to you in a far healthier state than it is now.'

Nathan shook his head. 'It is not that, Father,' he said. 'It would never be that.'

Windover was his home, but he had not consciously thought of it as his inheritance. He hoped his father had a long life before him. And given the dangers of his current profession, it could be a lot longer than his own.

'This will always be your home, you know that. And for Alex, too, as long as you wish it.'

Nathan nodded his appreciation of this, but it was not the greatest weight on his mind.

'Have you told my mother of your intention?' he enquired.

'Not yet. I wished first to inform my son.'

Nathan acknowledged this courtesy though it was small consolation for what lay ahead. Divorce cases were always notorious. They were lewdly reported in the popular journals and the court transcripts published in vellum-bound volumes for the edification of future generations. The marital exploits of the Spencers would doubtless entertain the reading public for centuries to come, and somewhere in this very library was an account of the divorce of Sir Charles Bunbury, which Nathan had read as a prurient adolescent. He could still recall the outraged, apocalyptic wording of the charge *that Lady Sarah Bunbury being of a loose and abandoned disposition . . . did carry on a lewd and adulterous conversation with . . .* He had forgotten precisely who, but he remembered that the servants had been called upon to give evidence against her.

'I suppose you know it will take years to contrive,' he pointed out.

'I am aware of that. But once the process is in train there is no reason why we should not live as if we were married already. Indeed, we have spoken of it.'

Nathan stared at him in astonishment. My God, but he was a sly old fox. And as for Fanny Wyndham . . . He wondered how long he had before she moved in.

There was nothing more to be said.

Nathan walked out upon the terrace and collapsed into one of the cane-bottomed planters' chairs his father had brought back from the Caribbean after the American War. The sun was slipping behind the clouds over Firle Beacon: a magnificent sunset that he was scarcely in the mood to appreciate.

Fanny Wyndham. Twenty-three with her childbearing years before her and his father still a vigorous fifty-six. The place would be swarming with their offspring.

It was not the loss of his inheritance that concerned him; he had been sincere in that. It was the loss of his home. Despite his father's assurance, once Fanny Wyndham moved in, it would never be the same again.

He did not know if he could face her. He doubted that she wanted to face him.

He was being childish. Petulant. A dog in the manger. If his father wished to remarry, that was entirely his affair.

But he wished it were not Fanny Wyndham.

He wished it did not involve a divorce.

He wished he was back at sea.

And of course, that was the answer. He must remove himself from the situation. Pointless hanging about the place with a long face. He must go back to sea. Indeed, he had a duty to do so.

As if to emphasise the point, the dying sun rose from its bloodied shroud to touch the lion and the unicorn with the semblance of the glaze they bore on the royal standard . . . save that by some trick of the light or Nathan's imagining, the unicorn's horn seemed to be tinged with red.

Then it was gone and the beasts were plunged in shadow.

He would write to the Admiralty to remind them of his existence – and the First Lord of his promise. And if Chatham pretended it had never been made then he would seek a lesser command.

One way or another, he would go back to sea – and the war.

Chapter Two

The Tide of War

———◆———

London. The hottest day of the year, as if summer had been saving herself for the last. One final searing show of strength before moving on, her unruly subjects subdued, stifled, sullen: dogged pedestrians plodding through a haze of heat and dust, St Paul's Cathedral an orb of burning gold above the silvered Thames and the City silent, somnolent, the great men of wealth slumped regardless at their desks and the clerks bent over theirs like melting candles dripping grease.

Nathan came up by chaise from Sussex, starting fresh at dawn, par-boiled by Croydon and set down at the Admiralty building in Whitehall as overdone as the lobster at the gate who rolled his poached eyes at Nathan's pass as if he cared not whether he were the Angel of Death or one of the Four Horsemen of the Apocalypse come to put the country out of its misery.

'If you will follow me, sir,' the hall porter instructed him, 'his lordship awaits you in the board room.'

His tone, though guarded, could not disguise a note of surprise, even outrage. Access to the board room was a privilege normally confined to the Lords of the Admiralty and those worthies as enjoyed their complete confidence: the hallowed sanctuary where grand strategies were devised for the confusion of the King's enemies, or such of his friends and relatives it was deemed advisable to confuse in these troubled times. It was not for the entertainment of mere commanders.

Up the stairs to the first floor and across the landing to a door of polished oak: the porter contriving to knock, open and step back in what was almost a single action, leaving Nathan bewildered in a sudden blaze of light.

'Commander Peake, my lord.'

'Ah, Peake, I trust I find you well?'

'And I you, my lord.' The tall windows, directly opposite, were only partly draped against the glare and Nathan saw the room through a haze of sunshine and a galaxy of dust. It was dominated by a long table covered in green leather where two gentlemen were engaged in the study of a chart.

'Come and join us,' said the First Lord of the Admiralty, as if Nathan had merely popped his head round the door on his way to lunch. 'We were just looking at a map of the Caribbean.'

John Pitt, Earl of Chatham, was in his late thirties, tall and slender with the bearing of a soldier, which was what he was, or had been, before his younger brother William, the King's chief minister, had plucked him from the obscurity of the 86th Foot, where he had achieved the rank of captain, and made him First Lord of the Admiralty and a member of the Privy Council. He had since added to these honours a full colonelcy in the 3rd Foot Guards, a promotion apparently deemed necessary by himself or his brother or both, to impress the half-dozen or so serving admirals who shared with him the onerous duties of com-manding His Majesty's fleets in war and who might otherwise have doubted his competence.

'I do not believe you have met Colonel Hollis.'

A gentleman approached, elderly and in the uniform of a Colonel of Marines but with more the look of a scholar about him than the military man. He peered above his spectacles with an expression that reminded Nathan of his classics master at Charterhouse during his brief period there before he joined the Navy.

After making his bow Nathan glanced briefly around the room, which he knew only by repute. The wall directly opposite was filled with a number of rolled-up charts, rather like newspapers in a coffee-house. Two bell-ropes hung down from the ceiling, presumably to summon servants and rear-admirals and other such underlings as should be necessary to take one of them down and unroll it upon the table. And on the wall to his left was a curious device very like a clock with a powder-blue face and a single hand – linked, it was said, to a weathervane on the roof so that their lordships might at any time be informed as to the direction of the wind in case they wished to set sail and cruise down Whitehall to the amazement of the populace.

'Your letter was fortuitous,' Chatham assured him with a beam that singularly failed to put Nathan at his ease. 'I am mindful that the last time we met, we discussed the possibility of your advancement to the rank of post captain.'

Nathan would not have called it a discussion. If his memory served him right – and he had called it to mind on no more than several hundred occasions over the intervening period – the First Lord had said: 'I suppose you must have your reward,' whereupon Nathan had been moved to thank him and been informed that: 'We can probably find one of the older frigates for you if someone dies.'

'Since when I have been considering how best to accommodate your considerable talents,' the First Lord continued, glancing toward the colonel. 'The taking of the *Vestale* in the mouth of the Seine, your heroic conduct aboard the admiral's flagship on the Glorious First of June, your secret work in France, of which Colonel Hollis has been informed, all recommend you for a posting of some eminence. Which is not so easy to contrive as some of your colleagues appear to think, even in time of war.'

'You are too kind, my lord,' murmured Nathan, wondering a little at this unexpected eulogy, clearly designed to impress the First Lord's companion, whose look of doubt had not escaped Nathan's attention when he had first entered the room.

'However, your patience is to be rewarded,' Lord

Chatham assured him. 'Fortune, or I should say, *Fate* has conspired to create a suitable vacancy at last and enabled me to offer you the command of one of our latest frigates: the *Unicorn*, of thirty-two guns, currently stationed in the Havana.'

Nathan was stunned beyond the power of speech. So much so, he almost missed the qualification to Chatham's last statement.

'Or *was*, when last we heard of her.'

Stumblingly, Nathan expressed his gratitude. He remembered the way the sun had struck the stone unicorn at Windover House only two evenings since, when he had been sunk in the depths of despair. He had thought it was portentous of some additional calamity, but far from it. He was to have the *Unicorn* – one of the new class of heavy frigates, armed with twenty-six 18-pounders and six 32-pounder carronades.

But what was it the First Lord had said?

His eyes focused finally on the point the First Lord had indicated on the map. La Habana, Cuba, the great haven of the Caribbean where the Spanish treasure ships gathered from Panama and Veracruz before sailing across the Atlantic under the heaviest escort the wealth of Spain could contrive. What was the *Unicorn* doing in the Havana? Had she been captured? Must he first take her back from her captors, cut her out from under the guns of the Spanish?

But the news had addled his brains. In this war, possibly for the first time, Spain was Britain's ally. The *Unicorn* must be stationed there.

'Well, I would send for a libation to celebrate your promotion,' beamed Chatham, 'but in the circumstances I feel it would not be appropriate.'

The beam faded. Here then was the catch.

'But before we come to that, there is something else about which you should be informed. Shall we be seated, gentlemen?'

Ten elegant red-upholstered chairs were arranged around the table for the ease of their lordships while they plotted the discomfort of the enemy. Nathan sat in one. He did not feel any more relaxed.

'Now – if you will permit me, Colonel, for this is familiar territory to you . . .' Chatham returned his gaze to Nathan. 'I expect you will have read of the recent encounter off the Île d'Obéron between Sir James Saumarez and the French squadron under Commodore Lafitte?'

As a naval officer Nathan certainly should have read of it – and he certainly would have remembered it, had he done so – but he searched his mind in vain for an account of the incident.

'The encounter was fully reported in the press,' Chatham assured him, 'but possibly you were in France at the time and I do not suppose they were eager to publish the news of yet another defeat. The French squadron consisted of three frigates, one of which was taken and another driven upon the shore. The third – the *Virginie* of forty-four guns – escaped into the Atlantic. But from certain captured documents, and from questioning the prisoners, Sir James ascertained that the squadron had been bound for the Caribbean. Assuming that the *Virginie* had continued with this objective, he sent word to Admiral Ford in Jamaica. Although the latter has quite enough to occupy him at present, it was not thought that a single enemy frigate would add greatly to his burden. However,' he glanced again at the colonel, 'a few days ago we received news from France which puts an entirely different complexion upon the affair.'

He contemplated the map for a moment before directing his attention once more to Nathan.

'Even if you are not a regular reader of the journals you must know from your own experiences on the continent that the war in Europe has reached a point of stalemate. The forces of Prussia, Austria and Spain have failed to turn back the tide of Revolution, and the French appear unwilling or unable to expand it beyond their own frontiers.'

Only give them time, Nathan thought, but he merely inclined his head in tacit agreement with the supposition.

'However, we on this small island have a reputation for looking beyond Europe – and there has been an understandable pressure from both press and Parliament for His Majesty's Government to take advantage of the current situation in the Caribbean. It is no secret that a large force is being prepared for despatch to the region – the largest ever to leave the shores of these islands. However, it will not be ready to sail until early next year, and in the meantime our own colonies may be in serious jeopardy from a different quarter. But perhaps, Colonel, you will explain the circumstances to our friend. Colonel

Hollis,' he told Nathan, 'maintains contacts with certain foreign nationals whose intelligence has been of use to us from time to time.'

The colonel acknowledged this judicious description with a small smile before addressing Nathan directly for the first time.

'You will doubtless be aware, Captain, that a number of revolts have already occurred in the region among the African slaves working on the plantations, the rebels being tutored and encouraged by agents of the Revolutionary Government in Paris . . .'

Privately Nathan doubted if the slaves of the Caribbean needed much encouragement, given the conditions they lived in, but he kept his opinions to himself in this instance.

'It appears that the French are intent on spreading anarchy and revolution not only throughout the Caribbean but in the Spanish territories in North America . . .' the colonel indicated them on the map . . . 'centred on the port of New Orleans where there is a significant number of settlers of French descent, known as Cajuns.'

Nathan nodded but kept his expression carefully guarded. His mother's family had been 'settlers of French descent'. He wondered if the colonel was aware of this.

'It appears that this was the particular objective of the squadron under Commodore Lafitte which contained a large contingent of infantry. And that despite his encounter with Sir John Saumarez, Lafitte has continued with his mission in the *Virginie*. I need hardly instruct you that the establishment of a new French colony on the

North American mainland – with a naval base on the coast of Louisiana or the Floridas – would be a serious threat to our trade in the Caribbean.'

'More than that, I think,' murmured Chatham dryly. 'I believe it is no exaggeration to say that whoever possesses New Orleans possesses the key not only to the Caribbean and the Floridas – but to the vast hinterland of North America west of the Mississippi. The tide of war has shifted decisively to the west,' he declared, in the tone he used to address Parliament, 'and we must swim with it or . . . or sink,' he finished lamely, doubtless making a mental note that some polishing was required before he delivered the speech to his peers.

'And the *Unicorn*, my lord?'

'Ah yes, the *Unicorn*.' Chatham sighed and glanced meaningfully at the colonel, who appeared to be lost in his study of the chart. Nathan braced himself. 'The *Unicorn* is a new ship, as I think I mentioned. Shortly after being commissioned she was despatched to the West Indies, to reinforce the squadron under Admiral Ford at Port Royal. The admiral, hearing reports of the *Virginie* in the region, sent the *Unicorn* in pursuit, though she was then very new to his command. Possibly she was the only ship he could spare. Or it may have appealed to his sense of humour. Or romance.'

Nathan remained unenlightened.

'To send a Unicorn in pursuit of a Virgin. Ha ha.'

Nathan smiled dutifully. He was not such a pedant as to point out that the French for virgin was *la vierge* and that *Virginie* was a woman's name, possibly bestowed in honour of the former British colony of Virginia, now part of the United States. But he reflected that, whatever Ford's reasons for his decision, it was typical of the Navy that they should send a frigate of thirty-two guns to engage one of forty-four with no expectation that there would be any result but a British victory.

'Your first duty on taking command of the *Unicorn* will be to seek out the *Virginie* and destroy her,' the First Lord instructed him. 'You will also support the Spanish authorities in the region in whatever actions they deem necessary to stamp out rebellion, either on the mainland or on the islands under their control.'

Nathan had no quarrel with the first of these instructions. The task of seeking out and destroying a heavily armed French frigate in the waters of the Caribbean with a ship of fewer guns and almost certainly fewer men was not without hazard, but at least he was in sympathy with the general sentiment behind the order. Stamping out rebellion was another matter – particularly when it was a rebellion directed against the Spanish colonial authorities. Nathan was not a great admirer of the King of Spain or of the Spanish planters in Cuba and Louisiana.

'Now to more practical matters,' the First Lord continued. 'Your previous command – the *Speedwell* – is, I believe, berthed in Shoreham.'

'She is, my lord.'

'Yes, well, there is some difficulty there. The Americans want her back.'

'I am sorry, my lord?' Nathan looked perplexed.

'I believe I have made myself perfectly clear. She is an

American vessel and her owners are pressing for her return. They claim she was "illegally detained". Well, the owners always do, of course, but in this case they may have a point. Besides, we have no more use for her in her previous capacity. I gather from your report that the French had already begun to suspect her credentials as a blockade runner. So it would be convenient if I could inform the American ambassador in London that she is on her way back to Boston or New York or wherever it is she came from.'

'I am sorry, my lord, I am being obtuse. You wish me to take her back to New York or Boston?'

'No, damn it, I wish you to take her to Cuba! So you may take command of the *Unicorn*. After that, the *Speedwell* may go to New York, Boston or the North Pole for all I care – but I can tell the American ambassador with perfect justification that she has resumed her voyage across the Atlantic. Is that agreeable to you? Or not?'

'Perfectly, my lord.'

'Very good. Colonel Hollis will arrange for you to embark a contingent of marines at Portsmouth, to reinforce those presently aboard the *Unicorn*. You may find them of use.'

Nathan kept his face carefully composed but he wondered how many there were and how he was supposed to accommodate them aboard the *Speedwell*. This was of minor concern, however, compared to Chatham's next instruction.

'You will also embark a certain gentleman in the capacity of political adviser. I believe you are already acquainted with him from your activities in France. His name is Imlay.'

'*Imlay!*'

Chatham arched his brow. 'I trust this is not disagreeable to you. You did not encounter any problems working with him in France?'

Nathan was lost for words. Imlay had been the American shipping agent in Le Havre, though Nathan had reason to believe he was much more than that. Where his true loyalties lay was still something of a mystery to him – and possibly to a great many other people.

Imlay. 'A man of many parts', as he had instructed Nathan on one occasion: soldier, adventurer, explorer and author of *A Topographical Description of the Western Territory of North America*.

And the man who had brought him news of Sara's death on the guillotine.

Nathan became aware that both men were observing him curiously.

'But . . . is Imlay not in France?' he enquired.

'Mr Imlay has recently arrived in London,' said the colonel. 'I believe you will find him helpful. He speaks excellent Spanish, even one or two of the local Indian tongues. He has spent several years in New Orleans and the Floridas, and has a great many contacts among the American settlers there.'

'Excellent,' beamed the First Lord, clearly anxious to paper over such cracks as he was aware of. 'Well, then, was there anything else?' He contemplated Nathan as if surprised to see him still sitting there.

Nathan collected his scattered thoughts. 'Only, my lord, that you mentioned certain "circumstances".'

'Circumstances?'

'Possibly connected with the previous captain of the *Unicorn*?' Nathan prompted him tactfully.

'Ah yes. Yes, indeed. Captain Kerr. I mentioned that he had died?'

'No, my lord, I do not believe you did, but I imagined that something of that nature might have occurred.'

'Yes. The details are somewhat vague at present. The news came to us from the British consul in the Havana. According to his report, the *Unicorn* arrived there in the first week of August with the news that Captain Kerr was missing.'

'*Missing?*'

'Quite. Missing, one ship's captain. Missing, one ship's cutter. That was the tenor of the first lieutenant's report, as conveyed to us by the British consul in the Havana. Be assured that if we knew more of the situation, you would learn of it.'

Nathan acknowledged the rebuke with a bow. But he was no closer to understanding.

'The incident occurred off the coast of Louisiana,' the colonel informed him. 'The first lieutenant – Mr Pym – stated that he had sent a confidential report of the precise circumstances to Admiral Ford. Doubtless there was a need for discretion – the French maintaining a great many spies in the Havana – and his account will be conveyed to us in due course. However . . .' He sighed again and resumed his study of the ceiling. 'A few days later, the

consul was informed that a body in the uniform of a
captain in the British Navy had been recovered off the
coast of Louisiana and conveyed to New Orleans in a
barrel of rum.'

'Rum!' Nathan raised his brow. Though why he should
express himself astonished at this particular detail, rather
than any other, was as much a mystery to him as it
possibly was to my lord Chatham.

'It is as good a preservative as any, I believe,' His Lordship commented with a frown, 'though brandy, perhaps,
would have been more fitting to his rank.'

Nathan nodded to himself a little as if this made
perfect sense and neither he nor the First Lord were
lunatics in the Bethlehem Hospital conducting an
amusing conversation for the benefit of the paying
visitors.

'There was no indication of how he might have died?'

'Oh yes. Did I not say? His throat had been cut.'

'By his own hand?' Nathan proposed, with a proper
expression of concern. 'Or . . . ?'

The First Lord considered him carefully, as if he were
reassessing his opinion of Nathan's capacity for
command.

'Whilst shaving? Unlikely, I would think – unless he
managed to cut his throat, walk to the side of the ship and
throw himself into the sea. I suppose a man of sufficient
resource might contrive to do that before he bled to death
– what do you think, Colonel?'

The colonel reserved his opinion on the matter,
confining his response to a wry smile.

'It is possible, of course, that it is the body of an impostor wearing the *uniform* of a captain.' Chatham's tone implied that he considered this unlikely. 'But whatever the explanation for this mystery, we must cling to those facts of which we are aware. Captain Kerr is missing. The *Unicorn* is without a commander. And unless he reappears in the near future with a suitable explanation of his absence, you, sir, are appointed in his place.'

'And I am to put myself under Admiral Ford's orders?'

'Did I say that?'

'I beg your pardon, my lord, I—'

'You are under Admiralty orders, sir. Which is to say you are to act upon your present instructions until such a time as . . . as they are amended.'

'And with the advice of Mr Imlay,' put in the colonel quickly.

'Admiral Ford will be instructed accordingly,' said Chatham, standing up to indicate the interview was at an end. 'The Second Secretary has your written orders. I believe you may just have time to provide yourself with a new uniform before you leave London.'

He extended his hand. 'And may I wish you joy of your commission, Captain.'

Chapter Three

Heroes and Whores

———◆———

Nathan stood at the head of the stairs and tried to collect his wits. His brain felt as if it had been shattered into a million pieces, all flying in different directions, but amid this spinning, colliding cosmos one bright star remained constant, solid and unmoving. He was made post captain.

The hall porter was looking at him strangely. Nathan pulled himself together and put on his hat, a semblance of order that would have worked better had he put it on the right way round. He corrected this deficiency and descended the stairs. He had sent away his chaise so the horses would not be left standing in the heat but it was only a short walk across St James's Park to his mother's house.

'I expect you will read of it in the *Gazette* sooner or later,' he addressed the porter with a carelessness that would have fooled no one, least of all a gentleman who had seen it all before, many times, 'but I have been made post.'

'I am very pleased to hear it, sir,' said the porter, with a surprisingly avuncular grin. 'Permit me to be one of the first to congratulate you.'

'Thank you. You are very kind. Perhaps you will take a glass of something with your colleagues to wish me luck.' Nathan slipped him a guinea.

'Be very glad to, sir, and I am sure we wish you all the very best.'

Nathan walked across St James's Park in a continuing state of bewilderment. Post captain. He was made post captain. The captain of a 32-gun frigate. He should be exultant and yet . . .

His principal emotion, now that it had sunk in, was one of grief. A terrible sadness. As if the news of his promotion had triggered the same alchemy of feelings as the news that Imlay had brought him on the Queen's Stairs in the Palace of the Tuileries. That Sara had died on the guillotine.

And Imlay was now in London.

Why?

'You look as one who has seen a ghost.'

Nathan started. There was a man standing a few feet in front of him, smiling.

Nathan looked about him guiltily to see if a crowd had gathered but there was no one else: just the two of them standing by the park lake in the heat of the sun.

'I am sorry.' Nathan shook his head to clear it. 'I forgot my directions.' He raised a hand in a deprecating gesture and made to move on but the man stood directly in his path. A short, thickset individual in his shirt-sleeves, wearing a broad-brimmed straw hat and carrying a large canvas bag by a strap over his shoulder.

'I, too,' he said, smiling still.

'I beg your pardon?' Nathan repeated, but frowning now. There was something in this smile that cautioned him. It occurred to him that the man was not all there.

'I, too, have forgot my directions. I am looking for Queen Anne's Gate.'

'Well . . .' Nathan hesitated. He was not eager for company but there was no way of avoiding it, unless he loitered in the park until the man had gone. 'As a matter of fact, I am going that way myself,' he admitted. 'If you would care to accompany me?'

'Willingly,' said the man, 'if you have now remembered where it is you are going.' He grinned widely to remove the possibility of giving offence. If he was not a simpleton, there was certainly something childlike about him, though he was well past his first youth. He had a snub nose and large brown eyes that had a look almost of rapture. Or mischief, it was hard to tell.

They walked on.

'Saint James's Park,' said the man in a tone of mild bemusement.

'Correct,' said Nathan. 'You are a stranger to London?'

'Oh, I have lived here all my life,' said the man. 'I was born in Soho and now I live in Lambeth. I have walked from one end of London to the other many times but I have not walked in Saint James's Park for many a long year. I find the lepers disconcerting.'

'The leopards?' Nathan looked for them in alarm. It was entirely possible they were a recent introduction. The park belonged to the Crown, though it had been open to the public since the days of the second Charles, and King George, in the present state of his wits, might readily conceive of leopards.

'Good gracious no!' The man laughed at the absurdity of this notion. *'Lepers.'*

'Ah!' Nathan nodded understandingly, as if they were a nuisance to most Londoners from time to time.

'I saw them the last time I was here down by the lake,' the lunatic assured him, 'and it disturbed me a little. Though in truth this was foolish.'

'Not at all,' Nathan corrected him politely. 'Lepers should not be wandering around Saint James's Park. They should be in a leper colony.'

'Oh, but it was a leper colony. Many years ago.'

'Truly?'

'In the reign of Edward the First.'

'Is that so?'

Imlay in London. As an American – a neutral – he could come and go as he liked, of course, provided he could obtain transport. But what had induced him to leave Paris? And what of Mary and the child? Had he brought them with him – or left them in France?

'I saw Edward the First once. In his coffin.'

And what was his interest in the Caribbean? For surely he must have an interest. He could not have been motivated purely by the interests of His Majesty's Government.

Somewhere in the back of his mind there was a clue to this – but he needed time and space to think on it. And here he was conversing with a madman.

'He had been dead for more than four hundred and fifty years.'

'That is a long time. And what did he look like?'

'Very old,' said the man.

Nathan laughed despite his unease.

'His face was dark brown, like chocolate, approaching to black. And so were his hands and fingers.' The man furrowed his brow in concentration as if trying to recall the exact detail. 'The chin and lips were entire, but no beard. Both the lips were prominent, the nose short, as if shrunk, but the apertures of the nostrils were visible . . .'

Nathan glanced at him in surprise. Clearly, this was no ordinary madman.

'A quantity of black dust was visible in the folds of the neck and jaw, but whether it had been flesh, or spices, could not be ascertained.'

'Spices?'

'Yes. He had been embalmed.'

'Where did you see this?' Nathan was genuinely curious now.

'In Westminster Abbey – in 1774 when they opened his coffin. I was making drawings of the tombs.'

'Really?' He began to perceive some sense in this. 'You are an historian?' A category of madman permitted to walk the streets, he recalled, being accounted harmless.

'No. But I have a great interest in history.'

They walked on in silence for a while and were nearing Birdcage Walk when the man spoke again.

'I hope you did not take it amiss, what I said to you?'

'What was that?'

'That you looked like a man who had seen a ghost.'

'Not at all.'

'It was not meant to be derogatory.'

'I am sure it was not.'

'I see ghosts myself, quite frequently. Though personally I do not use the expression. I think of them more as visions, or visitations, of what has been and what is to come. And then there are the angels, who have a different relationship with time.'

'And what form do they take, these angels?' Nathan enquired, more with a view to humouring him than from any genuine need for information on the subject.

'Oh, many forms. But, in general, more human than not.' He beamed and tapped the side of his head. 'It is in here,' he said. 'In the mind. In the imagination.'

Nathan was relieved to know it. He smiled and nodded in apparent agreement.

Thus encouraged, the stranger continued: 'Though sometimes I wonder if there is more than one universe – perhaps many others – that exist beside our own, but in another dimension of time and space. And maybe sometimes, some of us are permitted a glimpse, as if through a torn curtain. No.' He frowned as if the comparison displeased him. 'Not a curtain. More – a mist that suddenly parts and then closes again.'

They were approaching Queen Anne's Gate.

'What number were you looking for?' Nathan asked him.

'Number forty-four. The house of Lady Catherine Peake.'

Of course. Nathan should have known. In a sense, he *had* known from the moment he clapped eyes on the man.

'Lady Catherine is my mother,' he said.

A collector of strays, dissidents, malcontents and madmen from many dimensions.

The man stopped and peered up at Nathan from under the brim of his hat. He was a good half a foot shorter.

'How very curious,' he said. 'But then again, perhaps not.'

'My mother is expecting you?'

'Indeed. I have some things to show her.' The man indicated the bag on his shoulder.

What things, wondered Nathan in alarm. Bones, relics, the remains of an embalmed King? His finger, perhaps – or worse?

'Some engravings. A mutual acquaintance was good enough to recommend me to her.'

'You are an artist?'

'An engraver,' the man replied firmly. 'As the world would know me. For all that it is not valued as art, it provides a living for such as I. "I have taught pale artifice to spread his nets upon the morning. My heavens are brass, my earth is iron."'

'I see.'

'And you, I see, are a naval man.'

'Indeed.'

'One who has been in the wars, I think.'

Did it show in his face? 'We live in troubled times,' Nathan remarked mildly.

'"I, all drunk with unsatiated love, must rush again to war, for the virgin has frowned and refused."'

'I beg your pardon?' Nathan regarded him with alarm at mention of the word 'virgin'.

'No matter.'

They walked on; Nathan shook off his superstition.

'Well, this is it,' he said as they reached the door of his mother's house.

'Perhaps I should knock at the tradesman's entrance,' said the man, with another smile, though Nathan did not think he considered the concept amusing.

'Nonsense,' he replied firmly. 'Not at all.'

They mounted the steps together and Nathan rang the bell. Phipps, his mother's man, opened the door, greeting Nathan with a smile and a bow.

'How very good it is to see you, sir.'

'And you, Mr Phipps. This gentleman has come to see my mother,' he added briskly, for he had noted the faintly raised brow. Phipps knew a tradesman when he saw one, and whatever the egalitarian principles espoused by his mistress, he was more than willing to direct him to the correct entrance. 'And is expected.'

'Lady Catherine is in the withdrawing room,' Phipps replied, stepping back a pace.

It occurred to Nathan that it might not be such a good

idea to greet his mother, after an absence of some months, with a stranger in tow.

'Perhaps you would be good enough to show the gentleman into the library while I pay my respects,' he said.

His mother was sitting in the window with a book on her lap but she leaped up at sight of Nathan and flew to him like a young girl.

'My dearest, darling boy!' Nathan succumbed to an assault of muslin and scent. Too much scent and too little muslin.

'Mother!' He stepped back, and inspected her. 'What are you wearing? Or should I say *not* wearing?'

'This? What on earth can you mean, sir? I assure you it is the very height of fashion.'

'It may very well be, madam . . .' He was about to add 'for a girl of seventeen' but thought better of it. Nathan was very fond of his mother and quite proud of her at times, but at other times he wished she might be a little more stately.

'And can it be,' he recoiled in pretended shock as he noticed another facet of her appearance, 'that you are not wearing stays?'

'Fi, sir, and who wears stays, these days, that is under forty?'

Nathan made no comment. It seemed a day for delusions.

'What a way to greet your mother,' she continued indignantly, 'after an absence of however long it is. I've a good mind to box your ears.'

'It is not permitted,' he informed her, 'to box the ears of a captain in His Majesty's Navy, especially when he is wearing the King's uniform. I believe it is regarded as a crime of *lèse majesté* and you may be put in the stocks for it.'

She regarded him warily. 'You? Post captain? But you are a mere child.'

'I am twenty-five, madam.'

'Nonsense. What would that make me?'

Nathan forbore to astonish her.

'Well, I am very pleased for you, little one,' she said, stretching her arms to reach around his neck, 'if only they send you back to me alive and in one piece. You will be an admiral before we know it, just like your father, though I will not disguise from you that while this dreadful war continues I would as soon you were with him in Sussex minding sheep.'

'You despise sheep,' he reminded her. 'You have often remarked upon it.'

'Yes, but at least they have the sense to remain upon dry land and do not engage in wars, if I am not entirely misinformed on the subject. Have you seen your father lately?' Nathan's father and sheep being entirely associated in his mother's mind.

'I have just come up from Sussex,' Nathan informed her with perfect truth, though he did not add that he had been there several weeks without paying her a visit. This was no mere churlishness on his part but he had been in too much pain and sorrow from his last visit to France – and besides, there was Alex to be considered. It had seemed to him that it was better for them to stay with his father in the country for a while. But not without regret. He wished he had been able to tell his mother about Sara – to unburden himself of the anguish and the grief. He would like to have introduced her to Alex. But this would have involved telling something of his secret work in France and invited a score of supplementary questions. Questions his father would never ask.

Nathan knew his mother to be warm, generous and kind hearted, a prey to every lame dog with a long face and a tall story. But she was famously indiscreet. Whereas his father rarely, if ever, revealed his feelings, much less spoke of them, his mother was of that gregarious faction that regarded a secret as of value only if it were shared with as many of her acquaintance as were in favour at the time. She was not a frivolous person – indeed, she was at times too involved in politics and the serious business of the country for her own good – but she was more inclined to sensibility than to sense.

Unlike his father, as she frequently observed.

'And how is he?' she enquired now.

'He is very well. Indeed, I would say, hearty.'

'Hearty. Yes. It must be all that country air, and the company he keeps.'

Nathan glanced at her sharply. He wondered if she knew anything of his father's plans regarding Frances Wyndham. It would not have surprised him. His mother maintained that gossip was merely a means of intelligence-gathering and she was as good at it as any spymaster. He felt guilty that he could not share his information with her on this point, or his concerns. But it would only worry her and it would not have been fair to his father. And besides, he still hoped the latter might change his mind or find the unpleasantness involved too difficult to contemplate.

She reached a hand to his cheek. 'Poor Nat, I do not want you to have to choose between us. Look at you, a captain at your age. Well, there must be something of your father in you, for all that you do not at all resemble him. Do you still paint? I had hoped once that you would be an artist.'

Nathan rolled his eyes. 'I had almost forgot. There is a gentleman waiting to see you. I met him crossing the park. He has some engravings to show you. I left him in the library.'

'Oh, that will be Mr Blake.' She glanced at the clock on the mantelpiece. 'I told him to come at two. Mr Flaxman recommended him to me. Hell and damnation. I will tell Phipps to send him away.'

'No, you will not,' Nathan instructed her firmly. 'Not on my account. Let him show you his work. I will still be here when you get back.'

'And for some time after, I hope.' She raised her brow in what was both query and reproof. He did not respond. 'Ring the bell and ask Phipps to bring you up some refreshment. You look as if you need it.'

Nathan did as instructed and was delivered in very little time with the best part of a chicken and a jug of cool ale. He took them over to the window seat where he could dine at ease while gazing out over the park. After a short time he observed his former companion trudging back the way he had come with his bag over his shoulder. Something in his gait advised Nathan that he had not been successful. His heart went out to him. And in that moment the man turned and appeared to look straight at him with a severe expression. Nathan raised a hand in greeting – unfortunately with a leg of the fowl still in it, which might be taken amiss. But either the man did not see him or declined to return the salute. He turned again and continued on his way.

A moment later, Nathan's mother returned.

'Well, that was a waste of time,' she said. 'But I knew it would be. I am too easily prevailed upon.'

'Nothing to your liking?'

'It may surprise certain of my acquaintance, but I do not care to gaze upon pictures of naked, muscle-bound men. I do not know what John Flaxman can have been thinking of. God knows what people have been saying to him about me.'

This was not a subject Nathan could comment upon with any degree of comfort.

'I should have come down with you,' he said. 'I might have been more interested.'

'Really?' His mother arched her slender brows. 'I had no idea you were so inclined. Indeed, there were some illustrations of the wanderings of Odysseus which, now I come to think on it, might have been somewhat to your taste, though the private parts were, I recall, veiled, when they were not being pecked at by harpies . . . Which reminds me, he begged me to give you a message. I was not

sure that I would, but as you are clearly smitten . . . He
said to tell you that you will find what you have lost – but
that you are to beware the Sirens, especially the one that
plays the lyre.' Her tone was sardonic but she watched
him carefully for a reaction.

'He said what?'

'Do you really wish me to repeat it?'

' "I will find what I have lost". What can he have meant
by that?' Nathan spoke lightly but he felt a prickling
among the hairs of his neck.

'I really have no idea. Odious man. How I hate these
self-proclaimed mystics and prophets who seek power
over others by claiming to have the ability to see what
others cannot. Like those wicked children of Salem who
did for your great-great-grandmother.'

Lady Kitty's mode of debate was famously erratic, but
for once Nathan knew precisely what she was talking
about.

Nathan's great-great-grandmother, Sarah Good, had
been hanged as a witch in Salem, Massachusetts,
shortly before it went out of fashion, she and several of
her neighbours having been accused of conjuring the
Devil. They had posthumously been pardoned, their
judges and accusers exposed to ridicule and retribution,
but Sarah Good had not risen from the grave and Lady
Catherine was disposed to harbour a grudge on her
behalf.

'*Have* you lost anything of late?' she quizzed Nathan,
sharply raising her brow.

'No. Nothing of any importance,' he lied.

'Well, then,' she declared in triumph, 'there you are! You must not allow yourself to be beguiled by charlatans, my pet. You are just like your father, who was always touching wood for fear of some heedless word that would sink a ship at sea, and he would have a seizure if one spilled a little salt upon the table and did not at once pick up every grain and hurl it over one's shoulder like a demented flagellant.'

'I wish you would not be forever accusing me of being "just like my father",' Nathan complained. 'You know you would hate it if I was.'

'Well, you are just as feeble minded when it comes to religion and all that stuff.'

This remark troubled Nathan more than he was prepared to reveal. He had been brought up in the same Anglican tradition as his father – and all his father's family since the Reformation – and had attended church with him every Sunday during his recent stay in Sussex as if his beliefs were as soundly entrenched as in his childhood. But in truth he merely went through the motions of worship. He admired the old church at Alfriston, which had been there when the last Saxon thane had marched off to join King Harold at Senlac, but the rituals of the Anglican service no longer reassured or comforted him. He would have drawn more consolation from walking by the sea, listening to the rhythms of the waves and the gentle growling of the pebbles on the shore, and he did not admire the vicar, a vain man who sucked up to the gentry and lorded it over the rest of the parish. His sermons seemed mere cant to Nathan, empty renderings of the Scriptures which were as impossible to comprehend as they were to sleep through, the Reverend Judd having a way of emphasising words and phrases with a total disregard for grammar or meaning but with a vehemence and unpredictability that was reputedly capable of waking the dead from their slumbers – and certainly had that effect upon the slightly more sentient bodies in the pews.

But a more accomplished preacher than the Reverend Judd would have struggled to impress Nathan in his current mood of pessimism and despair. He could discern no divine plan in the slaughter he had witnessed during the time of the Terror in Paris. And yet he could not bring himself to believe in the opposite: that all was random. Chaos. Or as the Reverend Judd and his father would have it: the work of the Devil.

As a student of astronomy, Nathan was inclined to believe that a certain Order prevailed in the universe. That the planets moved in a certain pattern that was not at all random. His rational mind persuaded him that this Order was predetermined by nothing more wonderful than magnetism or clockwork (though these were wonderful enough in themselves), but his more romantic disposition longed for something more human. A clockmaker perhaps. Or a regulator. A benevolent old gentleman, by no means as magnificent as the Christian god, but whose function it was to keep the parts in working order and make delicate adjustments from time to time, when he felt they were called for.

But Nathan was obliged to admit there was little

evidence for such a benign presence, at least on Earth –
rather the opposite, in fact – and he sought solace in signs
and portents and other such mysteries that hinted at some
sort of order, if only it could be perceived.

He knew that in many ways he was as superstitious and
as whimsical as his father, or old Abe Eldridge – and
almost every mariner and countryman he had ever known
– and he knew his mother knew it too. So he told her he
considered it harsh of her to condemn a man as odious,
simply for issuing a warning that was doubtless intended
kindly, and mean spirited of her to send him packing
without a purchase, just because her great-grandmother
had been hanged as a witch.

She regarded him thoughtfully for a moment.

'Well, as to the former,' she said, 'I stand by what I said
earlier. It *is* an odious expression of self-importance and a
pathetic desire for attention that can cause much distress
to those gullible and weak minded enough to give
credence to it. And as to the latter, it is not that I am mean
spirited but that I find his images not at all to my taste
and, indeed, quite offensive. And besides,' she added,
turning her face away and gazing at some distant point
beyond the window, 'I have no money.'

'You have no money?' Nathan repeated foolishly. 'What
do you mean, you have no money?' He glanced around at
the rich furnishings of the room. Nothing appeared to be
missing since he had last seen it. Not that he would have
noticed.

'Oh, I have not yet been obliged to sell the furniture,'
she reassured him, 'but your war has played the very devil

with my investments. And now my bank has failed. Failed utterly, to the ruin of all.'

'My God.' Nathan was shocked, for he had always known his mother to be wealthy. 'Can nothing be done?'

'Oh, I suppose they will save something from the wreck but I have been told I can expect no more than a few pence in the pound. So,' she smiled brightly, 'we must dine on porridge and pease pudding and gather sea coal from the beaches.'

'What of your family in America? Can they not help?'

The Bouchards were as rich as Croesus, he had always supposed. Certainly this was his father's opinion and Nathan had seen the houses they kept in New York.

'Oh, I expect I could throw myself upon their mercy if I were so minded, but they have enough troubles of their own at present.'

Nathan raised a brow.

'My family has always made its living from the sea,' she informed him as if they were poor fishermen and not the richest merchants in Manhattan, 'and the sea is a desperate place at the best of times, you know, while at time of war its perils are considerably multiplied.'

'This is something we in the Navy have often remarked upon,' Nathan agreed. 'But their lordships remain unmoved.'

'And you are doubtless aware that the British blockade is the ruin of all honest traders.'

'Only those who trade with the enemy,' he retorted. 'Those who trade with Britain are well rewarded.'

'If they manage to evade the privateers and the French

national ships and the English captains who would rob them of their crews for the King's service as if they were still his subjects.'

But Nathan did not want a row, especially upon such uncertain ground, so he merely shook his head and expressed his genuine sorrow for her losses.

'I will transfer five thousand pounds into your account at once,' he assured her, 'or perhaps, in the circumstances, you would prefer it in coin.'

She regarded him in astonishment. 'How come you by five thousand pounds?' she demanded. 'Did your father give it you? And how did *he* come by it? Not by selling sheep!' Lady Catherine had a very low opinion of the value of sheep.

'No, it is by my own endeavour,' Nathan assured her, and when she remained sceptical: 'Prize money.'

'Prize money? You mean you are one of those pirates who prey on merchant shipping?'

'Not at all,' he insisted, though his views on the practice were more liberal than hers. 'It is from the sale of the French national ship I took in the Baie de Seine. The *Vestale*. A frigate of thirty-two guns. You read the report.'

'So I did. When you near lost a leg. And they paid you five thousand pounds for it?' She still sounded dubious.

In fact, the *Vestale* had been valued at £18,000 and he had received his full three-eighths share as commander of the sloop *Nereus*, being under the direct orders of the Admiralty at the time and with no flag officer to take his cut. But his prize agent had taken the proper percentage and Nathan had distributed a thousand pounds among the crew of the *Speedwell* who, being American, had not been included in the official division of the spoils.

'No, I'll not take your money,' she insisted, 'for I am not yet so destitute and you may have need of it.' She said this with such a look he was convinced she was better informed of his father's affairs than Sir Michael might have wished.

'I tell you what,' he said, 'I will share it with you. Fifty-fifty. That is fair.'

But she shook her head firmly. 'No, it would be against my principles to profit from the war, which I have always opposed, as you know – though you must do your duty as you see fit and I do not blame you for it.'

'But what will you do?'

'Oh, I will find myself a wealthy admirer, which is perfectly within my capacity, you know.' Nathan frowned, never doubting it. 'And in the meantime I will carry on pretty much as before, for it is never advisable to advertise one's poverty to the world. Save that I will not buy pictures I do not want, wretched boy.'

'I am very sorry,' he conceded, in all sincerity. 'I spoke out of turn. It is only that I have always known you to have money. I wish you would let me give you some. I hate to see you distressed.'

'Oh, I am not distressed. Nothing like as distressed as the great mass of the populace. Or the poor people of France, who endure even greater privations.'

Nathan shared her concern but she had presented him with an opportunity he could not despise.

'Do you ever hear from your friend Mrs Wollstonecraft,' he enquired casually, 'that was in Paris?'

Lady Catherine regarded him with suspicion. 'Why do you ask after Mary Wollstonecraft? You have never expressed the least interest in her before.'

'Only that you mentioned the poor people of France and I wondered if she was still there and what had become of her since the war. I am surprised she has faded from view for she enjoyed a degree of celebrity, I recall, when she was in London.'

'"A degree of celebrity"?' his mother echoed mockingly. 'She was notorious! "A hyena in petticoats", that rogue Walpole called her, and all because she spoke for the rights of women. Did you ever read her book that I gave you?'

'I started it,' he began defensively.

'You started it. And were the words too long for you, my pet?'

'Mother, I merely asked if you had heard from her. I did not wish for a critical assessments of my faculties. Or to become involved in the rights of women, of which I am generally in favour, whether or not I have read Mrs Wollstonecraft.'

'Mrs Imlay,' she corrected him absently.

'I beg your pardon?'

'She married. An American. By the name of Imlay.' It did not appear to be a name she approved.

'So you have heard from her?'

'I did correspond with her for a while,' Lady Catherine replied cautiously, 'while the post remained operative. You know she was in Paris to write about the Revolution?'

Nathan shook his head, though he knew it very well – and a great deal more he was not prepared to reveal.

'Well, she was in great danger, of course, when war was declared. And then I heard that she had married an American called Imlay. I understood it to be a marriage of convenience, if that is the word, for as the wife of a United States citizen she was safe from arrest, but apparently she fell in love with the man and the last I heard was with child.'

Nathan affected surprise, though he had met Mary several times in France and on the last occasion he had even met the child, a baby girl called Fanny. He had wondered if Mary had mentioned this in her letters to his mother, but either they had failed to get through or she had been discreet. Marriage to Imlay would have taught her the value of discretion.

At any rate it would appear his mother knew considerably less than he, or was dissembling as shamelessly. Then she said: 'And now the scoundrel has deserted her and is living with an actress from a strolling theatre company in Charlotte Street.'

Nathan blinked, for this was a genuine surprise. 'How do you know this?' he enquired.

'We have acquaintance in common. Indeed, I saw him at a soirée only a few nights since, bold as brass with the hussy on his arm. I should not call her hussy,' she shook her head at the iniquity, 'for I doubt he told her he was married, and if any is deserving of the word it is he. But, of course, it is not applied to a man.'

'And did you speak with him?'

'I did not. I snubbed him most severely. And so did most of the company, for Mary was well liked among those with half a brain and they know something of her circumstance.' But she looked a trifle concerned. 'The trouble is that from what I have heard, the marriage was not quite regular. I mean, it was not conducted in a church or by a member of the clergy but by the American Ambassador in Paris, who apparently has that authority vested in him, like the captain of a ship. But if it is disputed – or Imlay denies it – there are those who would think the worst of her. They already call her whore and this will merely confirm them in their opinion. Not that one should care a hoot, of course.'

'And would Imlay be likely to deny that he was married to her?'

'Assuredly – if he felt his present association reflected badly on him.'

'With the actress, you mean?'

'Not that it seems to trouble society when men behave like whores,' Lady Catherine reflected bitterly, 'and he is reckoned to be something of a hero, I believe, in certain circles. I suppose being a womaniser only adds to his "heroic" qualities.'

'So he is well known in London?'

'Oh, quite famous, even. Not notorious, like poor Mary. He is received everywhere, even with an actress upon his arm. Such are the times we live in.'

His mother was an unlikely moralist but for once
Nathan agreed with her. He had a great regard for Mary
Wollstonecraft, even if he had not read her *Vindication of
the Rights of Women*. He admired her pluck and her
sharp wit – and then, she had been a good friend of Sara's
and had looked after Alex when Sara was in prison.

As for Imlay, Nathan had few illusions where he was
concerned, but they had shared a number of adventures
together and for all his duplicity the man was not without
charm, or conscience. Nathan doubted he had abandoned
Mary and her child for ever. But nor did he for a moment
doubt that Imlay would take advantage of their absence to
amuse himself with an actress in Charlotte Street.

'I hope if you ever meet him,' said his mother, 'you will
treat him with the contempt he deserves and not be
fawning upon him like other men.'

'Oh, I expect I would be obliged to call him out,'
Nathan replied lightly, 'but I am unlikely to have that
honour unless you have invited him for dinner, for I must
leave London at crack of dawn to join my ship on the
south coast. We will be sailing on the next tide.'

This was not entirely true. He needed to collect some
things from Windover and to bid goodbye to his father
and Alex. But he had already sent Gilbert Gabriel ahead
of him to prepare the ship's company and to instruct his
First Officer, Martin Tully, to get in supplies for a lengthy
voyage.

His mother's face fell and he moved quickly to her side
on the couch and put his arm around her shoulder.

'So come, bring on the porridge and the pease

pudding,' he said, 'and we will make the best of it until I come roaring home with my fortune made – in a manner you cannot but approve – and all your problems will be over.'

'Just come back safe and sound,' she said, squeezing his hand and close to tears. 'Other problems I can deal with.'

Chapter Four

Pirates

———◆———

The log ship splashed over the leeward quarter and shot swiftly astern in a millrace of white water, watched with eager eyes by as many of the company as had secured a place along the rail.

'Turn!' yelled Francis Coyle as the ribbon crossed the rail; his voice, which had recently broken, pitched a little higher than he might have wished in the presence of so wide and critical an audience.

His young associate Mr Place dutifully turned the 28-second timer and held it level with his eye. An expectant hush from the audience. The wind played its endless music in the taut rigging. The last grain of sand . . .

'*Stop!*'

Coyle nipped the line between finger and thumb, measured the distance from the last knot with a practised eye and ran back to the little group of figures at the stern with a look of barely suppressed excitement upon his freckled features.

'Twelve knots and three fathoms, sir. If you please.' Remembering to snatch off his cap only at the conclusion of this astonishing revelation.

'Thank you, Mr Coyle,' replied Nathan coolly, keeping his own face straight with an effort. He turned away with his arms clasped behind his back but not before he had seen the grins on the faces of the nearest hands and heard the gleeful repetition along the rail.

Twelve knots and a half, near as damn it: the best yet by almost two knots. Nathan caught the eye of the mate, and his particular friend, Martin Tully, and permitted his face to relax a little. He would have laughed aloud had he not feared the wind might take it amiss. For the past three days the *Speedwell* had been running before a brisk north-easterly that had taken them far out into the Atlantic to some hundred leagues north of the Azores, rarely dropping below seven to eight knots and often exceeding that. In the past few hours it had shifted somewhat to the east without diminishing in intensity. Nathan restrained himself from reckless remark, but could not help thinking that at this rate they would make the Havana in little more than a month from now. But of course that could never be – his innate pessimism reasserted itself – and even then it would be nearer three since Captain Kerr first 'went missing' with his cutter. Three months for the *Unicorn* and the *Virginie* to conclude their dalliance in the waters of the Caribbean or the Gulf of Mexico or wherever they chanced to meet.

The *Virginie* had been Nathan's particular study since he first heard of her from the First Lord of the Admiralty. She was a new ship, almost as new as the *Unicorn* but armed as Chatham had said with forty-four guns – forty 18-pounders and four 36-pounder *obusiers*: a short-barrelled weapon not unlike a carronade but with a higher elevation more in line with a mortar. He could learn little of Commodore Lafitte but her captain was a man called Delarge who had risen from the lower deck, and although many of Nathan's colleagues were inclined to sneer at the new breed of officers thrown up by the Revolution, there was no reason to doubt his competence. If it had, indeed, been a humorous conceit of Admiral Ford to send a unicorn in pursuit of a virgin, it could be the French who had the laugh on him. Nathan could not help but recall that in the myth, it was the beast that came off worse from the encounter. Yet here he was, exulting in the headlong rush to battle, curbing his impatience lest it should not be fast enough to find the *Unicorn* before she found her *Virginie*. As if his presence alone would make the difference between victory and defeat.

He was not normally so sanguine. His recent promotion had done little to address a somewhat negative assessment of his abilities as an officer: a doubt that had persisted since first obtaining his commission. He had some ability as a commander, if only in the command of detail, but he privately considered he was more suited to the role of purser. He constantly failed to measure up to his own standards of what he considered to be outstanding leadership, and his skills as a navigator were far eclipsed by Tully, who could take in a chart at a glance as if the rocks and shoals came leaping out at him, and was possessed of an almost mystical sense of direction and their position upon the map as if sextants and quadrants were mere playthings for the less gifted. A natural-born sailor, he had an instinctive feel for the sea and the wind and their effect upon hull and sail which Nathan could only labour dully to emulate, struggling with the mathematics, his brain relentlessly obsessed with calculation.

He was good with men, too. Nathan watched him covertly as he leaned against the rail, conversing amiably with the second mate, Jonathan Keeble. He appeared to be at ease with most of his acquaintance, whether they were old salts like Keeble, born and bred on the waterfront at Marblehead, or the Honourable Philip Whiteley, the lieutenant of marines who had joined them at Portsmouth and was the second son of a viscount.

But perhaps this was not surprising, given his own background.

Tully was a Channel Islander: the son of a Guernsey fisherman who had married the daughter of a local *seigneur* – and though the young woman had been disowned by her family for the offence and died soon after, Tully had been taken into his grandfather's house to receive the education and upbringing of a gentleman.

But some recalcitrant strain had inclined the boy to take his father's part and at the age of sixteen he had quit the seigneurial home to become first a fisherman and then a smuggler, in which latter occupation he had been

surprised by a British sloop and given the choice of
serving in the Navy or assisting in the colonisation
of Botany Bay. He had been master's mate on the *Nereus*
and Nathan had formed a sufficient respect for his skills
to retain his services on the *Speedwell* during her covert
missions to Le Havre.

If and when he assumed command of the *Unicorn* he
had resolved to make Tully up to acting lieutenant.

'Mr Place, there!' Tully broke off his conversation with
Keeble to fling out a rebuke to the senior of the two boys
who were clowning about some fifty feet above his head in
the futtock shrouds. Place had just snatched at Coyle's
cap, missed, and almost lost his footing on the ropes. 'If
you must contrive to kill yourself, sir, pray indulge me by
doing so over the sea so we will not be obliged to scrub
you off the deck.'

The two boys grinned but climbed into the maintop
where they were safer and less noticeable.

Coyle and Place. An unlikely alliance. Nathan
wondered if it would endure until they reached the
Havana where, inevitably, they must part – for Coyle
belonged to the *Speedwell* and Place . . . Place belonged to
King George.

Place's mother had by some divine process learned of
Nathan's appointment to post captain and surprised him
at Shoreham with young William in tow. She was the
widow of one of his father's old shipmates who had been
killed at the Battle of the Saints when his son was barely a
year old and she had often been a guest at Windover. She
had begged Nathan to take her son into the service as a

volunteer, for he had his heart set on it, she said – and after some feeble protests Nathan had agreed. He had been much the same age himself when he had joined the Navy, taken on by another of his father's old shipmates: it was the way the system worked. And if Nathan did not entirely approve of it, he had not declined to take advantage of it for most of his life.

And so young William Place would join Nathan on the *Unicorn* as a captain's servant, Volunteer First Class: the first step on a ladder that could make him an admiral, if he did not fall off it and break his neck – and his mother's heart.

But Coyle was a different case. He had been cabin boy on the *Speedwell* when Nathan first took command of her. Just turned twelve. A by-blow of the mate, it was said, who had jumped ship – or been taken by the press, it was not entirely clear. Either way, Frankie had been left to fend for himself, though he was in the way of becoming a ship's mascot even then. An engaging lad. They both were: he and his new friend. Willing and able. But Nathan could not look at them without thinking of Alex – and remembering the expression on his face when Nathan told him he was going back to sea and leaving him at Windover.

'Take me with you,' he had begged, fighting back the tears. 'Please, *monsieur*, I will try not to trouble you.' But Nathan could not take a seven year old into the Navy.

'I will be back soon,' he said, with no means of knowing if it would be this year or next – or ever. 'And you will be a good boy while I am away and apply yourself to your studies so that your mother would be proud of you.'

Feeling that he had deserted him. And betrayed her.

He had left early the next morning, before Alex was up, and he did not dare look back for fear of seeing his desolate face in the window.

Three bells into the afternoon watch. Nathan turned at the stern rail, braced against the sharp cant of the deck as the barque leaned into the long Atlantic swell. And the unknown figure at her bow – Diane the huntress or some lesser deity? – hurling the spray from her flowing locks as she hurried back to her home waters.

Nathan would be sorry to see the *Speedwell* go. She and all her dissolute crew. He watched them now as they lounged about the deck. He knew them all by name and character, though he might flatter himself as to the latter for they were born smugglers and dissemblers: blockade runners who had almost certainly been running contraband into France when they were taken by a British cruiser off La Rochelle. Most were from Salem or Marblehead, a few from Boston, all Massachusetts men and some old enough to have fought against the Crown during the Independence War – yet they had been willing enough to serve King George, if only for the bounty it paid them. And they appeared well enough disposed to the thirty marines the *Speedwell* had taken aboard at Portsmouth, inasmuch as any seaman could tolerate so alien a species.

The marines had been accommodated in the hold – with hooks rigged for their hammocks and gratings to give them light – much to the amusement of the Americans, who said they had never shipped redcoats before: though they did not call them guffies or jollies or Johnny-toe-the-liners as a British crew would. In fact, with Nathan's consent, the marines had shed their coats and wore their chequered shirts or seamen's slops, mixing freely with the hands on deck, far more freely than would have been tolerated on a British man of war where they might at any moment be called upon to assist the captain and officers against a mutinous or even mildly subordinate crew.

Nathan was perfectly aware that this service might be required of them if and when he assumed command of the *Unicorn*, for the fate of her previous captain remained a mystery. At least to him. And if members of the crew had been involved, an extra contingent of marines would be useful.

Nathan had wondered if the First Lord of the Admiralty knew more of the affair than he was prepared to admit. It would not be the first time he had kept Nathan in the dark about things, but on this occasion it seemed unlikely. No. He was persuaded that Chatham had told him as much as he himself knew – at least as far as the former captain of the *Unicorn* was concerned.

But Imlay was a different matter.

Nathan shifted his gaze to the companionway that led down to his cabin – and the cabin next to it where Imlay was accommodated.

'I fear I am but a poor sailor,' he had announced, shortly after leaving harbour, the pallor of his complexion suggesting that for once he was not dissembling. For the first two days he had protested he felt too queasy for either food or conversation, and as the wind freshened he had retired to his cabin and remained there for most of the time since, his continuing presence announced by the sounds of one in the throes of violent nausea. Nathan had sent Coyle and Place and even the Angel Gabriel to attend to him on numerous occasions. They had ensured he drank sufficient water to stay alive and even to take a little dry bread with a thin gruel, but anything more substantial was strenuously resisted. And the last thing he required, he assured them, was company.

Nathan was sympathetic but it was almost a week since he had seen Imlay for more than a brief moment and he was beginning to wonder, perhaps unfairly, if the American had taken lessons in playacting from his recent companion in Charlotte Street.

For the last two days he had been quieter – sleeping, Gabriel had assured Nathan when sent to ensure he had not expired. But he had slept long enough. It was time he took some air. And applied his mind to their mission.

Nathan's written orders confirmed that he was to count on Imlay for advice on all matters pertaining to the territories of the King of Spain in North America and the Caribbean. It would be some time, even at their current progress, before the need for such advice became urgent. But there were other questions pressing upon Nathan's mind.

'Mr Place,' he raised his voice so that it carried to the boy in the maintop. 'When you have finished your business aloft I should be glad of your company upon the deck.'

A brief – a very brief – interlude and Place came sliding down the mainmast backstay as if it had been designed for the express purpose of delivering small boys from one sphere to another in the minimum possible time, short of pitching headlong to their doom.

'My compliments to Mr Imlay,' Nathan instructed him in quieter tones, 'and if he is feeling a little better I would be glad to have a word with him, either in my cabin or his or upon the deck, whichever he prefers.'

'Sir.' Place turned smartly about but then checked and turned back, a troubled frown contorting his youthful features. 'Beg pardon, sir, but if he is not?' Nathan raised a brow. 'Not feeling better, sir.'

It was in Nathan's mind to suggest that Mr Place might then seek the assistance of two stout marines in dragging him up on deck by the scruff of his neck, but of course he merely inclined his head and responded that it might be appropriate to consider that problem if and when the need should arise.

Place was back within the space of a minute. Mr Imlay returned the captain's compliments and was feeling some-what recovered, thank you, if still not strong, and would contrive to attend upon the captain as soon as he had finished his dinner.

'His *dinner*?'

'Yes, sir, Mrs Small having prepared him a little dish of rice and coddled eggs which she is feeding him in his cabin, sir, owing to the delicacy of his stomach.'

Nathan caught Tully's eye and knew what he was thinking.

Mrs Small was the cook's wife, a Frenchwoman whom he had met and married in Le Havre – and a far better cook than he would ever be if he lived to be a thousand. But she was not handsome – in Nathan's view she rather resembled an amiable troll – and he was inclined to think she was safe from Imlay's attentions, especially in his weakened state.

'I trust she has not coddled the eggs in too much butter,' Nathan remarked, 'or we will not see him for the remainder of the voyage.'

But within a few minutes of this exchange the invalid appeared on deck, looking appreciably paler and thinner than when he had come aboard and a little unsteady on his feet, but sufficiently the master of his inner self as to contemplate the sea if not with equanimity then at least without bringing up his dinner.

Nathan had a chair lashed to the 6-pounder at the stern where Imlay might repose in a degree of comfort and where they might converse with as fair a chance of privacy as anywhere on the vessel. They were partly shaded by the sails at mainmast and mizzen but the sun found the gaps between canvas and yard, and the play of light and shadow made it particularly difficult to read an expression that was enigmatic at the best of times.

Nathan had known Imlay over a period of fifteen months in France without ever forming more than the haziest impression of his true character. He wondered sometimes if Imlay knew himself any better. He appeared to change his nature as others changed their coats to suit the current fashion, or the climate, or the company.

'I am a man of many parts,' he had told Nathan once, on a journey from Paris to Le Havre. Nathan had seen several of them: the urbane man of letters, the romantic frontiersman forever seeking new challenges and new horizons, the war profiteer and the resolute, if not quite reliable, man of action . . . But above all he was a gambler with an eye to the main chance, an improviser who would make use of any situation, or individual, to his own advantage.

Nathan began by making some general observations about the *Speedwell*'s progress and her present position on the charts.

'That is indeed gratifying,' Imlay acknowledged, though dully. Possibly it was not a subject on which he could engage with any degree of complacency.

'I suppose there have been times when you wished you had never left London,' remarked Nathan. 'Or even Paris.'

'That thought had occurred to me once or twice over the past few days,' Imlay acknowledged dryly, 'though there have been times when I have been uneasy in Paris, as you know.'

'Indeed.' Imlay had been in hiding for long periods during the Terror. 'But surely not under the current regime. I was under the impression that some of them were friends of yours.'

'I would not go so far as to say they were friends,' Imlay replied, 'though I was able to do them a small service at the time of the coup.'

'You helped them seize power,' Nathan pointed out bluntly. 'I would say they were considerably in your debt.'

Imlay studied him from beneath a raised hand as the sun flashed on to his face from between the sails. He seemed amused.

'You are surprised I did not stay to take advantage of their gratitude?'

'A little.'

'I had affairs of my own to attend to in London.'

Nathan was about to ask after Imlay's wife and child when he became aware of a lingering presence on the periphery of his vision, hesitant but clearly requiring attention, his lips moving in rehearsal.

'Yes, Mr Place?'

'Mr Tully's compliments, sir, and he would be obliged if you could spare a few moments in the maintop to view a sail that is causing him some . . .' The frown of concentration deepened in search of the missing word.

'Concern?' proposed Nathan, squinting toward the mainmast.

'Disquiet,' finished Place at much the same time.

'I did not wish to trouble you unnecessarily,' said Tully, handing him the glass, 'but she has altered her course since sighting us and I do not at all like the look of her.'

Nathan trained the telescope upon the distant sail. She was hull up on the western horizon and, as Tully had intimated, on a converging course.

'What on earth is she?' he said, for he had never seen such a strange rig.

'She is a polacca. Square-rigged at the main, lateen sails fore and aft. Parker was took by one off the south coast of Ireland on a Boston trader. They are very much favoured, he says, by the Barbary pirates, especially for a distant cruise. Would you like to speak with him, sir?' He raised his eyes to the topmast where Ismael Parker was waiting respectfully.

'You have seen her like before then, Parker?' Nathan prompted him when he came dropping down.

'Aye, sir, and hoped never to again. She took us off Kinsale Head and we were like to have been pulling oar still or taken for the slave markets in Algiers save for a British frigate that came up on her. They threw us over the side by way of a distraction. I was one of the lucky ones that could swim.'

Nathan nodded as if in sympathy though it was their present plight that occupied him more. The Barbary pirates operated from ports in North Africa – most notably Algiers and Tunis – and their normal cruising was the Med, but he had heard tales of their atrocities in more distant waters, even as far north as Iceland. They were crewed almost entirely by Moors and Turks but with Christian slaves at the oars. Christians were much in demand, too, as house servants, he had heard, all along the Barbary coast. Many of the Italian states paid the pirates bribes and they were wary of major powers that had a strong navy, but the American traders, not having any navy at all, suffered more than most from their attentions. It was said that Americans now formed a sizeable minority among the slaves of the region.

Nathan raised the glass once more to his eye. She was noticeably closer. He could make out the strange over-hangs at bow and stern – and the gun ports along her side. If they kept to their present course and the *Speedwell* did not alter hers, they would be in range within the hour.

'What guns do they carry, normally speaking, and crew?'

'Well now, the ship that took us, sir, she was a twenty-four, mostly 6-pounders, with swivel guns at prow and stern. And a crew of three to four hundred.'

'As many as that?' Nathan took the glass from his eye. This was a far bigger crew than a frigate in most navies.

'Aye, sir, not counting slaves. They go for boarding, do you see, sir. They'll not use the guns 'less they have to.'

This made sense. They would not wish to damage a potential prize, and with so big a crew they could board even an East Indiaman with impunity, unless she could keep them at a distance with her own guns. Not much chance of that in the *Speedwell*'s case, with three 4-pounders to each puny broadside and the single 6-pounder at the stern. Better to try and outrun her.

'And fast?'

'Very fast, sir. Built for speed, you might say. And with that rig they can sail as close to the wind as I have ever seen.'

'And with the wind on the quarter – as fast as us?'

'I'd not like to say, sir. That is, I'd not like to stake my life on it, nor any man's.'

No. That was Nathan's job.

'What do you think?' he asked Tully, when Parker had

been dismissed. It was his job but he was not above seeking advice on how to do it, not from Tully at least.

'We could run for the Azores.' Tully stated the obvious: the only course that would give them any kind of a chance.

'You think we have the legs on her?'

'If we start the water, ditch the guns . . .'

Even then, they both knew it would be a damned close thing. And every mile would take them far off their present course with a substantial risk of being stuck for days, even weeks, in the Azores Highs.

'Load the guns with chain shot,' he instructed Tully. 'And tell Whiteley to arm his marines.'

A flicker of surprise. Tully would never question an order but Nathan gave him the answer all the same.

'We cannot fight her,' he admitted, 'but if she comes close enough we might be able to cross her stern, then make a run for it.'

At least they would be running in the right direction. And he might damage her rigging enough to give them a flying start – if she did not damage them more.

Tully nodded and was gone. But there had been another question in his eyes and it lingered in Nathan's mind.

Would she come close enough without firing on them?

He could not count on it. *Run*, his more cautious voice urged him. *Run to the south and use the sternchaser when she comes in range.*

He slid down the backstay to the deck. The men were loading the guns under the supervision of Solomon Pratt, who had once been a gunner in the British Navy, Nathan had always suspected, and knew what he was about, though he complained a lot. He complained now when Tully told him to load the guns along both sides. Where was he to find the crew to fight both sides, he wanted to know.

And now here was Imlay, out of his chair, his face creased with concern.

'How can I be of assistance?'

You may stay below until we are took, was Nathan's initial thought, after which you will doubtless persuade them to drop you off at a convenient port in return for a substantial ransom to be paid at some future date. But of course he said no such thing but proposed that Imlay put himself at the service of Lieutenant Whiteley and his marines who were now below deck, preparing for battle. They would be useful in a close encounter but against three hundred . . . ?

'Mr Place.'

'Sir?' The boy had lost some colour but appeared steady enough considering the future he faced on the Barbary coast. Not quite the career Mrs Place had had in mind for him when she had brought him to Shoreham but steady employment, for all of that; and a good-looking lad could go far, he had heard, in the seraglios. 'Compliments to Mr Whiteley . . .' Was there ever a circumstance where you did not begin every blessed sentence with this courtesy? 'And beg him to arm ten of his marines with grenades, upon a short fuse.'

He caught Tully's eye. 'I mean to bring us right across

her stern,' he said, 'as close as we can get. You will take the con and I will take the guns. And as soon as we are past, bring her back upon our present course.'

Tully nodded as if it were as simple as that.

'We will keep the marines out of sight until the last minute,' Nathan said, thinking aloud. And then it came to him. By God. He almost laughed with the sheer reckless wantonness, the absurdity of it. But what could they lose?

Quite a considerable amount. Best not to think on that.

'Mr Tully?'

'Sir?'

Nathan nodded to himself as the questions raced across his brain and he ticked off the answers one by one. Or some of them.

'I want every man below deck.'

Tully stared at him. Was he mad? Very probably, Nathan thought.

'When I was on the *Hermes*,' he said, 'off the Mosquito coast, in eighty-nine, we sighted a schooner without a single soul on deck. Just a cat.'

Tully inclined his head attentively as if he had nothing better to do than listen to his captain's anecdotes of his time on a survey vessel off the Spanish main, with a Barbary corsair closing on them by the minute and 300 heavily armed Moors in her crew.

'The wheel was lashed, the sails set and she was moving at three or four knots. But not a soul to be seen. We came alongside, very close, and put a party aboard her. They came back very fast – for they had found the crew. Dead, every one, below deck, with the yellow fever.'

Tully nodded as if he had guessed.

'We will steer by the tiller ropes below deck,' Nathan said. 'You and I will keep a watch from the launch with a tarp thrown upon us and devise some means of signalling so that they will know when to turn.'

Tully nodded again but said nothing.

'So what do you think?' Nathan invited him with a grin, for he knew that Tully would not say he was mad even if he thought it. 'Is there anything I have overlooked?' He meant this to be ironic.

'I think it is a pity,' said Tully, 'that we do not have a cat.'

'Closer,' said Nathan softly. 'I need you closer.'

He was crouched with Tully in the bottom of the launch with the tarp over their heads, but he did not mean him. The polacca was about a cable's length to leeward, sailing on a parallel course. Bigger, far bigger than Nathan had thought when he saw her through the glass. Heeling over with the wind – as was the *Speedwell* – but he could see the people on her rail and in the rigging. So many people. Dark faces and beards, turbaned heads. Officers in flowing white. And he could see her guns: twelve 6-pounders in her waist, more of a lesser calibre on the quarterdeck. One broadside at this range . . .

A flash and a bang. Nathan flinched. But it was just one, fired from high in her forecastle. He did not see where it went. The first shot across the bows.

'She is using her mizzensail as a rudder,' Tully murmured in his ear, as if they might hear him on the polacca. 'A giant rudder to keep her bows up into the wind. If she loses it she will fall off to leeward. It will give us a few hundred yards at least.'

Nathan had to think about this. Tully always seemed at least one step ahead of him. But even when he worked it out he could not see what difference it would make, unless they could bring the mast down . . .

He could see her officers staring toward them from the quarterdeck. Jihadists, for the most part, dedicated to cleansing the seas of infidels – and making a tidy profit into the bargain. Just as Drake and Hawkins had served their Protestant god and filled their pockets in earlier times.

If she was going to fire into them it would be now. His whole body was tensed for the flash and roar of her guns. The thin planks of the launch all that stood between him and—

A sudden squeal in his ear. Nathan almost jumped. He turned his head. Tully had got hold of a rat. He was holding it by the neck, between finger and thumb, close to his face.

Nathan stared at it, took in its red eyes and its sharp teeth, then looked at Tully.

'We have no cat,' said Tully, 'but I dare say this will do as well.' With a flick of the wrist he tossed it through the gap in the tarp.

Nathan watched it drop to the deck, pick itself up, and make a dart for the scuppers. He looked back at the pirate. She was closer, surely. He could discern features clearly now. The ring in a man's ear, a scar, the jewel on the hilt of a sword, catching the sun . . .

'Now!' He jerked the lanyard leading over the far side of the launch and down to young Coyle below deck. Felt the answering jerk. Waited. *Now. It had to be now. What in God's name was keeping them?* And then he felt the lurch to leeward, almost a jolt as the tiller bit and the bows came round and dug into the trough. Saw the expressions on the faces of the Moors as the unmanned craft came swinging towards them, heard the shouts . . . And then he was throwing back the tarp and springing down on to the deck and sprinting for the nearest gun.

The hands were pouring up through the hatches. And the marines in their red coats: Whiteley had dressed them properly, as if they were on parade. It was to be hoped he had remembered the grenades . . . But he must leave the marines to Whiteley. And Tully would look to the sails. He could hear him bawling a stream of orders as the few hands that had been left to him took up the sheets.

They ran out the first gun. Slammed in the quoins to bring the muzzle hard up against the top of the port. The polacca appeared to be directly ahead of them, her sails filling the sky. For one terrible moment Nathan thought he had misjudged and they were going to crash into her. He froze with tension as the *Speedwell*'s bowsprit caught in the shrouds of her mizzen but it ripped through and now they were astern of her. Faces glaring down from the overhanging poop. A crash of musketry and a screech of metal on metal as something struck the breech of the gun by his hand and shot off past his ear.

He waited until he saw the big lateen sail at her mizzen and then tugged at the lanyard, arching his body back like a bow as the cannon roared and came hurtling back under him. Then he was running aft, past the second gun, taking in the paunchy figure of Solomon Platt squinting down the barrel. One of his men fell back, a hand to his head, blood spurting beneath his fingers. The Moors were firing from the tops but Whiteley's marines were firing back at them from the rail and the rigging, and Nathan saw Imlay with them as he brought a musket to his shoulder. Then he reached the third gun: the third and last unless they could bring the sternchaser to bear.

'Prime!' he roared, though he knew it was not necessary – they all knew what must be done, and none could hear him above the sharp crack of the musketry and louder bangs that must be the grenades, or the swivel guns up in the polacca's tops. Ismael Parker thrust the priming iron down the touch-hole to pierce the cloth bag and then poured fine powder from his powder horn into the quill. Nathan felt as if he were counting every grain. And the polacca was moving away from them, the gap widening by the second. A grenade burst in the air between the two vessels, showering both with hot metal. He could see it smoking on the deck.

'Heave!' he yelled at the men on the side tackles, pointing the gun as far aft as it would go. He could see the gunports on her starboard side. Closed, thank God. He had been counting on it, and that the guns would not be loaded, but there was no way he could have been sure. He crouched down and sighted along the barrel. A glimpse of lateen sail . . .

'Fire!' he bawled as he pulled on the lanyard, and he

knew, even as he arched his body back, that he had fired too soon, too low.

A thin jet of fire from the touch-hole and a greater blast of flame and smoke from the muzzle, blocking his view – and then, when it cleared, nothing. Nothing, all as before – and then slowly, ever so slowly, as if making some vain attempt at sobriety, the mizzen topmast began to topple forward bringing the yard and the topsail with it.

The hands were cheering but Nathan stared in frustration and disbelief, for the mizzen sail was still there. How? With the topmast down and the peak halliards surely parted? And he had no more guns, save the 6-pounder at the stern. He took two steps toward it but then whatever was holding the boom suddenly parted and it came down like a signal arm swinging at the mast and the sail with it. And without its leverage she was dropping off to leeward as Tully had said she would, but faster, further than Nathan could ever have hoped for. Then he saw why. The tangle of yards and canvas had come crashing down over the helm – and the grenades had started a fire.

Nathan could see men running aft with buckets but it was burning fiercely, burning as only dry canvas and tarred rope can burn. A tongue of flame ran up the mizzenmast shrouds and one of her guns went off as the powder caught.

The last he saw of her she was still burning, but they had managed to bring her up into the wind so the flames would not spread forward.

'Pity to leave her to prey upon another honest trader,'

he informed Tully, as if he considered going back to finish her off.

'Honest trader?' Tully raised a brow. 'D'you think they would call us that?'

'No,' Nathan agreed. 'I suppose not.'

He congratulated Mr Whiteley on the conduct of his marines.

'And thank *you*, Mr Imlay. We will have to find you a red coat.'

Imlay inclined his head coolly.

'And the crew behaved pretty well, do you not think?' Nathan said to Tully privately.

'Very well,' agreed Tully.

'I will be sorry to lose them when we reach the Havana.' Nathan allowed himself to admit of this possibility. He assumed his captain's pose, hands clasped behind his back, chin raised to contemplate a distant horizon, in this case smeared with smoke from the burning polacca. He might fool some people, even if he did not fool himself. 'I only hope the people on the *Unicorn* behave half as well.'

Chapter Five

The Havana

———————◆———————

They came into the Havana on the morning tide, forty-two days out of Portsmouth: neither as soon as Nathan had hoped nor as late as he had feared. But it would not have made the slightest difference had he flown on the wings of Pegasus, the British Consul informed him, for the *Unicorn* was not there.

'Nor has been since early August and I have had no word of her since,' the consul admitted, 'for all that I have made enquiry of every vessel that has entered the port these past two months or more.'

Robert Portillo was a tall, elegant man of about fifty with the dark complexion and distinguished manner of a Spanish grandee who had spent the best part of his life in the tropics. Don Roberto, his servants called him, but whatever his ancestry, he was a subject of King George and had represented His Majesty's interests in Cuba for over twenty years. His house occupied a corner of the

Plaza de Armas opposite the Palacio de los Capitanes Generales and was a veritable palace itself, built in the Moorish style, its three floors surrounding a large central courtyard with tropical palms and an ornate stone fountain. On this occasion, however, the consul had chosen to entertain his two companions on the roof, where he had caused a small garden to be built and where they could talk in total privacy, he assured them, while catching a little of the sea breeze.

The breeze proved an empty promise but they sat under a striped awning with a magnificent view of the vast harbour, from the fortifications of El Morro at its neck to the Bay of Marimelena far over to their right, where the *Speedwell* was moored among a host of other vessels. They had walked some distance in search of the consul's house and Nathan was drenched in sweat, despite the informality of his dress.

'Let us have no ceremony,' Imlay had begged him as they prepared to enter harbour, 'for we shall discover nothing by such means. Rather let us sail under the Stars and Stripes, in the guise of an innocent merchantman. For should we enter harbour in all the dignity of your estate, with the Royal Navy ensign streaming proudly at our stern, firing off all our guns in salute to His Most Catholic Majesty – which I am sure you are longing to do – you will be obliged to present yourself to the captain-general and will become a virtual prisoner in his house, forced to dine every day with Don This and Donna That, and you will learn a thousand opinions of their daily lives here and not one fact pertinent to our mission, while every

French spy upon the island and its nearest neighbours will know our business before the week is out. So instead, let us sneak ashore like a pair of eager young tars anxious to sample the local harlotry and we may pay our respects to the British consul in total discretion and discover the true situation here and what has transpired since he wrote to their lordships.'

So no ceremony it was, though Imlay's notion of what an eager young tar might wear to go a'wooing would have astonished the tarts of Wapping or any other harbour in the civilised world, consisting as it did of white shirt and breeches with a wide red sash at the waist, black Hessian boots with silver tassels and a wide-brimmed straw hat. As accessories to this ensemble he clenched a long black cheroot between his teeth and carried a canvas bag over his shoulder with what he called his 'duds', assuring his astonished companion that he would pass unnoticed in the exotic atmosphere of the port. The fact that they were escorted through the streets by a crowd of unruly urchins did not appear to modify this opinion.

The consul unrolled a map on the table before them. 'We had information that the missing cutter had been sighted in the Old Bahama Channel some three hundred miles east of here,' he informed them, 'among the islands of Jardines del Rey.'

Nathan was familiar with the Old Bahama Channel – or as familiar as he ever wished to be. It was the route they themselves had taken to the Havana: a narrow strait between Cuba and the Bahamas, several hundred miles long but no more than fifteen miles at its widest, hedged about with hundreds of small islands. Even with the aid of the one Admiralty chart available to them – drawn by Captain Elphinstone in the year of the British siege – it had taken them almost four days to navigate and they had come near to disaster on several occasions. You could hide a fleet in the islands of Jardines del Rey, let alone a small cutter.

'Lieutenant Pym determined to investigate the report,' the consul continued, 'but the day after she sailed I heard news of the body found in the Rigolets.'

'The Rigolets?'

'The gutter – in English.' It was Imlay who replied, in the lazy drawl of the expert, the celebrated author of *A Topographical Description of the Western Territory of North America* published by Debrett's of London at two guineas. 'A narrow channel from the sea to Lake Pontchartrain and thence to New Orleans – by the back door, as it were.'

The consul shot the speaker a look from beneath his brow. Nathan had introduced him merely as 'my friend, Mr Imlay', not quite knowing how else to put it.

'That is correct. The body was found by a fishing boat and taken to a small fort the Spanish have built there, whence it was delivered to the governor-general in New Orleans. I understand that it has since been given a decent burial.'

'So we cannot be perfectly assured that it was the captain of the *Unicorn*.' Imlay's tone verged on the sardonic.

'No. Only that it wore the uniform of a captain in the

British Navy and the *Unicorn* is the only British warship to have visited these waters for some while.'

'But Lieutenant Pym did not know of this when he left the Havana?' Nathan confirmed.

'No. I did not then have news of it myself. And as I have not been able to locate him since . . .'

'The mystery deepens,' Imlay commented, heedless of Nathan's warning frown. 'In addition to a missing captain and a missing cutter, we now have a missing frigate.' He drew complacently on the cigar he had acquired from the consul and blew smoke toward the roof of the awning.

'Well, we have had news of the cutter,' Portillo announced, 'but none that you will wish to hear. An English brig – the *Charlotte May* out of Kingston, was chased by pirates a little over a week ago in the Bahama Channel. There seems little doubt from their description of the vessel that she was your missing cutter.'

'I had thought that piracy was no longer tolerated in the Caribbean,' observed Imlay dryly, 'not since the days of Henry Morgan.'

'It is uncommon,' Portillo conceded, 'but the offshore islands are a notorious refuge of brigands and escaped slaves, and now, I fear, mutineers. You may count yourselves fortunate you did not encounter them on your journey through the channel.'

'We are not unduly concerned by pirates,' remarked Imlay, with a nod and a wink towards Nathan which he did his best to ignore.

'At present I am more concerned that there has been no word of the *Unicorn*,' he announced coldly.

'Well, there may be an explanation for that,' the consul sighed. 'I do not wish to be thought a Jonah, but within a week or so of her leaving La Habana the island was struck by a hurricane – one of the most severe I have known. It caused extensive damage in the city. I fear that if the *Unicorn* was in its direct path . . .'

'A hurricane now?' Imlay rolled his eyes drolly. 'She is not what you might call a lucky ship, your *Unicorn*.'

'Hurricanes are not unknown at this time of the year in the Caribbean,' Portillo reminded him. 'And for a sound ship in open sea, not necessarily fatal. But if the *Unicorn* was in the Old Bahama Channel, surrounded by reefs and small islands . . .'

Nathan shook his head. He might have known. He had been promoted to the command of a ghost ship.

He stood up and leaned both hands on the parapet of the roof, staring out over the harbour towards the distant sea, tranquil enough at present but especially treacherous in these parts and at this time of the year. A well-found ship with 250 officers and crew . . . yet the *Unicorn* would not be the first to have vanished without trace in the waters of the Caribbean during the season of hurricanes.

Why had she not stayed in the Havana and waited for word from the Admiralty – and for the arrival of her new captain?

From where he stood, he could see almost the whole sweep of the harbour except for the very tip where it curved round to the west behind the city walls. It was the best harbour in the Caribbean: a vast haven where the treasure ships from Mexico and New Spain could berth in perfect security, it was believed, safe from the depredations of storm and pirates both.

Since the days of Francis Drake it had been guarded by three great castles – the Morro and the Punta at each side of the harbour entrance and the Fuerza in the city itself, near the Plaza de Armas. But they had not been enough to stop the British from taking the port in '62, and since then the Spaniards had built another fort, bigger than all three – the Castillo de la Cabana on the heights above El Morro. So big – and expensive – that the King of Spain had informed his ministers that he hoped to be able to see it from Madrid. He had been disappointed in this expectation but it looked awesome enough to Nathan from the roof of the British consul's house. If the British tried to take the Havana again they would have a much harder job of it.

'And what of the *Virginie*?' he asked, returning to his chair and the welcome shade of the awning. 'No news of her either?'

'I wish that were so,' replied the consul with a weary smile, 'but the latest report was a little above three weeks ago when she took a Spanish schooner among the islands of Bocas del Toro off Panama. It is the sixth merchant vessel she has taken since we first heard of her from Captain Kerr back in July.'

'So you have met Captain Kerr?'

'I have. Briefly. When he called into La Habana.'

'And did he appear in good health?' Imlay enquired. 'And in possession of all his faculties?'

Nathan closed his eyes briefly. Whatever else he was, Imlay was certainly no diplomat.

'There was no indication of any problem in that regard,' Portillo replied blandly, 'but we barely spent an hour in each other's company. There had been reports of an unnamed French frigate off the coast of West Florida and Louisiana. He was impatient to be on his way.'

'And she has taken six prizes?' Nathan mused.

'I did not say prizes. In each case the vessels were burned, after first permitting the crew to take to the boats. I must assume her captain does not wish to reduce his crew.'

So much for that small hope.

'Do we know how many of her victims were Spanish?'

'Four, at the last reckoning.'

'That cannot have pleased the Spanish authorities. Have they taken any action?'

'If they have, I have not been informed of it.'

'Despite the forces at their disposal?'

There was room for above a hundred ships of the line to moor comfortably in the Havana, it was said, though there was nothing like as many here now. Nathan had counted just two ships of the line, three frigates and a sloop o' war. But why were they not out looking for the *Virginie*?

'The captain-general has other concerns. You are aware of the slave revolts in Hispaniola?' Nathan nodded. 'We have had a number of refugees from the island – both French and Spanish – bringing tales of massacre and rape. There is a great fear that the infection will spread to Cuba.

I doubt the captain-general is anxious to reduce his forces in pursuit of a mere commerce raider.'

'Even if she has other duties that are, shall we say, less commercial?'

Imlay spoke lazily, his eyes almost closed. The consul observed him steadily for a moment as a tutor might regard a pupil who might become irritating, given time and indulgence.

'I beg your pardon?'

'You were not aware that the *Virginie* has a more subversive role than that of a mere predator?'

'I was not so aware. I take it you mean in support of a rising among the slaves?'

'And other disaffected elements of the populace.'

'I see. That is very interesting. Well, I am not in the captain-general's confidence but I know he has received report of some problems in New Orleans.'

'What problems?' demanded Imlay sharply.

'I imagine among the French settlers – but it is not my province. However . . .' Portillo paused a moment, considering. 'I may be able to introduce you to someone who knows a good deal more about it. I will enquire if he is prepared to meet you, without revealing your true character, of course. In the meantime,' he spread his arms in a gesture of hospitality, 'what small comforts I can offer are at your disposal. I hope you will stay here as long as you are in La Habana. Your rooms have been prepared and whatever else you require, please do not hesitate to ask and I will endeavour to obtain it for you. La Habana, as I hope you will discover, has a great deal to offer.'

*

'Intriguing,' remarked Imlay, as they stepped out into the square. 'To what, do you suppose, did he refer?'

'When?'

'When he proposed to obtain "whatever *else* we required".'

'I imagine he meant in the way of home comforts.'

'And yet he mentioned that the city itself has a great deal to offer.'

'Well, I am told the architecture is very impressive.' Nathan gazed across the square toward the imposing frontage of the captain-general's Palace.

'Bugger the architecture,' Imlay retorted, 'have you seen the women?'

Nathan had been trying not to notice the women, though he could no more have succeeded in this lofty ideal than in remaining ignorant of the beggars who had assailed them as soon as they stepped ashore, or the flies or the half-dead donkeys.

'I have not yet been to Asia,' confided Imlay as they followed the consul's directions back to the wharves of San Pedro where they had left the gig, 'nor India, where I am told the *houris* would have made Alexander the Great reconsider his sexual predilections. Nor have I sampled the delights of China or Japan whose concubines, I am assured, are adept in the arts of pleasuring a man, but for pure physical perfection I do not believe there is a more refined creation than the *mulata* of the Caribbean.'

'I am sure she would be grateful for your approbation,' murmured Nathan, but Imlay was in full flow and Imlay in full flow was not to be diverted by any mere murmuring . . .

'Indeed, one might say that the female form has reached its apogee – or is it apotheosis?' He creased his brow in thought but before Nathan could instruct him, he was off again: 'And in so many pleasing shades from pale ochre to ebony, though if I must state a preference it is for the quadroon, whose delicate colouring is complemented by a nature that combines the most seductive qualities of the Latin and the African – and that hint of *hidalgo* blood, do you see?' He touched the brim of his hat to a particular example of the species who had caught his eye, sauntering by under the shade of a parasol, accompanied by a darker companion who might have been her maid. 'The straight nose, the tilt of the chin, the hauteur in the eyes – and the promise . . . Oh Lord, when one considers how guarded, how grand, how *unapproachable* is your pure Castilian beauty and yet how *available* those of her descent here in Cuba, where the precious blood of Madrid and Segovia is distilled with that of the Niger and the Bight of Benin and filtered through several generations. Why, it is as if God had designated these islands as a breeding ground to perfect the Rib of Adam.'

'The Rib of Adam is like to give you the Kick of Venus,' Nathan remarked, 'if you are unfortunate in your choice.'

'Upon my word, you are become a dull dog,' retorted Imlay, stepping back a pace and viewing him askance. 'Let us admire the architecture, forsooth!'

Nathan shook his head. But the criticism was not unjust. Yet he could not desire a woman without thinking on Sara and what had happened to her. Besides, even without such horror to distract him, there was his concern for the *Unicorn* and his own anomalous position: a captain without a ship. Thank God he had listened to Imlay and was not now strutting about in his uniform for the entertainment of the populace. They were, in any case, attracting more attention than Nathan desired: a circumstance that he was inclined to blame on Imlay, gazing around him with his fatuous smile and touching his hat to every attractive female he saw. Thus far no one appeared to have taken exception to this, but it was only a matter of time, Nathan considered, before he bestowed his favours upon someone's wife. Or mother.

Fortunately there were other distractions besides Imlay. The street they were in was as crowded and as narrow as an Oriental bazaar, with coloured awnings stretched from building to building and all manner of produce displayed for purchase at stalls on either side or on carpets laid upon the ground. After weeks at sea the surprising solidity of the surface made their step unsteady and Nathan's senses were further bemused by a riot of colour and sound and the jostling, indisciplined crowd that pressed upon him from all sides. A babble of voices in a language he did not understand; a multitude of unfamiliar faces; hands reaching out to pull at his clothes in a bid to make him stop and buy or only look, *señor*, only look . . . He was in constant danger of knocking his head on a cage of songbirds or a dead fowl hanging by its legs from a hook, or of tripping over the produce at his feet: exotic fruits and vegetables, fish still in the fishermen's baskets, husks of maize, barrels of meat in brine, strange trinkets, obscure offerings, religious icons, rosaries . . . Women swayed towards him with great wicker baskets on their heads overflowing with produce. Old crones with toothless gums held out what could be roots or shrivelled foetuses – to be consumed or used in witchcraft?

And glimpsed through dark doorways or sauntering brazenly through the street, those other women that so excited Imlay's passions . . .

'Well, I grant you there is more to please the eye here than I have seen in Portsmouth or any of our home ports,' Nathan conceded, 'but I confess I have never been easy in my mind with a relationship that is based entirely upon lust on the one part and cold commerce on the other.'

'But why should there be any more disgrace in purchasing a woman than any other commodity necessary to one's comfort? Or composure? Or need?' Imlay leaned towards him, almost shouting in his ear, his gait so unsteady he constantly lurched into him. 'Besides, I am persuaded that the *commerce* between a man and a woman is more honest than most. The goods are openly displayed for one's inspection, the price is agreed in advance, the job is done in the wink of an eye, or some-such, and generally both parties declare themselves satisfied with the result. And there is no continuing bill for maintenance – as there is with a horse, for example, or a house or indeed a wife. You are scandalised?' Nathan had drawn back a little, more to avoid this constant lurching into him than from any moral reserve. 'But consider – we both abhor slavery, do we not? But what is marriage – is it not comparable, at least from the woman's point of view? And from the man's, how much more satisfying – and simple – it is, to pay an honest wage for an honest day's work – or in this case, an hour's intercourse, if not less – than to be burdened with the expense and inconvenience of keeping a slave for life.'

They had finally reached the waterfront of San Pedro where the street was wider and they could move with less constraint, though the bustle here was, if anything, more industrious. Gangs of sweltering slaves unloading cargoes from the vessels, moored three or four deep against the wharves, a constant procession of carts and mules. A cross-hatching of spars and masts against the backdrop of La Cabana and the pelicans gliding above the limpid water, stretching their leathery necks like great lizards that had learned to fly.

'I say nothing against marriage for those that are inclined to it,' Imlay added after a moment's reflection, possibly recalling that Nathan had seen him in this happy state when they were in Paris, 'for it can bring much solace and satisfaction to both parties, but I maintain that no educated, intelligent woman can be easy in her mind with an institution so unfairly biased against her.'

No *educated, intelligent woman*. The shadow of Mary Wollstonecraft. Imlay's wife. Her name had not been mentioned throughout the long voyage from England.

Nathan, knowing what he did, was too cautious, too polite – unless Imlay referred to her first, and he had not. On a previous journey – across France – he had denied they were married. He had merely given her the protection of his name and his nationality when she was in danger of arrest as an Englishwoman living in Paris. But the couple had lived openly as man and wife in Neuilly and Le Havre – and she had a child by him.

'An educated, intelligent woman,' Imlay mused, apparently lost in thought. 'A Portia or an Heloise, the ideal of every thinking man – and yet, I confess I am as often attracted to the frivolous in woman. The swish of skirts, the *frou-frou* of silk and satin. I never cease to wonder at the devotion of certain women to their toilette: the exact positioning of a curl, the application of patch and powder, the exposure of an ankle. Such artifice! And the intricacies of the wardrobe – the attention lavished upon the purchase of a hat, a piece of ribbon. The delightful *silliness* of women. And yet,' he sighed, 'how swiftly it palls. And how one longs for intelligent conversation, the company of an intellectual equal.'

He lapsed into melancholy, doubtless in the grip of some personal torment or indecision, torn as he was between the author of *The Rights of Women* and an actress from a strolling theatre company; not to speak of the several dozen whores he had encountered whilst strolling the streets of the Havana.

The crew of the gig approached along the wharf – swaggering a little, or possibly as dizzied as Nathan by the stability of their new environment. But then he saw that they were drunk, with a levity of manner he would have frowned upon had they been in the King's Navy. But they were not in the King's Navy. They were free men, free from care and responsibility, with money in their pockets, grins on their faces and rum in their bellies – no longer bound in service to King George or any other power save their own lusts and inclinations and the need for gainful employment. And at that moment he envied them.

'So there it is,' Nathan concluded his narrative to Tully in the privacy of his cabin. 'And we are little better informed than when we left Shoreham.'

'Save that we know the *Virginie* is still at large,' Tully pointed out with a sigh that reflected the impossibility of doing anything about it.

'What I cannot understand is what possessed Lieutenant Pym to take the *Unicorn* into such dangerous waters at a time notorious for hurricanes in search of a missing cutter when his clear duty – his direct order, indeed – was to track down an enemy frigate.'

Tully could offer no explanation and was too conscious of his own duty to offer criticism of a fellow officer other than by a sorrowful shaking of the head.

'Did the consul have any idea how the cutter came to be missing in the first place?' he enquired.

'None. Or if he did, he chose to keep it to himself.' Nathan ran his fingers through his hair, scratching the back of his neck where it prickled in the heat. 'And it seems that Mr Pym chose not to confide in him. But clearly it is not so much *missing* as *took* – and whoever took it has since taken to piracy.'

'And there is no word from the admiral?'

'None,' Nathan repeated. 'So either he did not receive Pym's message or felt it unnecessary to reply.'

The *Speedwell* swung at her moorings, bobbing in the wake of some unseen vessel passing by in the crowded anchorage and they heard Keeble shouting some instruction on the deck above.

'I think we must sail for Port Royal,' Nathan announced in the silence that followed, 'and put ourselves under the orders of Admiral Ford, for we cannot remain here forever hoping for news of the *Unicorn*. I fear she must have perished in the storm.'

Tully did not trouble to contradict him. 'Shall I make it known to Keeble and the crew?' he enquired.

'No, I will tell them myself. Or rather petition them, for we are only passengers, after all, and if they decide to sail for Boston on the next tide we must find other means of transportation.'

Tully cocked his head as if listening for something on the deck above. The barque was taking in stores and fresh water from several bumboats sent out from the port.

'And if they agree – as I am sure they will – are we to sail as soon as we are provisioned?'

Nathan considered. 'There is someone the consul wishes me to meet before we leave, but it should not delay us long. Let the crew have the night ashore and we will leave tomorrow upon the evening tide.'

Nathan's optimism was ill founded. This was Cuba, the consul reminded him, and in Cuba events moved at their own pace and would not be hurried. His informant was on a mission to the interior and was not expected back for several days.

Was it worth the wait, Nathan wondered. Imlay was in no doubt.

'Apart from the *Virginie*'s movements, we must learn what we can of the political situation,' he intoned with a sober countenance but the hint of a twinkle in his eye. 'My lord Chatham was most pressing in this regard.'

The political situation in La Habana occupied Imlay for the next few days. On several occasions Nathan observed him emerging from an establishment in the Plaza Vieja with a female companion of precisely that shade of colouring he claimed most to admire. Happily the crew of the *Speedwell* appeared equally content to enjoy the delights of the Havana at the expense of His Majesty and to deliver Nathan to Port Royal or wherever else he wished to sail whenever he declared himself ready.

Nor was Nathan immune from the city's charms. With his dark hair and complexion he could pass for a Spaniard, though much to his regret he could not speak more than a few words of the language and understood less, and he wandered freely about the streets and squares of the city, sometimes with Tully, occasionally with Imlay, most often alone, dressed like an ordinary seaman in a plain white or chequered shirt and sailcloth trousers, sometimes with a faded blue jacket and a battered straw hat upon his head, untroubled by officialdom or even casual enquiry. He would have liked to paint, but to have set up his easel and oils would have smacked of indulgence and attracted too much attention to himself so he confined his endeavours to sketching in a little book, merely taking note of the colours — the washed-out reds and blues, greens and yellows, the subtle shades of antiquity. He could have been in Ancient Rome or one of the cities of the Greeks, he reflected, his eyes raised to the elegant if sometimes crumbling façades while his feet stumbled on the uneven cobbles or splashed through some stagnant pool left from the afternoon rain. But of course this was a Christian city and many of the buildings were churches or convents, some dating from the time of the conquistadors, others still under construction, and one, the Basilica of San Francisco de Asis, used as a warehouse because it was considered to have been defiled by the heretic English who had worshipped here when they took the city in '62.

So many churches, so many processions swaying through the streets behind some saintly statue, so many priests and monks and nuns ... And the half-naked children and the flies and the over-burdened donkeys shivering in the heat and the spavined horses ... Dogs sprawling in the shade. The stench of rotting fruit and vegetables. A brigade of ants swarming about a fish head. Lizards darting up the walls or suddenly stopped, still as statues, alert for danger or prey. A dark, shadowed doorway leading to an open courtyard filled with plants; the sense of being watched by hidden agents – and sometimes catching the white of an eye among the shadows.

Nathan would enter these shadows himself sometimes, finding out the little oases, the little sanctuaries, taking refreshment in some cool, tiled courtyard while the smells of cooking drifted out from the dark interior and a serving girl crushed herbs or spices in a stone mortar.

He continued to notice the women; and they, as Imlay informed him, noticed him.

'You are become something of a celebrity in certain quarters,' he remarked slyly at one of their rare encounters in the corridors of the consul's house. 'I have heard you described as *El Pintor Hermoso*, the Beautiful Artist. Bets have been laid on the first woman to steal your heart – I believe it was your heart that was mentioned, though the local patois is sometimes beyond my comprehension. The current favourite is one known as La Princesa Negra, whom you may have observed while you were sketching your groins and pilasters. She has certainly been observing you. It is said that she has made offerings to Lady Ochun, the Goddess of Love and Passion, and made an image in your likeness upon which she may work her magic, lacking only a clip of your hair or the parings of your nails, or even a scrap of your clothing, to make it effective.'

'You and La Princesa would appear to worship at the same shrine,' Nathan remarked dryly. 'But I take it this is not one of our Catholic deities.'

'By no means. Lady Ochun is the Madonna of the African slaves and those of mixed descent. Have you not seen her acolytes about the city?'

'How would I know them?'

'They are usually dressed entirely in white – though red is also a colour they favour, the shedding of blood playing an intrinsic part in their rituals. It is normally the blood of a cock, though there are ugly rumours of human sacrifice, doubtless put about by the Papists.'

'I saw a woman in red only this morning,' Nathan recalled thoughtfully. 'An old woman in the marketplace. She was sitting on a chair at the rear of one of the stalls with a white cat on her lap dressed in a large red ruff. I thought her a witch.'

'So would the Papists. Not so long ago they would have burned her for it. She would have been a devotee of Palo Monte, the magic of the Bantu who are from the region of the River Congo. Or of Abakua or Lucumi, the religion of the Carabali and the Yoruba.'

'You have made this your particular study, I see, while you have been in the Havana.'

'I like to keep abreast of the native customs: the dark undercurrents, as it were, that flow beneath the surface of society. You never know when it might prove useful.'

Nathan acknowledged this with a small bow. Imlay was not to be scorned for his knowledge of the local underworld and the secret societies that inhabited it. It had saved their lives on at least one occasion in Paris.

'So tell me more of this – what is it? – Palo Monte?'

'One might categorise it as the worship of the forces of nature. Concentrated, I believe, in a large cauldron guarded by the Muneca de Talanquera, a doll chained to its chair so it cannot escape. The Lucumi, which is by far the most interesting, is devoted to the worship of a whole host of saints, or *orishas*, as they call them, which are the counterparts of the Catholic saints: their alter egos, one might say. The Papists call this *Santeria* and affect to despise it as heathen, idolatrous and heretic, though I am perplexed to see how it differs from their own practice, except in the names of the particular idols, and some trifling distinctions of appearance. However, I am from New England Puritan stock and may be biased in my opinion.'

Nathan made no comment upon Imlay's religious susceptibilities other than a faint raising of the brow. He had seen him make the sign of the cross on more than one occasion in Paris and had wondered at it. But it might have been part of the elaborate game he was playing.

'And do the authorities tolerate these ceremonies?'

'They are inclined to look the other way, provided it does not impinge upon the orderly running of the colony. However, they have become more concerned, I am told, since the arrival of the French refugees from Saint Domingue, some of whom have brought their house servants with them and their darker practices which involve the raising of the dead and other peculiarities. However, it is La Princesa Negra you should look out for,' he advised Nathan with a grin, 'for she can raise more than the dead, I am assured.'

And with that he was off to gather more scraps, as he put it, from the less salubrious quarters of the city.

Nathan felt less contentedly employed but he had to admit, at least to himself, that he was in no great hurry to leave the Havana, especially when all he had to report was failure. He was possessed of that same fatal lethargy he had experienced in Sussex after his return from Paris, exacerbated by the heat and the indolent atmosphere of the city: a sense that Fate would take its course irrespective of his own futile attempts to alter it one way or another.

It was partly in a bid to shake off this lassitude that he rose early the next morning with the intention of strolling along the city walls before the sun was up and the populace about its business. His intention was to make a survey of the city's defences on the westward side, which had been ignored by the British in '62 but might be of more interest now that La Cabana protected the eastern approach and the direct route from the sea. He was convinced that sooner or later England and Spain would again be at war and the treasure ships of the Americas once more the legitimate prey of His Britannic Majesty's Navy.

He was successful in beating the sun, which had not yet risen above the rooftops, but not the people – or at least a substantial number of the lower orders, and their livestock. Indeed, the city resembled a farmyard at this time of the morning, with cows and goats driven from door to door and milked straight into the jug; long trains of donkeys, tied nose to tail with great panniers of fruit and vegetables slung over their backs; great two-wheeled farm carts with high wooden sides, piled high with hay or loaded with hogsheads of wine or spirits and pulled by gentle, slow-moving, cream-coloured oxen; a crowd of children driving a flock of geese before them; a giant Negro with a live pig slung over his shoulder.

All were apparently heading for the Plaza Vieja, which was in the process of being transformed into a vast marketplace, the live produce contained within ramshackle hurdles or wicker cages and the rest spread out on the ground in a manner that appeared entirely random but was clearly to some pre-ordained plan for there were no arguments about who or what went where, and although the goods were laid out in no particular order or classification, there were clear paths left between the stalls for the customers who were even now ambling down from the great houses about the square.

Nathan sat at a pavement café with a coffee and a fresh-baked roll, watching the activity with a kind of wonderment at the regularity of it all, as if stalls, animals and people were so many planets and their satellites orbiting the sun, or in this case the fountain that formed the focus of this mercantile universe: save that the fountain itself was not immune from the laws of commerce, for a crowd of Negroes were filling barrels with the murky water that flowed intermittently from the gaping mouths of its four stone dolphins. On enquiring from one of his fellow customers in his poor Spanish, Nathan gathered that it was taken to those houses that did not have their own supply and was sold at half a silver *real* per barrel.

'And does it never run dry?' he managed to ask with some difficulty and the aid of his empty coffee cup, miming the act of pouring.

'Only when the British come,' replied his informant, in English, a remark which Nathan was inclined to take amiss, assuming some personal slight was intended, until he recalled that during the siege of '62 the British had succeeded in diverting the Chorera River which supplied the city with its water: an action which, whilst perfectly justified at time of war, might well induce a lasting sense of grievance among the deprived citizenry.

This, in turn, recalled him to his present duties. Bowing stiffly to his cantankerous informant, he paid for his breakfast and set off in the direction of the city walls.

He was navigating the rough stone cobbles and potholes of Calle Muralla when he chanced to glance down one of the open doorways or passages that led, as did most, into a small courtyard with the floors of the building rising up above and saw, in the centre of this inner sanctuary, his woman in red – or another woman similarly attired – sitting in her chair with a white cat in her lap, just as before. He stopped and stared. She stared back.

Some compulsion, something more than mere curiosity, made him turn into the dark passage and advance slowly towards her. She was a very old woman, he saw now, with the face of a wrinkled walnut, but black as jet, the skin of her face drawn so tight about the bones it could have been a skull save for the bright light in her eye, beady as a crow's. She was smoking a cigar. He greeted her respectfully, in Spanish. But to his surprise she replied in French – or at least a form of French that was presumably local to one of the islands. And though it differed somewhat from the French Nathan had learned from his tutors he took it to mean: 'What are you looking for?' Or perhaps – 'What have you lost?'

'*Excusez-moi,*' he said, beginning to back out of the building.

And then she gave him a toothless grin and said: 'You will not find her here, my child.'

And then she laughed. A raucous cackle that shook her

meagre frame and the cat sat up, startled and alert, on her lap and Nathan smelled a sudden noxious stink: more noxious, less innocent than a fart – a terrible stench of decay that might have come from the very bowels of Hell. He turned and strode quickly back into the sunlight, shaken more than he would have cared to admit.

'I swear it was as if I had opened the lid of a coffin,' he told Tully when he met him later that morning on the roof of the consul's house.

'One of the decayed offerings they make to their heathen gods, perhaps,' suggested Tully. 'I have heard they are quite gruesome.'

'Or something of my own imagining,' said Nathan, almost to himself.

You will not find her here, my child.

What on earth had she meant by that? Most likely she thought he was looking for a woman, a whore. La Princesa Negra, perhaps. Or that he had mistaken *her* for one in her red dress – and then seen her face.

That was the rational explanation. But then there was the stench of death – and he could not but help think of Sara. Sara, after three months in the grave, or whatever foul place they had buried her.

He stood up quickly and walked to the edge of the roof, pressing his hands into the hot stone parapet, almost as hot as an oven. Pain, physical pain, anything rather than the agony in his mind. He had felt like this as a child when he had first thought on eternity. The concept of the neverending. His mind could not cope with it and he would pace about almost angrily, shaking his head to free it of that impossible thought.

'This place is beginning to plague me,' he said. 'I will be glad to see the back of it.'

'Well, we are ready to sail as soon as you are,' said Tully gently.

Nathan wondered how much he knew of Sara. Nathan had not told him much. Only that he had met a woman in Paris, and that she had died on the guillotine, and that Alex was her son. But Imlay might have told him more.

'We will give it one more day,' he said. Then, whatever Imlay had to say about it, they would sail for Jamaica and leave the whole unhappy business for Admiral Ford to resolve.

But for now here was the major domo with Don Roberto's compliments and he would be happy to see the gentleman in the library when he had a moment.

'Ah Captain, I am glad we found you!' exclaimed the consul with apparent relief, Imlay being there already with the silver-headed cane he had acquired for walking out. 'My informant is back from the interior and has agreed to meet with us in the Cathedral an hour from now.'

Nathan had not entered the Cathedral during his wanderings about the city. Perhaps he feared to defile it as the Basilica of San Francisco had been defiled. Now, as his eyes adjusted to the poor light and the smoke from the guttering candles, he gazed about him with interest. Here were the graven images he had been warned off by his Anglican tutors – but in more quantity and arrayed in even more finery than they had described to him; the stations of the cross and the confessionals – grim little cabinets of dark, intricately carved wood set at intervals along the walls; and the huddle of crones in the Lady Chapel mumbling over their rosary beads like a coven of witches. And everywhere the gaunt figure of the crucified Saviour: on the altar where it might be expected but also hanging from the walls and the roof; elaborate effigies and images, all painted in great detail and in vivid colours so you could not miss one small drop of blood, one precise degree of pain. Christ carrying the cross, Christ hanging from the cross, Christ taken down from the cross . . . Even the images of Christ in heaven revealed Him as if fresh from His terrible ordeal, dressed in a purple robe but with the wounds still raw about His wrists and ankles, while from beneath His golden crown the blood still oozed from wounds made by the crown of thorns. Blood, so much blood that to Nathan's reserved Anglican mind it more resembled a charnelhouse than a church: a charnelhouse with dolls.

'I see what you mean about the worship of the saints,' he murmured in an aside to Imlay, for he had imbibed enough of the prejudice of his tutors to make him uneasy.

'Quite,' replied Imlay, not quite so softly. 'And I am told that the Africans frequently conceal their own idols behind those on display so that though they appear to be worshipping Saint This or That, they are in fact paying their respects to Chango, the God of Thunder or Queen Obatala or some other of their *orishas*.'

'Gentlemen, pray keep your voices down,' murmured the consul. 'And try not to attract attention to yourselves.' This to Imlay, who was attempting to lift the skirts of a Madonna with his cane so he might peer into the recess behind.

'I beg your pardon,' replied Nathan, mortified. 'I did not mean to be offensive.'

'There is no need to apologise to me,' said Portillo, 'for I am not of their faith. By birth I am a Jew.'

Nathan could not help but show his surprise and Imlay started as if the roof might fall upon them.

'My family were displaced from Barcelona many years ago by the Inquisition,' the consul explained. 'They made their homes in England at the time of Cromwell.'

Though Imlay had discussed Chango and Queen Obatala with perfect equanimity, the name of Cromwell, following so swiftly upon the word 'Jew', caused him to start and look swiftly about him as if the officers of the Inquisition might be advancing upon them from along the aisles.

'But I have many friends among the Catholic community,' Portillo continued, in the same low voice, 'and they assure me that the saints are but a useful form of mediation between God and man, that the icons are mere aids to concentration and that a prayer to Saint Francis or Saint Christopher is not at all to be confused with the worship of Chango the God of Thunder. Ah, Brother, were you looking for us?' This in a slightly louder tone to a presence in black that had materialised beside them, much to Imlay's consternation.

'Don Roberto,' murmured the apparition with a bow. '*Señores*. If you will come this way . . .'

They followed the cleric along the back of the nave, down the side aisle and through a passage that opened, surprisingly, into a large courtyard filled with tropical ferns and palms and with a stone fountain in the centre gushing water of a clarity that compared favourably to that of the Plaza Vieja. Here, after murmuring something in Spanish to Don Roberto, their guide left them and glided off into the surrounding cloisters. Looking up, Nathan saw that the building rose above them to the height of several storeys, each with its own balcony, and higher still, above the height of the roof, the fronds of the four palms moved gently in the slight breeze.

This was clearly a palace of some magnificence and Nathan raised his brows enquiringly to the consul, who smiled as if at some private joke and told him: 'The Seminary of San Carlos and San Ambrosio.' Then, as another figure emerged from the shade of the cloisters, 'And here is our host, Brother Ignatius.'

Their host, it appeared, was also their informant: a Franciscan monk of middling years with a long, thin countenance which, had it not been browned by the sun, would have resembled an icon of the Early Christian martyrs or ascetics, Nathan thought. His first words, however, suggested a more genial nature.

'What will you have to drink?' he asked of them in perfect English. 'I usually have a *mojito* about this time of the day. The drink of El Draco, which would be appropriate to the occasion, do you not think?'

And so it was *mojitos* all round – a blend of white rum, lime juice and sugared water with mint which, legend had it, Francis Drake had introduced to Cuba. It was served to them at a small wrought-iron table by the first monk of their acquaintance, who reappeared briefly with a tray bearing an elegant pitcher and four tall Venetian glasses.

'To His Majesty, King George,' said their host, raising his glass. 'I understand it is appropriate in the service to deliver the loyal toast seated.' Brother Ignatius had been well briefed, and not only regarding the loyal toast.

'I am told,' he continued after setting down his glass, 'that you are interested in the movements of a certain French frigate and the nature of her business in the region.'

Nathan inclined his head politely, while privately wondering at the nature of the monk's own business, for clearly it was not entirely directed towards religious matters.

'I regret that I can add very little to what Don Roberto has already told you,' continued Brother Ignatius, 'and my information is now somewhat dated. However,' he drew his hands together as if in prayer, 'the vessel was first mentioned in a despatch to the captain-general, sent by the governor of New Orleans early in July.' The hands opened and closed like the wings of a butterfly. 'He did not then know her name, but it was reported that a French ship of war had landed men and a quantity of arms upon the coast of Louisiana, in a small inlet known as the Bay of Saint Louis, off the Mississippi Sound.'

Nathan exchanged a glance with Imlay. This was a

significant addition to what they had learned from the consul – and there was more.

'The arms were delivered to a group of settlers who had moved south from the French colony of Arcadia, on the Canadian border. They are normally referred to as Cajuns. You are familiar with the breed?'

Nathan nodded. Many of his Grandfather Bouchard's servants and farm labourers on his estate on the Hudson had been Cajuns: refugees driven from their homeland after the British victory in the Seven Years War. Many more had made the long trek south by ox-cart and flatboat down the Mississippi to New Orleans and Louisiana. They were a restless, restive, romantic people. As a child Nathan had heard their stories and learned to speak their tongue. They had sung him their songs. He still heard the rhythms in his head.

'Only a handful of men were landed from the ship,' the monk continued, 'but we believe they proposed to make a study of the terrain between the coast and New Orleans. And possibly they intended to train the settlers in battle, though I would have thought the Cajuns require very little tuition. As you may be aware, they are organised in military groups, each led by a captain or chief. Many are experienced Indian fighters and some have fought the British.'

'And this was in July?'

'About the second or third week.'

'Around the same time the *Unicorn* was anchored off Ship Island,' Nathan mused.

'A little earlier than that,' the monk said. 'I believe the *Virginie* had been and gone before the *Unicorn* arrived.'

'You have heard about the *Unicorn* then, and the mystery of her missing captain?'

'I have – mainly from Don Roberto here. I am afraid I know no more than he has already told you.'

'Leaving the *Unicorn* aside for a moment,' said Imlay, a trifle impatiently and with a sidelong glance at Nathan, 'what of the French settlers – and the agents who were put ashore. Is there any news of *them*?'

'None. They have, as you say, gone to ground.' Brother Ignatius smiled at the English phrase. His command of the language was near-perfect. 'Certainly there has been no report of any unusual military activity, though the governor in New Orleans has warned of the dangers.'

'And there is no further news of the *Virginie*?' Nathan persisted.

'None. Other than that she has been attacking shipping further to the south in the region of Panama. However, if you will permit me to speculate, I would say that having dropped off the men and weapons, her captain took her out of harm's way until such a time as her assistance was required. And so she avoided the hurricane that struck the region in the second week of August.'

Unlike the *Unicorn* . . .

'It is the governor's belief – based either upon information received or his own reasoning – that she will return when certain preparations, or dispositions, are made, and throw her weight into the equation.'

'So the governor is convinced that an uprising is inevitable?'

'Well, he has certainly taken precautions against such

an event. He has strengthened his fortifications in New
Orleans and is presently on a tour of the forts along the
coast.'

'And the reinforcements from Cuba?'

'None. Not as yet.' There was something in his tone
that hinted at criticism here, or·more to be said on the
subject.

'Do you have any idea why not?' Nathan pressed him.

Brother Ignatius inclined his head towards the consul
with an indulgent smile. 'Don Roberto thinks it is because
the captain-general is preoccupied with the danger of a
revolt among the slaves here in Cuba. I believe he has
other concerns.'

'Such as?' Imlay's manner was more direct than Nathan
would have preferred – or countenanced, had he been able
to check him without embarrassment.

The monk regarded him evenly. 'I am sure it is known
in London,' he began, 'and it may even be known in
Philadelphia, that there is a faction in Madrid that favours
a rapprochement with the French Revolutionists, followed
in due course by an alliance.'

'So you are saying that the captain-general is of their
opinion?'

The praying hands opened again. 'I say no such thing.
Only that the captain-general is not a reckless man. He is
not inclined to jump before he is pushed, especially if he
does not know which *way* he is to be pushed.'

'But if there were such a rapprochement,' Imlay carried
on, 'how would it affect the situation here in Cuba – or in
New Orleans?'

The monk smiled. 'We are in the realms of speculation once more, but the Spanish government has for some time been aware of the difficulties involved in securing its territories on the North American mainland. There are those who believe they were in jeopardy from the moment that your countrymen obtained their independence from Great Britain.'

'The United States has no present interest in expansion westward or to the south,' Imlay countered in a tone that surprised Nathan, so altered was it from his normal air of bored indifference.

'Really?' Brother Ignatius queried with another smile. 'And do you speak in a private or an official capacity?'

Imlay shrugged and reverted to his earlier manner of easy apathy. 'It is merely my opinion,' he confirmed, 'as a private individual.'

'Well, this is merely mine own, but if it were not forbidden I would wager that it is only a matter of time – and a very short time at that – before the United States controls the entire region. The governor in New Orleans suspects this process is already advanced and that agents of the United States – I should say agents *from* the United States – are already seeking the means by which it may be accomplished.'

'In collusion with the French settlers?' put in Nathan. Imlay shot him a look from beneath his hooded eyes – of warning or alarm?

The monk was shaking his head. 'That I cannot say, but I believe the governor has alluded to the possibility in his reports.'

'I would be very surprised if they had any official backing,' Imlay insisted.

'I am sure they do not. Officially. But it is the Spanish attitude that concerns us. Privately they are convinced that sooner or later the United States will expand into their territories – either through immigration or invasion or both. Those in Madrid who seek a rapprochement with France are certainly of this opinion. And they believe it may be in Spain's interests to make the first move, as it were: to offer New Orleans – and possibly the entire region – to France in return for concessions in Europe and other parts of the world.'

The base of the nearest palm swayed towards them as if eavesdropping. Nathan looked up to where the distant fronds moved in the hidden currents above the roof.

'And what do the French think of this?' enquired Imlay.

Brother Ignatius spread his hands again. 'I am only a poor monk,' he said. 'What can I know of the French?'

'Surely they would be foolish to take on the burden of a new empire in America,' Nathan suggested, 'after what happened to the last one. *And* risk alienating their friends in the United States.'

'Surely,' agreed the monk. 'And just as surely they have their reasons.'

He was looking straight at Imlay when he said this and Nathan wondered if he knew something about the American – or the interests he represented – that Nathan did not.

'But if the Spanish are not anxious to cling to their territories,' Imlay retorted, with a hint of impatience, 'why is the governor in New Orleans so active on their behalf?'

'Because that is his job, as he understands it. Baron Carondelet is a Fleming in the service of the King of Spain. He has family land on the borders of France and the Low Countries – land that is presently occupied by the French. Also, he is an aristocrat from an old Burgundian family. He has no cause to love the Revolutionists. Besides, I did not say that all Spaniards were of the same mind. Far from it. I am a Spaniard and I am by no means anxious to see my country allied to an atheistical, Revolutionist government in Paris. Nor, I should add, is His Holiness the Pope or those who put the interests of the Catholic Church above those of nationality – or mercantilism.'

Nathan nodded as if he entirely understood, though the tortured diplomacy of the Vatican had perplexed older and wiser heads than his. At the risk of appearing banal he brought the conversation down to a more prosaic level.

'Your English is excellent, sir, if I may make so personal an observation. As good as I have heard from any man not born in England.'

'Thank you, sir.' The monk's eyes glinted with amusement. 'In fact, I was born in Dublin. You may detect a little of the lilt.'

Nathan, who had detected no such thing, was about to frame another question when they were interrupted by the roar of a cannon. Followed swiftly by another – and another. It seemed to be coming from the direction of the harbour.

'Are we under attack?' the consul wondered, and though he smiled his eyes betrayed some uncertainty.

'Let us go and look,' proposed Brother Ignatius cheerfully.

They followed him across the courtyard and up two flights of stone stairs to a landing with broad windows overlooking the harbour.

And there, midway between the forts of La Punta and El Morro, they saw a ship of war gliding slowly into the harbour under reefed topsails, her bow wreathed in smoke as her guns roared the customary respects to the King of Spain.

Then the smoke cleared and they saw the flag at her stern.

The consul clutched Nathan by the arm. 'Good God,' he said. 'It is the *Unicorn*.'

Chapter Six

The Captain's Log

---

*D*espite the instruction of my lord Chatham, Nathan had neglected to purchase a new uniform during his brief stay in London. Indeed, after learning of his mother's misfortune, he would have considered it in the nature of a criminal extravagance. However, the Angel Gabriel had contrived to transform Nathan's old uniform by the simple expedient of moving the epaulette from the left shoulder to the right and fronting the lapels in white felt fringed with gold lace. And so it was in the full dignity of his estate as a post captain in His Britannic Majesty's Navy that Nathan greeted the first lieutenant of the *Unicorn* in the dining room of the consul's house in the Havana.

Judging from Pym's expression, something more convincing was required.

'Perhaps you would care to see my commission from their lordships,' Nathan suggested kindly.

The lieutenant, clearly embarrassed, protested that this would not be necessary, not at all; he knew the captain by reputation, of course, had read of his encounter – his *daring* encounter – with the *Vestale* in the Baie de Seine (a nervous smile), was perfectly prepared to take his word as a—

But the Angel Gabriel was at his shoulder and the document laid on the table for the lieutenant's inspection. The smile faded as he considered it in silence for a moment. He was sitting at one end of the long table with Nathan at the other, flanked by Imlay and Portillo. Nathan had decreed that the consul should be present, partly because they were guests in his house but mostly because he thought it ridiculous that Portillo had not been told the full circumstances of the incident involving Captain Kerr when the *Unicorn* had last put into the Havana. But he could not help feeling that the seating arrangement could have been better contrived. Save that the lieutenant's sword was not placed upon the table, it might have been a court martial.

Pym was an odd-looking individual, to Nathan's eye: short and stocky with a round, bullet head that emerged from his tight collar without the apparent aid of a neck. He had passed for lieutenant in '82 – ten years before Nathan – at the end of the American War, and had passed the years of peace serving with the East India Company. He was probably in his early thirties but looked older. He had arrived at the consul's house with a certain air of authority – or at least truculence – and at first sight Nathan had taken him for a bully, full of bluster and the sense of his own importance. He was exactly the kind of naval officer Nathan most disliked – at least in appearance and manner – but he warned himself against early prejudice. He was obliged to work with this man – and depend upon him – for months, even years to come.

Pym was still staring at Nathan's commission and the silence had become embarrassing.

'I very much regret the circumstances of my appointment,' Nathan assured him, 'and you may consider it premature, but it was his Lordship's decision and I am persuaded we must learn to live with it.'

He was already become pompous, he reflected, and had not been wearing the uniform more than an hour.

'You have brought the logs?' he enquired.

'I have.' Pym fumbled at the button of a pocket and removed three notebooks. 'The ship's log which is kept by the master, Mr Baker, my own . . . and Captain Kerr's up to the time of the incident off Ship Island.' After some slight hesitation he held them out to Gabriel.

'Thank you, Lieutenant, but for the moment, let us have your verbal report.'

Pym laid the three documents down on the table in front of him and moved them with the flat of his hands so that they were lined up more or less to his satisfaction.

'I scarce know how to begin,' he said.

'Ship Island would seem to be as good a place as any,' Nathan prompted him. 'I gather that is where the incident occurred.'

A nerve twitched at the corner of the lieutenant's mouth, or it may have been an effort at another unhappy smile. He had been told of the body found in the mouth of the Rigolets.

'Ship Island,' he repeated. 'Yes. You know it? I beg your pardon, sir,' as he recalled his situation and their relative status. 'But are you acquainted with the area?'

'Only from the charts,' one of which was open on the table in front of him, 'and from what I have read.'

Pym nodded. 'It is one of several islands that separate the Gulf from Mississippi Sound – and the most important. As you may be aware from your reading, sir . . .' *was there a note of sarcasm in that phrase? But Nathan told himself not to be over-sensitive . . .* 'larger vessels cannot proceed directly to New Orleans, the water being too shallow. They are wont to anchor off Ship Island or further out in the Sound and transfer their cargoes to smaller vessels for transport through the Rigolets.' He glanced from Nathan to Imlay to make sure they had understood this and the implication. Neither gave him the slightest indication that they had, and after a moment he added: 'It is a natural target for a cruiser intent on preying upon allied commerce.'

Nathan waited patiently.

'So the ship was cleared for action and the guns run out. There was a slight breeze, but it scarce ruffled the surface of the water and we were under full press of sail.' Pym's expression was remote, as if he was transported back there. The ticking of the clock was like a distant echo of the drum, beating to quarters.

'The anchorage was empty, but the *Virginie* had been there – five days before, or so we were informed.' His eyes focused on Nathan's again. 'There was an official on the island, a Don. He told us the French had come ashore to water and provision. He was not in a position to refuse them, he said. Then she left, heading south.

'We were about to follow when a boat arrived from the mainland with a Spanish officer and some soldiers. The officer spoke to Captain Kerr in private. Then the captain ordered that the cutter be prepared for a journey to New Orleans by way of the Rigolets.'

'Did he say why?'

'No, sir, he did not.' A small silence. The lieutenant flushed. Perhaps he interpreted the silence as a criticism of his commanding officer. 'Doubtless he would have, had he . . . had he the opportunity. But it was at this point that . . . that the incident arose.'

He paused to wipe his brow. He was sweating profusely but Nathan himself was by no means cool in his unaccustomed uniform. Nathan saw Pym's swift glance towards Portillo. He does not like him being here, he thought. He wondered if he should have spoken to the lieutenant in private but then he thought, no, damn it, he would not be party to a prejudice because the man had a Spanish name – and was a Jew.

'You may speak freely, Lieutenant,' he pressed him.

'I beg pardon, sir, only I am trying to remember the exact sequence of events. The cutter was alongside. It was provided with food and water and . . . and one of the carronades was secured in the bows.'

'Did you not find this surprising?'

'The gun . . . I . . . It was not for me to question a direct order. And doubtless, as I have said, it would have been explained in due course. But then, it all happened so quickly, I scarce . . . I was up forward – there was a problem among the forecastle men. I think now it might have been contrived as a diversion but,' he moved his hand wearily, 'there was a sudden rush of men to the quarter-deck. It took us all by surprise. I ran back and I saw they were holding the captain – with a pistol to his head.'

'They?'

'Some members of the crew.'

Well, of course some members of the crew, Nathan cursed him silently. Who else would they have been?

'How many?'

'As much as a score or more. The quarterdeck was crowded with them and there was a great deal of shouting and confusion. We have learned since that they were twenty-two in number.'

'And armed?'

'Yes. We had beaten to quarters, do you see, and small arms issued in expectation – I should say, in anticipation – of finding the *Virginie* in the anchorage.'

'And then what happened?'

'Well, the captain . . . Captain Kerr said to do as they said.'

'Which was?'

'To make off in the cutter. It was difficult to know what else we were to do.'

'That's all right, Lieutenant. This is not a court of enquiry.'

Pym did not look entirely convinced.

'I said they must first let the captain go, but of course they would not do that. By now the marines were drawn up with their muskets. They said they would put him ashore. I never thought, not for a moment, that—'

'So they made off in the cutter?'

'Yes, sir.'

'Toward the Rigolets.'

Pym nodded. 'We could not fire into them, when they had the captain. And they said if we tried to follow them – I mean, we could not follow in the frigate because the water was too shallow – but if we tried to follow in any of the other boats, they would blow his brains out.'

Silence. The clock again. More like a heartbeat now. Then, just as Nathan was about to prompt him, Pym resumed: 'The light was fading and there was a mist. In the morning I sent out in the other boats and we searched the shore, but there was no sign of the captain, or of the cutter. We searched further along the coast in both directions, but could not take the frigate too close inshore for fear of running aground. We had to send the boats in. Two days we searched and then, well, it is in the logs.' He touched the documents as if he were preparing to slide them down the table. 'I came to the conclusion that they must have doubled back in the darkness, slipped past on the far side of Ship Island, and headed east.'

'Why east?'

'Because I figured that if they were to seek sanctuary they must make for one of the French islands – Saint Domingue being the nearest – or the United States. And in any case they would head for the Florida Straits. It appeared I was right in this supposition, for when we entered the Straits we encountered a Spanish vessel that had been attacked by a cutter off the coast of Cuba.'

'So that is why you put into the Havana?'

'Yes, sir. Also, I was anxious to send word to the admiral of what had transpired.'

'These men – the mutineers . . .'

'I have a list of their names here, sir.' Again the hand went to the flap of his pocket. This time Nathan nodded and Gabriel took the proffered fold of paper and brought it down the table to him.

'At present, I am less interested in who they are,' Nathan declared as he reached for the list, 'than in why they did it.'

'They are all Irishmen, sir, every one.'

Nathan looked at him sharply. 'And is that a reason?' He had no accurate figures but he would have reckoned more than a third of the Fleet to be Irishmen, including several admirals.

Pym flushed. 'I have reason to believe, sir, that they are members of the Society of United Irishmen.'

Nathan knew of the United Irishmen; he might even have met some of them at one of his mother's soirées. He was imperfectly acquainted with their political aims but his understanding was that they wished for a greater voice in their own affairs: a circumstance that had aroused the resentment of His Majesty's Government who had accused them of terrorism, or at least of having an association with the terrorists in Paris, and acted accordingly. Many were in jail. But he had not heard of them enrolling in the Navy in very large numbers.

'So this was in the nature of a political protest – is that what you are saying?'

Pym looked taken aback by the notion. 'As to that, sir, I have no idea of their motives.'

'So what *are* you saying?'

'Only that I believe them to be members of an illegal organisation, dedicated to the overthrow of the British constitution and to make common cause with the Revolutionists in France.'

'That might be taken as political,' put in Imlay, unhelpfully.

'The question that concerns me,' continued Nathan with a frown, 'is how they came to be aboard one of His Majesty's frigates.'

'Well, as to that,' Pym was looking uncomfortable again, 'I believe it had been represented to them that it was either the Navy or a prison hulk on the Medway.'

Nathan raised his eyes to the ceiling.

'We had very little choice in the matter,' Pym conceded, 'being but recently commissioned and sent, in haste, to the West Indies.'

'But you had no intuition of violence?'

'There were . . . mutterings. Against which Captain Kerr felt compelled to take action on several occasions. But there was no reason to suspect a conspiracy to mutiny.'

Mutterings. Nathan glanced down at the list of names and his eyes widened in surprise.

'One of these men is an officer,' he observed.

'A warrant officer,' Pym corrected him.

'Declan Keane. Master's mate.'

'Yes. He was to have navigated the cutter.'

'But – he was involved in the mutiny?'

'Yes, sir. Indeed, I very much suspect that he was the leader – or at least one of the leaders. The main culprit, I believe from his behaviour, to be a man called O'Neill: James O'Neill, one of the gun captains. He it was who held the pistol to the captain's head.'

So it was carefully planned. And involved a warrant officer with a good knowledge of navigation, presumably. Sufficient to take them anywhere in the Caribbean – or to the South Seas.

'And you had no inkling of any conspiracy?'

'I am sorry, sir, if you feel there has been any dereliction of duty on the part of the captain or officers . . .'

'I did not say that, sir, nor do I think it. We are simply trying to discover how this unfortunate business occurred.'

Pym's expression was a mixture of truculence and pure misery.

'Well, sir, I do not see how it could have been avoided. And once it had occurred, what else were we to do?' His voice was become plaintive. 'What other action might have been taken? They had a gun to the captain's head. He ordered me to comply with their wishes.'

'And after?'

Pym looked confused. 'After? Well, I did all that could be done in the circumstances, and then I . . . I did not know at that stage, nor at any point these last few months, that Captain Kerr was dead.'

Nathan sighed. 'I would not presume to criticise the conduct of anyone at this point, but it has been over two months since your last visit to the Havana and not a word as to your whereabouts.'

'Which is accounted for in my log, sir. However,' he forestalled Nathan's interruption, 'if I must explain myself before these gentlemen . . .' a definite note of criticism there . . . 'having heard report of the cutter in the Old Bahama Channel and in the belief that my captain was still in the power of the mutineers, I ventured to take the *Unicorn* in pursuit, only to encounter a violent hurricane within days of leaving the Havana.'

'We feared you were lost,' Nathan said, in the hope of putting him more at ease.

'This was very near the case. We were then upon the eastern edge of the Channel and were like to have been smashed upon the rocks. However, we succeeded in taking the ship into deeper water and managed to ride out the storm.' He tapped one of the documents with a stubby forefinger. 'It is all in the log.' And then, catching Nathan's eye and with a note of defiance, 'Three days with all hands at the pumps, near dead upon their feet, eighteen inches of water in the well and the rigging a shambles.' The bracing went out of his shoulders. 'But as the storm subsided we had the ill luck to run upon an uncharted reef just north of Ragged Island.'

Nathan looked for it on the map but needed Portillo to point it out for him: a mere speck to the north of the Old Bahama Channel.

'We were forced to unload the ship of all her stores,

water and guns, and make camp upon the island for above a week when we managed to float her off upon the next spring tide. But our timbers were sprung – we were leaking like a sieve – and she had lost her rudder. We rigged up one of the sweeps, but it was not . . .' He shrugged. Nathan should know what he was up against, if he was any sort of a captain. 'And the wind then blowing from the south-west, I judged it better to head for Nassau on New Providence, rather than try to beat against it.'

It made sense, of a sort – if you could not make for Port Royal or the Havana or even Port-au-Prince, which was now in British hands. Nathan wondered if he would have done any differently. Or better.

'We worked the pumps night and day and reached Nassau on the last day of August.' Nassau, once the pirate capital of the Caribbean, was now not much more than a watering-hole. 'Whereupon we careened her upon the shore.'

He could have done little else, for if there were any dockyard facilities in the port, Nathan had yet to hear of them.

'Over the next few weeks we patched her holes, fashioned a new rudder, mended her rigging – even procured new boats, for the old ones were smashed to pieces and the cutter . . .' But they knew what had happened to the cutter. 'And then we sailed back for the Havana. And she is in as good order, I dare say, as when she left Chatham Dockyard.'

And after all that, to find a new captain waiting for

him – the jumped-up son of a rear-admiral with friends in high places.

Nathan nodded. 'Thank you, Lieutenant. I congratulate you upon saving your ship and your crew.' He hesitated a moment but it had to be said: 'It is a pity, however, that you did not see fit to send a message to Mr Portillo here advising him of your situation. It would have saved much anxiety . . .'

'Oh, but I did. I sent it by a British vessel – a slaver – the *Marie-Anne* of Liverpool, bound from Nassau to the Havana.' He glared at Portillo accusingly. 'You did not receive it?'

Portillo shook his head. 'I know the *Marie-Anne*,' he said, 'but she has not put into the Havana for six months or more.'

'Well, I assure you I sent it.'

'I am sure you did, Lieutenant. Clearly, it did not arrive. However, it answers the question. Gentlemen?' Nathan glanced to left and right but the others had nothing to add. The consul was looking down at the table, Imlay gazing into the middle distance as if he had other things on his mind, better things to do with his time. 'But now we must decide upon our future course of action.'

No. *He* must decide. And be judged for it – as Pym would be judged in the course of time by their lordships of the Admiralty.

'The *Virginie* is still at large and we have been instructed to find and destroy her.' He looked down at the chart. 'The last sighting was off Panama and I propose to take the *Unicorn* across the Yucatan Channel and down the Spanish Main in the hope of meeting up with her there.' He met Pym's eye and was about to add, 'If you have no objection,' but thought better of it. He was the ship's commander, not Pym: it was his decision and his alone. To pretend otherwise would be to add insult to injury. 'When, in your opinion, will the *Unicorn* be ready to sail?'

'Whenever you wish it, sir. We watered and provisioned in Nassau, and the ship, as I have said, is in good order.'

'And the crew?' It slipped out almost without his meaning it to, and Pym flushed a darker shade of red.

'The crew will do their duty, sir, for all that we are some sixty short of a full complement.'

'Sixty?'

'Which is, I admit, cause for concern.'

Quite right it was cause for concern. 'I believe you said there were but twenty-two involved in the mutiny?'

'I did, sir, but we were short handed to begin with and have lost a few more in the cause of our misfortunes. Two men overboard in the storm and three more injured whom we had to leave in Nassau. And ten men with the fever.'

'The fever?'

'The yellow fever.'

Dear God, it got worse. Yellow fever was the particular dread of every seaman and soldier who was sent to the region, but it was unusual to contract it at sea.

'All of which occurred when we were on New Providence.'

'And there have been no other cases since?'

'No, sir. Not so far, by the grace of God.'

Indeed. For nothing else known to man could prevent it
– or cure it.

'Very well.' Nathan levered himself up from his chair at
the head of the table. 'I suggest you return to the *Unicorn*,
Mr Pym, and I will join you there presently – with my own
people.'

His people. He had forgot to mention the marines. But
it was too late now. The lieutenant was on his feet and
preparing to leave. It would look like an oversight on
Nathan's part, which it was. And besides, it was a bad way
to end the meeting. He thought of a better.

'And let us hope our *Unicorn* does better than the last.'
He meant the last beast – that had become extinct. But he
could see that Pym thought he meant the frigate under its
last commander and took it amiss.

Nathan was mortified but an apology would only have
made it worse. The lieutenant bowed stiffly and left the
room with the consul in attendance.

'If you have no objection,' Nathan said to Imlay, 'I
think it would be of benefit if I were to spend some time
studying the logs.' He indicated the notebooks that Pym
had left. 'And do you send to the *Speedwell*,' Nathan
instructed the Angel Gabriel, 'and ask Mr Keeble to send
the gig for us in about an hour.'

Nathan began with the first lieutenant's log, if only because
it was the topmost book when Gabriel brought them to
him. The first few pages described the sea trials off the Isle
of Wight and were of little interest, though even at this
stage the *Unicorn* appeared to be dogged by misfortune.

Friday March 28th: At four o'clock this evening an order was brought us from Spithead by a cutter to proceed to sea under the command of Commodore Pasley in the Bellerophon *but a thick fog coming on forced us to remain at station off St Helens for the night.*

Sunday March 30th: Fresh gale and cloudy. At six AM split our foresail. Got it down and got up a new one; lost contact with squadron.

Monday March 31st: Heavy seas, wind SSW. Lost man overboard, later reported as John O'Driscoll, landsman. Not possible to launch ship's boats. Saw coast of Normandy on our weather bow.

Nathan skipped to the more recent entries which described the series of disasters that had befallen the *Unicorn* since the incident off Ship Island, but they were so sparse in their detail – and so dry in their style – that had Nathan not met the gentleman who had written them, he would have suspected him of irony.

Monday August 11th: Old Bahama Channel, off Cayo Coco. Flat calm. Heavy cloud to NE. Close reefed main topsail and reefed foresails. Set course NNW to clear islands. PM heavy rain. Visibility very poor. At half past twelve PM strong winds with heavy squalls: carried away larboard main-brace and starboard main topsail sheet; foresail blown to pieces, mainsail split and blowing from yards; got it down and set storm staysails. Heavy gale with squalls. At three PM took in staysls. Running before wind under bare poles. A prodigious high sea which threatens and endangers the bow. Carpenter reports four inches water in well.

Wednesday August 13th AM: Continuing heavy wind and seas. Carried away the chain-plate of the foremost main shroud. Mainyard sprung. Mizzen mast sprung in consequence of vangs of the gaff giving way. At half past eleven struck with a sea on the starboard quarter; stove in four of the main-deck ports, filled the waist and stove in the launch. Lost two men overboard later reported as John Doyle and James Plant. Carpenter reports lower-deck timbers sprung. Eighteen inches water in well. All hands at pumps. Six men injured in falls, one severe.

Friday August 15th AM: Storm abated somewhat. Lowered fore course under double reef and hoist staysls. At eleven AM sighted Ragged Island off starboard bow. At half past eleven ran upon uncharted reef . . .

A tale of unmitigated disaster told by a pedant. Had Pym endured the ordeals of Ulysses on his return from Troy, Nathan suspected that his account of them would have read something like this and the *Odyssey* been consigned to oblivion.

He took up the next document: *Ship's Log of the Frigate* Unicorn, *32 guns, Captain Lawrence Kerr, kept by Robert Baker, ship's master, March 17th to October 31st 1794.*

This was a typical ship's log with little to recommend it to a reader wishing for some insightful comment save that it was written in a legible hand. Baker had divided the pages into three columns for Course, Winds and his Notes. The latter were scanty and reflected Pym's view of events, even to using the same words at times – 'prodigious' being a particular favourite. Nathan suspected collusion but this was by no means unusual aboard a ship of war.

Nathan put the notebook to one side, meaning to study it in more detail when he had the time, and took up the last of the documents: Captain Kerr's log, dated from the ship's commissioning in Chatham in late February to the fateful day in July when he was taken by the mutineers.

From the first few days it was clear that Kerr was not a happy man, nor the *Unicorn* a happy ship.

His first cause for concern was with the crew. Inevitably, with a newly commissioned ship in the second year of the war, it had been difficult for him to find experienced seamen or any to man the ship at all. He had been obliged to accept *the sweepings of the jailhouse . . . and in consequence the ship is very poorly crewed, with nothing approaching a full complement and above a third of the people landsmen – with a good many Irish among them.*

Here was the first mention of that race that was to so

aggravate him in the ensuing weeks and months. But why was he so opposed to the Irish? There was no real clue in the early pages of the captain's log, save that he found them 'ill disciplined in their appearance and manner, much inclined to idleness and disorder'.

He had attempted to recruit more experienced seamen during the *Unicorn*'s voyage to Spithead, printing off posters to display in the taverns, but he had been unable to attract more than a handful of volunteers – *having but a poor record of piracy* – by which he must mean the taking of prizes. An indication that he disapproved of the practice – or was he chagrined that he had not yet profited by it?

He had been obliged to resort to the press, which had given the *Unicorn* something of an evil reputation during her progress along the south coast and without conferring much advantage. Kerr's gangs had seized fewer than a dozen seamen from almost as many ports and fishing villages in Kent and Sussex, and the ship had arrived at Spithead with her captain complaining he was still some two score men short of his full complement of 250. *And I doubt there is above a fifth of them that know what they are about.*

The situation improved slightly when they reached Spithead and were allocated a score of prime seamen taken by the press in Portsmouth from a recently arrived convoy. But Kerr was far from satisfied. The ship performed badly in her trials – which was only to be expected from such a new and diverse crew – but what really upset him was her appearance.

Kerr had determined views on orderliness. Everything must be 'shipshape and Bristol fashion' – as he asserted – although 'Jamaica fashion' were the words that sprung to Nathan's mind, for Kerr's obsession with gleaming decks and squared-off rigging was reminiscent of the most fanatical martinet on the West Indies station.

Nathan recalled that Kerr had spent some time on the station during the eighties, and presumably this was where he had acquired his respect for outward show. He was most concerned that the appearance of the ship and her crew would let him down and shame him in the eyes of his superiors and fellow captains. He bemoaned the fact that he could only afford to dress the crew of his barge in uniform and that the rest go *about in all manner of slops and some with rags on their backs more appropriate to the backstreets of Dublin than the deck of a ship in the King's Navy.*

And then there was the poor handling of the ship.

He described the petty mishaps that had occurred in the Channel when the *Unicorn* was at exercise with the ships of Pasley's squadron, and though the actual incidents were described in much the same bland terms as Pym, it was possible to discern his underlying anger with the incompetence of the crew. Time after time he referred to the need to *make an example of someone before the ship's company.*

Doubtless he felt himself to be under pressure. Nathan could sympathise with that. He had felt much the same when he had first assumed command. He felt it now. And he detected in Kerr the same anxiety: the sense of impending failure – and public disgrace. But whereas Nathan was naturally disposed to blame himself, and to perceive his own inadequacies in sharp relief, Kerr was inclined to blame others. And gradually something worse emerged: a tendency to regard the failings of the crew as sabotage – a deliberate conspiracy to do mischief. To do him down.

And this had fostered a determination to break them before they broke him. It began in the second week after leaving Spithead.

Sunday April 6th AM: Fresh breeze and fine weather. Performed Divine Service. Read Articles of War. *Afterwards rigged grating. The following made example of before the ship's company: Petr Flynn, landsman, disobedience; James O'Driscoll, neglect of duty; Patr Farell, drunkenness; Neil Quinn, filthiness; Donld O'Brian, sleeping on duty; M.^{ch} Connor, drunkenness, pissing upon the deck . . .*

And that was just the start of it. Nathan read on with increasing astonishment. In the course of the frigate's voyage – her *maiden* voyage – from Spithead to Port Royal, Kerr had listed over a hundred individual punishments. In one single day – July 25th – Nathan counted twenty-eight. There was no record of the number of lashes the men received – he would have to consult the punishment book for that – and Kerr invariably used the euphemism *made example of before the ship's company*, but there could be no doubting his meaning,

and the fact that he chose to record it so often in his log
indicated that he took some pride in the severity of his
regime.

Nathan had never ordered a man flogged – in his short
period of command he had never had reason to – but he
had been forced to witness many a flogging as a junior
officer and he detested it. The King's regulations laid
down that an individual captain – as opposed to a court
martial – could not order a man to be given more than
twelve lashes for a single offence, but many got round this
by claiming to punish more than one offence at a time.
Nathan had seen punishments of thirty-six, sixty, even
one hundred lashes meted out for a whole series of
offences, many quite trivial, but he had never encountered
such sustained punishment as that inflicted on the crew of
the *Unicorn* on her maiden voyage – and apparently
directed towards one sector of the crew. For almost all of
the victims – or 'miscreants' as Kerr called them – were
Irish.

What was going on here?

It soon became clear. According to Kerr, there was a
conspiracy afoot. The seeds of rebellion had been planted
in the good ship *Unicorn*, and in Kerr's view they were a
species native to Ireland.

As time went on, he became even less circumspect in his
opinions. The log had become less an account of the
voyage than a private diary in which he described his
hopes of success in tracking down the *Virginie* – and his
darkest fears of failure. Failure – and betrayal.

On 25 July he wrote:

Was approached by one of my informers among the crew with a note that he said was being passed among his fellow countrymen. It is in the form of a secret catechism, such as the Papists use, and reads:

What is that in your hand?
It is a branch.
Of what?
Of the Tree of Liberty.
Where did it first grow?
In America.
Where does it bloom?
In France.
Where did the seed fall?
In Ireland.
When will the moon be full?
When the four quarters meet.

The meaning is clear until the last two lines. I take them to indicate that some mischief is contemplated 'when the four quarters meet'. But what are the four quarters? I am resolved to play a waiting game to see what I may discover.

So Kerr had informers among the crew. Irishmen, by the sound of it, informing upon their fellow countrymen. It was a pity they did not inform Kerr that the four quarters referred to the four provinces of Ireland; it might have relieved his mind somewhat. For though he was right in saying this was a form of catechism, it was by no means secret. Nathan had seen it circulated in London, quite possibly in his mother's house.

But Kerr's was clearly a mind in torment. That same day, despite his suspicions and his resolve 'to play a waiting game', he had ordered twenty-eight men lashed for the usual range of trivial misdemeanours.

Two days later, he was taken by the mutineers and his throat was cut.

Nathan closed the journal with a sigh and stared down the empty table. Kerr was clearly a tyrant, and he had suffered the fate of many a tyrant before him – but was he naturally predisposed to tyranny or had the conditions of the *Unicorn* brought him to such a pass?

Nathan had discovered what he could of his predecessor before leaving London. It was little enough. He had passed for lieutenant in '76 at the start of the American War and six years later, just before it ended, he had been appointed commander of the sloop *Shannon*, named after the river in Ireland. Had *she* been unlucky for him, too? Kerr and the *Shannon* were on the West Indies station when the war ended, and he had stayed there until '86 when he brought the sloop home to be decommissioned. For several years he was ashore on half pay until the Nootka Crisis when the Navy was mobilised to meet a supposed threat from Spain, and he had secured command of another sloop, the *Cormorant*, of sixteen guns. The crisis had ended without war but Kerr was among those retained in service. The situation on the continent was uncertain; many expected war with Revolutionary France. In '93 it came. And the following year Kerr was made post and given the *Unicorn*.

Why? He appeared to have done little to distinguish himself in a lengthy career and there were more promising candidates on the waiting list. Many would have shed blood for a brand new frigate – their own blood and that of any who stood in their way.

Nathan had asked discreet questions in the Admiralty and been informed that Kerr had family influence. Apparently a cousin had recently become a board member of the East India Company – a nabob with several parliamentary boroughs in his pocket. Votes in Parliament: the secret of many a man's success – in the service and elsewhere. But Nathan could discover little else about him, save that he was aged about forty and single. Evans, the Second Secretary at the Admiralty, whom Nathan had gently interrogated whilst in London, thought he might have been recently widowed.

The whisper of a knock upon the door and the Angel Gabriel ghosted in to inform him that the gig was waiting for him in the harbour – and they might leave as soon as he was ready.

Chapter Seven

The Unicorn

———•——•———

Nathan changed back into civilian clothes for the walk down to the harbour not wishing to excite the populace beyond reason in his gold lace and trappings. They made quite enough of a spectacle already, he thought, with the consul come to see them off and one of his servants pushing a handcart with their trunks and the Angel Gabriel glaring about him for fear of footpads and Imlay strolling ahead like a benevolent despot with his court, the inevitable cigar clenched between his teeth and his hand raised from time to time in fond farewell – or benediction – to some lady in a window. Nathan thanked his stars they were not throwing roses.

'You must come aboard before we sail,' Nathan urged the consul in all sincerity. He had become quite fond of Portillo – or Don Roberto as he thought of him – during the course of their stay in the Havana: as appreciative of his generous hospitality and dry good humour as he was respectful of his insight. Certainly he would have preferred him to Imlay as a 'political adviser' for all that the latter complained that he was 'wedded to the Spanish interest'.

'I think you will have quite enough to think on when you are aboard the *Unicorn*,' Portillo said now, 'without having to worry about visiting dignitaries, even so humble as myself.'

They had almost reached the waterfront when Nathan became aware that they were being followed by another, more curious entourage. It was led by a tall black woman in a long red robe, her face shaded by a large red parasol held aloft by another woman, almost as tall, who walked a step behind her. To their rear came a small boy dressed as an Oriental page in a golden turban and embroidered robes, followed by a small monkey in a red waistcoat on a silken lead. And bringing up the rear was a massive black man in a long white robe and a tall white hat wielding a staff like a symbol of office.

At first Nathan thought they might simply be heading in the same direction, but there was something in their purposeful tread and the fact that they maintained exactly the same distance between the two groups that made him fear the worst.

He strode forward to catch up with Imlay.

'For God's sake, man, it is like a travelling show,' he complained.

'I am not sure I quite follow you,' Imlay replied courteously.

'Why, have you not seen what is following *us*?' Nathan admonished him, stopping and looking back.

The other group had also stopped.

'Good God!' exclaimed Imlay – and then he smiled and raised his hat.

'I wish,' said Nathan, 'that you would not encourage your harem to follow you around as if you were some Oriental satrap on a royal progress. Perhaps you would be so good as to conduct your farewells in private – unless you are planning to bring them with you.'

'Well, as to that, it is not my harem, worse luck, nor is it me they are following.'

'Then who . . . ?'

'You, my dear fellow. You.' He turned and continued on his way, and after a moment of astonished perplexity, Nathan hurried to catch up with him.

'What do you mean, *me*? Who are those people?'

'I cannot answer for all of them,' replied Imlay smoothly, 'but the woman in red is La Princesa Negra. I told you she had lost her heart to you. I imagine she has gotten wind of your departure and has come to grieve at the waterside. The least you could do is give her a wave.'

'Be damned,' said Nathan faintly.

They had reached the wharf where the gig was waiting for them, with four of the hands to pull oar and both Place and Coyle to instruct them. Place wore his blue naval jacket with a dirk at his hip, quite the midshipman already, and Coyle was chewing his lip and appearing close to tears: the two boys had cemented their friendship on the voyage out and within the hour they would part.

Nathan could see the *Unicorn* at her mooring under the guns of La Cabana, with the blue ensign at her stern lifting in lazy obedience to some faint breeze on the far side of the harbour. Pym must have given her a new coat of paint during her enforced stay on New Providence, for she looked as good as new with the broad yellow stripe along her hull and the gunports picked out in black and the shrouds so freshly tarred they almost gleamed. '*In as good order, I dare say, as when she left Chatham Dockyard.*'

If only in appearance.

'Let us first row out to the frigate,' Nathan instructed, or rather requested of the hands, for they were now under Mr Keeble's orders.

'To go aboard her, sir?' piped Place, with enthusiasm and alarm in equal measure.

Nathan knew exactly how he felt. 'No, we will content ourselves to sit up at half a cable's length where we might admire her without drawing attention to ourselves.'

As they pulled out into the crowded harbour Nathan looked back and saw the small entourage that had followed them, standing on the wharf, as still as statues, and then the woman in red stepped forward, clear of the shade of the parasol, and for the first time he saw her features and he felt almost as if he had been kicked in the stomach. He looked at Imlay to share his wonderment and Imlay smiled.

'Did I not say she was beautiful?' He sighed and raised his hat one more time in ironic farewell. 'And yours for the asking.'

Nathan shook his head and turned his back, but he was more disturbed than he cared to show, or would have wished to admit, even to himself, and the image stayed with him as they rowed out into the harbour: that tall figure in the flowing red robe at the water's edge and the finely sculptured features of a goddess. It was an effort not to look back.

Instead he looked to the frigate. *His* frigate. Another beauty. Riding at anchor in the sparkling blue water against the splendid backdrop of La Cabana, as if the biggest, most expensive fortress in the Caribbean had been provided merely as a setting for her own more decorous splendour.

They lay off her a while, holding against the tide, while he observed her. The bumboats were clustered about her, bringing produce from the shore: bananas, pineapples, melons, women . . . It was unlikely Pym would permit the latter commodity with his new captain preparing to come aboard, but certainly some bargaining seemed to be in progress. Nathan ran his eye along her gunports, restrained himself from counting them like a small boy – but only just. He knew how many there were. The faint breeze lifted the ensign in a desultory wave and then let it fall again. Pym had moved it from the peak of the gaff to the flagstaff at her stern – the ensign of a rear-admiral of the blue, reminding Nathan that he must write to Admiral Ford in Port Royal, if only out of courtesy, to inform him that he had taken command and was in pursuit of his orders from their lordships of the Admiralty.

They had rigged awnings on the quarterdeck and in the waist as a shade against the sun: so white they looked as if they had been painted or pipe-clayed like the belts of the marine sentries. Nathan could see one of them on the forecastle by the belfry, and as he watched he heard the distant sound of the bell: three bells in the afternoon watch.

Even this close he could not see a single scratch or stain on her hull, nor any rust from the metalwork. And the hammocks in their side netting with not a trace of bedding or clothes. Sure she hid her wounds well. No one looking at her could have imagined that she had been battered by a hurricane, near wrecked on a reef, blighted by yellow fever and suffered the disgrace of mutiny with her captain kidnapped and dumped on a foreign shore with his throat cut.

Stainless she most certainly was not. She should have Kerr's blood dripping from her scuppers.

'Row me around her if you would,' he begged the crew, and he leaned eagerly forward as they crossed her bow, close enough to see the proud white face of the unicorn with its golden horn.

They came down her starboard side – the side he would board as her captain – and he could see the steps rigged ready for him with red side ropes: he would have to wear gloves for fear of leaving a stain upon the least object he touched. He checked himself sternly, recognising an old enemy in this tendency to mock and belittle when he was feeling personally threatened and on the defensive: fearful of himself being judged. And then as they came round the stern he saw Pym, leaning over the side and shouting down to the bumboats to clear away and mind they did not scratch his precious paintwork, the whoresons.

'Very well, enough of this,' he said to the crew. Then, remembering his manners: 'Thank 'ee, but let us not keep Mr Keeble waiting.'

And so they rowed to the *Speedwell* and he stepped aboard her for the last time with his heart in his boots. He could never have imagined when he took command of her in Bristol a little more than a year ago that he would be so sorry to be leaving her. Or that her crew would be so sorry to see him leave.

'We have had some adventures together,' said Keeble, the second mate who was now her skipper as they sat in what was now his cabin going through the ship's papers and sharing a last tot of rum. 'And I am sorry they are ended, though there were times I confess I never thought I would live to say it.'

'Well, I suppose you will not be sorry to be quit the King's service,' Nathan countered, 'and free to go about your lawful business again.'

This was intended as ironic, for the *Speedwell* had been steeped in villainy long before she came under Nathan's command. But the Americans, he had discovered, were immune from the vice of irony – *if* they ever recognised the nature of the beast, which was doubtful.

'If them that's in the King's service would only let us,' muttered Keeble darkly, then, remembering himself: 'Begging your pardon, sir. I was forgetting.'

Nathan had resumed his uniform for the trip to the *Unicorn* but it was the first time Keeble or any of the crew had seen him in it, or even knew him in his true occupation as a captain in the King's Navy. He had come aboard in Bristol in the guise of their new owner, a Mr Turner of New York, engaged in running contraband across the English Channel to Le Havre, and though they had not taken long to smoke him, he had acted more like a privateer captain or a smuggler – one of their own – than a representative of His Majesty, strutting the quarterdeck in his bicorn hat and his gold lace.

And yet throughout his commission the *Speedwell* had been under Admiralty protection – a hired vessel, safe from the depredations of any zealous King's officer who aspired to take her as a prize or press half her crew to supplement his own. There was more reason to regret his departure than the force of sentiment.

'Well, you are at liberty to continue in the service if you wish,' Nathan assured him, with a smile. 'And the same goes for any of the crew.'

If not spoken entirely in jest – for he would have taken as many of the *Speedwell*'s crew as his conscience and Keeble's compliance would have allowed – this was a whimsical notion. None but the most reckless or feeble minded would have considered the prospect for an instant. The lowest-paid deckhand aboard the *Speedwell* earned far more than the six shillings a week available to him as an ordinary seaman aboard the *Unicorn* – *and* without the risk of being flogged senseless for drunkenness or pissing upon the deck, should such degenerate conduct ever occur to him.

But surprisingly there was no answering smile from Keeble, or even an embarrassed shrug of the shoulders.

'I know of at least one who might take you up on that,

sir,' he replied evenly. 'And that is young Frankie Coyle.'

'Ah.' Nathan recalled the way he had looked in the gig and William Place in all his finery with a dirk at his hip. 'I did wonder if he were so inclined. But you are in the nature of *loco parentis* to him – as a father figure, that is,' he added hastily, for Keeble's frown indicated he might take this amiss. 'Would you not wish him to remain aboard the *Speedwell* and return to his home in Boston?'

'Well, to be blunt, it was not much of a home he had there,' replied Keeble with a shake of his head. 'And if to join you was his wish, I would not be the one to stand in the way of it.'

'Then if you have no objection I will offer him a position as one of the captain's servants,' said Nathan, who had been thinking along these lines, 'which is to say with the same status as young Place, that of Volunteer First Class.'

The frown again. Keeble had little notion of the ranks accorded in the King's Navy but he knew the status of William Place was somewhat higher than that of a servant.

'But Billy Place is a gentleman, I think,' he observed, 'for all the swearing he's learned from I know not who.' With an even fiercer frown, for Keeble was from Marblehead and a man of determined morals.

'Aye, and will berth with the other young gentlemen aboard the *Unicorn*.'

'And Frankie with them?'

'Frankie with them. Do you have any objection to that?'

Now he did look embarrassed. 'No, no, only that he is not what you might say, used to being among gentlemen. His mother, well, not to put too fine a point on it, was a whore. And likely has remained so, if she still be alive when we come to Boston.'

'Well, he will not be the first whore's son that was an officer in the King's Navy,' Nathan assured him cheerfully. 'And some have been made admiral. Do you not think he merits the opportunity?'

'Oh, he does that, sir. He does that. And I wish him joy of it. It is only that I did not want you to be in ignorance and think I was making game of you if it came out.' Keeble squared his shoulders. 'But he is a good freeborn lad from Boston, Massachusetts, and as good as the son of any English gentleman, I dare say.'

'I am sure of it,' Nathan calmed him hastily, 'so let us put it to him and give him the choice.' Of berthing with the young swine aboard the *Unicorn* or remaining with a parcel of Yankee rebels and reprobates, he thought of adding humorously, but it would have been the wrong note on which to have ended the conversation and he had played enough of that music for one day.

And so there were five passengers beside Nathan in the gig that finally pulled for the *Unicorn* – Imlay, Tully, Gabriel, Place and Coyle: the latter proud but self-conscious in the smart blue jacket that Place had lent him, and Nathan's dirk that he had worn as a midshipman aboard the *Hermes*, and which had been presented to him as a gift to commence his new career. Their old shipmates were lining the rail to see them off with 'Three cheers for the captain!' and Mrs Small alternately waving her handkerchief and pressing it to her tearful face. Nathan would dearly have liked to take her with him but lacked the nerve to impose a female cook on the crew of a man of war, and besides, she and Small had a notion of opening a small French hotel in Boston.

'And you will come and see us there,' she had said, 'and I will cook you the best meal you ever had, as good as we had in Le Havre when you got us out of prison.'

'That I will,' he had said, knowing it was unlikely he would see her or Small or Keeble or any of them ever again.

This time they approached the frigate from her starboard side and Gilbert Gabriel hailed out '*Unicorn*!' to let them know her captain was aboard.

Thus Nathan came up the steps to the unearthly shriek of the boatswain's call and the stamp and crash of the marines as they presented arms, and as his head came level with the deck he was met with a startling spectacle of red, white and blue with the side boys all in white and the marines in red and the officers assembled on the quarterdeck, every one whipping off his hat as Nathan made his entrance, gazing about him as if he had every right to be here. Pym stepped forward with a bow.

'Welcome aboard, sir. Shall I present you to the officers, or do you first wish me to read your commission?'

His commission. My God, where was his commission,

without which he was nothing? An impostor, a mere pretender, a mountebank. He had a brief, tragic-comic image of being sent back to the *Speedwell* to find it. But Gabriel, the Blessed Angel Gabriel, was holding out the necessary item and Nathan took it with a brief roll of his eye for Gabriel's private consumption.

'Perhaps we should get the formalities over with first,' he proposed as he presented it to the first lieutenant, instantly cursing himself for not asking to be introduced to the officers, which would have been the right thing to do – his first decision and it was the wrong one – and now they must all stand there like lemons while the boatswain's call summoned all hands aft: a great rush of people from every part of the ship and most – for all Kerr's complaint – in blue jackets and white sailcloth trousers and pale straw hats with a neat black band and the name of the ship inscribed in white lettering. And as the weird keening died away, a shout of 'Off hats!' and in the silence with only the faintest of breezes ruffling the flag at her stern, Pym read out their lordship's commission: formally appointing Nathaniel Peake Esquire to the command of His Majesty's ship *Unicorn*, 'willing and requiring all the officers and company belonging to the said ship to behave themselves in their several Employments with all due Respect and Obedience to you their captain . . .'

And the silent ranks of attentive faces and the great walls of La Cabana towering above them and the pelicans rising and falling on the currents of air and the harbour going about its business as if nothing untoward was happening in their midst. Nathan could not stop himself from glancing towards that part of the waterfront where he had left the woman in red, and he did not know whether to be relieved or sorry that he could not see her.

'And you are likewise to observe as well the General Practical Instructions and what orders you may from time to time receive from any of your superior Officers for His Majesty's Service. Hereof nor you nor any of you may fail as you will answer the contrary at your Peril. And for so doing this shall be your Order.'

The set, stoic expressions. Some eager faces, most not. Most with that look about them that said, 'Let us wait and see, let us hope for the best while expecting the worst.' Much like the crew of his first command, the *Nereus*. A cagey regard under a mask of compliance. Wondering what the tide had brought in. But there was something more, something he had not seen on the *Nereus* or any- where else in the Navy: what was it? A kind of despond- ency. They looked . . . whipped. Whipped into shape by a tyrant of a captain who had had his throat cut.

So that was that and now the introductions. As many commissioned officers and warrant officers, seamen and civilian, as the entire crew of the *Speedwell*, and Nathan could have sworn he was the youngest amongst them, save for the midshipmen – and even one of them looked his senior by several years.

Mr Webster, second lieutenant, Mr Maxwell, third lieutenant, Mr Baker, master, whose log book he had read, or skipped through in the consul's house. Nathan repeated the names as he heard them, as if committing them to memory, when in truth they sank into the murky waters of his brain without a ripple and the faces like so much flotsam and jetsam passing before his drowning vision.

Mr McGregor, lieutenant of marines, a grim-looking Scot with a scar on his cheek – from battle or a duel? How would he react when he discovered that Nathan had brought his own Myrmidons with him? Would he take it as a slight or be relieved at the reinforcement? Mr McLeish, the surgeon, another Scot, young and sober looking, unlike many a ship's surgeon of Nathan's acquaintance. Mr Sawyer, master's mate – only one master's mate, the other having taken off in the cutter: Declan Keane. Yes, there was one name he could remember. Four midshipmen: Holroyd, Meadows, Fleetwood and Lamb. Mr McIvor the purser, Mr Bailey the schoolmaster, Mr Shaw who was to be his clerk, Mr Clyde, the gunner – Mr Lloyd, the carpenter and at last Nathan found something to say that would not cause offence or reveal him as a complete fool.

'Well, Mr Lloyd, you have had your work cut out, I believe.'

'Aye, sir, we have that.' Bobbing his bald head and exposing a reef of broken teeth. A man of about forty, Nathan guessed, ancient by comparison with the rest of the crew, a tide of frowns rippling up from his bushy eyebrows to halfway up his shining pate, a man who knew more about the ship, the solid oaken core of her, than any other man present and might have cause for his worried expression.

'Well, from what I have heard and seen so far, you have worked wonders,' Nathan assured him, 'and I would never have known the blows she has took.'

Careful now. Move on. Worried already that he might have offended Mr Pym, who doubtless considered he was owed the credit for it and was doubtless right.

Oh, what uncertain waters he sailed, what shoals and reefs, what quicksands. Better to say nothing but to bob his head this way and that with the occasional benediction of a repeated name like the god he was.

William Brown, master-at-arms, Jacob Young, coxswain, who had command of his barge – a bright enough lad, probably Nathan's own age or thereabouts, his eyes less guarded than the rest. The boatswain and his mates, the quartermaster and *his* mates, William Kerr, captain's steward . . . No trace of a falter in Pym's neutral tone and yet it dropped like a grenade upon the spotless deck.

Kerr. A coincidence of names or a poor kinsman taken into service? Almost certainly the latter. The captain's steward. The man who had waited upon him at table, run his errands, washed and ironed his clothes, kept his razor stropped, might even have shaved that vulnerable throat. A thin, pinched man with a prominent Adam's apple and a reedy voice. Had his captain, his kinsman, looked like this? What was Nathan to do with him? Consign him to outer darkness or make him subject to the Angel Gabriel? He might prefer the outer darkness. Nathan would.

Gun captains, captains of the foretop, maintop and mizzen. The smiling, perspiring faces and the guarded eyes. And that uneasy look about them that he recognised now as a look of defeat.

And with the *Virginie* still to fight.

If they ever found her.

He looked to his guns. Blomefield pattern, like the sternchaser on the *Speedwell*. Twenty-six 18-pounders on her upper deck; two 6-pounders and two 32-pounder carronades on the forecastle and four of each on the quarterdeck; save that one of them was missing – Nathan could not help looking and noting that one significant gap, like a missing tooth, on the starboard side of the quarterdeck. But apart from that, everything was in its place: the wheels of the trucks greased with cook's slush and the wood looking as if it had been polished with beeswax. And every gun fitted with a flintlock, Nathan noted with approval. But how fast could they fire, and how accurately? It was not a question he would ask but he would find out soon enough, just as soon as they were at sea and out of sight of the land, in case it was not as good as he hoped.

And now below. Starting with the captain's quarters – *his* quarters – and such a wealth of space and light and polished wood and gleaming brass he stood for a moment in the door, staring as if stunned, struggling to take it in. Day cabin, sleeping cabin, dining cabin. The sunlight lancing in through the stern windows and the motes of dust circling in the still air and the reflections of the water dancing on the ceiling. The long polished table and the chairs, the wood panelling. The only ornament the big 18-pounders on either side. A smell of soap and beeswax and coffee – fresh coffee. He wondered if Pym had made his home here during the interregnum or whether he had been

too respectful, too hopeful of recovering his lost captain.
Almost certainly the latter, and so it must have remained
almost exactly as Kerr had left it when he had stepped out
on his quarterdeck for the last time, all unknowing, to see
if the cutter was prepared and ready. And yet there was no
hint of his presence now, no ghostly coat hanging upon
the door, no nightcap in his cot, no pictures on the walls,
or any other personal effects: all cleared away, no doubt,
barely hours before Nathan had come aboard. So he
would not be troubled by the ghost of the hapless Captain
Kerr.

As if he had not felt him at his shoulder from the
moment he had stepped aboard, breathing his dying
breath in his ear, the dry death rattle. Reminding him that
all honour, all distinction, all possession was but fleeting
and could be snatched away at any moment, even upon
the instant of attainment.

He turned his back upon it.

'Very good. Now let us see the rest of the ship.'

Down to the lower deck. Cramped to a landsman or
the captain of a 74, he supposed, but vast to one whose
last two commands had been a brig sloop and a merchant
barque. All the more room because there were no guns –
they were all on the main deck – and the mess tables and
the mess kits had been secured to the sides and the
hammocks lashed and stowed in the netting up above.
The officers' cabins lay on either side of the gun room:
canvas-and-wooden coffins eight feet square. Shafts of
light pouring down from the gratings in the waist.
Nathan nodding and peering about him this way and that

with his curious stooping walk, his head tucked into his neck to avoid banging it on the timbers and his eyes darting about like a bird of prey, while Mr Pym, who was a good six inches shorter and had no neck and walked more or less upright, pointed out whatever he thought might be of interest: the galley with its stove and its boilers and its coppers; the animal pen with its goat and its pig and its chickens. The carpenter's store and the boatswain's store . . .

Down to the orlop deck and no light at all here, save for the eerie gleam that pierced the gratings from the deck above and the feeble glow of the candles in the lanterns that were carried by the quartermaster and his mate. Here was the midshipmen's berth where Place and Coyle must make their quarters: a rank, unsightly place for all the wrath that Pym must have visited upon them to make it more seemly. A table with a much-stained cloth of green. Sea chests for chairs. A row of broken-backed books on navigation and seafaring. Nails with clothing hung upon them, a pair of boxing gloves, a hanger for a sword. A cage for some small animal that they were probably intending to eat: now empty, the animal escaped or consumed. They moved on. The magazine and the store rooms, the sick berth – and here was McLeish again: rather to Nathan's surprise he remembered the name. A smiling young Scot, unlike the lieutenant who was an unsmiling old Scot. And now it came to him that Captain Kerr had very likely been a Scot himself. A Scot who had a poor opinion of the Irish. Had he filled the ship with officers of a like mind?

'So, Mr McLeish, you have no patients, I see?'

'No, sir, not at present.' The smile fading a little.

But of course, they were all dead.

Could he say nothing that was not injurious aboard this unlucky ship? But everything was neat and tidy and very clean, the dispensary filled with medicines and ointments, the implements all present and correct.

'Very good, Mr McLeish. Carry on, Mr Pym.'

But for once Mr Pym did not seem at all anxious to carry on and there on the deck ahead, halfway between the slops room for the seamen and the kit room for the marines, Nathan saw the reason why.

He stopped and stared. Glimpsed in the half-light, he had thought at first that they were heaps of dirty clothing, marvelling that Pym had allowed such an outrage upon his decks even here in the orlop. But they were not. They were men. Three of them. And in irons.

'What is this?' Nathan's voice was soft.

'They are associates of the mutineers, sir, who have given cause to be restrained,' replied Pym stiffly.

They were shackled by the leg to an iron bar set into the deck, and as Nathan's eyes grew accustomed to the gloom he saw the marine sentry standing to attention in the shadows with his fixed bayonet.

'And what was their offence?'

'Their offence?' Pym seemed surprised at the question.

Nathan waited, his eyebrows faintly raised.

Pym looked at the men and they gazed back at him without movement or expression.

'They are kept as a precaution.'

It was not unusual to clap men in irons on one of His
Majesty's ships – with no cells to secure them – though
they were usually kept by the gun room under one of the
gratings which would provide some air and light.

'A *precaution?*'

Pym looked as if he suffered some mental anguish.
'May I speak to you in private, sir?'

'By all means,' Nathan agreed. He said nothing more
until they returned to his cabin and Pym and he were
alone. Then: 'Let us have a glass of wine,' he proposed.

Pym looked somewhat startled at the suggestion.
Perhaps he was not a drinking man. Or perhaps it had not
been his previous captain's style.

'Why, yes – that would be . . .'

But where in hell's name was Nathan to find wine? He
solved the problem much as he would have done on the
Speedwell by turning slightly aside and bellowing:
'Gabriel! Gilbert Gabriel there!' in a voice that would have
carried to the topmasts, though the Angel Gabriel had not
so far to travel, having been lurking as close to the door as
was possible without actually leaning his ear against it.
He was with them with an alacrity that startled Nathan
almost as much as it did Pym, who had not had the
advantage of knowing him from the age of five.

'A glass of wine for myself and the lieutenant,' Nathan
instructed him, callously avoiding his eye for he did not
care to think what negotiations might be involved in the
transaction.

'Well, I congratulate you, Mr Pym,' he said, as soon as
the Angel had departed on his quest. 'The state of the ship

does you credit and despite all that you have had to endure.'

Pym lowered his head in acknowledgement of the compliment but his expression remained guarded.

'My one concern at present,' Nathan went on, 'is the morale of the crew.'

'I am more concerned myself, sir, that we are so short handed.'

'And yet you have three of them in irons,' said Nathan with a smile.

'I regret the necessity but I felt it incumbent upon me—'

'What are their names?'

'Connor, Murphy and O'Neill.'

'More Irishmen?'

'And known associates of them that took off in the cutter.'

'Known associates.'

'Aye, sir.'

'And is that their only offence?'

'I beg your pardon, sir?'

'Is that the only reason they are confined?'

'I would have thought it sufficient, sir. With what happened to the captain I felt it necessary, for the safety of the ship, to confine any men that were suspect.'

'My God.' It dawned on Nathan at last. 'You mean they have been confined in that hold since the cutter was took?'

'They were allowed ashore when we were on New Providence and Ragged Island,' replied Pym stiffly, 'though kept in irons with a guard on them at all times.'

'But they took no part in the mutiny?'

'No. Not in the mutiny as such.'

'You have evidence that they intended to take part in it?'

'No, but—'

They were interrupted by the return of the Angel Gabriel with a bottle of red wine and two tall glasses of cut crystal. Also a small plate of cakes. Nathan had not timed him but he reckoned it could not have been above two minutes.

'Thank you, Gabriel. Set it down and I will see to it.'

Nathan waited until he was gone. He kept his voice low. 'I mean no criticism, Mr Pym, or disrespect, and I beg you will not be offended, but I think they must be freed.'

'I must advise against it, sir. In my view they constitute a grave danger to the safety of the ship.'

'And yet there is no charge against them. And they were in no way involved in the mutiny.'

'Not in the incident itself, but all three were . . .' he saw by Nathan's eye that he had no need to remind him that they were known associates of the mutineers. 'And the big one, Connor, was the particular companion of Liam Brady, gunner's mate, who was the ringleader with Keane. I do not know why they did not take part in the mutiny, but they are all three, in my opinion, steeped in sedition and Connor – I do not know if you saw the size of him – is a great brute of a man and dangerous, a danger to the ship, and to let him free to practise his sedition upon the crew . . .'

But Nathan was shaking his head firmly. 'We cannot keep men locked up indefinitely for the fear that they may one day rise up against us.' He forestalled Pym's protest by raising his hand. 'God, man, we would have to lock up half the crew on every ship in the fleet.' He poured the wine into two glasses, noting with satisfaction that his hand remained steady. 'No, I think we may declare an amnesty, which is customary when a new regime, as it were, comes to power and then it will not seem as if it is a criticism of the old one.'

Pym looked like to explode but this resource being denied him by the law of physics and a recalcitrant Fate, he took the glass his captain had extended to him.

Nathan raised his glass. 'Again, sir, I congratulate you upon preserving the ship, against all odds. To you, sir, and the *Unicorn*.'

'The *Unicorn*,' muttered Pym, if not quite through clenched teeth then with some considerable reserve.

'Very good,' said Nathan, who was finding this expression most useful in his new capacity and adaptable to almost every occasion. 'And now to more trivial matters. I have brought thirty marines with me from England . . .'

Pym started. 'Thirty? Marines?' He looked about him as if Nathan might have concealed them upon his person and distributed them throughout the cabin when no one was looking.

'Thirty-two with their lieutenant and sergeant – all of whom will have to be accommodated. But being short handed I suspect this will not be too much of a struggle for you, and indeed, they will be of assistance in deterring any further disturbances among the people.'

'But . . . where . . .'

'I left them aboard the *Speedwell*. They will arrive shortly. Then there are my own people. Mr Tully, whom I should have introduced, was my number one aboard the *Speedwell* and master's mate on the *Nereus*. Unless you have an objection I would like to make him up to acting lieutenant. He is entirely capable of keeping a watch. The two youngsters are in the capacity of volunteers and will berth with the midshipmen. Then there is Gilbert Gabriel, my steward, whom you have met. I would wish him to continue in this capacity and to be quartered nearby. I will speak to Kerr privately about this and see if there is any other capacity in which he would care to serve. Otherwise, as one of the captain's servants I suppose he must be set ashore with the means to seek passage for England. And finally there is Mr Imlay . . .'

He drew breath, but before he could embark upon Mr Imlay there came a knock on the door and a midshipman was admitted, nervously clutching his hat.

'Mr Webster's compliments, sir,' he addressed Nathan, 'and the British consul is coming aboard.'

'Mr Portillo.' Nathan greeted the consul with a broad grin as he stepped upon the deck. 'I am glad to welcome you aboard, sir.'

He assumed it was in response to his invitation but the consul had a more practical reason for his visit.

'I have news for you that I deemed too important to

leave to a messenger,' he told Nathan when they reached the sanctity of his cabin. 'The *Virginie* has been sighted off the coast of the Floridas, a little more than two days' sailing from here.'

Chapter Eight

The Headless Corpse

———◆◦◆———

'Fire as you bear.'

A moment when the wind seemed to hold its breath, the sails flapping idly against masts and spars and the tackle creaking gently in the blocks . . .

Then the tremendous rippling broadside, splintering the torpid air into a million pieces and rolling away across the calm waters of the Gulf.

Nathan kept his countenance severe, his hands clasped composedly behind his back as was befitting for the captain of a 32-gun frigate and a veteran of the Battle of the Glorious First of June, though it was hard not to betray his emotions.

Silence. A bruised, battered silence. A greater silence than before after the deafening roar of the great guns, secured but still smoking against the open ports. Nathan bent his head towards Mr Shaw, captain's clerk, who stood at his side with his chronograph and his notebook.

'Four minutes, sixteen seconds, sir.' Shaw's funereal features were exactly right for the conveyance of bad news and this was very bad indeed.

Nathan stared at him in astonishment and asked him to repeat it. He had thought they were taking their time, but not as much as this. Could Shaw have miscalculated and added a minute, even two, by mistake?

'That is from the command "Cast loose your guns"?'

'Yes, sir.'

Four minutes, sixteen seconds. A crack frigate, it was reckoned, might fire three broadsides in the space of five minutes.

Nathan met the eyes of his first lieutenant. Did they appear a trifle disconcerted? It was hard to tell. Pym, at the best of times, exuded an air of prim indignation.

'Very well, Mr Pym, let us see if we can do any better on the other side.'

For the purposes of the practice Nathan had the gun crews firing both sides, six men to a gun, though in a duel with one other ship they would normally double up and fire one side at a time. They had obviously drilled for the most part without verbal commands – useless in battle conditions when no one could hear a word – with the gun crews numbered off from one to six, the lower numbers the most senior and skilled. They should have functioned like automata, each to his allotted station, but watching the next rehearsal with a new, more critical awareness, Nathan concluded that the majority functioned more in the nature of headless chickens.

Powder was spilled upon the deck, rounds were

dropped, men tripped over the tackle and their own feet, they got in each other's way, once they even got in the gun's way as it sprang back on the recoil, causing one man serious injury. Nathan was tempted to suspend the operation at this point but he steeled himself to an unnatural callousness. In a day or two they might be fighting the *Virginie*. They had to be better than this or they would have more than one broken leg to contend with.

He watched the gun captains as they fished for the cartridge with their priming wires. Some were better at this than others but it seemed like an age before they had all cried 'Home!' In went the wads and the rounds. And now the captains began to measure out the fine priming powder from their powder horns. Again, this took an impossibly long time. What was wrong with them? It was almost as if it was the first time they had done it. Yet he knew from the logs that they had practised every day – and been flogged for getting it wrong. Was this the trouble? Were they nervous? They *looked* nervous.

The one thing they were good at was heaving at the tackle. No problems at all there. They were quite good at the swabbing and the ramming too. And he could not fault the guns themselves. They were beautifully maintained, not a mark on them, the tackle meticulously laid out and shining white. Even the cook's slush from the galleys that was used to grease the wheels on the trucks looked as if it had been put through a sieve to remove any impurities.

'Four minutes, twenty-five seconds,' announced Mr Shaw lugubriously.

Nathan ran his tongue over his teeth for want of a more satisfactory form of expression.

'Very well. We will have them fight the starboard guns only, doubling up the crews,' he informed Pym, 'and this time we will give them something to aim at.'

They had made a small target from a dozen empty casks with a black flag flying from a stub of a mast and they had it towed about a cable's length to starboard. Perhaps having something to fire at would make for an improvement, Nathan thought. But it did not.

The target was still there when the last gun had fired. Untouched.

'Four minutes, forty-six seconds,' reported Mr Shaw.

'Have they ever fired guns before?' Nathan enquired with deadly irony. He was looking directly at Pym as he said this and he saw the expression on his face.

Then he realised.

'My God, they haven't! They have never used powder, have they?'

'Captain Kerr felt it would be wasteful, sir, to use powder in practice. At the price it is. And I saw no reason to change his orders.'

Nathan shook his head. 'No wonder they're bloody useless,' he snapped. Not wise. Not conducive to good discipline but he was seriously out of patience. He could not believe the *Unicorn* had sailed halfway across the world to fight a war and had never fired its guns until now. Nor was it true. Not quite.

'We fired them half a dozen times when we were with the squadron at Port Royal,' Pym informed him. 'But that was as much as the Admiralty allowed for practice. After that, it had to come out of the captain's pocket.'

'Very well. But from now on we will practise at firing the guns every day. And this time we will really fire them.' Even if it cost him the rest of his small fortune and he and his poor mother could go whoring together on Haymarket.

The bell rang. Eight bells in the forenoon watch. Dinnertime – at least for some. But not for Nathan. He had to eat alone, an hour after the first watch. Unless he was invited to join the officers in the gun room. He took himself off to his cabin to sulk, leaving Pym to scowl over his stained and sullied decks while Nathan sat at his empty table and brooded upon the ship's inadequacies.

She was a beautiful ship. He had had himself rowed around her five or six times on the pretext of studying her trim but in reality simply to admire her and take pride in his possession. Pym had done an excellent job of repairing the damage she had suffered. There was not so much as a scratch in her paintwork nor a yard out of line. Her canvas was immaculate, her scantling as elegant as an emperor's yacht and she rode the water like a swan. However, she might be the most beautiful ship in the King's Navy, but she was no fighting ship.

In the final resort, a ship of war was a floating gun platform, designed to sail to any place in the world and deliver a devastating broadside. And this the *Unicorn* clearly could not do.

Not in anything less than four minutes sixteen seconds, and then she'd be lucky if she hit anything.

What could he do about it?

He could give them more practice, of course. He would achieve some improvement, he was sure of it. But it was not just a case of practice. There was something fundamentally wrong with the ship. Or rather, the ship's crew. They were like men in a dream. Or a nightmare. There was a glazed, wary look about them. As if they were always looking over their shoulders.

What at? The ghost of their murdered captain?

If that was the problem, it had to be exorcised. He had already made a start. He had told the officers there was to be no more flogging – not for anything less than a brawl – and even then there was to be meticulous enquiry into who was at fault.

'I am not singling anyone out for criticism,' he had informed them, 'nor do I say anything against the practice of flogging in general' – it would not do for them to take him for a radical – 'but there has been altogether too much of it on this voyage, and it would be well if there was no more of it.'

The officers had taken it well on the whole – some of them even seemed to approve it – but it had made precious little difference to the attitude of the crew.

Perhaps it was too soon to tell. But he did not have much time. The *Virginie* might be waiting for them at Ship Island, a mere two days' sailing to the south-west.

He thought about his officers. Pym. He had not liked him when he had first met him, and the man did not improve upon further acquaintance. Prim, prickly, pompous Mr Pym. 'Mrs Pym' as Nathan called him privately, for he was more like the housekeeper in a great house than the first lieutenant of a ship of war. But, of course, he was probably more like the majority of first lieutenants than not. Sticklers for good order; obsessed with discipline and neatness and cleanliness. He could do nothing with Mrs Pym. He just had to work around her.

Then there were the other two lieutenants: Webster and Maxwell. Both older than Nathan, if only by a few months. Webster was a clergyman's son from Dorset. Lanky, tow haired, eager to please. Perhaps unfairly he reminded Nathan somewhat of a spaniel. Maxwell was from Norfolk farming stock, quiet in his manners, almost brooding, though he showed occasional flashes of dry humour. But for the most part he was as subdued as the midshipmen and warrant officers – as if they were all wary of drawing attention to themselves.

Strangely, the only one who looked you straight in the eye and appeared reasonably cheerful was Lamb, the youngest of them all. What's more, he had taken Nathan's protégés in tow, though as the most junior in the midshipmen's berth it was hardly his job.

But altogether they were a sad bunch. There were none of them Nathan could warm to, except perhaps for McLeish, the ship's doctor. Not that he knew the man, but McLeish had an air of independence, of detached observation, that Nathan tended to admire in people. Thinking of McLeish recalled him to his duties – for there had been a man seriously injured in the gun practice and he should enquire after his welfare. Taking up his hat, Nathan made his way down to the sickbay.

He arrived as McLeish finished taking off the man's leg a little above the knee. The only reason he had not heard the shrieks was because the patient had passed out at the first touch of the knife. One of the loblolly boys wrapped up the severed limb in a cloth as McLeish straightened up and wiped his bloody hands and saw Nathan standing there in the door.

'I am sorry I could not save it,' he said, 'but it had been through the mangle.'

'I had not realised he was so badly hurt,' Nathan confessed.

'Yes, it is amazing what a ton or so of iron and timber will do if a body gets in the way of it,' the doctor remarked.

Nathan looked at the poor wretch on the table. 'And will he . . . I mean . . .'

'Oh, he will be right as rain in a week or two. May limp a bit, of course.'

'Dear God,' Nathan murmured, turning away.

'I beg your pardon, sir. It is my damned dark sense of humour if you can call it that. It is a butcher's trade that numbs the senses, I fear. Stay, if you will, and have a glass with me. I need one if you do not.' He took off his blood-soaked apron and opened a cabinet where he kept his medicines – and several other objects that caused Nathan to stare somewhat.

'A little hobby of mine,' the doctor remarked, observing his expression. 'I usually keep them in my cabin but it was removed for the practice at the great guns. I hope you do not mind.' He scrutinised Nathan's face which had lost a little more of its colour. 'It is purely in the interests of medical science, I do assure you.'

'But you cannot – surely they are not . . .'

'Oh, they are not human. No, I do not cut off men's heads. Only their limbs and such other of their extremities that they can shift without at a pinch. No, they are simians, largely of the family *hominidae*. I am making a study of the similarities with the human skull, of which I have several in my study in Edinburgh, though I thought better of bringing them to sea with me for fear it might offend those of a more tender disposition. How do you like your usquebah, straight or with water?'

'Straight, if you please,' replied Nathan, who was not sure if he liked it at all, never having sampled the stuff, whatever it was. 'They appear very human.'

'Only in the shadows. If you look closely you will see that the elongated jaw and the narrow forehead are quite dissimilar from the human. At least in the majority of cases, though I have observed a few of our shipmates who might pass for a species of ape, especially when swinging through the rigging. And there is one there – over on the right – that you might very easily take for a human skull, being an infant of the genus *Pongo*, of Batavia, known by the natives of that region as the orang-utan – which I am assured means "person of the forest". Your very good health, sir, and my apologies once more for my foul temper. You would have thought I had cut off enough limbs by now not to mind but I find I do. Though not as much as the amputee, no doubt.'

Nathan cautiously tasted the amber liquid in the glass

the doctor had handed him. 'It tastes very like whisky,' he confided.

'That is indeed gratifying as it is from the family distillery in Bladnoch, and they try to make it as very like whisky as they can contrive, though as we are close to the border, some of our rivals in more heathenish climes have been known to dispute it.'

'But you said—'

'*Usquebah*. In the Gaelic, *the water of life*. I find it lifts the spirit a little even in the face of death. Now if you will excuse me I will away to my cabin, if it has been restored to me by the brutes that pulled it down, for I see that I have blood on my cuffs and must change my shirt before I join my fellows in the gun room; they have been known to object if I come fresh from the slaughterhouse, as it were. Or did you wish to speak with me?'

'No, no. I just came to see how your patient was doing,' Nathan said. A groan from the individual in question indicated that he was coming to his senses. 'But as it happens, I would appreciate a word in private. Indeed, if you would care to join me for dinner, I could repay your hospitality with a glass of wine.'

'That is very kind of you, sir, but if it is a consultation you require . . .'

'Oh no, no, it is nothing like that, I do assure you, nothing in the medical line. I would just appreciate your – well, your company as a matter of fact,' he finished shyly.

'Then I would be honoured to accept, sir, just as soon as I have made shift to change my shirt.'

*

Nathan's cabin had been put back together again, and he had Gabriel set the table for two and bring up a couple of decent bottles from the late Captain Kerr's store of wines which he had decided to inherit.

'And what is there to eat?' he enquired anxiously.

'Well, we have a fine pair of porgies to start with that was caught this morning, before the practice at the great guns scared all the fish and fowl for miles around even if it would not have troubled the French.' Nathan scowled but Gabriel was a law unto himself and the gunnery would have disgusted him, as a former highwayman, as much as it did his captain. 'Then there's a boned leg of lamb with anchovy sauce to follow, and after that a Cuban bread pudding with raisins, if it pleases Your Honour.'

'Thank you, Gabriel, that will do very well. And break out the *mariquitas* that we had from the consul's house,' Nathan instructed him, conscious that he was playing host for the first time aboard his new command. Perhaps he should have invited the entire gun room but he had not been in the best of tempers when the practice had ended and the atmosphere would have been dreadful. People would accuse him of favouritism in singling out the doctor, but be damned to them – and it was better than if he had invited Tully.

'Ah, Doctor. Come in, please, make yourself at home.' Nathan waved expansively at the great table in the stern window. 'And what may I get you to drink, failing the usquebah?'

McLeish had changed, not only into a clean shirt but the new surgeon's uniform approved by the Navy Board.

He looked around him as if it was the first time he had been here – and perhaps it was. Gilbert solved the question of what they would have to drink by bringing up a bottle of the late captain's Jerez with a plate of the consul's *mariquitas* – a form of fried plantain – and some stuffed olives. They had a bottle of muscadet with the fish before moving on to a Burgundy for the lamb: raising their glasses in turn to King George, the *Unicorn* and all who sailed in her, the union of England and Scotland, the confusion of their enemies, the poet Burns and then, as they became more light hearted, the Clan McLeish, the genus *Pongo* and a young lady the doctor claimed to know in Kirkcudbright called Catriona.

As they were well into the lamb and contemplating a second bottle of the red, Nathan remembered what it was that he had wished to discuss, or at least one of the things.

'I read in the ship's log,' he ventured, 'or it may have been the captain's log, I forget which, some reference to a corpse that was discovered in the chain store shortly after leaving Kinsale and heading out into the Atlantic.'

'Oh aye, that would be our waif,' confided McLeish.

'Your waif?'

'As in stray. Waif and stray. Our headless waif. Our "orfing" as the people call him.' He lapsed into apparent melancholy until he raised his eyes and saw that Nathan was still observing him with an expression of attentive interest.

'It was found during a rat hunt instigated by the midshipmen,' he went on, 'the creatures having offended Mr Holroyd by consuming the best part of a cheese his mother had given him and then pissing upon the plate.'

'The midshipmen?' queried Nathan, frowning, for he did not like to think of the young gentlemen behaving so badly, even before his accession to the command.

'The rats,' McLeish assured him, after giving him a look.

'Quite so.'

'Well, it was practically a skeleton by then.'

'Excuse me, what was?'

'The waif, the orfing, that we were discussing.'

'Ah yes, the waif.' He was a little confused about the waif but comforted himself with the thought that enlightenment might be forthcoming if he let the narrative continue.

'I examined it at my leisure – what was left of it, for it was negligible to begin with and had been half eaten by rats – whereupon I ascertained that it was the body of a young male, an infant, of between six and nine years.'

'A boy?'

'A boy. Yes. What did you think it was?'

'I am sorry. Go on.'

'I was unable to ascertain the cause of death owing to the absence of the head, but my supposition was that it would be starvation and disease. I shudder to think that the rats played any part in it.'

'Indeed, but—'

'You will want to know how it got there.'

'It was on my mind to enquire.'

'The theory was that he was on the run from a cruel parent or guardian and that he climbed into the chainstore during the construction of the vessel in Chatham with a view to making his escape or possibly simply seeking a refuge.'

'A stowaway.'

'Yes. I have no idea why he did not make himself known when the ship was at sea, unless he was already dead or so weakened he could not bestir himself, but alas, when he was eventually found he was at least a month gone.'

'And headless.'

'Ah yes. That was the most distressing part. And something of a mystery.'

'Perhaps . . . the rats?'

'That was a popular theory, but I think not. They would not remove the whole skull without leaving a trace. My own supposition was that it had been removed by certain dissident elements on the lower deck who wished to play upon the fears of the more susceptible among their brethren, but I may be speaking out of turn.'

'Not at all, Doctor, please go on.'

'Well, it may have suited their purposes, do you see, in stirring up discontent. Certainly it proved an effective means of making mischief.'

'In what way?'

'Well, the waif was buried with full naval honours off the southern coast of Ireland, but the absence of a head deprived the ceremony of dignity, as it were, or conviction, not to say consolation.'

'I suppose it would. Though after a battle I have seen worse.'

'People are inclined to be tolerant after a battle.'

'That is true.'

'And there were those who claimed that the spirit would not be at rest, as it were, until the head was found.'

'Which was not achieved?'

'Alas, it was not. And in the days and weeks to come, a number of the people claimed to have seen the ghost of the poor boy wandering the lower decks in search of the missing part of his anatomy. Wailing most piteously the while.'

'Good God, McLeish.'

'Aye. They are more superstitious than a gaggle of girlies, for the most part, your average seamen, and a great many of the ship's subsequent misfortunes have been laid at the door of this apparition.'

'So they fear the ship is cursed.'

'Cursed *and* doomed. And until the ghost is laid to rest they will continue to believe it, in my humble opinion.'

'These dissident elements that you mentioned,' Nathan continued after a moment. 'They were mainly Irish, I understand.'

'Exclusively Irish.'

'And in your opinion, between ourselves, might they have had any valid cause for their discontent?'

'Besides being flogged half to death, you mean, for every trifling misdemeanour?'

'Yes. I have read the punishment book, and it does seem as if the Irish contingent suffered, one might say, disproportionately.'

'One might well say that.'

'You think Captain Kerr had it in for them?'

'One might well say that,' McLeish repeated dryly. 'In an unguarded moment.'

'Do you have any idea why?'

'Only that, speaking as a Lowland Scot, there are certain of my countrymen who have for some years harboured a particular suspicion of the Irish, especially those of Catholic persuasion.'

'So I understand.'

'And Captain Kerr's family being Covenanters had suffered very harshly at the hands of the Irish under Montrose during the Civil War.'

'I see.' Nathan was in fact very far from seeing, but the origins of the grievance were possibly too obscure for his mind to deal with at the present moment in time.

'The memory of a Scotsman for a grievance is very long,' explained the doctor gravely.

'Thank you, Mr McLeish, you have enlightened me considerably.'

'Well, I hope I have not spoken out of turn.' The doctor leaned both hands upon the table and began to heave himself up.

'But before you leave, there is just one more thing.'

McLeish sank back into his seat with a sigh.

'At the time of the mutiny, I believe the captain instructed his officers to do as his assailants ordered.'

'Did he so?'

'It is recorded thus in the log.'

'Which log?'

'The first lieutenant's log.'

McLeish's expression was ambiguous.

'Possibly you were not there at the time?' Nathan suggested.

'Oh, I was there all right.'

'And is that what you heard?'

'The words I heard were "Do your duty".'

'"Do your duty"?'

'Of course, I may have been mistaken.'

'Not, "Do what they say"?'

'No. And I would propose that this would not be in the late captain's character, as it was generally perceived.'

'Well, thank you again, Doctor. I appreciate your confidence.'

'Not at all, sir, and thank you for your hospitality.' This time the doctor made it to his feet and proceeded somewhat unsteadily to the door.

A moment later, Gabriel appeared. Nathan wondered how much he had heard. All of it, most probably.

'Shall I light the lantern, sir?' he enquired with the suspicion of a rebuke in his tone.

Nathan noted, with surprise, that it was almost dark. They had been eating and drinking and talking for the best part of four hours. He sat there for a moment longer contemplating the remains of the last bottle, but thought better of it. Instead, he made his way to the quarterdeck for some fresh air. Tully had the watch. Nathan nodded to him with a secret smile.

'All well, Mr Tully?'

'All well, sir.'

'I think I will go aloft.'

Tully considered him gravely but was too courteous to suggest a more sedentary activity. Nathan felt his eyes upon him, however, as he groped his way down the ladder to the waist and so to the mainmast shrouds.

He climbed more carefully than was his wont – conscious of the drink he had consumed – and paused just below the maintop, considering that it would be prudent to go up through the lubber's hole for once, but his pride would not permit it – especially with the furtive, measuring eyes he knew would be watching him from above and below. He reached for the futtock shrouds above his head, inclining back at an angle of about 45 degrees. Right hand over left, left over right, his feet searching for the ratlines in the dark . . . and now he was hanging backwards while the mast described its long, lazy arc through the night sky. He did not look down but knew what he would see . . . The distant deck in the moonlight and the rushing sea, the bow rising and falling, rising and falling, and the spray flung back over the unicorn's head, over the unicorn's flowing mane, the unicorn rushing through the forests of the night, rushing to meet its mate – no, its virgin, its waiting virgin. For Christ's sake, no poetry, not now. Concentrate. Right hand over left, left hand over right . . . he missed his footing in the dark and only the desperate strength in his arms stopped him from plunging fifty feet to the deck. The stabbing pain in his arms brought a sudden memory of hanging from the manacles in the *maison d'arrêt* in Paris . . . He scrambled over the edge of the top breathing heavily, and the lookout scuttled away, knuckling his forehead.

For a moment Nathan considered going higher but a gleam of commonsense penetrated the fogged particles of his brain and then the lookout went swarming lithely up the ratlines to a higher level like one of McLeish's *hominidae*, leaving him in sole possession. He stood, swaying slightly with the rhythm of the ship, his arm hooked into the shrouds, and looked up at the stars. They seemed strangely close. And all in the wrong place. But of course, it was the latitude, the unfamiliar equatorial latitude. He should know them though, if he put his mind to it.

He sat down to study them better, searching for one of the planets that he might find his bearings.

No. He shook his head firmly.

He was much impressed by Sir Isaac Newton's opinion that the planets were rocks hurled out from the sun: blobs of liquid fire that had cooled over the millennia and were now held in place by the balance between their own momentum and the magnetism that pulled them back. Doomed to circle in a perpetual orbit, neither going forward nor going back. Like mortal beings compelled to seek their own destiny but held back by their origins, their loyalties, their sense of belonging . . . their love.

A quick burst of light caught his eye. A comet or fiery meteor? A falling star? Gone, already. What did it mean – if anything? Vainglorious though it was, it was not hard to believe that it had some personal meaning: that someone or something was trying to communicate with him. Waving. Perhaps he should wave back. The crew would love that. First a tyrant and then a lunatic who climbed to the top of the mast and waved at the stars.

There were those who would say it was a portent of disaster. Or that someone great had died. But did you have to be great for the heavens to acknowledge your passing? Were there not enough stars even for the insignificant? Or were they entirely indifferent to the fate of men and of nations, mere inanimate lumps of rock or liquid fire, hurtling through the heavens in obedience to the laws of gravity? Just as the rushing sea was indifferent to the fate of those who sailed upon it. People prayed. They lit candles before plaster saints. *Deliver us, Oh Lord, we pray Thee, from the perils of the sea* . . . Did it make the slightest bit of difference? If he let go of this slender lifeline, he would fall to the deck below and he would die.

Would a star fall from the heavens to mark his passing? *What had happened when Sara died?*

Had she ceased to exist the moment the blade sliced through her slender neck? A terrible image of the guillotine on the Place du Trône . . . of Sara climbing the steps to the scaffold, her hair shorn to the neck, her chemise torn to the breast and the terror in her eyes. Seized by the greedy hands of the executioners and borne down on to a bloody plank, wet with the blood of those who had gone before her, and slid under that terrible blade.

Sara.

How could it have happened? Why could he not have prevented it?

And what had happened next — apart from the executioner holding up her head to show to the crowd?

Was she in Heaven or Hell? Or projected into the vast crowded infinity of the universe? Transported to one of those distant glimmering specks of light?

Or nowhere.

She had once told him about her homeland in Provence. He could hear her now, a whisper on the wind . . .

'There is a little town called Tourettes. Near where we lived in Provence. I used to go there as a child. To the market with my father. Tourettes-de-Vence. A walled town on top of a hill. It is very beautiful. I used to love going to Tourettes. There is a café in the square where I drank lemonade and ate the little cakes, made of oranges, and watched the people coming to market.'

If she ever left Paris, she had said, that is where he would find her. In Tourettes, drinking lemonade and eating little cakes made of oranges.

And that is where he saw her in his imagination as he gazed up at the stars. Bleary now from the tears in his eyes.

The first captain we had was a tyrant who flogged us half to death; the second climbed into the rigging at night and gazed at the stars and cried.

He let go of the shroud and stood, balanced precariously on the swaying platform as the ship rolled. If it was in the stars that he should fall, then fall he would. And if it was not . . .

He threw out his hand as he felt himself go – and grabbed the rope.

As all drowning men do.

Chapter Nine

The Big Liar

———◆◆◆———

The *Unicorn* moved like a ghost ship through the amber haze shrouding the waters of the Mexican Gulf; under a full press of sail but the wind so light, the sea so calm she seemed almost to glide over its silken surface with scarcely a ripple to mark her passing . . . And the men standing by the guns and the lookouts double-posted at the tops, so like Pym's report of her last, fateful visit to these shores that even Nathan, who had not been there, felt an eerie sense of history repeating itself.

They were sailing parallel with the coast of West Florida and on a course that should bring them in sight of Ship Island within the hour, according to the master, Mr Baker, who went on to undermine the force of this prediction by muttering, 'If it were not for this blasted fog,' in an anxious voice while peering over the rail in the direction in which he clearly hoped it would materialise.

Nathan had to trust to his judgement, though he had
taken his own readings and checked them with Tully and
pored over the chart countless times in the privacy of his
cabin. He was far more informed on the topography of
the region than had been the case during his original
briefing at the Admiralty, but it was hard to make much
sense of it for the simple reason that the sea and the land
did not observe the simple rules of nature and keep to
their respective spheres as they did in every sensible part of
the world. It was impossible at times to know where the
one ended and the other began, for the coast was cluttered
with a myriad of offshore islands while the mainland
itself, if it *was* mainland, was riddled by hundreds of
rivers and creeks and inlets, many of them containing even
more islands, so that the entire region resembled a giant
jigsaw with pieces that did not quite fit. A devil's jigsaw. It
was a region that might have been better left to the swamp
creatures and those Indian tribes that had long made their
home here and doubtless would have been left in peace
had it not been for the existence of New Orleans.

*'The key not only to the Caribbean and the Floridas –
but to the vast hinterland of North America west of the
Mississippi.'*

Nathan recalled the words of Lord Chatham in the
board room of the Admiralty. But for all its importance,
New Orleans was as perplexing as the region it inhabited.
The port occupied a narrow strip of land between a river
and a lake: the Mississippi and Lake Pontchartrain. Yet for
all the water surrounding it, it was a damnable place to
reach by boat. There were two main routes: the front door

upriver from the Delta; and the back door through the Rigolets and the lake. Both were hazardous and slow, being afflicted with shallow waters, dangerous currents and shifting sandbanks. A fleet of small barges and rafts was required to convey cargoes between the port and the larger seagoing merchantmen waiting offshore, either at Chandeleur Island off the Delta or Ship Island off the Rigolets.

A French national ship such as the *Virginie* – or indeed a well-armed privateer – had only to wait at either of these locations to snap up a score of rich prizes – or cause the trade to dry up altogether, whilst enjoying ample opportunity of communicating with the Cajuns on the mainland.

Which was why Nathan had taken the precaution of clearing the ship for action and drumming the men to quarters – though it smacked of the same nervous apprehension as had possessed his hapless predecessor. The next few hours could very well see the long-awaited encounter between the *Virginie* and the *Unicorn*. Nathan only wished he were more confident of the outcome.

There were other causes for concern. The waters off the coast shoaled rapidly, even several miles out from the shore, and the depth varied dramatically so that he was obliged to maintain a seaman in the chains to cast the lead at frequent intervals for fear of running aground. And with the wind blowing from the south-west, as at present, there was a great danger of becoming embayed – though for this reason their approach had been timed to coincide with the ebb which should help to carry them offshore.

And then there was this wretched haze: an opaque

crystal ball shot through with sunlight, revealing nothing. As the *Unicorn* glided slowly onward, Nathan had the impression that the heavy, liquid air parted before them and then closed after, drawing them in toward whatever menace lay in the hidden waters ahead.

'Land ho!'

A shout from the lookout in the foretop and it took all Nathan's self-control not to rush to the rail, as he would almost certainly have done on the *Speedwell*.

'Ten points off the starboard bow.'

Slowly, painfully slowly to his straining vision, it emerged, not so much land as a denser patch of haze lying low in the sea to the north-west.

'Ship Island,' said the Master at his shoulder, as much relief as satisfaction in his voice. But how could he be sure, with not a single identifiable feature to mark it out from its neighbours? There was only one chart of the region available to them: drawn by the Swiss engineer Des Barres for the British Navy during the American War. It showed Ship Island as a thin strip of land, five miles long, a few hundred yards wide and shaped like an eel with a projection near the head that could have been its gills. Otherwise it was quite without character – little more than a sandbank composed of fine white quartz eroded from granite in the Appalachian Mountains, carried seaward by the rivers and creeks and dumped a few miles offshore. But there was a good anchorage at its western end – at least according to the chart – with four fathoms of water before the shoals began and the land and the sea began to play their tricks.

They crept closer to the island and a few sketchy details emerged: the white sand, the waving grasses bleached almost the same colour by the sun, great flocks of seabirds along the shore, even a clump of brushwood here and there on the higher ground toward the middle. But nothing else, no sign of human presence now or in the past.

They followed this desolate shoreline for several miles until at length they sighted a small hill, or large dune, on its westward point. And at last there was a trace of human activity in the few crude shacks that huddled in its lee – and a wooden jetty with a flagpole but no flag.

This was presumably where the *Unicorn* had encountered the Spanish official on her previous visit, but there was no sign of him now or any of his fellows.

More to the point, there was no sign of the *Virginie*.

'Let us come about,' Nathan instructed Pym, 'and try our luck at the Candle Isles.' However, before they could begin the manoeuvre there was a shout of 'Sail ho!' from the foretop and Nathan's heart missed a beat as he peered in the direction of the lookout's outstretched arm.

But he was pointing the wrong way.

'Dead ahead.'

It could not possibly be the *Virginie*, not from that direction, with scarcely enough water to float a barge. Then Nathan saw the pale triangle of sail and heard the sharp intake of breath from Pym at his side.

It was the cutter, emerging from the haze into which she had vanished over three months earlier with their doomed captain and his mutinous crew.

'It cannot be,' murmured Pym.

Nor was it. As the vessel bore down on them they saw that though it resembled the cutter in size and rig, it was a much broader vessel with a blunt, rounded bow, not unlike a Dutch barge but with the Spanish flag flying from her stern.

'Mr Imlay,' Nathan called over to his 'political adviser' who was lounging against the rail on the far side of the quarterdeck, 'perhaps you would be so good as to help us with your excellent Spanish and bid them come alongside.

'Let us heave to,' he instructed Pym in a quieter voice, 'and see if she has any news for us.'

She did. And it was not good.

'The Spanish fort on the Rigolets is under siege,' Imlay declared flatly. 'He says it was attacked three days ago by Cajun rebels. They are armed with heavy cannon and mortars. The fort is low on powder and shot and he does not think it can hold out for much longer. Two days at the most.'

'He' was the young Spanish officer who had come aboard from the sailing barge and who now sat in Nathan's cabin peering hopefully if uncomprehendingly at them with his large brown eyes. His name was Antonio de Escavar, Imlay had reported, and he was an aide to the governor-general, Baron Carondelet.

Nathan studied the map open on the table before him.

The Rigolets. The gutter. The back door into New Orleans. The fort was on Coquilles Island at the western end of the channel where it entered the lake, less than twenty miles from their present position. There was no way they could take the *Unicorn* into the Rigolets, but it was entirely possible that they could reach it in the ship's boats.

'Does he know how many cannon the rebels have – and where they are sited?' he asked Imlay.

Nathan curbed his impatience as the two men conversed at length. He found it extremely frustrating to depend on Imlay as an interpreter but Escavar spoke no English and very little French.

'He says they have eight cannon on Coquilles Island itself and four more on the far side of the Rigolets covering both approaches to the fort.'

'Twelve cannon? How did they get twelve cannon?'

Imlay put this to the Spaniard. Then: 'He says they were landed on the coast by a French warship.'

'The *Virginie?*'

Imlay shrugged. 'It would appear likely.'

'Ask him if he knows where she is now.'

It took a while.

'He says that after landing the guns and the men she headed south toward the Delta.'

'How does he know that?'

'He says they have a spy among the Cajuns who told them of the plan. When the French take the fort they will attack New Orleans, and the *Virginie* will stop any help from coming upriver.'

Nathan's frown deepened. 'So the governor knew of the plan but did nothing to try to prevent it?'

This seemed to require several supplementary questions. 'He says the governor is trapped in the fort,'

Imlay reported finally. 'Apparently he was on a tour of inspection and he was interrogating this informer of his when they were attacked.'

'Do you believe all this?'

'I don't know why he should be making it up.'

Nathan glanced once more at the map. The Mississippi emerged into the Gulf of Mexico about a hundred miles south of their present position. They had been making barely two knots with the wind on their larboard quarter. Beating against it would take them at least two days, probably three.

'Two days, he thinks, before it falls?'

'Two days at most. The governor has given up hope of saving the fort but will hold out as long as possible. He sent Escavar to alert the captain-general in Cuba in the hope that he would send ships and soldiers in time to save New Orleans.'

'And how did Escavar get out?'

'He slipped out at night with two Indian guides – the men who came aboard with him. They led him through the swamp to where they had concealed a canoe. When they reached the coast they found the *goelette* – the fishing boat. He was hoping to find a ship to take him to Cuba.'

Nathan studied the man thoughtfully. He looked as if he had been through a swamp. The man spoke. Imlay translated.

'He wants to know if we will take him there. He says there is not a moment to lose.'

But Nathan was shaking his head. 'Our job is to find the *Virginie*,' he insisted.

'And what about the fort?'

Nathan showed his irritation. 'What can we do? We cannot send the ship's boats through the Rigolets, not with cannon covering the approaches. I cannot sacrifice half the ship's company for an obscure Spanish fort.'

Imlay spoke with rare gravity. 'If the fort were to be taken – and the governor-general of Louisiana with it – it would be a great encouragement to the rebels. Others would join them. New Orleans would be next. And if New Orleans falls . . .' He spread his arms as if the consequence of such a calamity must be apparent to even one of Nathan's limited perception. But in case it were not, he added: 'Such a victory would resound through the Americas. It would be seen as a victory not only for the French but for the forces of revolution. It would encourage many others to rise up against their colonial masters. And in Europe, it would appear as if the French were irresistible. The Spanish would almost certainly sue for peace. They might even join the French in a war against the British.'

'So what would you have me do?'

'Well, we can at least send word to New Orleans.'

'How – if the Rigolets is closed to us?'

Imlay leaned forward over the map. 'There is a small bayou called the Chef Menteur to the south of Coquilles Island. It is little used but it joins Lake Pontchartrain here, near Point Herbes. Much closer to New Orleans. I could take the guides and be in New Orleans in two days.'

'You?'

'I speak French and Spanish – and several of the local

dialects. I am familiar with the terrain. That is why I am
here with you.'

This was true.

'But what will you do when you reach New Orleans?'

'I will tell them of the attack on the fort and warn them
to look to their defences. They might even be able to send
help to Carondelet, if it is not too late.'

'Why did *he* not do that?' Nathan nodded toward
Escavar.

'You want me to ask him?'

'That might be helpful.'

Another lengthy exchange.

'He says he could not escape inland because that is
where the French have posted most of their force. He had
to go towards the sea. Besides, the governor feared that a
force sent out from New Orleans would be ambushed –
and only weaken its own defences.'

'You sound sceptical.'

'I am.' Imlay smiled. 'I think it is possible he may have
felt that the Havana was a more attractive proposition for
him personally than New Orleans at the moment.'

Nathan returned to his study of the map. He could just
make out the bayou that Imlay had indicated: a thin blue
line among many, meandering through that impossible
land- and seascape.

'Menteur,' he repeated. 'French for liar.'

'Chef Menteur. The Big Liar.' Another smile. 'That is
what the Indians call the Mississippi because of the way it
twists and turns and is full of tricks. The French gave the
same name to the bayou.'

'But you think you can find your way through it?'

Imlay nodded. 'I can try. I did once before. And I will have the guides.'

He did once before? When? And in what circumstances? But Nathan did not ask.

'The Indians – you speak their tongue?'

'No. But one of them speaks Spanish – and French.'

'He speaks *French*?'

'Creole French. Patois. Pretty nigh impenetrable.'

'Let us have him down here.'

Gabriel brought both guides down to the cabin and lingered at the door, his eyes making a swift inventory of whatever objects he had left on display to attract their venal attentions. As a former highwayman he entertained a poor opinion of human nature, and their appearance was unlikely to encourage a more tolerant view. They were dressed in animal skins: breechclout, leggings and a form of waistcoat tied loosely with leather thongs. Their hair hung long and lank to their shoulders and appeared to be heavily oiled. One of them had a cloth tied around his forehead, perhaps to keep the sweat out of his eyes for it was not decorative. Both wore rings in their ears and one a necklace made from the teeth of some animal. They carried knives at their belts but no other weapons that Nathan could see. He stood.

'Thank you, Gabriel. Perhaps you would contrive some refreshment for our guests.' Then, addressing the latter in French with a polite bow: 'My name is Nathaniel Peake and I am the captain of this vessel.'

One of them stared back at him without expression. The other bowed in return.

'My name is Jean Desmarais,' he said.

John Who-Lives-in-the-Marshes. A not very original choice: he could have lived nowhere else in this part of the world. But he seemed remarkably composed – and well mannered – for a creature of the swamps. Far more so, indeed, than those natives of the English Fens that Nathan had encountered.

Jean Desmarais indicated his companion with a nod. 'This is my compatriot, Joseph Bonnet, and we are in the service of the Spanish Governor. I am afraid we smell somewhat of the Bog. And a grease we have used to deter the flies and other insects.'

'Not at all.' Nathan was vaguely embarrassed. Would he have apologised if he felt in need of a wash – as his mother frequently assured him he did, even at twenty-six? He thought not. He complimented the man on his French, for here was none of Imlay's 'impenetrable patois'.

'Thank you,' replied this prodigy with another small bow. 'I was educated by the Franciscan Brothers in New Orleans.'

Nathan wondered if Brother Ignatius had been one of them and whether John Who-Lives-in-the-Marshes was one of his sources of information. He invited them both to sit.

The Spanish officer looked perplexed and said something to Imlay in Spanish. Imlay's reply was brief.

The two guides took not the slightest notice of the

Spanish officer. They were studying the map with interest. Nathan drew his finger along the blue line indicated by Imlay. 'I believe this is known as the Chef Menteur. Are you familiar with it?'

'It is a name the French use,' said Desmarais. 'But it is a very little stream and a poor deceiver of men. We call it the Little Snake. Who drew this map?'

'A man called Des Barres,' Nathan told him.

'A Frenchman?'

'Swiss, I believe. From Switzerland.'

'Switzerland,' repeated Desmarais wonderingly.

'A land in Europe. Of many mountains.'

'Ah.' He said something to his companion and raised his two hands to form a peak a little above his head. They both laughed.

'So . . .' Nathan attempted to bring them back to the subject of the Big Liar, or the Little Snake as it had now become. 'Would you be confident of finding your way by this route to New Orleans?'

Desmarais looked at him with a frown as if this was a trick question. 'Is there a reason why I should not?'

'I wished only for your assurance.'

'Why yes, if I wished to do so.'

'And how long would it take?'

'By canoe, two days perhaps.'

'And if we did not go so far? If we went only so far as Coquilles Island?'

Desmarais raised his eyes from the map and studied him thoughtfully. 'Nine, ten hours perhaps.'

'Why should we want to do that?' Imlay frowned.

Nathan ignored him. 'And it would be possible to reach the fort from there?'

'But yes. Of course. That is the way we came here. With this one,' he indicated the Spanish officer, sulking at the far end of the table.

'And we could travel, at least part of the way, by night?'

'By night it is more difficult, but yes – with one who knows the way.'

'And how big a boat could you take there?'

'Not as big as this,' said Desmarais with a glint of amusement in his eye.

'But the ship's boats that we are towing astern?'

'This is possible.'

'What are you suggesting?' demanded Imlay in English.

'I am suggesting,' said Nathan, 'that we might be able to save you a trip.'

Chapter Ten

Into the Swamp

———◆———

The swamp had its own kind of mist: a grey-green fungus that clung to the surface of the water, rolling away from them in every direction as far as the eye could see. The boats moved through this vapour almost silently, the oars rising and falling like the wings of some clumsy, amphibious bird that could not gain enough momentum to take off. Looking up, Nathan could see stars and a full moon, but there was so much moisture in the air he had the impression he was looking down on them like shells and tiny stones at the bottom of a rock pool, dimly reflecting the light of the sun.

There were five boats in the expedition, each with its complement of marines and seamen, joined to its neighbour by a long length of rope in case they lost sight of each other. They were crossing a lake – Lake Borgne, the French called it, according to their guide – The Lake with One Eye. Why? Nathan's enquiry had elicited a small shrug. Ask the French, Desmarais said. In fact, it was not really a lake at all but a lagoon, separated from the sea by a chain of sandbanks and small islands: more pieces in the Devil's Jigsaw.

Nathan shifted slightly in his seat, moving the sword at his hip to make himself a little more comfortable. The air was oppressively humid and he was soaked in sweat already, though he had none of the rowing to do. Despite the protests of Lieutenant Pym, he had insisted on leading the expedition himself, arguing that he must take the responsibility if it all went wrong. In truth, he could not have borne to have stayed behind on the *Unicorn* while Pym led half his crew into the swamp. Besides, he knew he was better at this kind of thing than Pym: better than he was at commanding a ship.

At Nathan's request Escavar had drawn a rough map showing the fort occupying a narrow promontory on the northern tip of the island overlooking the Rigolets where the channel merged into Lake Pontchartrain. It looked impressive on paper. A timber stockade with blockhouses at each corner surrounded by earthworks in the shape of a five-pointed star – and inside each of the points, two 6-pounder cannon firing through embrasures. The garrison was normally about eighty men but there had been fifty more in the governor-general's party. The main problem for the garrison was the quality of their powder – much of it was damp and unusable.

The rebels had come up through the Rigolets: several hundred of them in a fleet of pirogues and flatboats, landing on the neck of the peninsula with their big guns: 12-pounders and four large mortars.

'Where did they get guns like that?' Nathan demanded.

'He says from the French frigate,' said Imlay, after consulting with Escovar.

Nathan nodded. He had thought as much. He wondered if they had brought extra weapons from France or sacrificed some of their own broadside. The mortars might be the *obusiers* the *Virginie* carried on her quarterdeck. It would make a difference if and when they encountered her.

Escovar was still rattling on in Spanish.

'The bulk of the force is concentrated on the right flank,' Imlay translated after a while. 'On a long stretch of beach, just out of sight and range of the cannon in the fort. But they have pushed their own cannon forward behind barricades of timber, back filled with earth, so they can bombard the fort from three positions.'

It was the mortars that were causing the greatest problem for the defenders, for it enabled the rebels to lob shells over the earthworks into the stockade itself. They also had them in the channel, mounted on *chalands-à-boeuf* – large flatboats driven by long sweeps and normally used to carry cattle. They moved them around the promontory at night, firing into the fort and then retiring across the Rigolets at dawn to cover the approaches from the sea and from Lake Pontchartrain.

Escovar estimated the total number of attackers at between five or six hundred.

Nathan had just sixty seamen and the same number of

marines under Whiteley and McGregor, but he was counting on the element of surprise and on attacking from the one direction the attackers had not covered.

Which rather depended on John Who-Lives-in-the-Marshes.

The guide had added to Escavar's account of the siege by explaining that the promontory on which the fort was built was composed of sand and silt washed up by the Rigolets. It was the only solid piece of land on the whole island. The rest was swamp, riddled with bayous. For this reason the French thought they were safe from attack in the rear and had posted only a few sentries. But Desmarais was confident of finding his way through the bayous and landing them on more or less solid ground within a few hundred yards of the French lines.

He was up in the bows of Nathan's barge now with his compatriot, Joseph Bonnet, peering across the rolling bank of mist.

Nathan could not have explained, even to himself, why he was prepared to put his faith in an unknown Indian guide when he could not bring himself to trust Pym, or Imlay – or even the ship's master Mr Baker. If he had been asked, he would probably have said it was no different from taking a pilot on board to guide them in or out of harbour. But he knew it was something more than that. He trusted Desmarais partly because of something about him, some indefinable quality that gave Nathan confidence. It had been the same when he had first met Tully. Perhaps he was drawn to rogues and outlaws: the sense of independence they had and their pride – the pride of the outsider who has no one to rely upon but himself, no other form of advancement. But he could not have said for sure what it was. Perhaps it was his own lack of confidence.

'What is the name of your people?' he had asked Desmarais when they were still on the *Unicorn*.

'In our own tongue we are the Taneks-hava, the first people,' he had said.

'And do you have a name, in your own tongue?'

'My family name is Itaanyadi.'

'Do you still have a family?'

'No. They were killed by the French. And I was taken to the mission in New Orleans.'

Did the fact that his family had been killed by the French make it more likely that he would help the British – or the Spaniards? It was useless to speculate. And too late.

They were approaching what appeared to be the mainland but was probably another island: a dense, seemingly impenetrable barrier of small trees or shrubs rising out of the mist, but as they came closer a gap appeared – or rather, the mist seemed to flow into a narrow channel between the foliage like a carpet unrolling before them, inviting them to enter. Desmarais seemed perfectly satisfied with this arrangement. And so on they went, into the swamp.

Nathan was no naturalist but it seemed likely from the salinity of the water that this was a mangrove swamp, and if his previous experience was anything to go by, it would be thick with mosquitoes and other stinging insects. Dr

McLeish had provided them with a repellent of rum and catnip to rub into their faces and Nathan had furtively added a sprinkling of vinegar and oregano which he privately believed would protect him from the miasma, a notorious breeding ground of disease. Otherwise there was only prayer.

The creek twisted and turned among the trees – was this the Big Liar? Or the Little Snake, as Desmarais called it. From time to time it forked left or right and the Indian would issue a command in French which Nathan translated for his coxswain. He was reminded of his journey through the catacombs of Paris with another guide, the man known as Jack the Mule. Imlay had been with him then, too, and the adventure had ended badly.

The insects had found them. They could hear them in the air, though they were not biting yet. Or if they were, the men were remarkably stoical about it. On his previous visit to the tropics Nathan had not been troubled by mosquitoes. He thought they did not like the taste of him; something in his blood – the French perhaps. Bats flitted in the air between the trees and from time to time they heard the cry of a bird or a large splash, and once a grunting cough betraying the presence of larger creatures but they remained invisible to their eyes.

They rowed for above an hour until the creek opened out into another lake, ringed in by distant islands. Desmarais came aft through the ranks of oarsmen and Nathan made room for him on the stern seat.

'The island is over there.' He pointed to the left but it could have been any of them; they all looked the same to

Nathan. 'If we wait here one hour we will reach the fort just before the sun rises.'

'Very well.'

And so they waited with the men resting up on their oars and the insects in a dense cloud about them, stinging now. There were muttered oaths, a slapping of necks and the backs of hands and frequent commands for quiet from the petty officers.

Nathan had not calculated for this delay, and the attentions of the insects encouraged his doubts about the wisdom of the enterprise. It seemed incredible to him now that he was prepared to risk half his crew and possibly the *Unicorn* herself to save an obscure Spanish official and an insignificant little fort – it was called La Petite Coquille, he had discovered: the Little Shell. True, he had been swayed by the wider strategic considerations proposed by Imlay, but he was inclined now to the belief that strategic considerations should be left to politicians and the more sinister agencies at their command. The last time he had agreed to support Imlay's grand designs was in Paris – and that had led to the loss of the one person in France who really mattered to him.

Did he blame Imlay for Sara's death? Partly. Though not as much as he blamed himself. And in all fairness he could not blame Imlay for their present situation. Imlay had been entirely opposed to Nathan's scheme of attacking the rebels – a 'rash conceit' he had called it, and that was the mildest of the expressions he had used. They had scarcely spoken since. He was now sulking in one of the other boats with Escavar.

Nathan would not have described himself as either rash or conceited, but there were times when he appeared to be possessed of some reckless demon that threw caution to the winds. He sometimes wondered if it was a means of escaping the more rigorous disciplines of command: that he preferred the throw of the dice to the more precise calculations of navigation and the day-to-day running of a ship of war.

He was brooding upon this failing – as he saw it – when he found himself staring into a pair of eyes. Indeed, he rather thought he had been doing so for some time before he became aware of the fact. Possibly the compartment of his mind occupied with such trivia as his immediate surroundings had categorised them as rocks. But no, they were eyes. Large reptilian eyes emerging from the swamp as if from the top of some creature's head, like a frog's. They observed him unblinkingly with what he took to be a cold, clinical regard, as if contemplating the mental torment of a fellow philosopher, though it was far more likely, he conceded, that the creature was considering whether he might be edible. The eyes were large enough to make this an immediate cause for concern, and in the instant this occurred to him, the creature apparently came to a positive conclusion, for without any further warning it lunged forward, rising some several feet out of the water to reveal a massive elongated jaw possessed of a truly astonishing quantity of teeth.

Nathan leaped up in the boat and fell backwards, the jaws snapping shut within inches of his face. The boat rocked alarmingly. The beast fell back into the water with a great splash and the thrashing of an enormous tail. Several of the seamen struck out with their oars. But there was no second attack. Nathan stood up shakily and gazed at the agitation in the water. He uttered a single awed expletive, then looked down the length of the boat. Saw the shocked expressions, reflecting his own.

'Fuck,' he said again with an embarrassed grin.

Several of the hands grinned back. Nathan laughed and then they were all laughing. He sat down, shaking his head but strangely pleased with himself. It was probably not commensurate with his dignity as a captain but he felt that the episode had united them somewhat. Certainly they all seemed more relaxed.

Desmarais came climbing towards him.

'It is time to go,' he said.

They had been rowing for almost a quarter of an hour across the lake when there was a sudden flash in the night sky to the north and a noise that could have been thunder. But it was not thunder. It was artillery. Again, and again . . . A battle in progress, or possibly the thunder was entirely at the command of the French. Either way, it indicated that the fort was still holding out.

Desmarais looked back at Nathan and raised an arm and they rowed towards the shore. As they drew closer Nathan saw that it was not as solid as it had appeared from out on the lake, but riddled with small inlets and creeks. On the guide's instruction they entered one, the trees pressing in on both sides and even meeting over their heads. No longer mangroves but more like a variety of

willow, and the ground appeared less swampy than in
other parts. As they glided through the muddy waters, the
glimpses of sky permitted them through the canopy of
trees changed from black to purple to indigo. Then the
creek widened appreciably and they saw the first streaks
of pink spreading from the east. Desmarais was peering
intently forward. For an irreverent moment Nathan
thought he might be lost. Then he pointed again and
Nathan saw a ramshackle wooden jetty standing up out of
the dispersing mist and a patch of muddy strand beyond.
This apparently was their destination.

They disembarked one boat at a time, the men moving
off rapidly for fear the jetty would collapse under their
weight, but there was scarce room on the shore for all of
them and there were some nervous glances towards the
murky water and whatever menaces it might conceal.
Indeed, the men appeared more apprehensive of the
swamp and the monsters that lurked there than the
unknown dangers ahead. The firing was continuous now
and much louder, the roar of the cannon accompanied by
the sharper report of musketry.

Desmarais was at Nathan's side. 'The fort is a short
march from here,' he said. 'I will go ahead with Joseph, in
case they have posted pickets.'

'Very well, but—'

Too late. They were already gone, melting into the
trees. And now here was Imlay, glowering after them.

'Where are they going?'

Nathan told him.

'And if they betray us?'

'Then we are betrayed,' replied Nathan evenly and with more composure than he felt.

They followed the narrow track the guides had taken through the trees, moving in single file in a long, stumbling column. The ground seemed to be a mixture of sand and shingle, and Nathan thought it was climbing slightly.

They had progressed some three or four hundred yards when they came across two bodies, pulled into the side of the track. It was light enough to see that they were white and that their throats had just been cut. They went on.

The track widened, the foliage not so dense. A low ridge ahead, almost a sand dune, topped with sea grass, at the bottom of which the two guides awaited them.

'The fort is just over the ridge,' said Desmarais. 'I think you must come with me to look.'

Nathan took McGregor and Whiteley with him. Up the little slope and then sprawling on their bellies at the top. And there was the battle arranged for their inspection, like a vast diorama.

As Escavar had said, the fort occupied the far end of a narrow promontory protruding into the Rigolets with a moat dug on the landward side so that it was entirely surrounded by water. Nathan could see the embrasures for the cannon but they were silent now, either knocked out by the enemy or out of powder or shot. A pall of smoke rose from the timber stockade and drifted out over the water.

It was the enemy cannon that were firing. From three batteries, so far as Nathan could see: one on each side of the promontory and a third directly in front of him at a distance of about two or three hundred yards. The individual guns appeared to be protected by mobile barricades of timber, mounted on large wheels. Ruts in the ground showed where they had been pushed forward and then backed up with earth.

Their arrival seemed to have coincided with a skirmish over to the right of the position. The garrison had made a sortie from the fort directed at the battery on this side but they were in the process of being thrown back by a large number of rebels who appeared to have sprung up from the ground. Focusing with his glass Nathan saw that they were emerging from a ridge – or sand dune – similar to the one he was lying upon but right on the water's edge. The beach Escavar had mentioned must be immediately below and clearly this was where the bulk of the enemy infantry was concentrated.

They were far too many for the Spaniards, who began to fall back. They fled over a crude bridge of timbers thrown across the moat, many dropping into the water in their panic. Nathan watched helplessly, thinking they would all be lost and the fort fall before his eyes, but then the rebels pulled back, possibly deterred by heavy musket fire from the fort.

Immediately the besiegers began to open fire with their artillery again, peppering the fort with shot and shell. Nathan looked more closely at the battery directly in front of him. These were the mortars or *obusiers*, not unlike the carronades carried by the *Unicorn*, but with a higher elevation that enabled them to lob their shells into the pall of smoke above the distant stockade. They were guarded by about twenty or thirty infantry, crouching with the gunners behind that extraordinary barricade. Or rather, series of barricades, each mounted on four giant wheels.

'Seen enough?' he enquired of the two marine officers at his side. They nodded and slithered back down the slope.

'Now I am not a soldier,' he said, 'but it seems to me we should attack the battery immediately in front of us, spike the guns, and then retreat to the ridge.'

'And then what?' McGregor appeared unimpressed.

'Then we must hold them off as best we can. At least until nightfall when we may face back in good order to the boats. Or did you have an alternative plan?'

'I doot there is an alternative,' McGregor conceded gloomily.

'Then that is what we shall do.'

They made their way back to where they had left the men and Nathan explained the plan to his officers, who took it back down the line. Then they advanced toward the ridge. It was decided the men should spread out in two ranks, the marines in the front and the seamen behind. Their muskets had been left unloaded thus far for fear an accidental discharge might alert the enemy, but now McGregor proposed that they should fire two volleys as they advanced, the marines first and then the seamen, the marines fixing their bayonets in between.

This was an altogether slower, more orderly procedure than Nathan had envisaged, being more accustomed to the desperate rush of a boarding party. He bowed to

McGregor's experience, however, hoping he would not regret it.

He loaded his own pistols, took one in each hand, looked about him to left and right, and nodded. 'Very well.'

It went badly from the start.

They had barely cleared the top of the ridge when one of the muskets went off, always a possibility where seamen were concerned. It might not have been noticed by the enemy, had their cannon still been in action, but it coincided with a lull in the fighting – occasioned, Nathan saw at once, by the fact that the fort was flying a white flag. The French immediately in front of them had emerged from behind their barricades and appeared to be engaged in a kind of celebratory dance, several linking arms and throwing up their legs while others made a large circle and rushed in upon each other, clapping their hands together.

But the sound of the musket shot brought an abrupt end to these festivities. They stopped dancing and stared back towards the men who had appeared on the dune behind them.

Nathan had a moment to consider whether the Spanish surrender made any difference or not from both a moral and a tactical point of view.

He decided not. On both counts.

'Charge!' he yelled.

The seamen immediately rushed forward in front of the marines, effectively blocking their fire. The French snatched up their guns. Most of the seamen, realising their error and rebuked in a terrible voice by McGregor, turned round and tried to get back behind the marines. A few of the more reckless ran on. Nathan, who had been converted to the more orderly approach, wavered between going back and going forward. He decided he could not abandon those who had already charged at his command and ran on.

The French fired a ragged volley. Then, seeing the seamen coming on with no apparent loss of impetus, they ran back toward the barricades, thus exposing the guns and their gunners, most of whom had climbed on the barricades to cheer and wave their hats at their comrades on the other batteries. They wisely decided to drop down on the far side.

The infantry, having reached the guns, turned about in some indecision. One of their number, presumably with the status of officer, was regaling them with spirit and thrashing those that were closest to him with the flat of his sword. Thus encouraged – and seeing how few of the enemy were upon them – they clubbed their muskets and charged.

A short, vicious engagement. Nathan fired both pistols, dodged a blow from a musket barrel, clubbed down his assailant with a pistol butt and received a blow in turn from someone coming up on his right. He fell, raising his arm in a desperate attempt to ward off the next blow. Then Gabriel was there, his guardian angel, laying about him with the old cavalry sword he favoured and swearing like a trooper. He was set upon by three bearded ruffians and Nathan struggled to assist him. But there was no need. A giant figure was there before him, an ogre with a great club which he wielded in both hands. Two of Gilbert's opponents went down before this mythical creature with no more protest or opposition than a pair of skittles; the third fled. Nathan recognised the Irishman, Michael Connor, whom he had freed from the shackles. He saw now why Pym had been so anxious to restrain him.

'You all right, sur?'

'Very well, thank you, Connor. Carry on.'

But the rest of his men had arrived in a wave of red and blue, all order gone to the winds but in sufficient force to put the remaining rebels to flight.

Nathan put a hand to his head and felt a bump the size of a hen's egg close to the crown but his thought processes seemed to be in more or less working order so he supposed that his brain was still intact. He staggered to the nearest gun, looking around for the seamen who had brought the spikes. But there were shells and cartridges stacked around the guns in neat piles. Also tubs with slow matches. This gave him a better idea. He peered through the timbers of the barricade. About fifty rebels were fleeing towards the fort, still with its white flag at the masthead. More over to the right, not fleeing. And to the left? He could see nothing through a haze of smoke.

'Belay there!' he roared to the seamen who were already at the guns with their hammers and spikes.

It had been in his mind to use the shells to blow the guns up but now he thought of a better use for them. They dragged them round to face the men on their right flank.

How did you fire shells? He could not remember that he ever had. Light the fuse and bung them down the muzzle, he supposed, much the same as you did with ordinary shot, and fire them before they blew up in your face. This, with a few technical embellishments, proved to be pretty much the case. Webster had been on a bomb ketch once and he said the thing to do was to load up with cartridge, drop in the shell, reach in to light it, then apply another light to the cartridge. This sounded plausible enough and Nathan invited him to demonstrate. The lieutenant's look was reproachful but he took off his jacket and approached the weapon with a determined frown. Although it was as short as any mortar, he was obliged to rest his head on the end, leaning down with the length of his arm to light the fuse. He shot out of the barrel with some alacrity and they scattered even further back as the gunner applied the match to the cartridge. A tense pause. Then the explosion. But the effect was as the manufacturers had intended. Nathan peered over toward the enemy lines to observe the fall of shot. For a moment, nothing; then another explosion, far more spectacular but a little short. Webster looked pleased with himself. Nathan nominated four volunteers to light the next ones. It took a little while to get the range; they then began to bombard the rebel position with serious results.

The French being hidden behind a ridge of sand it was impossible to observe the effect. But after some little while a boat emerged from the shore, filled with men. Another followed – and another. Nathan wondered for a moment if they planned to put ashore at a more suitable point for a counter-attack, but they seemed intent only upon retreat.

But now here was McGregor bellowing in his ear and pointing back at their own ridge. Nathan looked and saw a number of figures – twenty or thirty perhaps – making their way along it towards the rear of their position, cutting them off from their line of retreat to the boats. And then a great many more appeared from behind the third battery, over on their left. Briefly Nathan considered hauling the guns around, but even had there been time, exploding shells were a poor weapon against advancing infantry. They had done far better with grape.

McGregor and Whiteley had their marines drawn up in two ranks facing the men on their left who appeared to be a more immediate threat than those in their rear. Perhaps as many as a hundred were advancing towards them behind the tricolour of Revolutionary France with a drummer beating the step – like regular French infantry. Nathan ordered his men to ensure their muskets were loaded and to line up behind the marines but Whiteley, seeing what he was up to, came over, touched the peak of his hat with a smile and said: 'Forgive me for appearing to instruct you, sir, but we will only have time for a volley. Then we will fix bayonets and charge. It would be helpful if your men were to advance upon the men on the ridge.'

In other words, put with all the courtesy at Whiteley's considerable command, 'For God's sake keep out of our way this time.'

'Make ready.' McGregor's voice was reassuringly

steady. The French were at full pelt now, yelling as they ran, in no particular order but with no apparent lack of enthusiasm. The French – Nathan had been informed – were invariably better in attack; the British when conducting a fighting retreat. On this occasion, with water on three sides and a swamp on the fourth, Nathan concluded that this strategy was not an option.

'Present.'

The twin lines of muskets swung down to the firing position, the right hand pulling the butt into the shoulder, the right cheek pressed up against the comb. In what appeared to be the same movement, the soldiers in the front rank took half a step back with their right foot and the soldiers in the rear half a step to the right. The only improvement Nathan could have asked for was in speed. The front runners were almost upon them.

'*Fire!*'

The crash of the volley, the enemy lost in smoke. Before it had cleared and Nathan could see what damage it had done, the marines had fixed bayonets and McGregor's voice was raised again in the command to charge.

Nathan pointed his sword towards the ridge. 'There is our enemy, gentlemen,' he instructed them – they probably knew, but it was as well to be sure. 'And there are our boats – the only means we have of reaching the *Unicorn*. I know you will do your duty.'

The charge started well but faltered at the foot of the ridge. Several men were down. More fell to their knees and began to fire back.

'Belay there!' Nathan roared. 'On your feet. *Up, up!*'

He saw Webster go down, hit in the head. Tully had almost reached the top of the ridge when he too fell back. Then they were among them. Nathan slashed about him with his sword, felt a roaring in his ears, realised it was his own voice, collided with a tree and went down. Gabriel hauled him up again. A glimpse of Tully, apparently none the worse for wear, parrying the thrust of a sword and thrusting in turn, quite coolly it seemed, wholly unexcited with one arm behind his back. Nathan appealed to himself for calm. He rehearsed a little move. Looked for someone to practise it upon. But they were all gone. Dead or gone. And down below he saw that the marines had put the rest of the rebels to flight. The white flag was coming down from the fort and a moment later the flag of Spain went up in its place.

Nathan gazed around his battered crew. Fewer than there had been. Who was not there that he knew? Webster, of course. But someone else who should have been. Then in a flash it came.

Imlay.

He could not see Imlay.

Chapter Eleven

Carondelet

———◆———

'Imlay? Did you say Imlay?'

It had frequently been observed, most notably by his French subjects, that His Excellency the Governor-General of Louisiana and West Florida bore a striking resemblance to a horse, especially when startled, as was now the case. Had he thrown back his head and neighed, Nathan would not have been unduly astonished.

'I did,' he said. 'Gilbert Imlay, an American who—'

'An American? And of your party?'

'Well, he was with us at the commencement of the business. Where he is now, I cannot say.'

Nathan gazed across the parade ground as if he might glimpse him among those members of the garrison employed there. The fires that had been burning when he entered the fort had now been extinguished but the smoke lingered in the still air with an ugly smell of charred wood

– and perhaps flesh. The governor had lost over fifty men in the attack, he had informed Nathan, and being almost out of powder and shot had been on the point of surrender when the British made their appearance. Nathan diplomatically forbore to mention the white flag he had seen flying from the masthead. Baron Francisco Luis Hector de Carondelet was a proud man: Nathan would have taken him for a *hidalgo* – a Spanish grandee of the noblest blood – had he not known from his conversation with Brother Ignatius that he was from Flanders and that his properties had been 'liberated' by the French. They spoke French now in deference to Nathan's lack of Spanish.

'You have made a thorough search among the dead?'

'I would not say thorough, Your Excellency, as they are scattered over a wide area, which is why I would be greatly obliged if your men were to continue the search after our departure. I would not like to think of him lying wounded in the swamp at night, a prey to whatever monsters lurk there.'

'No,' agreed the governor, but there was something in his tone that indicated to Nathan that the prospect would not overly disturb him. 'No, we must certainly avoid that eventuality.' He spoke a few sentences in Spanish to the fort commandant, whose quarters they had appropriated, and the officer left the room, hopefully to relay Nathan's request as it had been stated.

'Is it possible that Your Excellency is acquainted with Mr Imlay?'

'Oh, we are not acquainted as such. But his name became familiar to us over the course of time – more familiar, indeed, than we might have wished. It first arose in connection with a plot to seize the territory for the United States with the assistance of a small army of frontiersmen from Kentucky and Tennessee.'

He observed Nathan's expression with interest. 'I suppose you were not aware of this?'

'Believe me, Excellency, I was not.'

'I am relieved to hear it. Else I might have feared you nourished similar ambitions on behalf of King George. Imlay is entirely mercenary, I believe, in his pursuit of employment and quite uncommitted in his loyalties. In what capacity is he retained by you? If I may ask.'

'He is . . . in the capacity of a translator. And to advise on the local situation.'

'And I am sure you will have found the advice most useful,' remarked the governor. 'Did he advise you to come to our assistance?'

'I . . . I had no reason to consult him on the subject.'

'I see. Yet his views might have been illuminating, I think.'

Before Nathan could ask him what he meant by this, there was a knock upon the door and two of the governor's African servants, or slaves, entered bearing trays with refreshment. Whatever the state of its powder and shot, the fort did not appear to be short of food and drink. There was cold fowl, a large pie, bread and butter, several cheeses, a pineapple and other exotic fruits, lemon water and wine.

Carondelet raised his glass. 'Your very good health, sir. I am in your debt. The fort must surely have fallen and New Orleans left at the mercy of these dogs. Who knows but that the French may have been celebrating the conquest of a new empire in the west, though I suppose they would not have called it that. I believe they use the word "liberate" when they plunder a man of his birthright. So to you, the English and King George.'

He took a delicate sip and contemplated the glass. 'There are those in Cuba – and in Spain – who would die before drinking to such an heretic. And would have me shot for proposing it, no doubt. I suppose you have heard that the English alliance is not popular among certain of my associates who would prefer an agreement with the French, being more disposed to tolerate the atheist pig than the Protestant swine. Your pardon, but it is their words that I use.'

Nathan granted his pardon, and conceded that he had heard a similar report.

'Doubtless it formed a part of Imlay's advice on the local situation,' remarked the governor with a sly grin. 'You need not answer that. Indeed, it was ignoble of me as a host to propose it. A captain must needs take advice from many unsavoury quarters.'

'Forgive me, Your Excellency, but I own I am somewhat disturbed by your suspicions where Mr Imlay is concerned. I have been given no cause to doubt his loyalty to the coalition against the Revolutionary Government in Paris.'

This was by no means true but it drew a satisfactory response.

'Pah! Imlay's loyalty is first and foremost to himself, I believe. And then to those of his inclination in the United States. The crowned heads of Spain and England, of Prussia and Austria, do not in the least engage his loyalties or his sympathies, believe me – though perhaps you know him better than I?'

'I know him only as well as any of my officers,' Nathan temporised, 'but he has never revealed any hostility to the King of Spain. And as I assured you, I knew nothing of his past activities in this region, other than as an adventurer and geographer.'

'Oh, adventurer he certainly is, that I don't deny. An adventurer, a freebooter, a pirate . . . well, I will not become agitated whilst indulging the appetite. It is not good for the digestion, I am assured.'

'Nor would I wish it, Excellency, but I would welcome an account of this conspiracy you mentioned, when you are at liberty to indulge me.'

'Oh, that is not at all disagreeable for it failed entirely in its objective. Indeed, the affair was of such an embarrassment to the Federal government they sought to arrest the leading conspirators for treason. General Washington, I believe, was apoplectic, though whether it was at the nature of the enterprise or its ignominious failure, I cannot say. Imlay, with other of the rogues, was forced to flee from United States jurisdiction – into East Florida, initially, where he offered his services to the Spanish authorities as a spy.'

Nathan confessed himself astonished. (This was an exaggeration. Nothing Imlay did could have astonished him.) However, he was alarmed at the extent of Imlay's previous activities. He wondered if Colonel Hollis had known of them when he had briefed him at the Admiralty.

'Well, given that he had but recently attempted to expel Spanish authority from the region it was certainly impudent,' the governor agreed. 'But as I believe I mentioned, one is forced to take advice from many unsavoury quarters. So my colleagues in East Florida availed themselves of the offer and he became a servant of the King of Spain. He was entered in the rolls as Agent number 37, with the code name Gilberto. Which reveals a certain lack of imagination among those who recruited him, I agree, but they are sometimes surprisingly inept. I am probably being indiscreet but one should know a little of the history of one's servants, I believe, for fear of further betrayal and it is quite possible he may survive the creatures of the swamp – with whom he has much in common. Let me help you to a little of this excellent pie. It is composed of pigeon breasts; the "passenger pigeon" is the name used by the English colonists, I believe, and though a common enough bird, it is quite delicious when cooked with the right herbs.'

Nathan allowed his plate to be replenished but his mind, for once, was not on his food.

'Forgive me, Your Excellency, for pressing you on this subject, but is it possible that Imlay is now working for the French?'

The governor considered for a moment. 'It is entirely possible,' he conceded. 'Our most recent information was that he has been residing in Paris for some years.' He shot Nathan a look but receiving no reply continued: 'However, he may be acting entirely on his own initiative. You know something of American settlement in the region?'

Nathan did not.

'Well, let me enlighten you. It began with those former soldiers to whom, as a reward for their services in the War of Independence, were given the uncultivated lands of Kentucky and of the southern bank of the Ohio. This vast territory, which twenty years ago was uninhabited, already comprises fifty thousand men capable of bearing arms and is increasing at the rate of more than ten thousand emigrants a year.

'This restless population, driving the Indian tribes before them, seek to possess themselves of the entire region between the Ohio and the Mississippi while demanding with menaces the right of free navigation to the Gulf.' Despite his earlier concern for the digestive system, the governor was continuing his discourse with increasing passion, knife and fork clenched in his fists like weapons and the pigeon pie helpless before him. 'And do you think this will be sufficient for them? *No*, sir, for their roving spirit acknowledges no obstacle or impediment, whether of peoples or physical barriers. A rifle and a little cornmeal in a bag is sufficient for an American wandering alone in the woods for a month.

'Our masters in Europe are preoccupied with the

menace of Revolution in France but I tell you, sir, it is nothing to the menace of these interlopers, for they are a new breed possessed of an independence, a notion of their own . . . *righteousness* . . . that brooks no dissent, no opposition, no obstacle to their progress. Unless they be stopped at their present frontiers they will advance westward to the Pacific, southward into Mexico and, indeed, northward into British Canada. And after that, sir, well, the world may look out for itself. And that is all I have to say on the subject.' He stabbed a pigeon breast with his fork and ate it with belligerence.

Nathan did not care to start him off again but it had occurred to him that Imlay might have sought the shelter and support of these prodigies – if any were in the immediate vicinity.

The governor shook his head. 'They have not yet penetrated so far south and show no desire at present to live in a bog. I think it is far more likely, if he is alive, that he is with the Cajuns. He speaks the language and he has worked with them before. Indeed, it may have been that they were expecting him.'

'How could that be?'

Carondelet shrugged. 'It would be interesting to put the question to Imlay,' he remarked evasively, 'if we are fortunate enough to apprehend him.'

'We have no evidence that Imlay has betrayed us,' Nathan replied cautiously. 'Or intends to do so. At present I am merely concerned for his safety. He is in the service of His Britannic Majesty and I would not wish him to suffer for any previous misdeeds while on Spanish territory.'

'Oh my dear sir, I said "put the question to him", not "put him to the question". I am not a member of the Inquisition. Here, your glass is empty and there is the bottle beside you . . .'

Nathan demurred. 'Forgive me, but it is high time I was on my way. We must get back to the *Unicorn* before nightfall. And then there is the *Virginie* to be found.'

'Ah yes, the *Virginie*. Whose virtues have been most generously distributed among these Cajun sons of whores. Their big guns came from her, you know, and most of the gunners.'

'So I believe. And I am told by Señor Escavar that she is now off the Delta, some one hundred miles to the south.'

'So we are informed. However, as the channels of the Delta have no more than thirteen or fourteen feet of water, we need hardly be concerned that a frigate of that size may come upon us by way of the river.'

'I confess I was more concerned with coming upon *her*.'

'Well, I wish you joy of the venture, though I had hoped I might prevail upon you to leave your marines here until I can bring up more of my own forces from New Orleans.'

'I am afraid that would seriously weaken my own force. But now that the rebels have fled, and you are in possession of all their guns, powder and shot . . .'

'This is true,' nodded the governor with as near cheerful an expression as his lugubrious features would allow. The guns had already been dragged into the fort and the mortars alone would be a sufficient deterrence to any future attack.

'Well . . .' He dabbed at his lips with the white napkin on his lap and rose from the table. 'I will be most fulsome in my report to Madrid and I trust it will be relayed to your own superiors in London. Who knows but that it may be the beginning of a greater understanding between our two nations, a greater willingness to combine our operations.'

The governor appeared ready to commence upon a long speech of farewell but he was interrupted by a servant with a message for Nathan. One of his officers desired to speak with him on a matter of some urgency.

It was Tully.

'I have been speaking with one of the prisoners,' he told Nathan, 'one of the gunners landed by the *Virginie*. He is a Channel Islander by the name of Tierney – Robin Tierney. A fisherman from Jersey. He says he and his shipmates were taken by the *Virginie* on an earlier cruise and forced into the French service. But he insists he has always been a true subject of King George and is anxious to serve on the *Unicorn*.'

'Well, if you think he is trustworthy, we need every man we can get. In fact—'

'I am sorry to interrupt you, sir, but he also has news of the *Virginie*. There were over a score of her men came ashore with the guns and about the same number of marines. He says she was to wait for them off the Chandeleur Islands – *not* the Delta as we were informed.'

'The Chandeleurs?' Nathan felt a knife turn in his

stomach. He had a clear mental picture of the Chandeleurs from the chart drawn by Des Barres. They curved in a long chain parallel with the coast of Louisiana, and the northernmost of them was barely twenty miles from where they had left the *Unicorn*.

Chapter Twelve

The *Virginie*

⸺◦•◦⸺

There was something wrong with the sea. Even among the shallows of Lake Borgne they felt it: a sluggish swell that seemed to come from nowhere for there was scarcely a breath of wind and otherwise the sea appeared perfectly calm with no wave crests, no white horses out in the bay. But still they felt it: that sleepy, sullen heave as if some giant reptile was moving in its sleep, stretching into wakefulness. Nathan could feel the heat rising from its back, an oppressive sweltering heat that distorted the air around them, cutting visibility to a few hundred yards. The sky was opaque, more bronze than blue, a vast metallic shield diffusing the light of an invisible sun. There was a storm brewing. They all knew it. Nathan felt the urgency in the silent rowers. He did not have to exhort them to pull. They pulled for all their worth, and even those who were resting and should have been slumped in an exhausted heap, were wide awake, staring dully towards the unnatural haze shrouding the western end of Ship Island where they had left the *Unicorn*.

That haze was suddenly shot through with flashing light; and close on its heels came the drum roll of thunder. But it was not the expected storm. With startling suddenness, the curtain parted as if blown away and they saw not one but two ships and the orange flames stabbing through the smoke as they pounded each other with their broadsides and the rippling roar of their cannon rolled back to them across the sullen sea.

'Pull!' Nathan roared now, leaning forward as if he could propel the boat with all the suppressed energy of his fury and self-loathing.

How far? A mile? A little less, perhaps. He prayed that it might be less; prayed that he might reach the *Unicorn* in time. If not to save her then at least to be there at the death and to die with her, for it was preferable to contemplate his own extinction than to face the living shame of losing his ship when he was not aboard her.

Pym had done the right thing in the circumstances. Which was to say, he had done nothing but kept the *Unicorn* at her anchorage, on spring cables, across the narrow deepwater channel with her bows pointing toward the island and the shoal water at her stern; and all her crew – all that Nathan had left him – manning her starboard guns.

The *Virginie* was about two cables' lengths to windward with her fore- and mainsails counter-braced so that she drifted slowly down upon her quarry. For there was no doubt who had become the hunter. With no room to manoeuvre – both ships reduced to mere floating batteries – it was all down to rate of fire and number of guns. And the *Virginie* was winning on both counts. She had more guns and more men to man them, and as Nathan's little fleet crept across the sea towards them it became clear that she was firing at twice the rate of the *Unicorn:* firing high, in the French manner, double-shotted and with chain.

Nathan watched in anguish as the main topmast came crashing down into the waist and the mizzen followed shortly after, like two great trees felled in a storm. Within minutes the *Unicorn* was a dismasted hulk and the French changed to round shot, firing directly into her hull and at almost point-blank range. God only knew what slaughter had been done to her crew, for her fire was spasmodic now, a single gun going off every minute or so while the fire poured into her was more or less continuous. Nathan's ship was being battered to death before his eyes.

It was a wonder she had not lowered her colours. But Nathan could see the blue ensign hanging limply at her stern. Had Pym, or whoever was in command, seen the boats closing on them to leeward? They were barely a cable's length from her now, coming up on her larboard side partly shielded by the clouds of smoke that drifted down upon them, all five boats in a ragged line as if in a race, with Nathan's barge fractionally in the lead. They could no longer see the *Virginie* now, hidden behind the looming bulk of the *Unicorn*, but they could hear the

relentless pounding of the broadside and the uglier
sounds of the shot hitting home. In those last 200 yards
Nathan could almost feel every blow landing, as if on his
own body.

But now at last they were at the frigate's side, the crew
shipping their oars and Nathan leaping for the shrouds
and tumbling his body over the rail, landing on all fours
and staring up at the bloody shambles they had made of
his ship.

The maintop had gone, bringing the mainyard down
with it and all of the sails and most of the rigging; the
mizzenmast, too, and most of the foretop which had
caught up in the starboard shrouds and hung at a crazy
angle, like a broken branch clinging to what remained of
the tree. The effect was rather as if a violent gale had torn
through a forest; the whole of the waist was filled with
debris, an impossible tangle of canvas and rope and
timber, and half of it hanging over the side, shrouding
what was left of the guns. Two were dismounted, two
more buried under the heap of wreckage – and their
crews, it must be presumed, with them. Other guns were
still firing from forward and aft, but how many or how
few Nathan could not guess, for the fire from the *Virginie*
was relentless. There was a great gap where two of the
gunports had been knocked into one, and this was where
most of the bodies were lying.

Yet some men were still alive, still on their feet, hacking
away at the wreckage with axes and knives. And
commanding them, it seemed, was young Place, hatless,
bloodied but still alive, yelling orders and almost capering

in what you might take for excitement or glee but was probably frustration at not being able to get at the guns, for he was pointing at what he could see of one of them, lost under a heap of cordage and canvas. He half turned as Nathan's men came scrambling over the larboard rail, reaching for the dirk at his belt, but then his expression turned from alarm to joy as he saw who they were and his eyes met Nathan's for a moment and he gave him a big boyish grin and shouted something unheard across the deck – and then a cannonball took off his head.

Shocked, stunned beyond belief, Nathan stared at the boy's headless body, still upright, almost posed in the act of drawing his dagger and then the blood came and it tumbled forward to join the carnage on the deck.

Nathan tore his eyes away and stumbled toward the quarterdeck: *his* quarterdeck, almost as much of a wreck as the waist, with the jagged stump of the mizzenmast like a tree on a blasted heath, still smoking from the lightning strike, the helm shattered and the bodies all around as if they too had been smitten down by the same bolt from heaven.

But it was not the whole picture. For all her wounds she was still a fighting ship. There were figures moving in the smoke. A boy running past him with powder for the guns. Another breaking open a cartridge box and struggling to carry it to the gunners. A gun captain crouched over the breech of a 6-pounder and a midshipman – Lamb – roaring soundlessly at the crew of one of the carronades – the *only* carronade on this side of the deck, for the other had been taken by the cutter.

Nathan threw a glance to larboard where the other two stood unmanned, calculating how quickly they could drag one of them across the deck . . . and then he saw Francis Coyle. He was propped up against one of the gun trucks, his chest soaked in blood but his eyes still open, one hand pressed to the wound, the other still clutching the dirk Nathan had given him. Their eyes met and Nathan saw the life in them.

He half turned. Gabriel was at his heels.

'Get that boy below,' he said, and then he saw Pym.

The first lieutenant was standing by the shattered helm as if posed for a painting, his hands clasped behind his back and his chin thrust belligerently forward; his hat, his overlarge hat, crammed firmly down upon his head and the blood trickling down his face from under it, spreading out across his cheek and pooling on his throat where it was damned by the tight collar. He had rigged a net to protect against falling tackle, but most of it had come down with the wreck of the mizzenmast, and a spar had fallen across the wheel: possibly it was this that had struck him. He looked at Nathan without recognition, apparently in a state of shock or wonder. Nathan called to him, went right up to him and spoke directly into his face but he did not respond. Just stood there, his hands clasped behind his back, his jaw clamped, his eyes screwed up as if staring into a blinding storm.

Nathan looked for Tully, but he had already taken command in the waist and he had most of the men from the boats hacking and heaving at the wreckage. Nathan saw the Irish giant Connor among them, picking up a great piece of spar and chucking it overboard as if it were a log or a lump of peat you might throw on the fire.

Where was Maxwell? His station was with the guns directly below the quarterdeck and Nathan could hear them firing still; he could even feel the reverberations under his feet, if it was not the shock of French round shot hitting the hull.

'Mr Lamb!' Nathan called over to the youngest of his midshipmen, who appeared to be commanding the quarterdeck guns, though it was doubtful if the men could hear a word he said and did not need to; they all knew what they had to do, and at near point-blank range it was no more astonishing than to load and fire, working like automata, white eyes staring from smoke-blackened faces, kerchiefs tied around their ears against the noise, worming and sponging, breaking open the cartridges from the wooden cases and ramming them down the muzzles of the guns, ramming the shot down after them and then standing back for the gun captains to do their work before they ran forward again. And the guns so hot the sweat sizzled and spat off them and the slush on the wheels of the trucks all melted so they screamed like banshees on a night out.

Nathan raised his voice. '*Mr Lamb!*'

And now he heard and looked about him – a brief expression of pure astonishment – and then came running up, touching his hat.

'I'm sorry, sir, I didn't know you were back.' As if he had been on a stroll ashore.

'My compliments to Mr Maxwell and I would be

obliged if he would give me a damage report.' Then, as he turned away: 'Mr McGregor, I would be obliged if you would distribute half your men among the guns and set the rest to help clear the decks. Mr Holroyd, let me know the state of the forecastle guns and who is commanding them.' And all the time wondering if he should haul down their colours that were still flying at the stern, still remarkably immune from the mayhem on the decks and in the rigging. Was that not the most useful, honest thing to do: to bring this slaughter to an end?

But first he crossed to the rail to see what the *Virginie* was doing.

For a moment he could see nothing for the smoke, but then a window opened and there she was in a glare of blood-red sun, apparently unharmed and most of her sails set, her hull intact and all her guns pointing towards him but not firing any more, not a single one and . . . and by God she was turning away! Incredibly. Her yards coming round and dropping off from the wind . . .

Why? But his relief was premature and he damned himself for a fool. It could only be to wear round and come across his stern. One raking broadside to finish them off. And it would, too. But did she have the space to do it? The *Unicorn* was moored in about twenty-five feet of water in a kind of trench, with her bows pointing toward the westernmost edge of the island and the seabed rising steeply at her stern so that in calm, clear water you could see the bottom. Was there room for a frigate to get past without grounding? Nathan strongly doubted it – but she was going to try. He would have to swing round on the spring cable to meet her – but how had Pym moored her? He looked for the hawser and saw it leading off through one of the after gunports on the larboard side. If Pym had used a dolphin or a kedge anchor they could pivot the stern round it . . .

But what if the French had a different plan? To wear round and come alongside. Fire one more broadside at point-blank range and then board. That is what Nathan would have done. He looked back at her, calculating the distance, expecting to see her bows crossing the wind and swinging back towards them, but she was leaving it very late. Impossibly late . . . All he could see was her stern. Why was she not coming round? And then a chink of light appeared in the dark stormclouds of his brain. She was not turning. She was running.

Impossible. He shook his head at such an absurdity. But still she ran on. Out into the open sea. The gap between the two ships visibly widening. And then as he stared, clutching the rail in an anguish of hope, her sternchasers fired. Two blossoms of orange flame flowering almost simultaneously. Aiming high again at what was left of the *Unicorn*'s foremast. A parting shot.

But why had she run?

Nathan looked to the south-east, looking to find a sail, a fleet of sails: the only possible explanation for this sudden withdrawal when they were at her mercy. And then he knew. No sail. No fleet. Just the biggest, blackest cloud he had ever seen. It filled the horizon to the south-east, reaching towards them and climbing high, so high and vast it was like the mushroom cloud of a genie he had seen emerging from a bottle in one of his childhood story-books. Save that it was shaped more like an anvil than a mushroom: a massive black anvil advancing towards them as if Vulcan himself had hurled it across the ocean . . .

'Hurricane.' Pym's voice, almost conversational, at his ear. Then, in case Nathan did not know the meaning of the word: 'Tropical storm. Had one a month or two ago, off Cuba. Never thought to see the like of it.' Staring at the great black wedge of cloud as if it was of only passing interest. A diversion from darker thoughts.

'Mr Pym . . .' Nathan's voice was a stranger to him, oddly husky; his tongue felt as if it was stuck in his throat. But Pym had turned away and walked back to his station by the shattered wheel.

'Please, sir, Mr Maxwell sends his compliments,' young Lamb, breathless from his mission, 'and wishes you to know he has nine guns that are still capable of firing, but he can use all the men you can spare him, sir.'

'Thank you, Mr Lamb.' It meant nothing now. The guns did not matter any more. Only the sails.

He looked aloft, knowing it was hopeless. The mainmast stripped of its yards, the mizzenmast and the foretop gone, the bowsprit alone intact, pointing like a spear towards Ship Island, their likely graveyard.

They still had the fore course. That last salvo from the sternchasers had missed its target. He supposed if they rigged a staysail they could just about run before the wind, but they would be running the wrong way: straight for that Devil's Jigsaw of a coastline to the north.

Their only chance was to head for the open sea, as the

Virginie had. That was why she had so abruptly broken off the battle, to give herself a faint chance of finding sea room; leaving her crippled adversary to the mercy of wind and waves.

Lamb was still there, waiting for his orders.

'Tell Mr Maxwell he is to cease firing and to join me on the quarterdeck with as many men as he can muster.'

'Sir.' Another voice. Baker, the sailing master, with his head bandaged and his arm in a sling.

'You are hurt, Mr Baker.'

'I am all right, sir. I have just come from the cockpit.'

The cockpit. What must it be like down there? He should send Gabriel and what others he could spare to help the surgeon – if only to hold the victims down while he worked on them with knife and saw.

But Baker had other priorities. 'We must cut the cables,' he insisted. 'Rig a jury mast, run to the north-east.'

Yes. Quite. Save that they would run upon Ship Island within the hour. Or one of the other islands in that grim chain between the Gulf and the Sound. There was not the slightest possibility of reaching open water in the state they were in, and Baker must know it. They had to find shelter. But where?

Then he saw Desmarais.

He had stayed to guide them back to the *Unicorn*, he and his companion Joseph Bonnet, and to claim the reward the pair had been promised, and now he was standing near the rail watching Nathan with a curious expression, as if interested to know what he would do now; as if it did not affect him one way or another. And yet he was no more immune from the power of the hurricane than any of them. Unless . . .

'We must find shelter,' Nathan instructed him. 'We need to find a bay, a deep anchorage with . . .' he gazed about him helplessly . . . 'some kind of a breakwater.' It was almost laughable. He heard the mocking cries of a seabird. Ship Island was the best they could do. This was it. There was nowhere else.

But the Indian was not laughing.

'There is the Isle of Good Feasting,' he said thoughtfully.

They found it on the chart, though Des Barres had given it a different name: Turtle Island. A scrap of land about three miles from their present position just off the northern shore of Ship Island, almost enclosed by the horns of a small bay.

'How high is it?' Nathan asked the guide.

A shrug. 'It is an island.'

'But . . . does it have trees?'

'Oh yes, it has trees. And many birds. Also turtles. And alligators. That is why we call it the Isle of Good Feasting.'

Nathan followed the line of soundings from their present position to the island. Twenty, twenty-two . . . It was just possible.

But Baker was shaking his head, repeating his mantra. 'In my opinion, our only chance is to head for the open sea.'

Nathan caught Tully's eye but for once it was

uncertain. He knew the rule as well as Baker. As well as Nathan.

'I know, Mr Baker. I know. But we cannot reach the open sea in our present state. I believe we must try for shelter, and judging from the chart, Turtle Island is the best that is on offer.' He turned back to Tully. 'We need a staysail from the foretop to the bowsprit.'

Tully nodded and was gone.

'And we will steer by the tiller ropes,' he instructed Baker — but the sailing master was looking beyond him and Nathan turned to see Pym standing in the open doorway. His face was still masked with blood but there was intelligence in his eye — and suspicion. And anger. He looked at the charts on the table.

'What are you doing?' he said.

Nathan told him as briefly as he could.

'Madness,' said Pym.

Nathan saw Baker's appalled, embarrassed countenance.

'Mr Pym . . .' he began.

'Pure bloody madness. And no more than five minutes back on the ship.'

'Thank you, Mr Baker, that will be all. Mr Pym, I will speak with you later.'

As if there was more than a faint possibility that either of them would survive the next few hours.

When he reached the quarterdeck the Angel Gabriel was waiting for him with the news that Frankie Coyle was dead.

Chapter Thirteen

Hurricane

————•◦•————

It began with the rain. Such rain as had convinced Noah of his divine purpose. A rain to cleanse the world of sin. Certainly it cleansed their bloodied decks within minutes of leaving the mooring, sluicing the carnage overboard through the scuppers in a pinkish torrent but continuing with such violence as if to erase the decks themselves and all that was upon them. Nathan fought his way up into the bows as they staggered around the tip of Ship Island under a reefed fore course and the scrap of a staysail Tully had set. He could barely see or breathe for the deluge and a stream of water poured from the front brim of his hat as if it had determined upon an alternative occupation as a gutter. He snatched it off in the hope of seeing better but it was impossible. Earth and sky had dissolved in a world of water.

He clung hard to the lifeline as the crippled vessel lurched, for without her masts she moved, as Tully had put it, like a drunken whore in the Haymarket, but she *was* moving and – as one might say of the whore – more or less upright and in the desired direction, with the wind obligingly off her quarter and not yet savage, though Nathan had no illusions about its true nature. He just prayed it would not reveal itself until they reached the Isle of Turtles: if they could find it in such conditions.

He struggled back to the quarterdeck, Baker was at the con, steering by compass alone – what he could see of it for the rain – with a line of boys relaying his directions to the men at the tiller. And the rest of them clinging to the lifelines or what rigging was left to comfort them. Pym, Maxwell, Tully, Holroyd, Lamb . . . the remnant of Nathan's officers, as helpless as he. It was impossible to take soundings. All they could do was follow that line of numbers on the chart and hope Des Barres had got them right and they had not changed since he first made them some twenty years before. Nathan looked for Desmarais and saw him squatting in the scuppers with a tarp held over him, apparently content to let others do the navigating though only he knew where the hell they were supposed to be heading.

And now a shout from Mr Lamb, clinging to the flagstaff at the stern. 'The boats, sir!'

Nathan ran to the rail. The ship's boats were strung out in a long line astern, for without the yards they had no means of hauling them aboard. But they should have covered them with canvas or tarps, for now they were awash with rainwater. They piped all hands and managed to haul the gig aboard, but there was no saving the others, and as they filled up they acted like a great sea anchor dragging at their stern.

'Cut them loose,' Nathan ordered bitterly, and he stood there and watched them fall away into the mist of rain. More guilt, more evidence of his gross incompetence. With the boats they might have made their way ashore before the sea grew too great, and though he lost the ship he would at least have saved the crew. He made his way back to the starboard rail and resumed his hopeless vigil, searching for some solid outline in that shifting palette of washed-out blues and greys. Ship Island was barely a half-mile off their starboard bow according to the chart, but you would never have known it and they dared not venture closer for fear of grounding.

He became aware of a presence at his side. Desmarais, still holding the tarp around his head and shoulders like a shawl, peering through the torrent. What at? What landmark was he searching for – and how could he hope to find it in such a flood?

'*Now*,' he said.

Nathan frowned. 'What?'

'We must go in. Towards the shore.'

Nathan stared to windward, clawing the water from his eyes. What shore? He could not see a thing. But it was a little late for doubts. He gave the order, saw the astounded face of Baker, turned back to the rail, and there it was: a line of white surf and sand, if it *was* sand, about two cables' lengths off their starboard bow and beyond. Could those be trees?

Desmarais was running forward, spinning along the

lifeline like a spider on a web, and Nathan followed more cautiously with his speaking trumpet. The Indian had shed his cloak and was clambering up into the bows, clinging precariously to the forestay. He seemed entirely at home on the sea – and if he had taken to the air, Nathan would not have been entirely astonished.

'There!'

Trees. A long line of trees, bending under the torrent of rain but Christ, they were close . . . Nathan turned back to face the quarterdeck and raised the trumpet.

'Hard a larboard!'

He heard the order repeated to the men down below at the tiller ropes and slowly, painfully slowly, the bows came round. But Desmarais was shouting again.

'Too far!'

'Starboard! Two points to starboard.'

Ridiculous. To manoeuvre a ship of this size in such waters, in such a storm. Pym and Baker were right. They should have made for the open sea.

But there it was – his breakwater. An unbroken line of trees almost at the water's edge but not mangroves. Pines. How had they got here? Birds must have brought the seeds, in their shit most probably, to mix with the mud and the sand. It did not matter how they got here. They were pines and they had stood the test of time and tide and whatever the weather could throw at them . . .

'Here! Now!' Desmarais screaming in his ear as if Nathan could stop her like a canoe, by digging his paddle in the water and spinning round. But Tully had his men along the yard, hauling up the course, and the frigate wallowed in the choppy water in the lee of the island with just the staysail to hold it off the shore. Nathan could deal with choppy. If choppy was the worst it could do.

They dropped anchor and sent the gig out with hawsers to make them fast to the trees. Pym's face was twisted into the semblance of a gargoyle spouting water.

'To moor in such a sea? It is pure—' But then he caught the look in Nathan's eye and did not finish. He did not have to. Madness it surely was, but what else was he to do, having brought them thus far? If they did not moor they would drift upon the shoals.

He had to trust his breakwater.

The gig made four trips in all with four hawsers. By the time they had finished, the rain had eased somewhat but the wind was worse. It howled and roared about them as if in fury at their defiance. But the sea so close inshore was less turbulent, or at least not so as to sweep their decks.

'I think, Mr Pym,' said Nathan, 'we may pipe the crew to dinner.'

A mere pretence at calm but it gave him some small satisfaction to see Pym's expression. It was a cold scrap of a meal, of necessity, with the galley fires dowsed, but they had the last of the fresh bread with a cheese brought from Havana that almost resembled Cheddar, along with apples and onions and a portion of plum duff which, though even stodgier than usual without the benefit of a hot custard, was helped down with a double ration of grog and generally found welcome. As meals went it would never have suited Mrs Small, but recent events had reduced her absence to a minor item in Nathan's list of regrets. He helped his own portion down with a bottle of Captain Kerr's claret which he shared with Tully in the privacy of his cabin, past caring if it smacked of favouritism or not.

'What do you think?' he asked him as the *Unicorn* tugged and strained at her moorings. 'Speak frankly. Have I done the wrong thing?' He did not add 'again'.

'There was little else you could have done,' Tully assured him. 'We would never have survived in the open sea.'

Nathan wondered if he meant that or was it merely said in kindness.

'Is there anything more we can do?'

'Not that I can think of,' said Tully. 'Only hope that the sea does not break over the island and swamp us.'

They went up on deck. The wind screamed through their sparse rigging and slammed into their raddled hull, forcing the ship to leeward as far as the protesting hawsers would allow. But the ropes held and the sea did not swamp them, though it heaved and foamed about them and hurled itself into the air in an explosion of froth and fury.

Nathan remained on deck throughout the night, huddled in his boat cloak, staring into the darkness towards the invisible breakwater. He felt that only the force of his will would maintain it there, that if he relaxed his concentration for a moment the sea would sweep it away and them with it. He felt every moan and groan of the hawsers like a man upon the rack. He spoke few words. Declined offers of sustenance or warmer clothing. In truth it was warm enough, for all the howling of the wind. Halfway through the midnight watch the carpenter came with reports of sprung timbers and eight inches of water in the well. Nathan set all hands to working at the pumps. They toiled all night.

A little after six bells in the morning watch the wind eased dramatically and then dropped away altogether. Nathan looked up at a hole in the raging clouds and knew it for the eye of the storm. It was a comfort to see a patch of clear sky and stars. A reminder that Order prevailed in some corner of the universe, if not his, and remained entirely unmoved by the unruly world below. There were those he knew that chose to blame the stars for whatever misfortunes befell them on Earth – and praised them when things went their way. Nathan was by no means free of this superstition but he was sufficient of a Christian to restrain himself from heretic prayer and merely wished them well, whatever element composed them . . . and then the black clouds wiped them from his view and Chaos resumed its tumultuous sway.

In the grey dawn they saw that the sea had broken right over Ship Island some three or four cables' lengths beyond their stern. But their own small island endured: their own little eye of the storm. It endured until a few minutes before noon, by which time they could see nothing of Ship Island beyond the small horn of the bay: just the tumultuous, victorious sea reclaiming its own.

Then before Nathan's astonished, anguished gaze the horn appeared to disintegrate and the sea came roaring through. It broke over the western tip of Turtle Island and came rushing towards them, led by a massive wave at least as tall as their broken foremast, curling at the crest. Nathan was running to the rail calling for axes, grabbing one himself and hacking at the nearest rope when it hit them. Half drowned in the scuppers, clinging to the tackle of the starboard carronade, he felt it lift them like a log and knew they had been torn from their moorings. He felt the speed of their passage through the water, felt the bows coming round to the north, had some vague notion of what was happening to his ship even as he fought for his own poor life . . .

And then they struck.

Chapter Fourteen

Marooned

———◆◆◆———

Nathan looked back from the stern of the gig as it pulled away from the shattered frigate. She looked like one of the prison hulks he had seen on the mud of the Medway, but not so homely.

He supposed he should not complain. She should not have been there at all: the waves should have broken her back, battered her to death and scattered the pieces over the Devil's Jigsaw, but that fatal surge had been the last. Nothing that followed had approached anything like the force of that single wave. It had torn a great swathe through their little breakwater, but this in itself had contributed to their survival, for if they had remained tied to the trees they would undoubtedly have been crushed by the great weight of water. Instead it had torn up the trees by the roots and hurled the ship onto the shoals about a cable's length beyond their mooring. They had passed a miserable few hours huddled on the dismasted hulk,

convinced that the next great wave would finish them –
but it never came. By first light they knew the storm was
spent, the sea heaving and pitching about them as far as
the eye could see but no longer threatening their
destruction.

Now it was almost calm and the sky a near-perfect blue
with just a few shreds of white cloud on the distant
horizon to the north. And the *Unicorn* held fast by the
bows amid the wreckage of her breakwater.

Nathan had resolved to save her if he could, though
there were those, he knew, who had already condemned
her. There was little or no tide on this side of the barrier
islands and they would never be able to kedge her off, Pym
maintained, in the soft sand, even if they possessed a boat
large enough to carry out the anchor. He and his ally
Baker advised Nathan to break her up and use her timbers
to build a smaller vessel that might ferry them to safety.
But the carpenter, Mr Lloyd, for all his head-shaking air
of gloom and despondency, had assured Nathan that the
hull was fundamentally sound and they could patch those
parts that were not. With a jury rig Nathan was confident
they could sail the ship at least as far as Pensacola in West
Florida where the Spanish had a naval dockyard of sorts.

But first they had to haul her off her present location.

They might not be able to use an anchor but Nathan
was hopeful of finding a secure enough lodging among
those few trees close to the water's edge that had survived
the late surge. Many of them had been snapped off at a
height of ten feet or so, but the roots appeared firmly
embedded and after inspecting them carefully he decided

they could take the strain, particularly if the cable was attached to one of the broken pines wedged behind three or four of the stumps growing in a more or less straight line.

It took them almost two hours to make ready but even with the entire crew heaving on the capstan-bars they could not move her.

'Very well,' Nathan told the first lieutenant. 'We will lighten ship.'

'Using what?' demanded Pym, adding quickly when he saw the look in Nathan's eye, 'Perhaps you have forgotten, sir, that we have lost the boats.'

'No, I had not forgotten, Mr Pym, but we will build a raft. In fact, we will build two rafts as there is no shortage of timber.'

The remaining hours of daylight were engaged in building them and they spent another restless night in the hull. At first light they rigged lines between ship and shore to haul their homemade rafts betwixt the two, but even with a hoist and tackle on the beach it took them the best part of the day to remove the guns and most of the stores and water. The sun was low above the sea before they were ready to try again.

And once more their efforts were in vain. Nathan kept them at it for above an hour, even after they had lost the light. He had the entire crew jumping up and down on the quarterdeck in the hope of shifting her, but there was not the slightest intimation of movement. She was stuck firm.

'In my view,' said Pym when they adjourned to the privacy of Nathan's cabin, 'we have no choice but to

abandon the vessel. The people are exhausted, sir, and I
regret to say very close to mutiny. If you will not permit us
to break up the ship, I respectfully submit that you send to
the Spanish Governor in New Orleans requesting his
prompt assistance. A fleet of five or six pirogues should be
sufficient to convey the entire ship's company to
Pensacola, where we may take ship for Port Royal.'

'Thank you, Mr Pym, I shall certainly send to Baron
Carondelet for assistance. If he is able to send us a couple
of hundred soldiers or labourers I have no doubt our
concerted efforts will haul us off the mud . . . and if they
do not, then we will do as you suggest. But I am resolved
to give it one more try.'

Pym visibly fought to control his temper. 'And in the
meantime, sir? What are we to do to keep the hands
occupied? For if they are confined here for more than a day
or two without useful employment, I fear the consequence.'

'Then we must set our minds to the problem, Mr Pym,
and between us I am assured we will contrive something
for their amusement.'

Nathan regretted this constant need to assert his
authority – and the manner that appeared to come with it
which was so alien to what he thought of as his true
character. Not for the first time he wondered if he was
suited to the business of commanding a ship of war, or
indeed any body of men, when his natural inclination was
to more solitary pursuits. He had long since come to the
conclusion that he was more suited to the life of a spy.
Like Imlay, whose absence he rather regretted.

Where *was* the man – and what was he up to? Nathan

stared out over the darkening Sound toward the invisible mainland. It was quite possible, of course, that he had become lost in the swamp, a prey to the monsters that lurked there. Possible but unlikely. Imlay was a survivor. He was alive somewhere, Nathan was sure of it, and up to no good. And yet, in a strange way he missed him.

He was aware that his doubtful authority was ebbing fast. The hands were at best sullen workers and Nathan knew they were not far from rebellion. If he did not succeed in freeing the *Unicorn* within the next day or two, he could expect serious trouble.

His immediate concern, however, was for the casualties of the recent battle. They had lost fewer men than he had feared when he first set foot on the ship: eighteen men dead, twenty-seven wounded, several of whom were not expected to live. McLeish wanted to move some of the less serious cases ashore where he considered their chances of survival were greater than in the foetid sickbay. Then, too, there was a pressing necessity to bury the dead before they grew noxious and it was clearly not possible to bury them at sea.

McLeish was one of the few people Nathan felt he could count on, but the poor man looked near dead himself. He had been on his feet in the cockpit for the best part of the two days and nights since the battle, aided by his assistant and a pair of loblolly boys. His lean features now more resembled a skull than a face and his eyes were deep pits that stared dully out upon the world. And if you looked into them, thought Nathan, you would likely see the image of Death staring back.

The first thing after breakfast, he joined Nathan in the gig to search along the shore for a suitable patch of dry land where they could throw up a tent for the wounded – and another, possibly not too far away, to bury the dead. But dry land was not much in evidence. Ship Island was become little more than a mudflat. Turtle Island, in its lee, had been spared much of the violence but it looked sorely distressed. The sea had mostly receded but it had left a great deal of mud, and the broken pines stuck up from patches of stagnant water like naked stumps in a bog.

They followed the shoreline right round the island, and close to the eastern point they found a stretch of beach rising to a stand of trees which had escaped more or less intact. This little sanctuary had attracted a fair proportion of the region's wildlife – mostly ducks and seabirds, but also a few alligators basking in the sun close to the water's edge. Although they seemed indifferent to the bird life, at least for the moment, there was no knowing how they might react to more substantial prey, but Desmarais resolved the problem by taking up the musket he had acquired after the battle with the French and despatching one of the largest with a single shot, causing it to writhe in spectacular death-throes while its companions slid with some rapidity into the sea and the entire bird population took to the air with a great agitation of wings and cries.

'Thank you, Monsieur Desmarais,' Nathan remarked dryly when the disturbance had abated somewhat.

They landed on the now deserted shore and walked back to view the corpse which was about seven or eight feet long from nose to tail, a good three feet composed entirely of mouth, jaw and teeth.

'Can it be eaten?' Nathan enquired of its killer, who was eyeing it thoughtfully and stropping the edge of his knife against his thumb.

'But of course,' Desmarais replied cheerfully, somewhat diminishing the value of this assertion by adding that it tasted very like snake.

McLeish appearing restless, they postponed further discussion of its culinary virtues and continued to the stand of trees which the doctor pronounced perfectly suited to his needs, if the crew could be prevailed upon to set up tents and dig a trench which would help to drain the ground and also serve as a latrine.

While this was accomplished Nathan returned to his cabin to write a letter to Baron Carondelet describing their present plight and begging him to send what men he could spare. Though he had spoken confidently to Pym he was by no means certain that help would be forthcoming, the governor having sufficient problems enough of his own. It took him several drafts to complete the letter to his satisfaction. Then he considered the problem of who to send with it. Reluctantly he decided it had to be Tully. Apart from anything else he was the only one of his officers who spoke sufficient French to execute the mission with any confidence and answer any subsequent questions that might arise. He sent him off in the gig with six of the hands and Joseph Bonnet as his guide – being reluctant to part with Desmarais whose expertise he had come to rely upon.

Then, with a melancholy heart, he took up *The Book of Common Prayer* and prepared for his next ordeal.

They had dug a trench on the far side of the stand of trees from McLeish's little hospital and the bodies were stitched in canvas in the traditional manner as they would have been at sea, with the last stitch of the needle through their nostrils to ensure that no mistake had been made but without the necessity of a cannonball at their feet. The people had been assembled in their divisions for the ceremony and they stood with hats off in the sun while Nathan began the ceremony.

He had never officiated at a burial service before and though he had attended many, the most recent had been at sea with all the proper formalities: the ship heaved to with her topgallant yards all a-cock-bill and her rigging all awry to signify mourning and each body placed on a mess table and covered with the ensign. At the appropriate point the captain, or chaplain if they had one, would depart from the conventional words in *The Book of Common Prayer* and intone: 'We therefore commit his body to the deep to be turned into corruption looking for the resurrection of the body when the sea shall give up her dead . . .' At which point the table would be raised and the shrouded figure slide from beneath the ensign and disappear beneath the waves.

And despite the mournful nature of the occasion there was invariably a sense of satisfaction, certainly among the hands, that their shipmates had been given a proper send-off.

There was none of that here. And though they used a

mess table and the ensign and slid each of the bodies individually into the trench they had prepared and Nathan repeated the same portentous lines for each, the ceremony was lacking in dignity. The sea did not close respectfully over the bodies and there was something pathetic and degrading in those sprawling, shrouded figures. It looked, Nathan realised with growing concern, like a pauper's grave.

'. . . we therefore commit his body to the ground: earth to earth, ashes to ashes, dust to dust . . .'

After the third or fourth occasion, as Nathan sprinkled the wet sand over the recently departed he became aware of a spirit of resentment among the living. A shuffling of feet and a muttering of voices. He distinctly heard the words: 'It is not right.' And the response: 'No, mate, it is bloody wrong.'

These phrases were not in *The Book of Common Prayer* or, so far as Nathan was aware, any of its variants.

He heard Pym's furious bellow for silence, echoed by his junior officers, but the damage was done. When the service was over Nathan made a short speech, informing the crew that he had sent for assistance and assuring them that they would shortly be sailing for Port Royal where the vessel would be refitted and they would enjoy a welcome spot of shore leave. But it did not go down well. Dismissed, the hands shuffled off with surly discontent watched with suspicion by their fuming but helpless officers.

Afterwards, they were put to work on building a palisade on the western point of the island where there were a number of fallen trees and from where they could mount a battery of guns to provide some defence against attack from the sea. It was little more than a gesture but at least it gave them something to do and provided a semblance of discipline. Then Nathan spoke to McGregor and Whiteley about their marines.

'I see no cause for immediate alarm,' he assured them, with more confidence than he felt, 'but can you trust your own men if it becomes necessary to restore order?'

McGregor looked despondent and though this was not far off his normal expression it was clear that he entertained serious doubts.

'In a conflict with the enemy they have nae equal,' he asserted, 'as I believe you have witnessed. And normally I would say they would be willing and able to maintain discipline aboard a tight-run ship o' war. But in these circumstances . . .' he indicated their present surroundings with a dismissive hand . . . 'and with men they have known since leaving Portsmouth, I doubt some o' them might prove a wee bit recalcitrant, though I cannae speak for Mr Whiteley's contingent that only came aboard in the Havana.'

'I think they may be counted upon,' said Whiteley quietly. 'They have fought in two battles under your command, sir, both of which have ended in victory, against all the odds, and their morale is reasonably high even despite our current difficulty. However, if I may make a suggestion, I think it might be wise to billet them ashore – perhaps building a small stockade close to where we have set the wounded. It would avoid any excessive fraternising with the men, especially during the hours of darkness when grievances are likely to fester and conspiracies be nurtured.'

Nathan agreed at once and the two men set off with their sergeants to find a suitable site.

Over the next few days as the stockade began to take shape the marines slept ashore under canvas and Nathan had them fetch the small arms and powder from the ship for safekeeping. It grieved him that he could not trust his own crew but he had not been their commander for more than a fortnight and why should they trust *him*: they had lost a score of men dead and their ship was wedged on a sandbank. It was clear that their discontent was growing by the day.

Pym was seriously worried and proposed a pre-emptive strike against those he considered to be the ringleaders but Nathan would not hear of it.

'It could provoke the very mutiny we fear,' he said. 'And besides, what would we do – hang them?'

It was clear from his expression that Pym did not consider this course of action beyond contemplation but he relapsed into a critical silence. The two men were now scarcely on speaking terms and to Nathan's regret most of the warrant officers seemed to have taken the first lieutenant's part. Indeed, the only men among the entire crew he felt he could count upon, in terms of personal loyalty, were Whiteley and McLeish, Maxwell possibly and Lamb, his servant Gabriel, of course, and surprisingly the Irishman Connor who appeared to have formed an attachment to him and assumed the unofficial role of bodyguard.

And then there was Desmarais, who continued to prove his worth.

The *Unicorn* being a little way offshore was not unduly troubled by mosquitoes and other stinging insects, but the first night ashore the wounded suffered greatly; hearing McLeish's complaints, the guide proposed taking the rafts over to Ship Island with a party of men and gathering certain grasses or weeds that he assured the doctor would serve as a repellent, either by being burned on a fire to make smoke or boiled up and mixed with tallow and then smeared on the exposed parts of the body. It stank to high heaven but McLeish said it seemed to work and more effectively than his own resources.

The guide also provided food for the pot, mostly fowl but supplemented by the occasional reptile. Several days after the storm the sea turtles had returned to the island in substantial numbers. The presence of humans did not seem to discourage them, despite the attentions of Desmarais – though he was selective, he said, in his execution. The creatures had been coming to the island since the dawn of time and he did not wish to encourage a change of habitat, he informed Nathan earnestly. They were the chief reason, apparently, why the Tanekshava – the first people – called it the Isle of Good Feasting.

McLeish said they were known in English as Loggerhead Turtles, adding – as a practical Scotsman as well as a naturalist – that they made an extremely nourishing soup. The first that Desmarais shot was almost four feet long and weighed over 800 pounds.

Fish, too, were plentiful. There was no shortage of rods and lines aboard the *Unicorn* and the men were detailed in parties and sent off on the rafts to the areas that Desmarais said would provide the best fishing. They mostly caught red snapper and grouper and once a swordfish. Crabs and shrimps were collected from the rocks – and oysters by the hundredweight.

This constant supply of fish and fowl, with the occasional reptile, probably kept the men from open rebellion more effectively than any employment that could be devised for them. Even so, Nathan put them to the lengthy task of dismantling the upper deck capstan and assembling it again on the shore, on the grounds that it must be easier to haul the *Unicorn* off her berth without the considerable weight of her crew aboard. He also set them to dredging a channel beneath the stern of the vessel by the simple if painstaking process of lowering buckets from the rafts and dragging them along the bottom.

But as the days went by with no word from Tully, the men became more agitated and Nathan braced himself for a confrontation. It was only a matter of time, he thought, before an order was openly disobeyed, or one of the officers abused, and then he would have to take action. The stockade, fortunately, was near completion and they had armed it with the carronades and four of the 6-pounders, pointing directly at the stricken vessel. But it would have broken Nathan's heart. And he knew he would always be remembered for it: the captain who had fired upon his own ship. In the eyes of his peers that would be more damning than firing upon his own crew.

He continued to sleep in his stern cabin at nights, even after the marines had removed to the stockade, but with Gabriel at the other side of the door with a pair of loaded pistols and his own close beside.

After ten days of sunshine the weather took a turn for the worse, and though the wind did not reach anything like the force of a gale and the waves did not disturb them, they served as a grim warning without in any way dislodging the frigate from her position in the mud. Once again Pym urged Nathan to consider breaking the ship up and using the timbers and spars to construct a vessel capable of carrying them to the mainland or even Port Royal. It would give the men something useful to do, he argued, and persuade them that they possessed the means of their own salvation, if only they maintained discipline.

But Nathan shook his head. 'Not until we have heard from Mr Tully,' he said.

But he was at a loss to explain Tully's continuing absence for it could not have taken more than a few days to make the journey to New Orleans and back in the gig, and Nathan could not believe he would tarry there without sending word. It was impossible not to fear that he had come to grief, perhaps by running into a party of rebels or hostile Indians. Indeed, it was not impossible that New Orleans itself had fallen to the French faction.

When the storm abated Nathan determined to make one more attempt to haul the frigate off, this time using the capstan they had built on the shore.

It was no more successful than the last two attempts.

But it was with a greater and more personal sense of defeat that Nathan finally called a halt to their efforts. He knew from the way the men turned away that there would be trouble.

It was not long in coming.

The men waited until they were back on the ship and safe from any immediate interference from the marines. Then, before the scandalised gaze of Mr Pym, three of the hands came aft and mounted the steps to the quarterdeck.

'That is all right, Mr Pym,' Nathan restrained him. 'I will speak with them in my cabin.'

They had removed their caps and their manner was respectful enough but Nathan saw the looks on the faces of their shipmates in the waist and knew they would not be satisfied with any common flannel. It was possible that Pym was right, he reflected, and there was no dealing with them at this stage save by punitive measures, but if it came to a fight he needed to pick the right moment and on his own terms with the marines at his back. He prevented Pym from coming down below with him but took Gilbert Gabriel as reassurance.

'Please be seated,' he instructed them, gesturing towards the table in his day cabin with Des Barres's chart still laid out upon it.

'Thankee, sir, but we would be happier standing, if it does not offend Your Honour.'

The speaker was diffident but firm. To his shame, Nathan could not put a name to him but he recognised him as one of the foretopmen – a tall individual with bony

features and a mop of tobacco-coloured curls, neither old
nor young, and though he looked like a seaman he did not
have quite the style of one in the King's service, nor the
lengthy tarred pigtail that accompanied it. A sea lawyer?
Nathan tried to summon up his memory of the man's
name and background; it was there somewhere if only he
could recall it.

'As you wish,' he said, 'but I will sit if you do not
mind.' He took his place at the table with Gabriel
glowering in the background close by the door. He did not
have his pistols in his belt but Nathan knew they would
not be far away. His own were in the drawer under the
table, and loaded.

'So what can I do for you?'

They were naturally uneasy – who would not be, with
the Angel Gabriel at his back – but the spokesman
answered briskly enough and it suddenly came to Nathan
who he was. Ringmer, or Ringwood, a Hampshire man, a
former merchant seaman taken from a homeward-bound
Indiaman shortly after the *Unicorn* had sailed from
Spithead, and possibly disposed to resent it.

'With respect, sir, the hands are of the opinion that the
ship ain't never coming off of this and that we ought to
think about using her timbers to make another, the like of
a cutter as it were . . .' He flushed at mention of this vessel
with all its connotations. 'We mean no disrespect, sir, but
we reckons we'll be stuck here forever else.'

'I appreciate your concern – Ringmer, is it not?'

He nodded, frowning; he would not like it that Nathan
had put a name to him.

'And I appreciate that we have not had a chance to get to know each other better, before the business with the Frenchman laid us aback, but you will understand that it is difficult for a captain to appear to take orders from the crew.'

'We mean to give no orders, sir.'

The others nodded vigorously.

'I know. But you see how it might look. And other captains might be disposed to resent it. And their lordships, too, were they to hear of it. However, I am prepared to take this in the nature of a friendly discussion among men who are, as it were, in the same boat, ha ha.'

They did not laugh but one of them nodded gratefully. The other two merely looked dogged.

'You know I have sent to New Orleans for assistance,' Nathan added, in a different tone, as if to take them into his confidence. 'And have every expectation of its arriving within the next day or two.'

'I'm sorry to say it, sir, but it seems to us that the gig has mislaid itself, as it were, else why have they not returned?'

'I cannot tell you that, but I am persuaded we must be patient a while longer – for the sake of the ship. She is practically new out the stocks. Do you not think we owe it to her and to the country to preserve her if we can?'

An uncomfortable shuffling silence.

'Well?'

'In point of fact, sir, she has always been something of an unlucky ship,' said Ringmer. The others nodded energetically.

'Everyone knows she is cursed, sir,' said one, 'and has been since she left Chatham.'

'You may not know it, sir, as it was before your time, but there was a skeleton found . . .'

'Of a little child . . .'

'I know all about that,' replied Nathan sharply. 'Do you think I have not read the captain's log?'

'And the missing head, sir?'

'And the missing head,' Nathan confirmed. But he could not leave it there, and besides, he perceived a small opening. 'Does it truly disturb the men?'

'Aye, sir, it does that. It disturbs them sorely. There's them that's seen it.'

Ringmer turned on the speaker. 'Stow that, Jacob Maplin. We don't want none of your old wives' tales.'

'Even so,' the fellow persisted stubbornly, 'there are them that reckon it be the cause of all our troubles and should be laid to rest one way or t'other. As is only right. An' if it don't get laid to rest it will find some way of doing so itself, for like, and take us with it.'

'We did not come here to discuss this,' snapped Ringmer with a glare at his companion.

'Nevertheless it is a valid point,' agreed Nathan, 'but I cannot see that the curse, if such it is, will be lifted if we were to leave the poor boy's head in the hull. Rather would it pursue us wherever we sailed and in whatever vessel, resolved to punish us for our iniquity in deserting it.'

'If we were to break the ship up,' proposed Ringmer cunningly, 'maybe we would find it.'

'You would like to find it? And give it a decent burial?'

A couple of nods.

'Very well. I will initiate another search.'

'We have searched already.'

'Not with the ship stable and with no other priority. We will search the hull from top to bottom. We will pump the bilges clean and disinfect her while we are about it. And I dare say we will find it and have the cleanest, sweetest-smelling ship that ever sailed into Port Royal at the end of it.'

Ringmer looked decidedly displeased but Nathan reckoned it would confuse the issue for a day or two.

As soon as they had gone he had himself poled ashore to warn McGregor and Whiteley to be on their guard. Then he went to see McLeish.

'We need a skull,' he told him. 'A child's skull.' He told him why.

'One of the ship's boys died last night,' McLeish mentioned thoughtfully. 'He lost both legs and gangrene set in. He has not been buried yet. I suppose we could boil the head and leave it out in the sun for a few hours for the ants to clean up.'

Nathan stared at him in horror. 'Good God!' he exclaimed. 'Is this your idea of a joke?'

'On the contrary, I am entirely practical. The boy has died. We can cause him no more pain. He is food for the ants whether you like it or not. He might as well do us some small service while he is about it.'

'It is unthinkable,' Nathan declared, shaking his head.

'Unthinkable, is it now?' McLeish observed him curiously. 'How is it that you can contemplate flogging a man, a living man, or hanging him or cutting him in half with a cannonball, but you cannot bring yourself to condone a simple chemical process performed upon a poor unfortunate who cannot feel a thing? And by so doing, satisfy the greater good?'

'I do not know how it is,' replied Nathan curtly. 'I only know that I can never approve such barbarous practice. We are not in Edinburgh.'

'Well, I do not know what else you are to do.'

'There is that skull in your cabin,' Nathan reminded him. 'Your monkey.'

'My monkey?'

'It bears a striking resemblance to the skull of a human child.'

'I take it you mean the infant orang-utan. From Sumatra.'

'I stand corrected. But it would answer perfectly.'

'Answer what?'

'I told you, to place in an obscure part of the hull so that some member of the crew might find it.'

'You would contemplate such a gross deception?'

'You seemed to find it perfectly acceptable if we were to use the skull of your recently deceased ship's boy, boiled in vinegar and fed to the ants.'

McLeish considered. 'And you would bury it – the head of an orang-utan – in the pretence that it is the head of a human child and pronounce the Christian burial service over it, from *The Book of Common Prayer*, in the full knowledge that it is the head of a beast?'

'In the interests of saving the ship, I would.'

McLeish shook his head sadly.

'And if you are concerned for your loss,' Nathan assured him, 'when we are done you may dig it up and restore it to your belongings.'

'I am astounded. I am deprived of speech.'

They began the search at first light. Each division took a quarter of the ship and Nathan offered a sovereign to whoever found the object.

It occupied them for most of the forenoon.

Then when it was almost time to pipe the hands to dinner, a solemn procession came aft led by one of the older seamen bearing the pride of the doctor's collection in both hands as if it were a birthday cake. His name was Jennings, Pym informed him – sailmaker's mate.

'Well done, Jennings,' Nathan congratulated him, taking the skull off him before anyone else could get a look at it in the clear light of day, and signalling Gabriel to give him the promised reward as a distraction. 'Where did you find it?'

'In the sailmaker's stores, sir,' said the fellow in an awed tone, 'under a pile of old canvas. It had been there all this time and none of us never knowing of it.'

'Well, well, and you can see the teethmarks of the rats, I fancy, in the bone.' Nathan bore it away before they could get a closer look.

They buried it with all due ceremony close to the trench where they had lain those slaughtered in battle, a carved wooden cross announcing that here lay the mortal remains of John English of Chatham, Kent, died 1794, and Nathan read the same solemn words as for the others;

but this time, except in some notable cases, the hands evinced every sign of satisfaction.

Nathan studiously avoided McLeish's eye as they returned to the ship for dinner. They had barely stepped aboard when they heard the shout of, 'Sail ho!' from the lookout in the bows.

But it was not a sail. It was a fleet.

Chapter Fifteen

The Price of Freedom

————◆————

'The *Lion* is come,' declared the Baron de Carondelet from the prow of the leading gunboat, sweeping off his hat with a theatrical flourish: 'the *Unicorn* to save.'

The reference was obscure but Nathan expressed his heartfelt thanks.

'I could do no less after the service you have given to His Most Catholic Majesty,' the governor assured him. 'And see, I have brought you my little fleet.'

Riding on their oars in the channel between the stranded frigate and Turtle Island were four slim galleys each with a 32-pounder in the bow followed by about a score of pirogues and other craft. Each of them loaded to the gunwales with men.

'Only tell us how we may be of assistance,' the governor proposed, 'and it shall be done.'

'Perhaps Your Excellency would care to come aboard,'

Nathan invited him, 'and we will discuss the problem in more comfort.'

'Comfort?' Carondelet repeated archly, raising his equine countenance to view the stricken vessel. Had he possessed a lorgnette Nathan was persuaded he would have used it. 'Is it safe?'

'Perfectly safe,' Nathan assured him. 'It is as steady as a rock and as incapable of movement.'

Tully came aboard ahead of him. 'I am sorry we could not be here sooner,' he told Nathan, 'but His Excellency was away from New Orleans and they told me nothing could be done in his absence. I found him at the mouth of the river, fighting the French.'

Nathan raised a brow. 'Cajuns?'

'And French marines that had been landed earlier – by the *Virginie*.'

Further discussion of this encounter was prevented by the arrival of the governor and his entourage, which included their old acquaintance of the swamp, Antonio de Escavar, in rather more finery and considerably better spirits than when Nathan had last seen him. Indeed, all the Spaniards appeared mightily pleased with themselves.

'We have been fighting the Devil,' the governor informed him cheerfully. 'And have been entirely victorious.' The Spanish fort near the mouth of the Mississippi had come under attack, he explained, and he had been obliged to go to its assistance with his gunboats.

'The *Lion*, the *Panther*, the *Crocodile* and the *Holy Ghost*,' he told Nathan proudly. 'The *Lion* is my flagship.'

Nathan expressed his admiration of the Spanish flotilla

and congratulated the governor on his victory.

'Had I been able to convey them to the Rigolets we would have had none of that nonsense on Coquille Island,' the governor assured him, 'but they are normally confined to the Mississippi. However, when your officer found us in the Delta I lost no time in leading them to your rescue. And here we are.'

He had brought 200 of his soldiers with him, he informed Nathan, and 300 African slaves: 'on the assumption that there is heavy work to be done.'

Nathan kept his face carefully composed but his heart sank. He had been brought up as a child to abhor slavery. It was the one thing on which his mother and father had been entirely in agreement, and from the moment she had set foot in England Lady Catherine had thrown herself wholeheartedly into the anti-slavery movement. For a while indeed her house in St James's had become a battle centre of the campaign and a refuge *'for those that would not be seen in Clapham'*, as Lady Catherine charmingly put it, and William Wilberforce had been a regular visitor there until he and Nathan's mother fell out over his continuing friendship with William Pitt.

Nathan could not abide the notion of using slave labour to free the *Unicorn*, but if he refused the offer of assistance on the grounds of conscience the governor would be deeply offended. It would be seen as a diplomatic affront: an offence against His Most Catholic Majesty, no less. Carondelet would take himself off in high dudgeon to write a scathing report to his seniors in Madrid – with a copy to the Spanish Minister in London

– and the *Unicorn* and her entire crew would be left to rot.

Nathan wrestled with his conscience. Slavery was repugnant to him but it was sanctioned by the law, it thrived in the British colonies and it maintained the quality of life enjoyed by many in Europe and the Americas. The Church then spoke in its favour; the Africans themselves practised it widely and the Arabs were its greatest proponents. Besides, what choice did he have?

Hang it, he thought, I cannot do it.

He was considering the most diplomatic way of framing his objections when an idea came to him. Or rather the germ of an idea, for he needed time to develop it. But it restrained him from his immediate impulse and he listened with apparent attention as the governor explained his own concerns.

'I am reluctant to put the military to hauling upon ropes,' he said, 'for it does not become fighting men to indulge in manual labour. I do not include seamen in this, of course,' he added hastily, 'as it is part of their normal duty, but your Spanish soldier is possessed of a . . . how shall I put it? . . . a certain *pride* that makes him ill suited to menial work. In short, he is quite useless. I am persuaded the Africans will prove more than equal to the task. Many of them are Yoruba and of impressive physique, as you will find.'

When they returned above deck they saw that the boats were now drawn up on the shore of Turtle Island and the Africans were squatting in a large group under the watchful eye of the soldiers. They appeared entirely indifferent to their fate, or their surroundings, but Nathan was relieved to see that at least they were not chained: possibly because there was nowhere to run to.

'I propose to haul entirely from the shore,' he informed his officers, 'using our own people on the capstan and the governor's hauling upon ropes at each side. But it is a question of where we attach them.'

After consulting with Mr Lloyd it was decided to attach one hawser to the lower deck capstan and wrap the other right round the hull and through each of the hawse-holes, with the Africans heaving upon each end from the shore. In addition Tully proposed they bring back one of the guns and mount it in the bows, firing it at the precise time they commenced hauling in the hope that the shock through the timbers might loosen the vessel from the sand.

'I hope you will not take it amiss if I beg the officers to join me at the capstan-bars,' said Nathan, 'for we are all in the same boat, as it were.'

The expression had grown stale in the repetition – and it had been none too fresh when he first used it – and the smiles of his officers were at best perfunctory, but none could object when their captain was so clearly willing to put himself to the task. He only wished it would shame the governor and his soldiers into overcoming their repugnance of 'menial work' but it was not to be anticipated.

The preparations took them above two hours and it was past six bells in the afternoon watch before they were ready to begin. Nathan took off his coat, folded it neatly and laid it on the ground as if for a prizefight or a game of cricket. Then he rolled up his sleeves, rubbed a little sand in the palms of his hands, and took his place at the capstan.

A final look about him to make sure everyone was ready, then he raised his hand for the benefit of the ship's gunner who had personally taken charge of the 18-pounder in the bows . . . and let it fall.

A collective grunt from the men as they put their weight into it. The gun roared . . .

And . . .

Nothing.

They might as well have tried to move a mountain.

Nathan's feet scrabbled in the sand as he leaned his body into the hard, unyielding timber. He was already soaked in sweat. Groans from the men as of those upon the rack or suffering the agonies of constipation. Nathan laid his cheek against the wood and looked toward the Africans to his left. Carondelet had been right about their physique. Their muscles bulged as they heaved upon the rope, leaning their bodies almost horizontally into the sand, driving themselves on with deep, almost ritualistic grunts. There were soldiers shouting at them in Spanish and by God, one of them had a whip . . . Nathan felt close to despair. He would have to call a halt to it and there would be no more diverting the men with monkey skulls. Then, through the pounding in his ears he heard the roar of the gun again and . . . a jolt. He almost slipped in the sand. Had the bar slipped in its housing; had the fibres of the cable parted? Another jolt. By Christ, she was moving. Or something was. No, the ship was moving. Slowly at first, an inch at a time, but then faster, further . . . and now it began:

'*I love a maid across the water . . .*
Aye, aye, roll and GO!'

The savage stamp on the word *go* lacked the impact of a stamp on a wooden deck, but Nathan's heart was bursting with emotion; he could have wept. And now the fiddler leaped up – the smallest man in the crew – up on to the drumhead with the fiddle to his chin, a little imp of a man, tapping out the rhythm with his foot.

'*Sally's teeth are white and pearly,*
Aye, aye, roll and GO!
Her eyes are blue, her hair is curly,
Spend my money on Sally Brown.'

It was not a familiar shanty – Nathan had first heard it when they weighed anchor in the Havana – and McLeish had told him it was a song the crew had picked up in Jamaica.

'*Oh, Sally Brown I had to leave you,*
Aye, aye, roll and GO!
Trust me I'll not deceive you,
Spend my money on Sally Brown.'

And from along the shore the song of the Africans: the deep, vibrant sounds in their own tongue as they hauled on the rope – but it was not a song of joy.

She was free! They were all on their knees and the *Unicorn* was floating free. A great cheer from the men, the hands and the jollies as one, and they threw up their hats and capered about the shore while the Africans collapsed in the sand with their heads between their knees. And then Nathan led the charge to the sea. He plunged in fully clothed, not waiting for the raft, delighting in the wonderful freshness of the water, striking out for the ship as she floated in mid-channel. He had left a skeleton crew aboard to let go the stern anchor so she would not drift on to another shoal, and they threw him a line and hauled him up the side.

'Well done, Mr Clyde!' he shouted up to the gunner in the bows. 'I swear it was your gun that did the trick.'

'Aye, sir,' grinning from ear to ear. 'I reckon it may've helped a bit.'

And for the first time since he had come aboard Nathan felt they bore some resemblance to a crew and that he was a part of it.

But there was a great deal of work to be done before she was a ship again.

'I am glad to have been of service.' Carondelet bowed when Nathan came to thank him. 'It is a small return of the debt I owe you. And did I not say my Africans were equal to the task?'

'We could not have done it without them, Your Excellency.' He hesitated a moment. 'I do not suppose they are for sale?'

Carondelet looked at him sharply.

'I mean no offence, Your Excellency,' Nathan assured him, 'but as you will have observed, we are desperately undermanned and I thought to ease the situation. But I should not have been so presumptuous.'

'Not at all, Captain. Why should I be offended? Any more than if you expressed a desire to purchase one of my horses? No, I am only surprised that you should countenance the use of slaves aboard a ship of His Britannic Majesty's Navy.'

'It is unusual, I agree, but I do not believe it is expressly forbidden in the regulations. In dire need we sometimes resort to pressing free-born Englishmen into the service,' he added with a straight face.

'And even Americans, I have heard.'

This was true.

'Well, the only offence is in proposing to pay for them when I am still in your debt. You must permit me to make you a gift. How many would you like?'

Nathan protested that he could not possibly prevail upon His Excellency's generosity in such a matter; the debt had been paid in full.

'You have your fort; I have my ship,' he insisted.

The governor gave in with a surprising alacrity. It soon became clear why.

'They are valued at four hundred Spanish dollars per man,' he was informed by the purser Mr McIvor, who had been given the task of negotiating the price with one of the governor's officials. 'That is in silver dollars, or pieces of eight as we call them in England.'

'How much is that in English money?' Nathan enquired with a worried frown. He had an idea it was rather a lot.

'Well, the rate of exchange varies considerably but we have agreed four shillings and sixpence to the dollar, which makes . . .' he glanced into his notebook . . . 'ninety pounds per man.'

'Good grief! For a slave?'

'That is the current price in the slave market at the Havana. It is a little more, he tells me, in New Orleans, but he is prepared to give us the benefit of the doubt, as it were.'

'I had no idea it was so much.'

'The price is a little higher than it was because of the war, but when you consider you are buying the services of a prime fieldhand for life – the price of a woman or a child would be much more modest, unless, of course, the woman was handsome – it may be considered a bargain. I believe a farmhand in Sussex can cost almost two shillings a day, at least in the summer months. If your slave lives for two years you will have broke even, though there is the cost of keeping him, of course – but then you can always sell him on, often at a considerable profit.'

'Thank you, McIvor, I will bear that in mind.'

He was making his own calculations. He had little more than £100 of his own money aboard the *Unicorn* but the Admiralty had provided him with £2,000 in gold sovereigns for the purposes of 'intelligence' and whatever emergencies might arise in the course of his more clandestine activities. He entertained serious doubts as to whether the clerks at the Admiralty would countenance spending it on slaves, but this was an argument he could have at a later date. If it came to it, he would have to recompense them from his prize money – the prize money he had offered to his mother. He felt sure she would understand.

The entire amount at his disposal would buy him thirty men. At best it was but a salve to his conscience.

In the event McIvor was able to obtain a considerable discount for gold and a further reduction if Nathan agreed to choose the men by lot, so that he did not pick the most powerfully built.

'How does that work?' he demanded with suspicion.

'Well, say we agree to buy thirty. A number of stones are put in an enclosed jar. Thirty of them are marked with a cross. Those that pick them out become yours.'

'I see.' He was become a slave-dealer. 'Very well. Make it so.'

The final price worked out at £68 per slave. Nathan watched them come aboard the *Unicorn* where the crew had already begun the task of fitting a jury rig.

'Am I to put them to work, sir?' enquired Mr Pym with a grim look. 'Or are they to be treated as supercargo?'

'I will speak to them,' said Nathan.

This was the first difficulty.

'Apparently they understand some Spanish,' McIvor told him. 'Command words, for the most part. For their normal discourse they converse in their native tongue and there is a form of patois, based I believe on the French, but it is impenetrable to most Frenchmen.'

In the event one of them spoke passable French and Nathan chose him as an interpreter for the others.

'What is your name?' he asked him.

'I am called Jorge, master.'

'You do not call me master,' Nathan informed him. 'You may call me sir.' It was to be hoped he appreciated the distinction. This was going to be difficult.

'Very well, Jorge. Now listen to me. I have bought your freedom, do you understand me? For you and your fellows.'

Jorge regarded him without expression.

'I have bought you into His Britannic Majesty's Navy. You are now a servant of His Britannic Majesty, King George, of England. George. That is the same name as Jorge.'

'Yes, master.'

'Sir.'

'Yes, sir.'

'Very good. While you are aboard this ship you will be rated as landsmen and paid . . .' he made a swift calculation . . . 'about five Spanish *reales* a day. When we reach Jamaica – which is an island owned by King George about a thousand miles from here – you will be released and I will give each of you what you are owed in wages and a certificate to say that you are now freed men.'

There was understanding now in the man's eyes, but also suspicion. Nathan could not blame him.

'In the meantime, however, as servants of King George – as are we all – you will be expected to do your share of the work aboard ship.'

But what work were they to do? And how in God's name were they to be given their orders, shown where to berth, how to get food from the galley – a thousand things he had not thought of when he had conceived his plan. He supposed they could do the usual work of a landsman if they were shown how, but every single order would have to be relayed through Jorge – and who was to do it, given that Jorge would have to be spoken to in French? Nathan could not be expected to do it himself, nor would he have the time.

Then he remembered Tierney – the Channel Islander Tully had found on Coquilles Island. Until they reached Jamaica he could act as Jorge's mentor – or slave driver, for Nathan did not suppose the work they would be doing would differ very greatly from what they had done before, save that they would be paid for it.

'If you please, sir . . .'

'Mr Lamb?'

'Mr Pym's compliments, sir, and there is a Spanish gentleman wishing to speak with you.'

It was Escavar with a summons from the governor who was about to take his leave and wished to have a private word aboard the *Lion*. Nathan had himself rowed over in the gig which had now been restored to him.

'I must return to New Orleans,' Carondelet informed him, 'but before I go I have news of Mr Imlay.'

Nathan braced himself.

'When we broke the siege of Fort San Felipe we took a number of prisoners – Cajun rebels and French regular soldiers: marines, landed by the *Virginie*.'

Nathan declined to mention that Tully had already told him so. He assumed the marines had been landed in the Delta shortly before the *Virginie* headed back to Ship Island – and her encounter with the *Unicorn*.

'Among them was your Mr Imlay.'

Nathan expressed his astonishment. He did not have to feign it. 'But how could he have got from Coquilles Island to the mouth of the Mississippi? It is above a hundred miles, across a swamp.'

'I assume he employed the services of one of the Cajuns as a guide. And he could have travelled most of the way by river. However, it does suggest that he was well acquainted with the French intentions before arriving on these shores – unless he ran into them by accident, as he declares.'

'You have spoken with him?'

'I have indeed. He maintains that he became lost during the engagement on Coquilles Island and was making for the Delta in the hope of finding you again when he was taken prisoner by the French.'

Nathan frowned. 'You believe him?'

The governor gave him a look. 'During my time in New Orleans I have met some of the greatest rogues upon the face of the earth,' he confided. 'And in my opinion Mr Imlay would be perfectly at ease among them.'

'Where is he now?'

'I imagine he is on his way to Hispaniola.' He corrected himself, 'I should say Saint Domingue for they are bound for the French part of the island where the Revolutionists are spreading liberty, equality and fraternity at the point of the bayonet. I sent him there in a Charleston trader, with those French nationals that survived our encounter.'

Nathan was stunned.

'And may I ask, Your Excellency, the reason for this decision?'

Carondelet sighed. 'I did not know what else to do with them. In the case of the French marines, they are prisoners of war. I am bound by certain conventions to either house them in a fitting manner until the end of hostilities which I am by no means anxious to do, to exchange them for Spanish prisoners of war or to return them under parole to the territory of France. I am unsure who is presently running Saint Domingue but I am perfectly prepared to concede that it is French territory for the purposes of this transaction. As for Imlay,' another sigh, 'he is a citizen of the United States. Indeed, I have reason to believe he is an American agent, though they have found it convenient in the past to disown him and doubtless will do so again. But I want no trouble with the Americans. I had rather send him to the French. Of course, had I known at the time of your current situation I would have brought him to you, but I did not know of it. Your officer did not arrive until the day after Mr Imlay had been sent on his way.'

'I see.' Nathan supposed he should be grateful. What would he have done – put him in irons? 'You say you believe him to be an American agent . . .'

Carondelet observed him shrewdly. 'I imagine you know a great deal more about Mr Imlay than you are at liberty to reveal,' he announced. 'And so you will understand that I am similarly compromised.'

'But you said . . . I am sorry, Your Excellency, but you implied he was in the service of the French.'

'Yes. And doubtless he is also in the service of the British from time to time. But it is my belief that his first loyalty is to the United States. Provided, of course, that it is in his own interests.'

Carondelet stood up. 'Now I must be on my way.' He glanced through the window of his cabin in the stern of the gunboat to where the *Unicorn* lay in her new berth. 'I trust I leave you in reasonable shape.'

It would be a while before they were in anything like reasonable shape but they were already hauling up the new mainmast.

'Will you take her back to the Havana?' enquired the governor. 'Because if you are, I will avail myself of your services as a courier to the captain-general.'

'I am sorry to disoblige Your Excellency, but I had determined to make for Port Royal in Jamaica and deliver my own report to the commander-in-chief.'

'Very well. It is of no consequence. I wish you God speed.' He extended his hand. 'If you are fast enough, you may catch up with Mr Imlay. In which case, you must be sure to give him my regards.'

Chapter Sixteen

The Sea of Sirens

———◆———

Port Royal, Jamaica: the most important British base in the Caribbean – and scarcely a ship of war in sight. In fact, the only one Nathan could see from the windows of the governor's mansion was French – the privateer *Atalante*, of eight guns, which had been brought in as a prize after coming off worse in an encounter with the *Antelope* packet in the Windward Passage. If he leaned out of the window he would just be able to see the *Unicorn*, or rather her masts – her *new* masts – above the cluster of merchant shipping moored in and around the North Docks. She would soon be ready for sea and he was aware that his present summons might be to receive some instruction as to her future – and his own. There had been no definite news of the *Virginie* since his encounter with her in Ship Island; it was possible, of course, that she had foundered during the hurricane. It was also possible that the *Antelope* had brought orders for him from Admiral Ford in Port-au-Prince.

Brisk footsteps announced the return of the young subaltern who had left him kicking his heels on the landing. His Excellency was sorry to have kept him waiting, he declared coldly, and was now ready to receive him. The fellow's manner suggested to Nathan that his star was not considered to be in the ascendant by those lesser nebulae that orbited about the august presence of the acting governor.

General Williamson was seated at his desk, framed by a somewhat larger view of the harbour than Nathan had been afforded from the landing. He did not stand when Nathan entered but looked up wearily. It had been several weeks since their last encounter and Nathan was shocked at the change in him. As acting governor of Jamaica and commander-in-chief of His Majesty's forces in the region he had a heavy burden of responsibility and it appeared to have aged him cruelly, unless he was prey to one of those obscure tropical diseases that had wasted many a governor before him. For the past few months he had been preoccupied with the situation in Saint Domingue where a rebellion among the African slaves – partly inspired by the Revolutionists in Paris – had caused the French planters to cede the colony to the British in return for their support.

Saint Domingue was the richest colony in the Caribbean: the 'Pearl of the Antilles'. It produced more than half the sugar and coffee consumed in Europe, more than all of Britain's West Indian colonies combined, and General Williamson had stripped Jamaica of most of its defences to claim it for King George. But after some initial success in seizing Port-au-Prince, the expedition had suffered a series of reverses. Yellow fever had decimated the British forces on land and sea, and the rebels – under their leader Toussaint L'Ouverture – had proved far more capable than Williamson or his commanders in the field had anticipated. In recent months the rebels had captured a number of small ports along the west coast which were being used as a base by French and American privateers, and were ravaging allied shipping in the Windward Passage. Nathan was half expecting to be asked for his assistance in curbing these mercenaries, and although he was officially under Admiralty orders he would have had difficulty in refusing such a direct request from the governor.

But the general, it appeared, had other concerns.

'We have a problem in Cuba,' he announced after a perfunctory greeting, waving Nathan to a chair.

Nathan inclined his head politely, anticipating some difficulty with the Spanish authorities – and indeed, this was partly the case – but it was far more serious than a diplomatic spat and of far greater import to him personally.

'I have received an official complaint from the captain-general regarding the activities of a nest of pirates presently operating on the southern coast of Cuba that are said to be British seamen – formerly of His Britannic Majesty's ship *Unicorn*.' He surveyed Nathan coldly as if it was his fault. 'Your mutineers, it would appear.'

He adjusted his spectacles to consult the document on the desk before him. 'About a month ago they seized upon a British vessel in the Old Bahama Channel, a slaver: the *Marie-Anne* of Liverpool, bound for the Havana. She carried eight guns but they took her at her moorings under cover of darkness, boarding her from small boats and a cutter – *your* cutter, it would appear. You frown, sir. Do you dispute it?'

'I beg your pardon, sir. It is the name of the slaver – the *Marie-Anne*, did you say, of Liverpool?'

'Is that significant?'

'Probably not. But it sounds familiar . . .' Then he had it: the vessel Pym had entrusted with a despatch for the British consul in the Havana.

'The assailants included a number of maroons,' the governor continued. 'Escaped slaves and other riff-raff who had found refuge on the islands of Jardines del Rey and joined forces with your mutineers.'

The use of the personal pronoun might be considered objectionable in this instance but it was probably not worth the effort of a protest.

'Might I enquire sir, but how is this known? That is to say, how we came to have report of the incident.'

'Twelve of the crew were taken prisoner but later released on to one of the islands, whence they made their way to the Havana. They say many of their attackers spoke English with an Irish accent and several spoke Gaelic among themselves.' Williamson bent his head over the papers. 'They describe the leader as being a tall, red-haired rogue with a scar on his cheek.' He looked up and surveyed Nathan over his spectacles. 'Very like the description of this O'Neill that your first lieutenant reports as having led the mutiny on the *Unicorn*. And another was wearing the uniform of a British naval officer – I imagine this would be Keane, your master's mate.'

'And may I ask, sir, when this occurred?'

'On the night of September twenty-sixth . . .' reading from the document . . . 'the survivors being held prisoner for several weeks and finally reaching the Havana on November seventh.'

Two days after Nathan had left.

'Since when they have taken to flying the black flag and have established their hunting grounds in the Sea of Sirens.'

Another name that struck a chord but for the moment Nathan could not place it, unless it was from his distant studies of the Classics. But it seemed to trigger more of an alarm than some memory of his schooldays.

The governor heaved himself from his chair and crossed to a large wall chart adjacent to his desk. He indicated a large indentation, or gulf, on the southern coast of Cuba.

'The Sea of Sirens, so called because of the great number of islands, rocks and hidden shoals, only a small number of which are marked on the chart. It is, as you see, conveniently close to the Windward Passage and on the direct route for shipping from Europe to the Spanish Main, which is presumably why the villains chose it, as have many pirates in the past. This is where they have made their base.' He placed his finger on a long, narrow peninsula about halfway along the eastern edge of the gulf. 'The peninsula of Serpiente. You see that small bay, or lagoon, on the furthest tip, almost like a mouth? It is *Boca del Serpiente*. The Mouth of the Serpent. A traditional haunt of pirates since the days of Drake, I am told. Indeed, there is a fort they have seized there – Fort Felipe – that was built not long after Drake paid a visit to the region. Somewhat run down since then, I am told. However it had, until recently, a small garrison of regular Spanish soldiers and up to a dozen cannon – 12- and 18-pounders. The captain-general says they were taken by surprise. He says your mutineers have made common cause with the maroons of the Sierrra Maestra who have had the impudence to declare a republic, calling themselves the Army of Lucumi. The captain-general is, as you may imagine, somewhat alarmed at the prospect of its becoming a rallying point for all the slaves in Cuba – not unreasonably, given that they now have a fort, an eight-gun sloop and the makings of an army. All they appear to be lacking is a sufficiency of small arms and powder.'

He returned to his desk and sank heavily back into his chair with a sigh.

'I need hardly stress that with the current situation in Saint Domingue, the last thing we need is a full-blown slave revolt in Cuba. The captain-general points out that as the instigators of the rebellion are British seamen, it is incumbent upon us to do something about it, particularly as Serpiente is a good deal closer to Jamaica than it is to the Havana.' The Governor observed him with a jaundiced eye. 'The *Unicorn* is almost ready for sea, I understand?'

'The repairs will be completed in the next day or two. I would like to put the new spars to the test of a full press of sail but other than that, yes, she will be ready for sea – but I had hoped to continue my search for the *Virginie* . . .'

'Quite so. However, as we have no knowledge of her present whereabouts – or indeed, whether she survived the hurricane in the Gulf – I am of the opinion that your clear and present duty is to put a stop to the activities of these pirates, the former members of your crew, the murderers of Captain Kerr. Do you not agree?'

'That has always been my intention, Your Excellency, once I had dealt with the *Virginie*. Indeed, those were the instructions of their lordships.'

'Yes, well, it has now become a matter of some urgency, as I am sure their lordships would agree. And I am also sure you can put your new rigging to the test on the journey to the Sea of Sirens. I can let you have a pilot who knows the region well – an Englishman who has lived here for many years. Also a gentleman who will be able to advise you on the situation regarding the Army of Lucumi. He is Spanish, a Spanish cleric, but I am assured that he speaks good English and has travelled extensively in Cuba, indeed throughout the Caribbean.'

Nathan said nothing, but his experience of Imlay had nurtured a prejudice against advisers, and gentlemen advisers especially.

The governor sat and fished around among the papers on his desk.

'There is another matter.' Something in his voice

alerted Nathan to the possibility that he had been keeping the worst news to the last. 'You are aware that your reports on the encounter with the *Virginie* and the expedition to Coquille Island were sent to Admiral Ford in Port-au-Prince, together with the officers' logs and what other documents appeared relevant . . . Well, I have now received a reply from the admiral by way of the *Antelope*.' He cleared his throat; had difficulty in meeting Nathan's eye. 'I regret to inform you that he is strongly critical of your decision to strip the *Unicorn* of half her crew – and all her marines – leaving the ship almost defenceless within striking distance of a heavily armed enemy. Indeed, he describes it as madness.'

Nathan felt the blood drain from his face. His body had gradually stiffened into attention.

'Although you are under the direct orders of the Admiralty he feels it incumbent upon him to deliver a severe reprimand and to make his feelings known to their lordships in his next despatch.'

General Williamson looked up from his papers. 'I find I am in agreement with the admiral's opinion on this matter and must, regrettably, add my own reprimand to his. Do you have anything to say?'

Nathan struggled to control his temper. 'Only, sir, that we had no intimation that the *Virginie* was in striking distance at the time, and that I took only a third of the hands on the expedition, not the one half that is reported . . . And my reasons for doing so were that otherwise, the fort would almost certainly have fallen to the rebels – and with it, very likely, the entire province –

with dire consequences for the Americas and for the war in Europe, as I was advised by Mr Imlay.'

'Well, as to Mr Imlay, it appears he was no more to be relied upon than—' But he thought better of saying more. 'And whatever your reasons, I cannot but agree with Admiral Ford that your decision to strip the *Unicorn* of even a third of her crew to aid a few Spanish colonists was rash in the extreme.'

'And yet, with respect, sir, you have stripped this entire colony of its defences in order to aid French colonists in Saint Domingue.' He should not have said it. He was wrong and he knew it. A good officer would have accepted the rebuke with stoic silence. But he could not help himself. He was not a good officer.

The governor had gone a shade of crimson. 'You dare to make such a comparison, sir – to hold *me* culpable!'

'I merely point out the similarity—'

'Shut your damned mouth, sir. How dare you speak to me in such a manner! By God, sir, I could have you dismissed the service. Indeed, I have a good mind to have you clapped in irons.' He flung a hand in the direction of the window and the harbour. 'I might have "stripped the entire colony of its defences", sir, but I can still find officers who could do a better job than you have – Lieutenant Pym for one.'

Nathan seethed at the injustice – and yet he was a damn fool to have spoken. He stood stiffly to attention, gazing at a point a little above the governor's head.

'I beg your pardon, sir. It was a vain, shallow remark and I deeply regret it. I can only request the opportunity to make amends by bringing the murderers of Captain Kerr to justice.'

'Indeed. Yes. Quite.' But he had begun to bluster and his hands flapped like the wings of some flightless bird. 'And you *shall* make amends, sir, believe me. You will bring me this, this . . . all of them, their heads on a plate. Or I will have yours, do you hear me, sir?'

'Yes, sir.'

'Yes, sir. Now get out.'

Chapter Seventeen

The American Agent

There had been the ghost of a suspicion in Nathan's mind when the governor had spoken of a 'Spanish cleric' but he had dismissed it as groundless — until he saw the hooded figure seated in the boat approaching from Kingston — and even then he could not be certain until the man stepped aboard the *Unicorn* and threw back his voluminous cowl to reveal the ascetic features of the monk he had last seen in the Seminary of San Carlos and San Ambrosio in the Havana.

'Brother Ignatius,' said Nathan dryly.

'I hope I am welcome,' said the cleric with a thin smile but a twinkle in his dark eyes.

'You are very welcome,' Nathan assured him — and was somewhat surprised to find he meant it. 'Though I fear you are among heretics.'

'We are a tolerant Order,' the monk replied with a small and possibly mocking bow.

Nathan left Pym to the practical task of getting the remaining supplies aboard – he was, after all, a practical man who enjoyed the confidence of his superiors – and conducted Brother Ignatius to the privacy of his cabin.

'I do not think we have the exact ingredients for a *mojito*,' he apologised. 'We have large quantities of rum, of course, though of a dark and viscous nature, and as we are a British ship, a plenitude of limes but not, I fear, the mint.'

'It is not the same without the mint,' the monk pointed out.

'I thought you would say that. One wonders how Sir Francis Drake managed to lay his hands on it.'

'Probably the same way he laid his hands on every other object that he came upon: by stealing it from someone else.'

Nathan smiled tolerantly. 'Whereas the King of Spain had so profound a respect for the property of others he removed all their gold to Madrid to safeguard it for them. A little wine, perhaps?'

'If I am not keeping you from your duties.'

Gabriel drifted off to raid the late Captain Kerr's dwindling supply.

They composed themselves contentedly upon the cushioned lockers of the stern window with its splendid view of Green Bay and Salt Pond Hill and the whole magnificent coastline down to Alligator Point.

'I will not ask how you are come to be in Jamaica,' Nathan assured him, 'for that would be impertinent in me, but I must enquire if you are officially in the service of

His Britannic Majesty, if only for this voyage, so that you might be included in the division of the spoils, as it were, should any be forthcoming.'

'I am in the service of God and my Church,' replied the monk mildly, 'and as to any division of spoils, unhappily I am sworn to a vow of poverty, though a small donation to the Franciscan Order would not be refused.'

'So God and His Britannic Majesty are on the same side in this war?'

'It is unusual, I agree – but yes, it would seem so, for the time being. As we face a common enemy.'

'Satan? Or the French?'

'You are splitting hairs. At least while the French pursue their current policies with regard to the Church of Rome.'

Gabriel returned with the wine. Nathan raised his glass.

'Well – let us drink to their confusion.'

'And the blessing on those that confound them.' The monk drank with satisfaction and raised the bottle to the light. 'An excellent Bordeaux. Seventeen eighty-three was, I believe, a very good year. Your own choice?'

'I regret not. I know very little of wines. It was in the stock of our late, lamented captain.'

'Ah yes. Whom we are about to avenge.'

'Let us hope so. You are to advise me on the Army of Lucumi, I am told.'

'Really?' The monk raised his thin brows. 'I fear someone must have taken my customary loquaciousness for knowledge. What was it you wished to know?'

'Well, an assessment of their number and disposition would be helpful, along with an inventory of the weapons at their disposal and an opinion of their ability to use them.'

'There you have me,' said the monk, shaking his head. 'I am an innocent in such matters.'

Nathan regarded him with a curious smile. 'Perhaps, then, it is as a spiritual adviser that you have been attached to me.'

'Do you *need* spiritual advice?'

'Very probably. But I have been exposed to so many heresies, it would only depress you.' He frowned. 'Lucumi? Now I think on it, is *that* not a heresy?'

'It is. Sometimes known as Santeria, the worship of the saints, and widespread among those of African descent. However, there are those in the priesthood that are inclined to tolerance, provided it poses no threat to the Roman religion and its adherents continue to observe the approved forms of worship. The Army of Lucumi may provoke a change of view.'

'Do *you* consider them a threat?'

The monk considered. 'It is a little early to say. Certainly, given what has happened in Hispaniola, one must be on one's guard.' He lapsed into a brooding silence, staring into his glass, but just as Nathan was about to speak he looked up and said: 'I am opposed to slavery, by the way. Probably as much as your Mr Wilberforce. But what has happened in Hispaniola – in both the French and Spanish parts of the island – is gross beyond imagining. What the whites have suffered is nothing to what the blacks will suffer – and are suffering – in retaliation. And were I myself black, I believe I would be wary of the promises of those that have been sent from France to stir the slaves into rebellion. The moment they are rid of the Spanish and the English, and the tricolour is flying in Port-au-Prince and the people of France are clamouring for their coffee and their sugar, there will be as much liberty, equality and fraternity as there was before – or there is in Paris now – and Toussaint L'Ouverture will be one of the first to know it.'

'That may well be the case, but I must be honest with you: my prime concern is with the mutineers. I have neither the desire nor the means to crush a slave revolt in Cuba.'

'Even if the French become involved?'

'Is there a danger of that?'

'A very great danger. In fact, I should not be surprised if Commodore Lafitte and your friend Mr Imlay were not discussing the opportunities at this very moment in the stern cabin of the *Virginie*.'

Nathan considered him carefully. He was aware that the monk would be telling him a mere fraction of what he knew.

'What does Imlay have to do with this – or the *Virginie*, for that matter?'

'A good question – and one that has been occupying my mind for some little while.' Brother Ignatius studied his glass thoughtfully and Nathan, seeing that it was almost empty, refreshed it from the bottle at his elbow.

'Thank you. Yes – Imlay . . . When I met him, in the

Havana, I could not be certain that he was the same man, though I had my suspicions.'

'The same man?'

'Gilberto. Agent number Thirty-seven. The *American* Agent.'

Nathan recalled what he had been told by Carondelet. Agent number 37 had clearly made something of a name for himself. But it was better to plead ignorance in the hope of learning more.

'I am afraid you will have to explain yourself, for I am entirely at sea.'

'As was I until recently, when I had news of Imlay's more recent activities in Paris.'

'Imlay's activities in Paris?' Nathan repeated slowly, as if these too were a total mystery to him. As indeed at times they had been. From the look he received in return he had to wonder if Brother Ignatius knew something of his own adventures in the French capital – but that could not be possible, even for a man of his insights and connections.

'Indeed. A veritable web of intrigue. It has taken me a little time and energy to unravel and even now I would not claim to comprehend more than a small part of it. However . . .' The monk took another sip of wine. 'Let me tell you what little I know. In 1783, the year that gave birth to the United States – the year of this remarkable vintage, in fact – Gilbert Imlay found himself unemployed in Philadelphia. He claimed the rank of captain in Washington's Army but no one seemed sure of what he did to earn it. Certainly he appears to have seen very little

active service. Some say he had been working as a spy
behind British lines in New Jersey; others that he had been
spying for the British. Certainly there are those in his own
family who appear to believe that to this day and have
entirely disowned him. But he retained – he still retains –
the friendship of a select group of former officers who are
loyal to General Washington and who are known
colloquially as "Washington's Boys". Those with an
interest in such matters speculate that he was a double
agent, working for both sides, though his true loyalties are
something of a mystery – if he *has* any true loyalties, save
to himself.'

Nathan made no comment, though he sensed from the
look he was given that the monk was rather hoping for a
contribution at this stage.

'Well, within a year or so of the war's ending he has
become an explorer, a frontiersman, a companion of
mountain men and adventurers. Oh, and a land speculator
too, for whatever else he is, there is always the hard-
headed businessman in there somewhere. And as the
frontier pushes westward and to the south, he becomes
involved in a conspiracy to invade Spanish Louisiana,
either to claim the territory for the United States or to
declare an independent republic – and to enhance the
value of his land. But alas for these adventurers, the
conspiracy is exposed by the Spanish authorities and
denounced by the United States Government who, fearing
that it may lead to war with Spain, order the arrest of the
leading conspirators, Imlay included. He goes to ground,
not for the first or the last time, and turns up – curiously

– in the Spanish territory of western Florida where he is employed as a spy – Agent number Thirty-seven. You do not appear surprised. Perhaps you have heard this story before?'

'It was the suspicion of the Baron de Carondelet,' Nathan admitted. 'But I am interested to hear what more you can add to the account.'

'Ah yes, Baron de Carondelet, an excellent man. His superiors should heed him more, but I fear that the Spaniards have a very poor estimation of the Flemish, considering them dull, even stupid. Much as the English regard the Irish.'

'I do not believe the English have ever considered the Irish dull,' Nathan informed him. 'Indeed, we would wish them duller at times. But do not let me divert you . . .'

'Well, let us stay with Imlay – inasmuch as we can. Some time in the early nineties he turns up in Paris, then in the throes of Revolution. He makes important friends on the Committee of Public Safety, in particular Citizen Robert Lindet and Citizen Lazarre Carnot, who have an interest in international affairs. At some stage, shortly after Spain and Great Britain have entered the war, he writes a memorandum for them in which he details plans for the invasion and conquest of Spanish Louisiana . . .'

He observed Nathan's expression. 'You had no intimation of this?'

'None at all. I am staggered.'

'Well, knowing that the French are more interested in sugar and coffee than they are in swamps and the creatures that inhabit them, Imlay proposed that the region of New Orleans and its adjoining coastline would make a perfect base for an assault upon the British and Spanish possessions in the West Indies. Indeed, he had plans for a general revolt, not only among the French settlers of Louisiana – the Cajuns – but also among the slaves of the West Indies. But . . .' Brother Ignatius shrugged . . . 'what becomes of this plan? The French have other preoccupations. It is the time of the Terror. The time of Robespierre. The only man of any importance who appears interested is Citizen Danton – but he is not in power. No, he is very much *out* of power, and in April of that year he himself becomes a victim of the guillotine. Imlay goes to ground – or underground, perhaps.'

Again that little smile of secret understanding, and though Nathan kept his expression carefully bland he felt that the monk could see the images that flashed across his brain, of himself and Imlay groping their way blindly through the catacombs under Paris, of the skulls that lined the Empire of the Dead and the macabre icon of the Beast under the palace prison of the Luxembourg.

'Until July, 1793, when suddenly . . .' the monk spread his hands in the manner of a conjuror . . . 'up he pops. It is the month of Thermidor. Robespierre is overthrown. The Terror is ended. New men come into power. Among them Paul François Jean Nicholas Barras: one of the most important of these new men, if not *the* most important. And who is Barras but a friend of Gilbert Imlay? Or at least, an associate, a drinking companion . . . who knows the extent of their intimacy? But Barras is a man of vision, very like Danton, whom he resembles a little, though he is not of peasant stock like Danton but very much the *ci-devant* aristocrat, a former viscount, in fact, and an officer in the King's army. We will hear more of this Barras, believe me.

'However, to the present: in the course of their acquaintance Imlay tells Barras of his plan – the Louisiana Conspiracy, let us call it, as others do. And Barras is intrigued. You appear sceptical. Well, yes, I am merely speculating – I was not privy to their conversation – but it is a speculation that fits the facts. Barras looks into the plan and discovers that far from being quietly dropped, it has been secretly activated. Citizen Carnot, also a man of vision, has despatched a flotilla to the West Indies under Commodore Lafitte, with a representative-en-mission, one Citizen Delarge, to advise him. Imlay is horrified. Why was he not told, why was he not consulted? Well, I imagine Citizen Carnot did not trust him. Do you think that might be the case? Possibly Citizen Carnot believed him to have other loyalties than to the French, especially as he was then on the run as a suspected British spy.'

His eyes regarded Nathan above the brim of his glass with an expression of pure mischief – but the glass was almost empty. Nathan reached for the bottle and poured.

'Thank you. So, let us say that Imlay tells Barras that the plan cannot possibly succeed without his participation, and the backing of his contacts in New Orleans – particularly as Barras has now discovered that the flotilla has been dispersed by a British squadron off the Île d'Obéron. So Barras makes a proposal. Or perhaps Imlay does. Either way, what is proposed is that Imlay travels to London – which he is free to do, of course, as an American citizen – and offers his services to the British. Perhaps he is already in their pay, who knows? At any rate, his task is to discover what the British know of the French plan – *his* plan – and what are Britain's own plans for the region. It is known in Paris that an expedition is being prepared – a great armada – "the biggest ever to leave the shores of Britain".'

Nathan started, for these were the exact words of Lord Chatham. Had he used them in public – or were there spies in the very heart of the Admiralty? But of course there were. Imlay for one.

'But what are the targets of this armada? Saint Domingue – or one of the other French islands? Saint Martinique – Guadeloupe – or the North American mainland? Or all of them? And if the Spanish make peace with the French, will the British also attack Louisiana and the Floridas? These are the questions which interest the French. And, of course, they are of some interest to the United States, too. So – Imlay comes to Britain and, with the ingenuity for which he is famed, manages to get himself employed as a political adviser to a certain young captain, bound for the West Indies.'

'So you think we were duped. You think he tricked us into giving him a ride to Cuba so he could go about putting this plan of his into effect.'

Brother Ignatius sat back in his chair. 'What do *you* think, my friend? You must know him a great deal better than I.'

'I think . . .' Nathan paused. What *did* he think and, more to the point, what did he wish to reveal of his thoughts? 'I think Imlay himself does not know half the time what he is about. And I also think I would be better occupied in considering how I am to deal with the situation in Boca del Serpiente.'

The monk sighed. 'Ah well, it is less interesting than the great affairs of nations . . . but though I can claim no great insight into the Army of Lucumi I do know someone who has a far greater knowledge than I. If you will set me down in the port of San Juan Bautista, some thirty miles south of our Serpent, I will endeavour to learn what I can.'

Nathan gave him a sharp look. 'Is that safe? Stupid question. But should I send people with you?'

'That would certainly *not* be safe. No, I will go alone and trust in my cloth to protect me – and of course my God.'

A knock upon the door. Mr Lamb.

'Mr Pym's compliments, sir, but the pilot is come aboard and he wishes to know are you ready to weigh anchor?'

Nathan twisted round to regard the view through the stern windows. The sea was calm: a shimmering crystal into which the grebes dipped their delicate beaks and the pelicans plunged with more deadly intent. As he looked, one of these strangely reptilian birds converted its body into a perfect spear and dived, entering the water at great speed and with scarcely a splash. For some reason Nathan thought of Imlay.

'Tell Mr Pym he may carry on and I will be on deck

shortly. I suppose,' Nathan continued, when the door had closed, 'you would have me believe that Imlay procured the mutiny on the *Unicorn* and the murder of Captain Kerr?'

'There are times, indeed, when Imlay appears to have an infinite capacity for mischief, but let us say that in this case it is more likely that Fate played into his hands.'

'Well, I hope you are right about one thing – and the *Virginie* is presently on her way to Boca del Serpiente, so we may encounter her on more equal terms in the Sea of Sirens.'

Then Nathan suddenly recalled why the name had triggered an alarm when he had heard it in the governor's mansion. *Beware the Sirens.* The message his mother had given him from the mad philosopher he had encountered in St James's Park, with his etchings of Odysseus . . .

Nonsense spouted by a lunatic, but Nathan felt as if someone had walked on his grave.

A run of footsteps upon the deck . . . a pause, a few chords on the fiddle – and then it started.

> '*Way, hay, up she rises,*
> *Way, hay, up she rises,*
> *Way, hay, up she rises*
> *Earleye in the morning!*'

Stamp and go, stamp and go . . .

> '*What do you do with a drunken harlot?*
> *What do you do with a drunken harlot?*

What do you do with a drunken harlot?
Earleye in the morning.
Give her a poke with the boatswain's starter,
Give her a poke with the boatswain's starter . . .'

No music for a monk's ears.

'Pray finish the wine,' Nathan instructed him as he stood, 'for they are raising the anchor and I must go up on deck.'

Chapter Eighteen

The Army of Lucumi

———◆———

'Two minutes twelve seconds.' Silas Shaw, captain's clerk, pressed the button on his pocket chronograph and looked towards Nathan with a rare smile of satisfaction upon his bitter-lemon features.

'Thank you, Mr Shaw.'

They had whipped up a perfect storm around the little raft of empty rum casks and timbers floating just over two cables' lengths off their starboard bow, and though the raft remained intact, there was some cause for satisfaction in the timing.

Nathan turned to his first lieutenant, who was glaring with displeasure at his scuffed and sullied decks.

'Very good, Mr Pym. Now we will come about and see if the larboard guns can do any better.'

A pounding across the decks as they began to wear . . . a disciplined frenzy of activity and then—

'Fire as you bear!'

Again the rippling broadside and at least two close shaves before the penultimate round demolished the raft entirely and the last scattered the debris.

'One minute fifty-eight seconds,' announced Mr Shaw.

It was repeated by those closest to him and a great cheer arose from the gun deck.

'Quiet there! Take that man's name.' A furious Pym pointed, red faced, at one of the more celebrant of the crew who was making lewd gestures with a rammer.

'Very good.' Nathan raised his voice so that it carried the length of the gun deck. 'But you all know it must be closer to a minute by the time we meet up with the *Virginie*, for we have shipmates to be avenged.'

He turned away, despising himself as he always did whenever he played the politician. But he sought out the ship's gunner to congratulate him privately.

'You have done very well, Mr Clyde, with a very mixed bunch but I believe the Africans are coming well up to scratch.'

'That they are, sir, and they take a fair pride in the guns.'

'I dare say they do. Certainly they make better gunners than foretopmen.'

All but five of the Africans had elected to stay aboard the *Unicorn* when she had left Jamaica, though Nathan suspected this had more to do with their reluctance to remain in a slave colony with little money, no prospects and very little English than with their enthusiasm for life aboard one of His Majesty's frigates.

Still, they were a welcome addition to the crew, and with his extra quota of marines and the score or so of 'volunteers' he had picked up from the jails and taverns of Kingston and Port Royal, the *Unicorn* was not far short of her full complement. With the improvement in her gunnery – they had been practising every day since leaving Jamaica – he felt a greater sense of optimism than at any time since joining the ship. But his talk of meeting with the *Virginie* was more for the benefit of the crew than from any private conviction, whatever Brother Ignatius had to say about it.

The notion of paying her back for the miseries she had inflicted upon them off Ship Island had taken hold on the lower deck as much as it had among his officers, and Nathan felt it advisable to nurture this ambition, rather than to reveal the true purpose of their mission as they threaded their cautious way through the Sea of Sirens. Only his lieutenants – and of course Brother Ignatius – knew of his intention of attacking the mutineers and their rebel allies in the Mouth of the Serpent. The rest of the officers and crew remained in ignorance. Sooner or later of course he would have to tell them, but he was still working on his speech – and that would have to be as political as any he had made.

He watched as Tully and Maxwell returned to the quarterdeck from their divisions. They were having an animated discussion about the performance of their respective guns and crews, and Nathan felt a sharp stab of envy – not only for their easy intimacy but for the technical nature of their discussion. He envied them their total absorption in the detail of things. He remembered it from when he had been a lieutenant – and a midshipman before that, conversing with another junior officer about some specific aspect of gunnery, or navigation . . . or what they were going to have for dinner. Larger issues, such as where they were going and why – or who they were fighting and why – had rarely entered into it. They could leave that to others – remote, godlike beings like their captain, who could never converse with anyone, not with ease, and who ate his dinner alone, an hour after everyone else – unless he invited them to join him for a formal meal in his cabin or was invited to join them in the gun room on some special occasion: and whenever he spoke he would be listened to with respect, his views treated with the deference due to his godly status.

Well, to hell with it; he did not have to play by the rules. He intercepted a look from Tully, vaguely questioning, perhaps sensing his discontent, and summoned him with a slight sideways movement of his head as he would have on the *Speedwell*.

Tully excused himself and joined him at the starboard rail.

'What did you think?' Nathan asked him.

Tully replied formally with an intelligent summary of the operation, adding one or two trifling criticisms and modest suggestions for improvement. Nathan half listened – the question had been an excuse, a means of introducing a different subject altogether, though it was, he supposed, related.

'And the diverse elements, they are working together?'

'Well enough. There are always diverse elements in any crew.'

'More so than usual, perhaps, with the Irish and the Africans.'

Tully knew him well enough to suspect there was a deeper reason for this line of questioning. It was not so unusual to have a significant proportion of Irish among the crew of a British man of war and even a number of Negroes.

'I have noted no particular tensions between them,' Tully said quietly, 'or with any other sections of the crew. Of course, there is a language difficulty.'

'With the Irish?'

'With the Africans.' In a tone of mild surprise until he saw Nathan's expression. 'Your pardon. Very good.'

A poor joke but it had broken at least part of the constraint that sometimes rose between them.

'The fact is,' Nathan confided, 'I cannot help but fear there will be an element of divided loyalty when I tell them the true nature of our mission. Both from the Africans and the Irish.' He kept his voice low but they were both looking out to sea, and unless Gabriel had his ear pressed to the cabin window below, there was little risk of being overheard – and Gabriel probably knew already what was the true nature of their mission. It could only be hoped he had kept it to himself for the time being.

'I think you are wise to wait until the last possible minute,' Tully agreed. 'But much depends on your plan for the encounter.'

'Right. Well, when I have a plan I will share it with you.

At present I have not the remotest idea what to do.' Tully smiled. Did he think he was joking? 'But whatever it is, it will involve some considerable violence – and to men with whom they have much in common, and towards whom they probably feel a great deal of sympathy.'

Tully said nothing for the moment. He looked away down the length of the deck. A considerably quieter deck than it had been a few minutes ago, though Pym already had the defaulters on their knees scrubbing at the marks on his precious planking.

'Well, as to the Irish,' began Tully at length, 'there are only twenty-eight of them left. If you fear, that is . . .'

Nathan sensed him choosing his words. 'Come on,' he urged him. 'I want to know your opinion.'

'Well, if you do not believe you can rely upon them, I suppose you may limit their participation in the affair. It does, as I say, depend on the eventual plan. If it is to be a cutting out . . .'

He left the sentence unfinished but Nathan nodded his understanding. If the *Unicorn* were to remain offshore and he or Pym – Maxwell or Tully – were to lead the boats in with the marines and some picked members of the crew, probably by night, the Irish need never know what they were about until they returned with their captives: such of them as survived.

'And the Africans?'

'The same goes for them.'

Nathan made a sour face. 'I hate it when I cannot depend on members of my own crew – and have to deceive them.'

'Well, take them into your confidence then. As you have me. I was once a smuggler, yet you did not appear to distrust me when we encountered the smugglers in the English Channel. Men who were my former shipmates, in fact.'

'Really? You did not tell me that at the time.'

'Did I not? Perhaps it escaped me in the excitement of the chase.'

They both grinned, remembering. Then Nathan sighed.

'To tell truth, Martin, I am not even sure of my own loyalties. Dear God. Look at us. We are entirely opposed to slavery. The King's chief minister is opposed to it, the leader of the Opposition and most of the Whigs, even a great many Tories. The Navy is opposed to it – I have yet to meet an officer who will speak in its favour – and yet here we are fighting to restore it, all over the Caribbean. In the next twenty-four hours we may be forced to fire on an army of escaped slaves.' His voice had risen a little and he saw one or two glances cast in his direction. He lowered his voice again. 'Why is it we are so often on the wrong side, Martin, killing men we should be fighting beside?'

But wiser heads than Tully's had considered this question without coming close to an answer. Nathan caught sight of a diffident figure, hovering at the extremity of his vision.

'Yes, Mr Godfrey?'

The pilot approached and saluted. 'I believe we will sight Cape Cruz in about an hour,' he announced, 'and then we will follow the coast north to Boca del Serpiente.'

'Very well, sir.' Nathan raised his voice so that the first lieutenant could hear him at the con. 'Mr Pym, I believe we will heave to.'

Nathan did not wish to take any chance of being observed from the coast and their presence carried to the rebels.

'Mr Lamb, oblige me if you would, by finding how Mr Lloyd is getting on with his virgin.'

A delighted grin from Lamb, who was young enough to find this amusing. He dived down the nearest companionway and popped up again a minute or so later with the semblance of gravity upon his youthful features and the information that, 'Mr Lloyd says her paint is still a bit wet, but if you are ready to see her he will bring her up on to the forecastle.'

Notice of the event had got about and the deck was more than usually crowded with idlers as their new figurehead emerged like Aphrodite from the waters – and with at least two of her most striking attributes.

'Dear God,' murmured Nathan to Tully. 'I believe I asked for a virgin, not the Whore of Babylon.'

He did not know if it was the bosom that disturbed him most or the violently rouged cheeks and the lewd and self-satisfied smirk she wore upon her countenance. Her creator came aft, the subject of ribald comment and with the look of a naughty Welshman who knows he has been found out and for once does not mind, aware that popular feeling is on his side.

Pym was beside himself, discipline shot to ruin. 'Mr Lloyd, you have disgraced yourself,' he said.

'I beg pardon, sir, but I am not sure I know what you mean.'

'You know very well what he means, Mr Lloyd,' put in Nathan. 'Did you have to give her such a distinctive . . . profile?'

'It was unavoidable, sir, if it is to go over the 'orse's 'ead, so to speak.'

'I see. Yes, I suppose that is a consideration.' As usual, when speaking with a Welshman, Nathan struggled to avoid mimicry, not from any desire to mock but from some compelling cadence in the language.

'And the 'orn will 'ave to come off, you know – that is, with your permission, sir.'

'I suppose it will. But cut it at an angle, if you would, Mr Lloyd, so it may be securely restored when we are done.' He observed the small twitch in the carpenter's brow. 'I beg your pardon, I do not wish to teach my grandmother to suck eggs.'

He was aware that something wittier might have come to him, but it hadn't and it was no use chasing it now.

'And Mr Pym, perhaps we may put some of the hands to painting the ship red, or that part of it as we have agreed.'

When all was done and the watch had gone to dinner, Nathan attempted to still his own hunger by having himself rowed out to a cable's length and looking back on his ship in her new likeness, the proud-bosomed figurehead at her bow and the broad red stripe down her side, for all the world the image of the *Virginie*, especially when they broke out the tricolour at her mizzen.

'I am sorry, Mr Pym,' he told the first lieutenant when he returned to the ship and caught his sullen eye – Mr Pym was an honourable man, like his former commander, the late lamented Captain Kerr, and had no truck with privateering or flying about under false colours – 'but it would not do to go hovering about the shore in our true identity and have it known from here to Port-au-Prince.'

'As you wish, sir. I am sure you know what you are about.'

It was a waste of time trying to make friends with the man or take him into his confidence. They were poles apart. Nathan sought out Brother Ignatius who had the freedom of his cabin and was reading a book in the stern windows.

'We have set sail for San Juan,' Nathan informed him, 'and will be ready to land you as close as we may, a little after dark.'

It was approaching midnight, in fact, the wind having dropped considerably in the meantime, before they were close enough to the port to consider launching a boat.

'Are you sure it is not too late?' Nathan enquired of the monk. He was concerned that he might attract the attention of the watch. There was almost certain to be a curfew with a rebel army camped on their doorstep.

'Oh, who would trouble a poor monk?' replied Brother Ignatius carelessly. 'And we are often about at night, upon some small errand of mercy.'

'I shall not rest easy until your return,' Nathan said, handing him down into the gig.

'I will try to be at the rendezvous this time tomorrow night,' the monk assured him. 'Failing which, perhaps you would be good enough to send back for me at the same time for the next two nights.'

'And after?'

'After that, I think we may take it that I am unavoidably detained and you should do what you can without me.'

Fortunately for Nathan's peace of mind they brought him back the following night none the worse for wear and indeed, looking considerably pleased with himself. From the smell about him, Nathan gathered he had discovered his favourite form of refreshment.

'Here,' said the monk, thrusting a bundle of mint in his face. 'I have brought us the necessary ingredient.' A bottle followed – unlabelled. 'And a more refined version of the stuff you are insensitive enough to call rum.'

Gabriel relieved him of both items and bore them down to the cabin in their wake while the monk subjected him to a detailed list of instructions.

'Remember you must pluck the leaves from one sprig and crush them with the sugar before you add the lime juice,' he concluded. 'Add another sprig for decoration in each glass and put the rest of the mint in water to keep it fresh.'

'So,' Nathan regarded him thoughtfully when they were alone, 'I gather you had a satisfactory trip – if only in the gathering of herbs.'

'Oh never fear, I did more than gather herbs. I have learned everything you wish to know. At least, I hope so – though as a seafaring man you are probably going to ask

me things about tides and currents and suchlike that will
entirely confound me.'

'I think we can safely leave the tides and currents to Mr
Godfrey,' Nathan assured him, 'if only you can tell us
about the Army of Lucumi.'

'Ask any question you like and I will endeavour to
oblige you.'

'Very well. How many are they?'

'A little over a thousand – though more are rallying to
them by the day. But they are very short of powder and
shot – and guns. Small arms, that is, for I am not counting
the cannon in the fort. I am informed that they have no
more than a couple of hundred muskets between them,
the few they brought down with them from the Sierra
Maestra and the rest taken from the garrison at the fort.'

'And what of the mutineers – the pirates?'

'They keep very much to themselves – in the boat which
they have moored in the bay. And they are somewhat
reduced in number since they left the *Unicorn*. I am
assured there are now no more than sixteen of them, the
rest having fallen in the battle with the slavers – or
succumbed to disease.'

'But do they not have the maroons they brought with
them from the Gardens of the King?'

'My informant believes that they have joined the Army
of Lucumi and are camped in and around the fort. If you
will provide me with paper, pen and ink I will draw you a
map.'

Nathan did as he was requested and watched carefully
as the monk drew the outline of the Serpent's Mouth with

the fort on the western lip and the shape of two boats in the small enclosed bay.

'Two?' he questioned him.

'One is the brig – which they have named the *Fabhcún* – which is to say the *Falcon* in the Gaelic. The other is your cutter, I believe. The maroons are mainly accommodated in Fort Felipe, which they now call Akaso – the sentinel – though some are under canvas on the beach below, just here, where there is a small jetty for landing supplies. The guns of the fort cover the entrance to the bay and there are more covering the principal approach from the shore, here.'

'And do they know how to use them?'

'Not very well, I am told. That is one source of aggravation with the pirates who wished to place one of their own number in command of the artillery, with others that were with them in the brig from the Jardines del Rey, but Olumiji is jealous of his authority.'

'Olumiji?'

'The leader of the maroons, those that were in the Sierra Maestra. There is further division with those that came from the Jardines del Rey who are Kokongo. Olumiji and his men are mostly Yoruba. The one thing that unites both groups is their dislike of the pirates. Certainly of being ordered about by them. O'Neill, your former crewman, has a reputation for being overbearing, I understand. He wishes the maroons to join him in his little fleet, under his command, and sail for Hispaniola to join with the French as a privateer. Olumiji is reluctant to relinquish his own authority and his power base in the

Sierra Maestra, His name means "one who awakens", by the way. And he has plans for a general revolt among the slaves of Cuba. Plans that appear to involve Imlay, you will be interested to know.'

Imlay again. 'But how can that be? Imlay has not been near the Sierra Maestra.'

'No, but he made good use of his time in the Havana, it appears. I am not sure, nor was my informant, but Olumiji knows all about him and his promise to support them with French ships and French arms.'

'Christ.' Then Nathan realised what he had said and to whom. 'I am sorry.' He shook his head. 'It is just that I cannot quite come to terms with the depths of that man's iniquity – or his . . . machinations. Or my own naivety. I had thought his only interest in the Havana was in women.'

'Well, that did occupy some of his time – and not only for his pleasure. Many of the leading savants of Lucumi are women and not a few of them are spies – including Olumiji's closest adviser, a woman by the name of Adedike. Which means "one who comes to fulfil our plea". It may be an innocent expression of gratitude on the part of her parents but I am inclined to suspect a more universal application. She also has a French name. Sabine. Sabine Delatour. I am told she came from Saint Domingue a little over a year ago with a boatload of refugees – and papers that established her status as a freed slave. It is thought that she was the mistress of one of the French planters, an aristocrat, who granted her freedom in his will. He was butchered by the rebels in Saint Domingue,

though there are those who say Sabine – Adedike – killed
him. Certainly there are many in San Sebastian who
consider her a witch. She arrived there recently by ship
from the Havana and has now established herself, as I say,
in the counsels of the Army of Lucumi. O'Neill tried his
luck with her once and I am told this is one of the major
sources of tension between the maroons and the
mutineers.'

'Your informant seems remarkably well informed.'

'She is.'

'She?'

'Yes. Do you have any objection to that?'

'No. It was just that I thought . . . no matter.'

'She, too, is a savant of Lucumi, but is opposed to
violence, certainly at this time and in this place. A very
interesting woman . . .' he grew thoughtful . . . 'quite
sincerely religious and wise beyond her years, though of
course, deluded in her beliefs. Ah, here are the *mojitos*. I
hope you have not spoiled it with too much sugar,' he
warned Gabriel sternly. 'It is a frequent fault of the
English to be putting too much sugar into things.'

Nathan pulled the map to him and studied it carefully.
A cutting out would be very tricky. The boats would have
to sail in right under the guns of Fort Felipe, or whatever
it was called under its new ownership, and then out again
with the brig and the cutter. He supposed they could burn
them at their moorings but the boats would still have to
come out again.

Alternatively, the *Unicorn* could sail into the Serpent's
Mouth and do the job herself. But she would sustain fire

from the fort and the brig. And she might have trouble manoeuvring in such a confined space. He wondered if Mr Godfrey had any idea of the depth of water in the tiny bay.

Brother Ignatius was at least partly satisfied with his *mojito*.

'Perhaps you took my advice on the sugar a little too much to heart,' he informed Gabriel. 'It is a little tart. But not bad for a beginner, not bad at all.'

'You say they are expecting help from the French,' Nathan cut in abruptly, quite oblivious to Gabriel's presence. 'Did you mean the *Virginie*?'

'I am not sure if Imlay was specific about the precise means of their deliverance, but certainly if they anticipate help from the French they would expect it to come by sea.'

'Thank you,' said Nathan. 'And thank you, Gabriel,' to his steward of the flapping ears. 'That will be all.'

But he knew now how it could be done. And with any luck it would not involve the necessity of a battle with the Army of Lucumi.

Chapter Nineteen

The Serpent's Mouth

———◆———

The frigate stood half a mile or so offshore, with Mr Lloyd's virgin at her bow and the tricolour hanging limply from her stern in the torpid tropic air. Nathan looked back at her from the stern of the gig as it pulled for the distant headland, trying to see her as the men in the fort would or, more critically, the men in the brig who had once served in her. There was nothing glaringly obvious to him – no small detail he had overlooked. The greatest danger was if there was a distinguishing feature of the *Unicorn* he remained unaware of, but it had been a good eight months since the mutineers had last seen her, and she had been through a lot since then. Nathan had taken the precaution of dressing the marines in slops and none of his officers wore their coats. He even had them wearing the tricolour in their hats, in case they could be seen with a telescope.

He turned back to gaze over the heads of the rowers

towards the Serpent's Mouth, aware that they would be watching him, too: in his civilian cape and his tall beaver hat; and Tully next to him at the tiller in the uniform of a lieutenant in the French Navy, specially knocked up for him by one of the crew who had been a tailor in his former life. The rowers were all men who had joined the ship in Port Royal – with Tierney, the Channel Islander, in the bow. It would have been too much of a risk to take any of the original crew of the *Unicorn* for fear the mutineers would recognise them, but Nathan could have wished for better oarsmen. Although he had waited for slack tide they were making heavy weather of it and they were closer to the eastern headland than he desired.

Tully snapped at them, uncharacteristically anxious – and in English. Nathan warned him to keep his voice down, fearful that it would carry to the men in the brig. He could see her clearly now – and the little cutter beside her – moored fore and aft on spring cables just inside the bay. Several crew members were staring towards him from the forecastle of the brig. He looked away at the fort on the opposite headland. Men were there, too, gazing down from the battlements. And the guns: eight of them – 12-pounders most likely – covering the approaches to the bay. Any vessel that tried to force a passage into the Serpent's Mouth would face a withering crossfire from the fort and the brig – and even the cutter with her 32-pounder carronade at the bow, *his* missing carronade.

They were directly in the entrance now, clawing their way towards the jetty on the western headland, directly beneath the fort. A great many men were standing in groups along the shore. A few uniforms, not many, no particular order or discipline, and not many guns. An encampment further back into the bay, all along the shoreline and climbing up into the cliffs. Forty, fifty tents. A lingering smoke from the cooking fires. Washing hung up to dry. Again, no military order. But the fort . . . the fort was a different matter and that was where the bulk of the army was accommodated – at least according to Brother Ignatius's mysterious informant in San Sebastian. How did she know? By intuition, by magic? Or did she have a more conventional means of communicating with them? And the greater question: could she be trusted?

Too late now. Tully directed the little gig towards the jetty. A steep flight of stone steps led up to the fort, or more correctly the gatehouse: a squat, square barbican with two small cannon flanking the entrance. Beyond, a little higher up the cliff, there was a steep chasm with a wide wooden bridge – a drawbridge – leading to the fort proper. The doors were open but the portcullis was lowered.

They were under the guns now. They could never depress so low. A small boat – or a flotilla of small boats – creeping close in by the western headland, would evade their fire. But – Nathan permitted himself a swift glance back over his shoulder – they would be in the direct line of fire from the brig and the cutter across the bay.

A sudden sound from the fort – very like the sound of an anchor chain running out – and he looked up to see the portcullis being raised. A file of soldiers came marching out, perhaps two dozen of them in good order, dressed in white uniforms and boots with bandoliers at the chest and muskets at the shoulder, and led by an officer or sergeant calling the step. A guard of honour or an escort for the prisoners? The soldiers marched across the drawbridge and into the barbican and then out again, forming up in two lines at the top of the steps.

A muttered word from Tully and the boatcrew raised oars as they approached the jetty. Tierney leaped ashore with the painter. None of the men on the shore ran up to help or greet them in any way. Nathan waited until Tierney had secured them fore and aft and then stepped ashore with Tully following. They walked on alone, past the silent army on the shore and up the steps to the fort.

The officer shouted a command. The guard presented arms – a good sign? They walked between the two disciplined lines of men, Nathan nodding and smiling amiably. The officer turned on his heel and marched ahead of them into the barbican. They followed him, through a dark passage and out again into a small courtyard and a glare of sunlight. More soldiers drawn up in ranks. But not with guns. A band. A military band. Fife and drum and what looked like a tuba. And as Nathan and Tully stepped through into the light, the band began to play.

The 'Marseillaise'.

Nathan stood at attention. He half wondered if he should sing. *Allons enfants de la patrie* . . .

They played the first verse and the chorus: a crude

rendition with a few false notes but Nathan had heard far worse on the streets of Paris. He sang to himself.

Aux armes, citoyens!
Formez vos bataillons!
Marchons! marchons!
Qu'un sang impur
Abreuve nos sillons!

The music ended.

A nervous silence. Nathan began to clap – enthusiastically. Tully, too. But now what? They could not go on clapping for ever, with their fixed grins. But at a word of command the band marched off to the side to reveal another guard of honour – and two figures standing a little in the shade. A man and a woman. The man in a white uniform, the woman in a long red dress.

Nathan stared for a moment and then advanced towards them, though every instinct urged him to run in the opposite direction, dragging Tully with him. It might surprise them. They might even get away with it. But still he walked forward.

And came to a halt a few paces from where they awaited him. He took off his hat. Bowed.

'My name is Imlay . . .' It came out as a croak. His mouth was dry.

He began again. 'My name is Citizen Imlay and I am sent by the National Convention in Paris . . .'

To do what? He paused. And I am come to bring you freedom? Liberty, equality, fraternity. Possibly this is what

Imlay would have said, and a great deal more. He was a good actor, good at making speeches. Nathan had once heard him speak to the Convention in Paris, though not with success on that occasion.

'I come . . .' But the words stuck in his throat. Not because he did not believe them, but because he knew *they* would not. They knew he was not Imlay. They knew he was not French. They knew he had not come to bring them their freedom. And they would tear his tongue out by the roots with hot pincers – when he had told them all they wanted to know.

There was a silence.

Then the man spoke.

'Welcome to Free Cuba,' he said. His voice was deep, his accent heavy. 'My name is Olumiji. But I do not speak well the French. This woman speak for me. Her name is Adedike.'

But Nathan knew who she was – by whatever name she called herself. She was the woman who had followed him to the waterfront in the Havana, the courtesan whom Imlay had called *La Princesa Negra* – the Black Princess.

Chapter Twenty

La Princesa Negra

―――・◆・―――

They were escorted to a room deep within the fort. A plain room with bare stone walls and a wooden floor; the only furniture a table and chairs. There were no bars on the windows but it was as good as a cell, or as bad. The only view was of an enclosed courtyard some thirty feet below and the steep walls all around.

'What was that about?' asked Tully.

Nathan shook his head.

'That woman,' Tully said, frowning. 'I think I have seen her before.'

'She was the woman who followed us down to the waterfront,' Nathan told him, 'when we left the consul's house in the Havana.'

Tully had lost some of his normal composure. 'Can you be sure?'

'She stayed in my mind somewhat,' answered Nathan

dryly. He had not told Tully what Imlay had said about her and her desire for him.

'They seemed to be arguing,' said Tully.

'There appeared to be some disagreement, certainly. But I could not understand what was said.'

'Do you think she recognised us?'

'I think she probably did.'

'So she knows we are English.'

'Well, she knows we were staying at the English consul's house. Though we came from an American ship . . . But I think she knows that I am not Imlay and that you are not French.'

'So what now?'

Nathan shrugged. 'Your guess is as good as mine. They have not taken our swords,' he pointed out.

Footsteps in the corridor outside. A knock at the door. Nathan remembered to speak French, for what it was worth.

Two women entered with trays of food and drink. They set them down at the table and left. No words were spoken. Nathan glimpsed a pair of armed guards in the corridor outside.

He inspected what they had left on the table. A ham, fried plantains, bread, olives, tomatoes, some unknown fruit or vegetable, wine and water.

'We may as well eat,' he said, sitting down and pouring the wine. He caught Tully's eye. 'Well, it is better than staring out of the window.'

They were left for some considerable time. The light faded from the sky. It had been late in the afternoon when they had landed.

'I wonder what has happened to the boat crew.' Tully broke a lengthy silence.

Nathan could offer no suggestions.

'Do you think Pym will do anything?'

'I hope not.' Nathan stood up and crossed to the window. Deep shadows in the courtyard. Soon it would be night. 'This is not good,' he said.

Footsteps in the corridor outside and another knock on the door. This time it was the officer who had brought them here – with two guards. He spoke to Nathan in Spanish and when Nathan looked blank, made a gesture towards the door.

Nathan stepped into the corridor but when Tully attempted to follow he was stopped by the guards. He began to protest.

'Leave it,' Nathan told him. 'I think it will be all right.'

He had no grounds for this belief but it would have been pointless to argue. He was led down several corridors and up a spiral staircase, glimpsing the sea through one of the slit windows – and the distant *Unicorn* in the light of the setting sun. A door at the top of the stair. The officer knocked, listened a moment and then pushed it open and with another abrupt jerk of the head, invited Nathan to enter.

The room was not dark but it was a tricky, hazy light: the dying light of the sun lancing from several windows through a thin, pungent smoke.

And then Nathan saw the woman.

She was sitting by one of the windows, framed against the blood-red sky. The door closed behind him.

'May I offer you a glass of wine?' She spoke French in a voice that was almost as deep as a man's – and brisk.

'Thank you,' he said. He stood just inside the door. The smoke, he saw, was coming from several candles – and an incense-burner that hung on a long chain from the rafters. The roof above was pointed. They must be at the top of one of the castle towers.

She moved from the window. She was wearing a long robe, not red this time but black, like a nun's. But she did not look like any nun that he had seen and her feet were bare. He had heard the expression 'feline grace' and had thought it trite, but not now; save that 'feline' was too gentle a word, 'grace' too innocent. She crossed to a small table at the far side of the room and poured wine into two tall glasses. She had not invited him to sit though there were chairs at the table; also a couch along one of the walls. The incense was not unpleasant but heady, almost overpowering.

For some reason he had a sharp memory of the old woman sitting in the courtyard in the Havana stroking the cat in the red ruff. Incense, he remembered, was often used to hide the smell of decay . . .

But why should he think of that?

He was aware that she was looking at him – as if inspecting him for flaws. He felt awkward standing there, and tense. Something else, too, that was more disturbing. He could not remember when he had last been in a room alone with a woman, other than his mother, but of course it must have been when he was last with Sara and he was shocked because he had to think about it.

'So – who are you?' Her voice was softer but not more gentle – if anything, there was a hint of menace in it. And she came towards him, leaving the glasses on the table, and stood, disconcertingly close.

It came to him to say, 'My name is Imlay,' and to repeat it stubbornly, as to an interrogator, every time he was asked. But something warned him that this would not be wise so instead he said, 'My name is Peake. Nathan Peake.'

'And you are English?'

'Yes.'

'Yes,' she said, and her lips stayed parted in what was almost but not quite a smile. Her features were as perfect as he had thought them when he had seen her on the waterfront in the Havana: sculptured, a black Venus, but a glow about her skin, a bloom like violets.

'If you had lied to me, if you had said you were Imlay, I would have had your tongue torn out by the roots,' she said.

So he had not been wrong about that, then.

'So what shall I do with you instead?'

When he thought about it afterwards, being honest with himself, he thought he had probably leaned, or swayed, towards her but it was she who kissed him. The first time. If that was in his favour. Then, it was more or less an equal endeavour. And more of a fight than an embrace. Broadside for broadside, as he might have put it, hammer and tongs. Simple black robe though it was, she was naked beneath it. His own clothes were more of a problem and there was some tearing, though not of his tongue. Some disturbance, also, to the furniture. They crashed into the table and knocked over the wine glasses. A candle ignited some powder and a small fire started which Nathan put out with the wine that was left in the bottle: a brief moment of clear-headedness.

He was not aware of the light fading from the windows but it was dark when next he noticed them, the room lit only by the flickering flames of the candles. They lay on the floor, apart but within easy reach, not touching. The rough matting prickled his back. He turned his head to look at her. She might have been sleeping. He raised himself quietly and stood by one of the windows. A distant light that was the *Unicorn*. A hint of yards against the evening sky.

He felt a touch, a fingernail drawn down the sweat of his spine, like a knife. He shivered. He had not heard her move.

He turned and cupped the angle of her jaw in his hand. He looked into her eyes but saw nothing there that he knew. He kissed her gently and she bit him. Not gently. He flinched away and swore, tasting the warm blood on his lip, trickling down his chin. He wiped it with his hand and looked at it in the light of the one remaining candle, the blood on his palm. He thought quite deliberately about this, not angrily at all, thinking what would be the best response. Then he spun her round by the shoulders and slapped her once, but hard, on her naked buttocks.

She was round in a flash, her eyes blazing, and he thought for a moment that he had a real fight on his hands. She seized him by the hair. It had long come undone and hung to his shoulders and she had plenty to pull. But she only pulled him to her and kissed him, violently, but without using her teeth this time, and then her legs were around his waist and he fell back against the narrow window-ledge, holding the weight of her. Where and how they went from there he did not know. Somehow they managed to avoid the broken glass. They ended up on the couch. It was darker now and the last fat candle flickered, making huge shadows on the distant rafters of the roof.

'Where do you come from?' he asked her, twining his finger in the tight curls of her hair.

'Hell,' she said.

He nodded as if this confirmed his suspicion. 'And what brought you to Cuba?'

'You,' she said. She kissed him, with surprising gentleness, on the mouth. 'But I have come to take you to Heaven.'

'Apparently,' he said. 'But both Heaven and Hell involve death, I am told, as an intermediate stage.'

'And you do not want to die?'

'Not yet.' He was superstitious enough to fear that their banter had become sinister and she would metamorphose into the old woman in the courtyard in the back streets of La Habana, and that he would smell that reek of death before it took him.

'And yet you flirt with it,' she said.

'Is that what I am doing?'

'You must have known it was a risk. Coming here. Pretending to be Imlay and with the French.'

He leaned on one elbow and looked down at her. 'Did you tell them who I am?'

'How could I? I did not know. I told them,' she corrected herself, 'I told *him* – since he is the only one who matters – that I needed time to think about you and to consult my spirits.'

'Is that what we have been doing?'

'Yes. Did you not know?' She looked up at him curiously and then with a sudden, fluid movement she stood up and walked to the window. He gazed at the beauty of her in the light of the moon and that one flickering candle.

He thought of Sara, too, and there was a great pain in his chest. He could not think of Sara. The pain went.

'Imlay spoke of you,' he said. 'In the Havana.'

'Did he so?'

'You know Imlay?' He was conscious of a feeling very like jealousy.

'We have met,' she said. 'Professionally.'

But that was not reassuring, given what Imlay had said of her profession.

'He said you were a princess.'

'He was right. My father was a king, so that would make me a princess, would it not? In your country.'

'And yet you became a slave?'

She turned then and he was aware of her regard, though he could not read her expression.

'Yes. My father was defeated in battle and I was sold as a slave.' There was that in her tone that warned him not to pursue the matter.

'I am sorry. I want to know about you.'

'Good. But there is plenty of time.' She looked around the room at the mess they had made. 'We did not have our wine.'

She clapped her hands.

One of the wall hangings moved and to Nathan's astonishment a figure promptly appeared, a woman. He sat up and tried to cover himself with the rug from the couch.

Adedike laughed. 'Too late for that,' she said. 'I would suppose she has seen everything now. She likes to peep.'

She said something to her then in her own language and the woman bowed and went back through the curtain into what must be another room or recess beyond.

'Was she there all the time?' Nathan asked, shocked.

'I very much hope so, or I will have her whipped. And if you had continued to thrash me she would have rushed in with a knife and cut your throat.'

'I did not thrash you.' He was indignant. 'It was what we call in English, a spank.' He blushed.

'Ah yes. I know a little English but not much. A "spank", is it not? It was not unpleasant. Is that what you do in England to your women?'

'No,' he said, grinning at the thought, and his own abrupt denial.

'Oh. Only slaves? But no, for slaves you use the whip, or the cat.'

He shook his head. No longer smiling. 'Not me. I would never do that.'

'No? Then why do you come with your ships and your guns?'

'I came only for the men in the brig – who killed my captain.'

The woman came back with wine and glasses and a small bowl of sweetmeats on a tray. She looked about her at the mess they had made of the room. Nathan righted the table, taking care where he put his feet for the broken glass and she set the tray down and smiled her thanks. He blushed for his nakedness and for what she might have seen earlier. Adedike spoke sharply to her and she left.

'And what would you do with them?' she said to Nathan. 'These men in the brig?'

'I would take them to Port Royal in Jamaica for trial.'

'And the Army of Lucumi?'

So this was the interrogation. Well, it was better than the last time, in the house of arrest in Paris. Thus far.

'I have no quarrel with the Army of Lucumi,' he assured her. He poured wine for them both.

'I don't know if I can believe you,' she said.

'Why would I lie?' He handed her the wine. 'I could not fight the Army of Lucumi, even if I wanted to.'

'No? With your fine ship and all your fine men? And you are their captain?'

'I am.'

'So young to be the captain of a ship.' She stepped up close to him and sipped her wine, watching him the while.

'Very well. You may take them.' She gestured toward the window with the hand holding the glass. 'With my blessing. You may take them for trial in Port Royal. And then you may hang them.'

She walked away from him and stood at the window

with her back to him. He looked at the shape of her in the flickering candlelight, no longer lustful but awed by her beauty. He supposed he could fall in love with her. He had never made love to a woman that he was not in love with, a little. And with Sara . . . But he must not think on Sara.

'You *will* hang them, I suppose,' she said.

'Probably,' he said. He stood up close to her. The window looked out over the bay and he could see the lights of the brig and the cutter.

'There is one, O'Neill, who is the leader,' she said. 'He is the one who cut the throat of your captain. The others . . .' he felt her shoulder lift in a shrug . . . 'they do as he says. Save one. His name is Keane. When O'Neill would have insulted me he was angry and not only because he feared what I would do.'

'They will all get a fair trial,' he assured her glibly, knowing it would be as fair as for any men accused of mutiny in the King's Navy. 'When we get them to Port Royal.'

She turned to face him. 'There is a price,' she said. Her voice as brisk as when he had first entered the room.

'What?'

'Olumiji will not let them go for nothing.'

'Olumiji?'

'Our general. We need guns. Muskets. Powder and shot. And a captain of artillery.'

'That is not in my power to give you,' he said.

'That is the price,' she repeated.

'You would fight the Spaniards?'

'Olumiji would fight the Spaniards.'

'They are very many. I don't think he can win.'

'Then he will go back into the mountains. Where they cannot follow.'

'And you?'

'I will go back to La Habaña.'

'You are not afraid of what they may do to you?'

'I have powerful protectors.'

'Among the Spaniards?'

'And the French.' She turned to face him then and he saw the mischief in her eyes. 'Are you jealous, my Englishman?'

He wondered then if she was a spy for the French. And others. An agent like Imlay who served several masters and was entirely his own.

'Would you not wish to return to where you came from – in Africa?'

She threw her head back and laughed, a deep, rounded chuckle, like a man's. 'Even if that were possible I could not live there now.' She considered him, still with the mischief in her eye. 'Perhaps I will go back to Saint Domingue,' she said. 'When they get rid of the English. Or perhaps I will go to Paris. Or England. With you.'

He could just imagine it. Taking her down to Sussex. He could almost see her in London though. She and his mother would make a formidable alliance – if they did not kill each other.

He looked past her to the lights of the two vessels moored in the bay and she twisted her head round to look at them.

'If you cannot pay the price you cannot have them,' she said.

'I have only the guns in my ship,' he said, calculating.

'How many?'

'A hundred. Muskets. Fifty pistols.' It was about half the total in the ship's armoury, not counting the side-arms for the marines.

'That is not enough.'

'It is all I have.'

She watched his face carefully. 'And powder and shot?'

'Yes. I could spare you that.' He could not believe he was offering to deliver guns to these people: rebels against his King's allies. Was she truly a witch?

'But how could it be done?' he asked.

'How many boats would you need to deliver them?'

'Three. Maybe four.'

'When you enter the bay you will be close to the brig.'

'We could be.'

'Then you may do what you want – and afterwards bring the guns to the shore. And you will leave the brig to us.'

'And then?'

'And then the boats will go back to your ship . . . And you will stay with me.'

He thought she was joking. He smiled. Then he realised that she was not.

'You will be our captain of artillery,' she said.

'But – I am the captain of a ship. In the King's Navy.'

'That is the price,' she said.

Chapter Twenty-One

Mutiny

———◆———

The three boats approached the Serpent's Mouth in what might just be described as line ahead but considerably slower than Nathan would have wished. He had a dozen oars to each boat but most of them were pulled by Whiteley's marines dressed in seamen's slops and they had as much idea of rowing as they did of taking in a reef in a storm. He had planned to go in with the flood and out on the ebb but now he feared he had waited too long and would miss his tide. If it turned now they would never get through the narrow gap between the two headlands, not with the tide against them and a parcel of guffies at the oars. He could sense the sharp, mistrustful eyes focused upon them from the deck of the brig but forced himself not to stare back as he steered for the centre of the gap, about half a cable's length from the moored vessel. He could only hope that what Olumiji had told them would gull them for long enough. He could see the men waiting at the jetty with two mule carts for the guns and the powder kegs stacked in the centre of each boat.

They were right in the middle of the gap now and the tide, thank God, still with them. He looked behind at the following boats: Tully in the second, Holroyd in the third with a scarf wrapped round the lower part of his face to avoid recognition. Just about keeping their station. A swift glance at the brig. She was pointing almost directly towards him, the gunports still closed and the hands lining the side, staring out at the approaching flotilla. The cutter swinging idly at her mooring about fifty yards beyond, with no one aboard that he could see.

He should start to turn now and head towards the jetty if that was his direction, but he kept on, holding on as long as possible to his present course. Three more strokes of the oar. Level now with the bow of the brig. He heard a shout from her decks, more questioning than alarmed, ignored it, carried on, still not looking. Another shout, angrier now, and he threw the tiller over, yelling an order to the rowers. They came round in a slow arc, painfully slow, until they were pointing directly at the brig.

'Pull!' he urged them. 'For God's sake, pull!' The other two boats had turned with him, all three rushing for their target at different points along the brig's side.

Shouts of alarm now and a louder voice raised in command. Nathan saw men running towards the 6-pounder in the bows but then the brig started to swing on her spring cable to bring her broadside to bear. Fifty yards. Less. The gunports flew open and they ran out the guns. One, two, three . . . How many crew did she have? Sixteen, he had been told. But enough to fire all four guns in her broadside if they did not have to worry about sailing her. And, Christ, they had them loaded! Loaded and ready to fire. He could see the smoke from the slow matches burning in the tubs. He had expected this. Expected it, but hoped against hope that they would not be so alert or as efficient.

He heard the orders, given in a calm, steady voice.

'Point your gun . . .'

Saw the squat black muzzles shifting in the gun ports. Saw his own particular gun, the one that was aimed directly at him. Saw the gun captain through the open port bent over the breech with his powder horn, carefully measuring the fine powder into the quill.

'Fire as you bear!'

The sharp crack of the report and Nathan flinched. But it came from his own boat – from Whiteley, lying full length in the bow with the hunting rifle he preferred to the Brown Bess musket – and whether it hit its target or not they gained ten precious yards before Nathan saw the spurt of flame from the powder quill in the breech of the cannon.

'Down!' he screamed. 'Everyone down!' He felt the scorched wind across his back, the brutal howling fury of the grape, but they had fired too high or else the gun would go no lower. He roared at the shocked marines to take up their oars again and pull.

Twenty yards, no more.

'Pull!'

A plume of fire through the smoke and a deafening report. Nathan gave an appalled look to his right, saw the grape tear through Tully's boat, and then he was pushing the tiller hard over to his right and yelling for his crew to ship oars. They bobbed close by the brig's side with an infuriating gap of three or four feet but one of the few seamen in his crew leaned over with a boat hook, gripped the mizzen shrouds and hauled them alongside.

A mad scramble up the side. Nathan leaped for the shrouds and hoisted himself up to the rail, but seeing two men running at him, one with a pistol and the other with a pike, wisely kept going in the direction of the mizzen top. The pike man attempted to foil him in this intent by thrusting the weapon up at his belly. Nathan let go with one hand to fend it off, arching his body back, but the curved blade caught in the ratlines and instead of gutting him, merely succeeded in piercing his thigh. The pain, though, was impressive. Nathan seized hold of it and pulled it out, appalled by the gush of blood, but short of dropping back into the launch he could only continue his advance, wrenching the pike out of the man's hands and dropping down on to the deck. The sudden pain in his leg caused him to stumble and almost fall, a fortunate mishap as his second assailant chose that precise moment to fire the pistol at his head. This, being lower than it was, avoided the worst effects of the discharge, only suffering an additional parting to the scalp. Nathan, still possessing sufficient of his wits, reversed the pike and thrust it upwards into the man's guts, pulled it out and, seized by a savage bloodlust, went after its previous owner. But his own blood was flowing freely now from the wound in his scalp and the former pikeman, observing his distraction, seized up a belaying pin and hurled it at his head. Then, noting the number of boarders now in contention, he sprinted for the opposite side of the brig, leaped up on to the rail and cast himself into the sea.

Nathan, severely disheartened by the belaying pin which had struck him a glancing blow on the temple, sat down on a hatch cover with some notion of reviewing the situation.

This design was thwarted by a large red-haired man with a pistol and a cutlass who came charging down the deck towards him, removing such obstacles as presented themselves in his path by the simple expedient of shooting one and disembowelling the other. Nathan moved to abandon his sedentary position with some alacrity and drew one of his own pistols with the intention of shooting his assailant in the head, but this excellent plan was betrayed by a singular circumstance.

The pistol was one that Nathan had acquired in Paris: one of a pair, in fact, which he had obtained from the armoury of the Tuileries on the day of the coup that had succeeding in toppling Robespierre and ending the Terror. They were short, stubby affairs made in Belgium, known as greatcoat pistols because they would conveniently fit into the pocket of such a garment, and he had kept them largely on this account. They were not accurate, he had discovered, beyond a range of about twenty yards but he considered them useful in close quarter encounters, and the configuration of the muzzle and the butt made for a satisfactory club after they had been discharged. They also had the facility of a small metal cap which fitted over the firing pan and preserved the powder from damp, a serious consideration when fighting at sea. The sole disadvantage of this device was that it had to be removed before firing and this Nathan had neglected to do, with the consequence that when he pressed the trigger the hammer fell upon the metal cap and the powder failed to ignite as effectively as if it had been thoroughly soaked in seawater.

With an oath directed as much at his own incompetence as at the manufacturers of the pistol and his intended target, Nathan threw the weapon at his opponent's head and sprang to one side with sufficient agility to avoid a blow from the cutlass that would have split his own skull from crown to chin. The force of this blow was so great, in fact, it caused the sword to lodge itself in the hatch cover and Nathan was able to draw his own sword and prepare a more adequate defence than he had hitherto been allowed.

Besides his naval training Nathan had been instructed in swordsmanship by no less an exponent of the art than Henry Angelo, son of the famous Domenico Angelo Malevolti Tremamondo of Livorno, whose fencing school in Soho was patronised by some of the most accomplished and aristocratic blades in England. Nathan had attended it at his mother's expense, she being in funds at the time, as a twenty-first birthday gift.

Signor Angelo's methods, however, being of the Italian school and laying heavy emphasis on subtlety, dexterity and the Machiavellian artifice of the feint, were possibly more suited to a duel on the palazzo than to the chaotic conditions of a hand-to-hand encounter on a ship of war, especially as Nathan's opponent, in this instance, had clearly been exposed from an early age to the Irish school.

'If you have the clear head,' Signor Angelo had maintained, 'you will find the point always has the victory over the edge . . .' A dictum with which Nathan was entirely in agreement. The proviso, however, was that you had 'the clear head' and this posed something of a problem when it was reeling from a blow to the temple, half blinded by blood and preoccupied with avoiding the series of wild, exuberant slashes and thrusts available to an energetic and enraged tyro of the Irish school.

Driven to the far rail and with no remaining room for manoeuvre, Nathan finally abjured his tutor's sophisticated techniques, seized his opponent by the throat and drove his knee into his groin, distracting him sufficiently to step to one side and pierce him neatly through the shoulder with a thrust that Signor Angelo and even his esteemed father might have approved.

The cutlass clattered to the deck and Nathan applied the point of his sword to the man's chin.

'Yield,' he instructed him, with some notion of chivalry.

'Be fucked to dat,' replied the Irishman, seizing the sword in a clenched fist and bending it away from him, while lashing out with his boot and catching Nathan a terrible clout on his right knee. Ill tempered from this blow and glimpsing an approaching shape to his right, Nathan wrenched the sword free of the man's grasp and drove it decisively into a point a little below his throat and above his breastbone. He drew it out to release a shocking amount of blood and turned to face this new assailant.

But it was Tully.

'You're alive,' Nathan observed with relief.

'So it would appear,' said Tully, 'and yourself?' Gazing in concern at the top of Nathan's head.

'I will let you know,' Nathan replied, 'in a day or two.'

This conversation, though brief, was permitted them only because the battle appeared to be at an end. Nathan crossed to the starboard rail. The cutter was still at its mooring, still apparently unmanned. He looked for Holroyd and saw him leaning against the rail, looking sick and holding something bloody in his hand.

'What have you got there, Mr Holroyd?' Nathan asked, distracted for a moment.

'My ear, sir.' He exposed his broken teeth in a shaky grin. 'I thought the surgeon might sew it back on.'

'Good man.' Nathan was warming somewhat toward the midshipman after fighting three battles together, if only because they had both survived them. He would be almost human without the spots – the scarf had been a considerable improvement – but now it was clutched to the side of his head where the ear had been, apparently in an attempt to staunch the flow of blood.

'In the meantime, do you see that cutter there?'

Holroyd indicated that he did.

'I want you to take it out for us – do you think you can do that?'

'Yes, sir.'

'Good man. Take the gig you will find tied to the stem and three seamen – not guffies – and sail her out to the *Unicorn* where she belongs.'

'Yes, sir.'

Nathan had promised Adedike the brig but not the cutter. It was his cutter. He had come all the way from England for it and put up with a great deal of inconvenience on the journey; he was damned if he was going to leave it here.

He looked down at his other boats. Two were intact, the third was filled with bodies and bloodied water. God only knew how Tully had survived. He called him over.

'See if any of them are still alive,' he instructed him, 'and bring them aboard if you can.'

But even as he spoke, the launch filled up and sank. Nathan swore an oath. He looked up at the sky, then around the shambles of the decks. Bodies everywhere, some his, most not. Most of the mutineers had fought to the death, knowing what would happen if they were captured, but his men had taken some prisoners. They brought them to him – three of them – one little more than a boy, another wearing the uniform of a master's mate in His Britannic Majesty's Navy.

'Take that off,' Nathan commanded him savagely.

The fellow struggled to obey but the right sleeve was soaked in blood, his arm slashed from wrist to elbow.

'Leave it,' said Nathan wearily. 'You would be Keane, I suppose?'

'I would,' said Keane. 'God help me.'

'And where is the man called O'Neill?'

'He is over there, the bastard,' said Keane venomously, 'with his throat cut just as he cut the captain's.'

Nathan saw that he meant his red-haired assailant. He went to look.

'So I killed him,' he said wonderingly to Tully as they stared down at the body. 'They sent me all this way for that.'

But it was not over yet.

They laid the dead and the wounded in the launch belonging to the brig. They had lost ten men, most gone down with the boat, and half a dozen wounded, two so badly Nathan did not think they would live.

Nathan permitted Tully to bandage up his wounds and then went down to the captain's cabin to see if he could find anything of interest. He took the log and a bundle of charts, a sextant and a compass, and some papers written in English and French. Then they climbed down into the boats and set off for the jetty.

The whole shoreline and the battlements of the fort were lined with men who had been watching the battle. Nathan caught a glimpse of red on the walls of the barbican. Adedike. She kissed her hand to him and then he saw her expression change to concern as she saw the state he was in. With one bloody bandana wrapped around his head and another around his thigh.

They unloaded the small arms and the powder and shot.

Nathan glanced up at the fort. Adedike was gone from the battlements. He saw Olumiji coming down from the gate with his bodyguard, doubtless to make sure he had his guns. Then Adedike came running out of the gate after him, her red robe streaming out behind her.

Nathan stepped ashore.

'That's the lot,' said Tully.

'Thank you,' Nathan said. He looked at him, then reached out a hand to Martin's neck and pulled his head to him, resting his forehead against him for an instant. He was too choked to speak. Then he began to walk towards the fort.

'Where are you going?' Tully called after him.

Nathan kept walking. He heard Tully running after him and felt his hand on his shoulder. He turned.

'I have to stay,' he said. 'That was the arrangement.' He managed a shaky grin. 'She needs a captain of artillery.'

'The Hell she does!' Tully took out a pistol and pressed it under Nathan's chin. 'Back in the boat.'

'What the fuck are you doing?' demanded Nathan, truly astonished.

'Back in the fucking boat.' Tully manhandled him off the jetty, yelling orders to the startled men in the boats.

Nathan could hear shouts from the direction of the fort.

'This is mutiny,' said Nathan. 'You could hang for it.'

Tully threw him down into the boat and jumped after him and held the pistol to his head.

'I gave my word,' Nathan told him. 'I said I would come back.'

'And so you did,' said Tully. 'Pull, you bastards,' he instructed the marines.

Nathan saw the men on the shore raising their muskets.

'Put down your weapons or I will blow his head off,' Tully shouted in French.

Tully cocked the pistol. Nathan prayed to God it was not loaded. He heard Adedike screaming orders in her own tongue. The men lowered their muskets. They were heading out into the mouth of the bay.

'Keep close to the headland,' said Nathan, recollecting himself.

Tully gave the order and the three boats crept along the foot of the headland under the guns of the fort. The cutter was already out, her sails set, heading for the distant frigate.

Nathan looked back and saw Adedike standing at the end of the jetty with her arms outstretched. She was shouting something – a plea or a curse. She looked so beautiful he felt a deep pang of regret. But it passed.

'You can put the pistol away,' he told Tully. 'I am not going to swim to her.'

'I would not put it past you,' said Tully, but then he remembered his place. 'I beg your pardon, sir. I am, of course, entirely at your command.'

But Nathan was past caring who gave the commands. He felt as if someone had stabbed him in the chest. He pressed his hand to the pain, doubling up in agony.

'Christ . . .' He felt the blood drain from his face.

'What is it?' Tully was leant over him, his own face creased with anxiety.

'I don't know,' said Nathan wonderingly. 'It feels like my heart.'

Chapter Twenty-Two

Enemy in Sight

———◆———

'Well, I do not think it is your heart,' concluded McLeish, after tapping at Nathan's chest and listening to it through a small instrument held to his ear. 'And you did not receive a wee knock in the scuffle?'

'I received several wee knocks in the "scuffle", as you call it,' Nathan informed him wearily, 'but not, so far as I am aware, upon the chest.'

'Well, let us be having a look at the others and I dare say you may find it a distraction from whatever discomforts ye in t'other region.'

A distraction it was, but when McLeish had finished stitching the wounds to Nathan's head and thigh, the pain in his chest returned as savagely as before.

'What in God's name can it be?' he demanded. He found it difficult to breathe.

'I can only suppose it is a spot of wind,' suggested

McLeish mildly. 'Have you eaten anything that might have disagreed with you at all?'

'Wind? *Wind?* It feels as if someone has driven a spike into my chest. And I have not eaten a thing for several hours. Dear God, man. *Wind?*' He rolled over on his side in the hope of easing the pain. 'Christ,' he groaned. 'I fear the wench has done for me.'

'The wench, indeed? And which wench would this be?'

Nathan did not answer but Tully, who had brought him down, murmured in the doctor's ear that he supposed he must mean 'the witch woman' who was a kind of shaman to the Army of Lucumi.

'And how might that relate to the pain in his chest?' McLeish enquired with the coolness of a professional whose diagnosis is questioned by an inferior. Neither Tully nor Nathan felt it incumbent upon them to reply and after observing them both for a moment with a frown, McLeish exclaimed: 'Dear God, man, never tell me you believe yourself to be hexed! By a witch, forsooth, God bless my soul.'

Nathan became aware of a new attentiveness in the crowded cockpit for they had not been speaking Latin.

'Is there anything I can do?' asked Brother Ignatius, who had been helping to attend the wounded.

'Well, it is more your province than mine,' replied the doctor. 'I received scant instruction in the treatment of curses at the medical faculty of Edinburgh, the last witch being burned somewhat before my time, though it was in my own home town of Kirkcudbright, I believe.'

'I had always understood that witches were hanged in

England,' the monk remarked with interest.

'That is as may be,' McLeish retorted, 'and I am not one to be critical of the English, but Kirkcudbright being in Scotland we have our own ways of dispensing justice, and doubtless those that concern themselves with such matters considered that burning was a more reliable means of disposing of a nuisance than hanging, though in a more enlightened age we have recourse to neither but merely consign the poor creatures to the madhouse.'

'It is nonetheless an interesting phenomenon,' Brother Ignatius observed, and resorting to the Latin in which both he and McLeish had been versed for their respective reasons, he added: 'The curse of a witch has been known to have a surprisingly potent effect upon the simple, superstitious mind. I have known otherwise healthy creatures to wither away in the course of a few days and frequently expire.'

'This is possibly true,' agreed McLeish, 'but I fear it is entirely beyond my powers to propose a remedy, other than a strong emetic. Do not feel constrained, however, if you wish to bestow a blessing. I do not believe he has any significant aversion to the Church of Rome. Indeed, I would have thought his religious propensity to be quite low.'

'I am perfectly conscious,' Nathan informed them both coldly, 'despite my considerable discomfort, and though I was the despair of my tutors I had the good fortune to receive a classical education – at least in the Latin – so if you wish to continue your discourse without regard to your patient's finer feelings, may I suggest you do so in

Greek, Hebrew or Aramaic – or whatever scholarly language you have had the leisure to pursue.'

This speech, though not lengthy, caused him some considerable effort but it was worth it to see the expressions on their faces and the protestations of regret, doubtless sincere on the monk's part.

'My dear sir, I meant no offence,' he assured Nathan. 'In fact, I am inclined to take your complaint a good deal more seriously than those who aspire to what they call "an enlightened approach" . . .' He slid his eyes disparagingly towards McLeish. 'And although medicine may apply itself to superficial physical injury with some success, it appears to me to be entirely at a loss when it comes to the more complex afflictions of mankind.'

'Aye well, when the Church of Rome discovers a cure for yellow fever or bubonic plague or those mental conditions that baffle us poor physicians, pray inform me of it,' retorted McLeish, and then, addressing himself to Nathan: 'In the meantime I would prescribe a bolus that I will instruct my assistant to make up for you. And a few hours' sleep would not come amiss, either, for you have lost a great deal of blood which, I have been told, can render the mind as feeble as the body.'

'As to that, I am of the opinion that a frank confession of sin and a sincere act of contrition frequently soothes the mind as effectively as it relieves the spirit,' remarked Brother Ignatius, complacently folding his hands within the copious sleeves of his habit.

'Thank you, sir, but if I am to die I would prefer to die in the faith of my fathers,' Nathan assured him, and then turning to the doctor and addressing him in Latin, out of consideration for his other patients: 'And as to your boluses, you may stick them where they will do more good, for I am perfectly aware of the palliatives offered to the "simple, superstitious mind". But I thank you for stitching me up and now, if you have no objection, I will go about my duties.'

And with some effort and all the dignity he could muster, he stood up and hobbled back to the quarterdeck.

The *Unicorn* was heading sou-sou-west under a full press of sail and Tully had the watch. He looked at Nathan in concern.

'A chair for the captain,' he instructed Lamb, who was at the con. Then, lowering his voice for Nathan's private ear: 'If you will permit me, sir, you look as if you could use some sleep.'

'So the doctor tells me. However, I would sleep better for knowing our present position and what speed we are making.'

Tully told him. They were at the edge of the Sea of Sirens and making a little over six knots with the wind in the north-east. 'And if you feel up to it, sir, one of the mutineers – Keane – has asked if he may speak with you.'

'Where is he?'

'Put in irons, sir, at your command.'

Nathan sank into the chair Lamb had brought him. He could not contemplate a trip below decks, unless it was to collapse in his cabin.

'Bring him up on deck,' he said.

Keane when he appeared looked as bad as Nathan felt.

He was a young man of about Nathan's age with features that would have been accounted personable, had they not been so drawn and pale.

'I beg your pardon, sir,' he began, 'and I do not wish to distract you from your duties, but I wished to make a plea on behalf of the boy.'

'The boy?'

'Dermot Quinn, sir, that was taken with me on the brig.'

'Oh, the boy. Yes. What of him?'

'Only to say, sir, that he had nothing to do with the mutiny but only came into the cutter out of loyalty to his fellow countrymen.'

'And what of his loyalty to King George?'

'Oh, sir, he is a young boy, barely thirteen years old, and a native of Dublin.'

'Old enough to choose better company, and is not Dublin a province of the kingdom?'

'It is, sir, and I doubt the boy would contest it for he is the son of a gentleman and a lawyer.'

'Is he indeed, then what is he doing—' But he bit his tongue for the fellow was in no position to answer his abuse.

'With the likes of us,' Keane finished for him with a grim smile. 'The fact is, sir, he was staying with his mother's sister's family on the south coast of England when his uncle was taken by the press and the boy would not be separated from him and so the officer said they should take him along as well.'

'And where is his uncle now?'

'He was knocked on the head, sir, in the fight with the slaver.'

'I see, so he was in on the mutiny?'

'He was, sir, and that may have been the reason the boy came with us.'

'Very well. I am sure the court martial will take this into consideration.'

Keane bowed his head. 'My God, sir, you know what they will do to him, and he was as opposed as any of us to the way O'Neill served out the captain.'

'I am sorry, Keane, but it is the best I can do.' He felt another savage pain in his chest and gasped.

Tully came to his side as they led Keane below. 'Are you sure there is nothing I can do for you, sir?'

'No. I will be all right.'

He was distracted by a shout from the lookout in the foretop: a sail coming up fast on their larboard beam. But she was a smaller vessel than a frigate and as she approached they saw that she was a merchant vessel: a snow brig flying the Union flag. She must have seen *their* colours but she altered course and ran to the south. It took them an hour to catch her and oblige her to heave to under their guns. Her captain came over in his gig and reported to Nathan on the quarterdeck. Mr Barnaby Leach, of the snow *Priscilla* out of Bristol, bound for Panama with a cargo of dry goods. He had thought they were French, he said, flying false colours.

'You were not heading for Panama when we sighted you,' Nathan pointed out.

'That is because we were running from a French

frigate,' Leach told Nathan, 'that we sighted in the Windward Passage.'

They had been sailing through the Passage, he said, when they were overtaken by the packet *Greyhound*, come from England with despatches for the governor in Port Royal. They had sailed in company for a while, exchanging news, but then they had sighted a strange sail bearing down on them from the east and so they had scattered, the packet running for Port Royal and the *Priscilla* to the west.

'But she went straight after the *Greyhound*,' said Leach, 'and at such a lick I'll swear she will have o'ertook her.'

'And you say she was a frigate?'

'I do. And a French national ship. To tell truth I thought you was her, somehow got ahead of us – for she had the same red band on her side. That is why we ran from you, even though we saw the ensign.'

'And when was this?' Nathan felt a fierce exhilaration; if only he was not in such pain.

'About three hours since.'

Nathan thanked him and sent him on his way. He instructed Baker to set a course for the south-west.

'You think she is the *Virginie*?' enquired Pym unnecessarily.

'Whoever she is, we must see if we can come up with her,' Nathan informed him briskly.

There was little chance of catching her up, given the start she had, but if she *was* the *Virginie* there was a fair chance she had been heading for Boca del Serpiente – even if she had permitted herself to be distracted for a while by the packet. He was considering whether he had the energy to consult the charts in his cabin when Gabriel approached bearing a tumbler upon a tray.

'Doctor says this is your bolus, sir, and you are to drink it at once, if you please.'

'Be damned to the doctor's bolus,' said Nathan. He peered into the glass and made a face. 'Does Mr McLeish think that if he makes something sufficiently disgusting, the more gullible among us will be convinced of its efficacy?'

'That would indeed be a futile exercise,' said McLeish dryly as he emerged from the companionway, 'given your immunity to the power of suggestion. But you will find it no more disagreeable than a cup of whey. If you will be so good as to take your medicine like a good fellow.'

Nathan drank. McLeish was right. It was not at all unpleasant, though he was conscious of a pressure in his innards.

He gave vent to a mighty belch.

'Be damned,' he murmured weakly, and was shaken by another.

The quarterdeck maintained a veneer of discipline. But the pain had eased a little and now he felt a stirring in his bowels.

'What in God's name is it?' he demanded, gazing into the empty cup.

'Bicarbonate of soda and a distillation of liquorice and senna,' McLeish informed him calmly. 'A concoction of my own devising which I have always found efficacious in cases involving the use of sorcery.'

'Dear God, get me to a privy,' Nathan commanded Gabriel as he struggled out of his chair.

'Wind,' he heard McLeish remark complacently to Tully as he limped from the quarterdeck. 'I told him it was wind. It can be surprisingly painful if trapped in the wrong place.'

Nathan was comfortably installed on the privy adjoining his cabin when he heard the shout from the lookout:

'Sail ho! Three points off the starboard bow.'

Chapter Twenty-Three

The Virgin and the Unicorn

Nathan stared intently at the approaching ship through his Dollond glass. At this distance all he could be sure of was that she was ship-rigged, almost certainly a ship of war, and that she might, just might, have a red stripe along her side.

And she was exactly on course to round Cape Cruz and beat back into the Boca del Serpiente.

He closed the telescope and made his way back down the shrouds, rather more staidly than was his normal practice, to where his impatient subordinates awaited him on the quarterdeck.

'Very well, Mr Pym, let us fly the signal – but in the meantime I think we may beat to quarters.'

At once came the stirring beat of the marine drum and the fiendish shriek of the boatswain's pipes down the companionways to summon up the watch from below.

But Nathan felt a deeper stirring.

'Carry on, Mr Pym,' he murmured to the bemused lieutenant as he hurried below to find McLeish.

More concerted activity all along the gundeck as they folded the bulkheads up to the deckhead and cast loose the guns, converting them from mere furnishings – convenient hurdles between mess tables – to deadly weapons of war; powder boys rushing up from the magazine with their paper cartridges; McGregor's sentries taking up their stations at the companionways to prevent others from leaving theirs; Nathan's own quarters entirely demolished and Gabriel supervising the removal of the breakables to the orlop deck. Nathan followed them below and found the doctor busy in the cockpit with his assistant and the loblolly boys, laying out the grisly tools of their trade: the scalpels and forceps, the tenon saws, probes, catlins, needles, nippers and turnscrews, the yards of bandage and cloth . . .

'So you want something to bind you now,' the doctor established after listening to Nathan's apologetic and somewhat oblique request. Out of respect for his captain's dignity he at least spoke in the language of his profession.

'I do,' Nathan confirmed, in the same tongue. 'For while I am much obliged to you for easing the apparent obstruction, I fear you may have loosened more than is advisable at the onset of a battle.'

'Indeed, and it would inevitably have an adverse effect on morale were you to unburden yourself upon the quarterdeck,' McLeish conceded unnecessarily. 'Well, I can supply the means of redress, but I must warn you that while it may render the bowels inactive for a limited period, the inevitable release, as it were, when the effect diminishes, may confine you to the seat of ease for some considerable time.'

'My dear doctor,' Nathan replied, 'if that is the worst unpleasantness I may suffer as a result of the forthcoming engagement then I may count myself fortunate indeed, and if it is not disrespectful to the Almighty I will make use of the enforced period of leisure to offer thanks for my deliverance.'

He returned to the quarterdeck with the small brown bottle that McLeish had delivered to him – 'Fifteen drops in a cup of water, no more, and if the engagement should continue for more than an hour or so you had better repeat the dose if you do not wish to make a spectacle of yourself in sight of the enemy.' A quarterdeck restored to its usual calm but considerably reinforced by a contingent of marines and the gun crews at the 6-pounders and the carronades. Nathan glanced swiftly to the south-east. Their quarry was noticeably closer and had not altered her course by a single degree. Twenty minutes and they would cross her bows, if they did not collide.

'She has not answered the confidential signal, sir.'

'Thank you, Mr Pym.' He applied his eye once more to the glass, thrusting a steadying arm through the shrouds. Yes, there she was. The chaste white figure at the bow and the broad red stripe at her gunports. After journeying so far and for so long. And this time he was ready for her.

He snapped shut the telescope.

'Send the word for Mr Lloyd.'

The carpenter hurried aft, dragging his cap over his sweating pate.

'Mr Lloyd, I believe we still have your virgin at our bow.'

'Aye, sir, which I was never instructed to remove.'

'I am aware of that and I do not blame you for it, but it will never do, you know.'

'I had thought, sir, that they might take it a form of mockery, do you see?' explained the carpenter. 'The way the Welsh archers would give the French the two fingers, you know, at the time of Agincourt.'

Nathan stared at him incredulously. The man had hidden depths.

'I am sorry, Mr Lloyd, but we cannot charge into battle with a smirking whore at our bow. You must get rid of her, sir. Cast her into the sea and give us back our unicorn.'

It was easier said than done, even with the carpenter's mate sawing away from the beak and two hands out on the bowsprit pulling at the noose around her neck, but at last she fell away and there was their unicorn, if not quite whole . . .

'The horn, sir, the horn!' exclaimed Nathan, who had gone up forward to see the job done. 'You must give him back his horn.'

'Oh, sir, but I do not know if we have the time.' The carpenter looked pointedly out toward the enemy, looming large off their starboard bow. But under Nathan's fierce frown he scuttled off with his mate to the carpenter's store and came back a minute later with the object clasped to his bosom.

'You will be glad now that you cut it off at an angle,' Nathan assured him as the carpenter leaned over the beak, holding it in position while his mate hammered in the nails. 'Perhaps a lick of paint to disguise the join.'

He grinned into the carpenter's appalled countenance. 'I am making game of you, Mr Lloyd, you may return to your station.'

And Nathan returned to his at the quarterdeck where Mr Holroyd begged his attention.

'Mr Tully's compliments, sir, and he wonders if you would free the prisoners who are in irons so that he may make use of them at the guns.'

Dear God, he had entirely forgotten them. It was to Tully's credit that he had not.

'By all means,' he said. 'Find the master at arms and have them freed. Let us see if they may redeem themselves somewhat,' he remarked to no one in particular. He doubted if it would count much in their favour at a court martial, but it might save them from a hanging, if only by getting in the way of a round of French shot.

'Sir, beg pardon, sir, but there is something I think you should see.'

Mr Lamb now with his telescope.

Nathan took it from him and crossed over to the leeward rail.

'She is full of soldiers, sir. I thought you should know.'

'Quite right, Mr Lamb.'

He could see them packed into the waist and crowded into her tops. French regular infantry and marines. Nathan wondered if they were the same marines who had been paroled in the Mississippi Delta, and with that thought he swung the glass up to the quarterdeck and there he was: Gilbert Imlay, large as life, standing a little apart from the huddle of officers on the weatherside and staring over towards the *Unicorn* as she bore down on them. His Nemesis.

It was to be hoped.

Nathan handed the glass back to the midshipman without comment and sought out the sailing master at the con.

'Mr Baker, when we have run past her we will wear ship and cross her stern.'

'Aye, aye, sir, wear ship it is, sir, to cross her stern.'

It was an obvious manoeuvre, even to Baker – and well worth conceding the weather gauge for that one raking broadside. But if it was obvious to Baker it must be obvious to their opponent. So what would they do about it?

Nathan stared intently at the approaching frigate. Who would make the decisions – Lafitte or Bergeret? Lafitte would be in command of overall strategy – where the *Virginie* sailed and why – but when it came to fighting, Nathan was almost certain it would be the former sailing master, Jacques Bergeret, who made the decisions that mattered. What would Nathan do in the same position? He knew very well that he would wear ship the moment he was past and present his larboard broadside: the guns that had not yet fired. He might get in a complete broadside while his opponent was still reloading and then they would run downwind together, exchanging broadside for broadside . . . and with all those soldiers available to him he would try to board at the earliest opportunity.

As he stared out at her he saw the sudden flash of fire from her starboard bowchaser and then the other. The two separate explosions rolled over the water towards them, chasing the hurtling shot, and he marked where they fell, about a cable's length short and just off his starboard bow.

'Tell Mr Clyde to fire as he bears,' he instructed Lamb absently: he was not going to be distracted by a duel between their bowchasers, not when they would be exchanging broadsides a few minutes from now.

'What is the time?' he asked his clerk Mr Shaw, who stood at his side with his chronograph and his notebook.

'Eleven minutes past four o'clock, sir,' replied the clerk precisely, but Nathan saw that his hands were shaking.

A hole suddenly appeared in their fore course. They were aiming high in the French tradition, hoping to disable him before he brought his broadside to bear or make him fall off from the wind. If they kept to their present course, the two ships would pass each other at a distance of no more than 100 yards, Nathan figured . . . And then, as he gazed out at her from the leeward rail, he saw her bows come round into the wind until they were pointing directly towards him.

He sought the master's eye. 'Bring her a little further into the wind, Mr Baker.'

'Aye, aye, sir, but she is already near as far as she will go.'

'Even so, I think she may take half a point.'

He watched the edge of the sails for the slightest sign of feathering, both ships now heading up into the wind as close as they could possibly sail.

What was she trying to do? She could not cross the *Unicorn*'s bow for she could not come so far into the wind. And if she kept to her present course the two ships would collide. Was that what her captain intended? A head-on collision might sink both ships. No, he was hoping Nathan would give way and forfeit the weather gauge – and if he did not . . .

He came to an instant decision.

'Mr Baker, prepare to wear ship.'

'To wear?' It was almost a wail. 'Now, sir?'

Nathan turned a furious face upon him and saw the despairing glance Baker threw at Pym.

They began to wear.

'Gun crews to larboard,' Nathan roared, loud enough for them to hear him on the gundeck below – and he heard his cry repeated in the waist and then the rush of feet, the creak of tackle and the screech of the carriages as they ran out the guns on the larboard side.

They were coming round, crossing directly ahead of the *Virginie*'s bows at a distance of about a cable's length. Nathan glanced down the row of guns in the waist.

'Fire as you bear!'

The rippling crash of the broadside. The *Virginie* disappeared briefly in the black pall of smoke.

'And now they will rake us,' he distinctly heard Pym mutter in the background.

'Right about! Mind you take us right about, Mr Baker,'

Nathan instructed the bemused sailing master in case he had it in mind to run downwind, but they were still coming round and the *Virginie*'s bow was pointing directly at their stern, the bowsprit barely fifty yards from them and closing. He could see the holes in her fore course, one of the bowchasers dismounted and by God, they had taken the head off her virgin . . .

'Gun crews to starboard,' Nathan bellowed, but they were already on their way, running back to their former positions as the bows came round, the sails filling and cracking as they took the wind from the starboard quarter, and the *Virginie* coming up fast on the same side . . .

'Fire as you bear!'

The two broadsides crashed out together and Nathan could barely see for the smoke, but he could hear the terrible sounds of the shot smashing home and the shrieks of the wounded all about him. He saw a series of individual tableaux, as if lit by flashes of lightning on a storm-black night: the starboard rail exploding in a shower of splinters; a piece of timber, a foot long, sticking out of Shaw's throat; his chronograph and his notebook falling from his lifeless hands; one of the quarterdeck 6-pounders knocked clean off its truck and its crew sprawled about it, dead and dying; McGregor red faced and roaring, pointing his sword toward the French marines in the tops like an enraged sorcerer who would bring them down with a curse; a helmsman reeling back with his hands to his face and the blood spurting between his fingers; and the look of surprise on Pym's face as a French round took off his hat and the top part of his head.

Then the *Virginie* was past, her greater way taking her ahead of them as Nathan had known it would, with the *Unicorn* still completing her turn, and he shouted in Baker's ear to make him understand they were to come as far into the wind as was possible, on exactly the same course as the *Virginie* had been.

'But stand by to wear again if she drops off from the wind.'

Would she? It was what Nathan would do. But she was holding to her present course with the *Unicorn* about half a cable's length behind her. Why? She could not be running from them, surely.

'Mr Lamb?' He looked round for the midshipman.

'Here, sir.' Popping up from behind him like a pantomime demon with a crazed grin on his face. Instantly changed to horror as he stared at Nathan's chest. 'Oh, sir, you have been hit.'

Nathan glanced down and felt his heart leap into his throat as he saw the spreading stain, and then raised his eyes to heaven as he remembered the little bottle of brown medicine McLeish had given him.

'Give me the glass.' He snatched it from Lamb's hand and sighted along the rail at the huddle of officers on the *Virginie*'s quarterdeck. They seemed to be arguing. He could see them waving their arms in the French manner, not that he had anything against that, he did a fair amount of arm-waving himself when he was excited; perhaps it was the French in him. He saw that Imlay was

involved in the dispute, if dispute it was. Could she be
running for the Sea of Sirens – hoping to carry out her
mission of aiding the rebels? But she would have to leave
him labouring in her wake and there was little chance of
that. The two ships were just about matched for speed –
and if she held to her present course, there was a danger
of running upon Cape Cruz. Besides, she had no
sternchasers and not much in the way of weaponry on her
quarterdeck either, for she had left her *obusiers* in the
swamps of the Rigolets. The *Unicorn*, on the other hand,
could fire with her bowchasers and – as she clawed into
the wind – the most forward of the forecastle guns.

Finally, someone on the French quarterdeck saw sense
– or won his point – for Nathan saw the *Virginie*'s stern
swing away from him as she fell off from the wind and he
yelled to Baker to follow suit and the two ships turned
together like two stately dancers and began to race
downwind, hammering away at each other with their long
guns and scarcely 100 yards between them . . .

The *Unicorn*'s crew had improved at their murderous
trade. All along the crowded gundeck they toiled without
ceasing, swabbing out the smoking muzzles, ramming in
the paper cartridge and the iron shot, heaving at the tackle
to run the heavy cannon back up to the open ports, the
iron wheels of the trucks shrieking almost as despairingly
as the wounded; the two ships running so close at times
the flame from the muzzles leaped across the space
between, the burning wads striking the sides and falling
back hissing into the rushing sea.

For the best part of an hour they ran on, the flash of

the guns brighter now against the darkening sky, the swirl-
ing smoke splintered by the blood-red light of the setting
sun so that at times Nathan had the impression he
was watching demons stoking the fires of Hell. Sometimes
a round would come straight through the gunports,
screaming off the metal surface, taking off a head or an
arm or a leg, but it was the great jagged splinters that did
the most damage, flying from the battered timbers and
exploding onto the crowded decks.

Both ships were firing double-shotted, mostly into the
hulls, though the French had a few guns loaded with chain
still in the hope of crippling them aloft. And with some
success. First the *Unicorn*'s mizzen topmast went and then
their gaff, and then they lost the use of the mainsail when
both leech-ropes were shot away. Twice the *Virginie*
steered towards them in the hope of boarding, but each
time Nathan saw her coming through the smoke and
veered off. But with the damage the *Unicorn* had suffered
aloft he could not back his mizzen to slow down that
headlong rush and cross her stern for one killer raking
blow. Still, he could see the blows they had dealt her, the
gaping wounds in her side where two or more gunports
had been knocked into one, the shattered lengths of rail
and the blood running from her scuppers. Her mizzen too
had gone by the board and a little after half past five her
main topmast fell, instantly followed by the fore
topgallant. The sudden loss of power caused the *Unicorn*
to shoot ahead of her, and the wreckage dragged the
Virginie to starboard so that Nathan feared she would
rake them. But she missed her chance and the two ships

drew apart and for the first time in over an hour the guns fell silent.

Nathan sent the topmen aloft to reeve new braces so he could work back to windward, but before they could finish, the *Virginie* had cut loose the wreckage and was moving downwind again, firing at their stern as she passed them; but a ragged broadside it was, at a range of four or five hundred yards, with no more than five or six guns of her twenty in action and not a single hit. Nathan wondered at this, for she could not have lost that many guns or men, even after the pounding she had taken. Was she short of powder then, or shot? It had been a long time since she had left Brest and he doubted there was much of either available to them in Saint Domingue, with the war that was raging there.

He ran up to the maintop while he had the chance, ranged his glass along her decks and saw the carnage that was there, and then up to her quarterdeck where a single officer stood at the con with the two helmsmen. Then, even as Nathan watched, they began to spin the helm and she came round to the west, leaning hard over as she took the wind on her beam. By God, they were running! Running to the west. He felt a momentary exhilaration, instantly dashed, for the *Virginie* was running straight into the setting sun, the dull orange orb visibly sinking below the horizon. With night falling as swiftly as it did in the tropics she had a good chance of eluding them. He burned his hands sliding down the stay to the quarterdeck but hardly noticed the pain, he was so anxious not to lose her. By the time they came about she was a mere shadow against what little light remained in the western sky. And by God she was cracking on – for the wind had freshened and she must be making four or five knots even with her reduced canvas. Nathan looked to his own sails, wondering if he could get more out of them by falling off the wind, for he was no longer afraid of ceding the weather gauge, and if he could only range alongside her, he might cut her capers yet.

He leaped down to the deck, looking for Mr Baker, but instead here was a madman yelling up at him, white eyes staring out of a smoke-blackened face. After a moment he recognised Mr Godfrey, the pilot; he had quite forgotten him – where had he been the while? Nathan shook his head and cupped his hand to his ear for the fellow's convenience and managed to comprehend that there was a very great danger that they were about to run upon an object called the Pissing Cay.

'What? What did you call it?' As if it mattered.

'Pisinoe – that is one of the Sirens.'

'Pisinoe,' Nathan repeated wonderingly and in fear. 'The one that plays the lyre.' Just as the mad philosopher had warned him. He heard the distant drone from his schooldays, when they had read by rote, stumbling over the translation.

Draw near, illustrious Odysseus, flower of the Achaean chivalry, and bring your ship to rest that you may hear our voices.

But where was she? He could not see her. The sea was clear for . . .

And then he did – and was astonished that he could

have run so close to her all unaware. A long, low spit of land off his starboard bow, just beyond the *Virginie*: a reef by any other name. And the sluggish waters folding lazily over, leaving the merest smear of white like the telltale cream on a cat's whiskers.

Nathan shouted out a string of orders that brought the *Unicorn* up into the wind, heeling hard over to larboard. Shot a swift glance at the *Virginie* and saw her running on. Had they not seen it? Ah, now they had. He saw her cleave to the wind as she put her helm hard over, and for a moment he thought she would make it and with fifty yards to spare – but there must have been an outcrop of rock just below the surface of the sea, for suddenly she struck, struck with shocking violence, her foremast crashing forward with a mighty crack and the main course shredding, blowing like rags in the Siren-singing wind.

Chapter Twenty-Four

The Place of Horror

———◆◆◆———

The *Unicorn* came as close to the wind as she could, the top sails feathering and the main course cracking like a gun and flapping back against the mast. They were less than a cable's length to windward of the stricken vessel, and when Nathan looked over the side he could see the rocks below their own hull, so close he was in a cold sweat until they clawed their way into deeper water.

He counterbraced the yards about 500 yards off and they dropped anchor on a spring cable with the guns still run out and looked back at the *Virginie* perched and listing upon the rocks. The tricolour still flew from her stern but there could be no question of her fighting on: her people already had the ship's boats lowered and were passing down the wounded. It was almost night and they had the great lantern lit at her stern and more in the boats at her side, the lights dancing in the water. Wisps of smoke curled from her guns, as from the nostrils of a great sleeping dragon, stretched out upon the rocks.

Nathan looked at his watch. Twenty past six o'clock. A little more than two hours since the *Virginie* had opened fire with her bowchasers. It seemed much longer. He stared around at his bloodied decks; the blackened faces of the gun crews, some more truly black than others for the Africans seemed to have colonised the quarterdeck carronades. They grinned as they met his eye and he smiled wanly back. His ears were deafened, his brain numbed.

'My compliments to Mr Maxwell,' he instructed Lamb, still dogging his heels, 'and ask him if he would step up to the quarterdeck.'

But Lamb came back with Tully.

'Lieutenant Maxwell has been taken below,' Tully said, 'to have his wounds attended to.'

'Is he badly hurt?'

'Bad enough, by the report I heard, but he would not leave his station until it was ended.' Tully looked towards their crippled rival. 'I wish you joy of your victory.'

Victory. But there was no joy in it, only a terrible weariness. And so much still to do.

'Take command here, Martin, if you will. I am going aboard the *Virginie*.'

She was listing hard to starboard when he came alongside in his barge with McGregor and Whiteley and a score or so of their marines. Her decks were shocking, even in the subdued glow of the lanterns: a shambles of blood and debris, worse than the *Unicorn* even after the battle off Ship Island. He found someone who looked like an officer.

'Where is your captain?'

A blank stare, though Nathan had spoken in French.

'Your commanding officers, sir?'

'Dead. Both dead.' He was practically a boy, his face white and bloodied, close to tears.

Nathan took Lamb and two of the marines and went below to the stern cabin. It was a foot deep in water but there was a lantern hanging from the beams and by its light they saw Imlay sitting at the captain's table reading some papers. He looked up with a smile when he saw Nathan and said: 'There you are. I wish you joy of your victory.'

Nathan was at a loss for words. But this was never a problem for Imlay.

'I was just going through their papers to see if any were of use to us,' calmly folding one of them and making to put it into his jacket.

Nathan drew a pistol from his belt and cocked the hammer. 'Get out from there,' he told him, 'or I'll blow your head off.'

Imlay looked surprised and a little hurt. 'My dear fellow, you cannot think . . . My God, I believe you do.' He gave a hard, harsh laugh. 'But I have been a prisoner of the French these past three months or more.' He waved a hand at the papers scattered around him. Nathan saw that more were floating in the water, screwed up like little paper boats. 'I was looking to save what I could before she went down.'

Which would not be long, judging from the sounds the ship was making and the water that was in her already. Once she slid off her uneasy perch she would turn turtle and take them all down with her. Nathan felt her shift and lean even further to starboard, her timbers groaning in protest or surrender.

'Take him up on deck,' he instructed the two marines, 'and do not take your eyes off him for an instant.'

When Imlay had gone, still mouthing protests of innocence and indignation, Nathan scooped up the papers from the table and crammed them into the bag he had brought for this purpose. There were several mail-bags in one corner and he told Lamb to bring two men down from the deck to carry them into the boats. Then he took the lantern and entered the adjoining cabin. A dead man here, face down in the water, in the uniform of a senior officer – Bergeret or Lafitte perhaps. What was he doing below decks? Had he come here after they hit the rocks – for the ship's papers and her code book – and had Imlay killed him? Nathan would not have put it past him.

There was a writing desk by the wall. Nathan yanked at the drawers and stuffed his bag with more papers. Found one that was locked. Blew it open with his pistol. Here was the code book and the signals book and . . . He stared at the bundle of letters in disbelief.

Captain Nathaniel Peake, *Unicorn*, care of His Excellency the Lieutenant Governor of Jamaica. With the Admiralty seal.

How?

But of course. They must have caught up with the *Greyhound* and this had been among her mail.

Another groan from the dying ship; the water was up to his thighs now. He stuffed the bundle into his jacket and struggled back into the other cabin where he found Lamb and a couple of the hands groping about in the darkness for the mailbags. A last look around and then he followed them up on deck: a deck now canting at an angle of thirty degrees or more, with the blood running down into the scuppers, a dark crimson in the lantern light. But all the people seemed to be in the boats or at least those still alive. He looked round again, strangely reluctant to leave. Lamb was at the stern cutting down the tricolour and wrapping it up into a clumsy bundle.

Nathan waited for him to finish and then climbed after him into the barge.

They had barely pulled away when the *Virginie* gave another great groan and slid off the rocks. She sank by the bow, her stern poking up above the foaming waters like the arse of a great dabbling duck. Nathan took his hat off and stared back at her as his boatcrew rested on their oars and watched her die. Then they pulled for the *Unicorn*.

When he reached the deck, the French prisoners were being herded below and the wounded conveyed more gently to McLeish's crowded cockpit. The master-at-arms, Mr Brown, was waiting to ask what he wanted done with Mr Imlay.

'Put him in chains until I have time to deal with him,' Nathan ordered curtly.

'And Quinn?'

'Quinn?' Nathan frowned. Who in God's name was Quinn?

'He was one of the mutineers, sir. The boy. The only one to survive.'

'I see. Well, let him be for the time being. I don't think he will trouble us, do you?' He glanced around his battered ship. Baker already had men up in the damaged rigging making what repairs they could in the dark and Tully seemed to have everything under control on deck.

'I am going below, Martin,' Nathan told him. 'If you have a moment, see if you can compile a list of our casualties.'

Gabriel had the lanterns lit in his cabin and a dry pair of trousers laid out for him. Nathan could have sworn he smelled toasted cheese.

'I thought you could eat a little supper,' the Angel said.

Nathan could always eat a little supper.

The galley fires were out but Gabriel had a little spirit stove of his own in the adjoining cabin.

'Bring a bottle with it,' Nathan told him. 'The best red you can find.'

He pulled out the packet of letters from his jacket and studied them in the lantern light. One from the Admiralty, two in his father's hand and one in his mother's. Not yet opened.

The Admiralty first. He ran his eyes down the brief missive in the elegant hand of the Second Secretary. He was hereby requested and required to return in the *Unicorn* with all possible despatch and present himself to the First Lord of the Admiralty in London.

For good or ill.

Nathan held it in his hands and stared at it for a long moment, seeing his disgrace in it. And yet it was too soon for Admiral Ford's reprimand to have reached their lordships. Why then, did they want him home – and without waiting for news of the *Virginie*?

Gabriel came back with the toasted cheese and a bottle of Burgundy.

'Thank you, Gilbert.' Nathan made rare use of his first name and was rewarded with a gap-toothed grin.

'Your father would have been proud of you this day, sir. And will be when he hears of it.'

'Well, it is better news than I thought to bring him.'

And may have worse yet, he thought. He stuffed himself with toast and cheese and knocked back the late captain's best Burgundy as if it were small ale. Gilbert watched him approvingly.

'Damned good,' Nathan assured him. 'Would you have a glass with me?'

'Not at present, thankee, sir, but I will in a while.'

'Then be so good as to give my compliments to Mr Tully and I would be glad to speak with him when he has a moment.'

Tully came down almost immediately.

'Martin, grab yourself a glass and join me.'

'Thank you, sir, a quick one if I may, for there is a deal of clearing up to be done. And I have brought you the butcher's bill.' He passed over the sheet of paper with the names of the dead. Seventeen of them, with Pym's at the top.

SETH HUNTER

'And we have our orders from the Admiralty,' Nathan told him. 'Courtesy of the *Greyhound* packet by way of the *Virginie*. We are to go home.'

Tully gazed at him blankly, as if it was a concept that was entirely alien to him.

'Home, Martin.' Nathan dinned it into him. 'And to the beauty you keep in Hastings. So, as soon as you have finished your wine, you may set the men to raising the anchor and tell Mr Baker to set a course for the Windward Passage.'

A great smile lit up Tully's face as he finally took it in. He threw down the wine as if he could not bear to waste an unnecessary moment.

'Then with your permission, sir . . .'

When he had gone Nathan poured himself another glass and ran his eyes over the casualty list again.

Shaw, of course, and Mr Midshipman Meadows and others he had never got to know and now never would. Then he saw the name of Kerr, the captain's servant, who had chosen to stay with the ship and serve under the purser.

And there was Declan Keane at the very end: the master's mate who had joined the mutiny.

Nathan thought for a moment and then he found pen and ink and wrote the name of Dermot Quinn at the bottom of the list.

Then he picked up the letter from his mother. It was thicker than she usually wrote – she was not a great one for writing letters and he wondered if it would contain news of the divorce – but she had enclosed another letter

with it and he saw with a shock that it was from Mary
Wollstonecraft. It was addressed to his mother, but after
reading the first page he saw why Lady Catherine had sent
it on to him.

I pray that your son Nathan may still be alive and in
good health, and that you will give him my good
wishes and inform him that I have received a letter
purporting to be from his friend and mine, Sara,
Countess of Turenne, who was believed to have
died upon the guillotine.

The letter was sent from the Vendée several
months since and reached me in Le Havre by a
most circuitous route, the region being plunged into
the most violent conflict between Royalist rebels
and troops loyal to the Republic. It is, as far as I can
tell, in Sara's hand – though I do not know it well
and have no papers with which to compare it.
However, it contains details of her escape from the
Place du Trône where she was to be executed among
the last of those condemned in the time of the
Terror.

According to this account, she and another
prisoner, also a woman, managed to free their hands
and jump from the cart as it approached the square.
Her companion was apprehended by the guards but
Sara escaped with the aid of some among the crowd
who smuggled her from Paris that same night.
Believing herself still to be in the greatest peril she
made her way by degrees to the Vendée where she

felt herself to be safe from pursuit. However, the situation there is extremely volatile and the region is under martial law which is why she has been unable to communicate news of her escape to her friends and most especially to her young son whom she still believes to be in Paris. It also makes it impossible for me to verify this account or to write back.

However, I am assured that Nathan will wish to know of this news as soon as possible and that she sends him her love and her hope that they will meet again.

That is all I know for the present and all I have time to write, but I trust I shall shortly be in England when you will hear in person from

Your very dear friend,
Mary Imlay

Nathan sat for a long, long moment holding the letter in his hand. The blood had drained from his face. He felt a mixture of emotions. There was joy – somewhere – but it was buried under a weight of doubt, and a terrible anxiety. How long since the letter had been written? He turned it over in his hands: 5 November 1794. Over three months ago. And how many months before that had Sara written her own letter? If it *was* Sara.

On the deck above, he heard the sounds of the men at the capstan and the notes of the fiddler finding his tune . . . And then they began to sing. And somehow news of their destination must have made itself known to them

– through Gabriel, most likely – for they were singing the
song of homecoming.

> '*Farewell and adieu to you Spanish ladies,*
> *Farewell and adieu to you ladies of Spain*
> *For we've orders to sail for old England*
> *Though we hope in a short time to see you again.*
> *Oh . . .*'

And now the great stamp and shout as they put their
backs into the capstan:

> '*We'll rant and we'll roar like true British sailors,*
> *We'll rant and we'll roar all on the salt sea,*
> *Until we strike soundings in the Channel of old*
> *England,*
> *From Ushant to Scilly is thirty-five leagues.*'

Acknowledgements

———◆———

Many thanks to Martin Fletcher and Jo Stansall at Headline; to Gustavo Placer Cervera, Ambassador John Dew, Richard Gott, Hal Klepak and Tim Marchant for sharing their knowledge of Cuba, past and present; to Fizz Carr for sharing her knowledge of sheep on the Sussex Downs; to Cate Olsen and Nash Robbins of Much Ado Books in Alfriston for providing me with obscure and invaluable reference books on 18th century life in Sussex and Cuba; to the staff of the Reading Room at the National Maritime Museum in Greenwich and especially to Brian Thynne of the NMM for digging out some remarkable 18th-century charts of the Caribbean and the waterways around New Orleans; to the captain and crew of the *Earl of Pembroke* at Square Sail in Charlestown and to Michael Ann and Ian Tullett for all their help with sailing and the sea; to Henry Escudero and Margaret Ann for their hospitality and guidance at the Jungle Lodge in

Bocas del Toro off the coast of Panama; and to Sharon Goulds for arranging my trip to Cuba and being such a stimulating and entertaining travelling companion.

History

The Tide of War combines fiction with fact – or at least what is known to be fact – and readers might like to know where the lines have been drawn.

In 1794, when the book starts, the French Revolution was five years old and had more or less run its course. The French had guillotined King Louis XVI and his queen Marie Antoinette and established a Republic based on the principles of Liberty, Fraternity and Equality. This had resulted in war with the rest of Europe which was still, on the whole, ruled by kings and queens, emperors and empresses. Faced with a war for their survival and undermined by royalists and dissidents in France itself, the leaders of the Revolution resorted to a rule of Terror.

By the summer of 1794, the majority of Frenchmen and women had had more than enough of this bloodletting. Robespierre and his closest allies on the Committee of Public Safety were overthrown in the coup of Thermidor and a new, more moderate government took power. But the war continued.

At the beginning of *The Tide of War* the rival armies had reached a position of stalemate and Britain decided to take advantage of its naval supremacy by launching an attack on the French possessions in the West Indies. A major armada was being prepared – the biggest ever to leave the shores of Britain at that date. The rest is fiction – but I have used two real-life characters who played a significant, if shady part in the true history of these times.

One of them is Baron Francisco Luis Hector de Carondelet who was governor-general of Louisiana and West Florida, then part of the vast Spanish Empire in North America, an empire covering most of the present-day USA from the Mississippi to the Pacific Ocean.

Carondelet fought a losing battle against the encroachments of the French and the British and, more particularly, the rapidly expanding population of the United States. In the National Archives of Cuba (No 48 Secret, Seccion de Floridas Legajos 2, 11) there is a despatch from Carondelet expressing his fear of 'the immoderate ambition of a new people, adventurous and hostile to all subjection, who have gone on gathering and multiplying in the silence of peace since the recognition of the independence of the United States'. Written in 1794, it is chillingly prophetic, at least from a Spanish point of view. In his letter to the Duke of Alcudia, Secretary of State in Madrid, Carondelet writes:

'This vast and restless population, progressively

driving the Indian tribes before them and upon us,
seek to possess themselves of all the vast regions
which the Indians occupy between the Ohio and
Mississippi rivers, the Gulf of Mexico and the
Apalache mountains, thus becoming our neighbours at the same time that they demand with
menaces the free navigation of the Mississippi . . .
Their roving spirit and the readiness with which
these people procure sustenance and shelter,
facilitates rapid settlement. A rifle and a little corn-
meal in a bag is sufficient for an American wandering alone in the woods for a month; with the rifle he
kills wild cattle and deer for food and also defends
himself against the savages; the corn-meal soaked
serves as bread; with tree-trunks placed transversely
he forms a house, and even an impregnable fort
against the Indians; the cold does not terrify him
and when the family grows weary of one locality it
moves to another and settles there with the same
ease . . . Who shall warrant that our few inhabitants
will not unite with joy and eagerness with men who
offering them their help and protection for the
securing of independence, self-government and self-
taxation, will flatter them with the spirit of liberty
and the hope of free, extensive and lucrative
commerce?'

One of these men was the other major historical character
I have used in the novel – Gilbert Imlay.
Imlay began his career as an officer in Washington's

army fighting for independence from the British. He was thought to have turned traitor and become a British spy but it seems likely that he was part of a select band of secret agents working for General Washington, a kind of pioneer CIA known as 'Washington's Boys'.

After the war, Imlay followed the great pioneer Daniel Boone across the Appalachians into the territories that became Kentucky and Tennessee and bought 17,000 acres of land on the Licking River. In the hope of encouraging immigrants to the area – and enhancing the value of his land – he wrote a book: *A Topographical Description of the Western Territory of North America* published in London by Debrett in 1792. But his enthusiasm did not stop with literature. It is likely he was one of the men Carondelet feared were planning to invade the region to 'liberate' it from Spanish rule. Fearful that their activities would bring war between Spain and the United States, President Washington ordered the arrest of the leading conspirators and Imlay disappeared for a while. He is suspected of being employed as a Spanish agent in Florida under the name *Gilberto*, or Agent Number Thirty-seven – though it is possible he was always working secretly for Washington. But at any rate, in 1792 he turned up in Revolutionary France.

In 1793, when France declared war on both England and Spain, Imlay set himself up in Le Havre and Paris as a shipping agent, importing goods past the British block-ade. He also became the lover of Mary Wollstonecraft, the British pioneer feminist who had moved to Paris to write about the Revolution and found herself in danger of imprisonment as an enemy alien. As Imlay's 'wife' – no one knows for certain whether they were married or not – Wollstonecraft became an American citizen and continued to live in France throughout the time of the Terror. In May, 1794, she gave birth to Imlay's child in Le Havre but shortly after this Imlay moved to London where he began an affair with an actress living in Charlotte Street. His activities over the winter of 1794–95 remain elusive. We know only that Mary wrote increasingly desperate letters to him from Le Havre, begging him to rejoin her and their child.

There is no evidence that he was either working for the British or that he returned to North America – but nor is there any doubt that his intrigues continued. In the Paris Archives des Affaires Etrangeres, Louisiane et Florides 1792–1803, there are two documents entitled 'Observations du Capitain Imlay' and 'Memoire sur la Louisiane' relating Imlay's plans for the invasion and conquest of Spanish Louisiana and New Orleans, written during the Terror in 1792 and submitted to Lazarre Carnot, the military expert on the Committee of Public Safety. It is these plans that form the basis for the plot of *The Tide of War*.

SETH HUNTER

The Time of Terror

1793: the French have killed their king and are about to embark on the violent period of bloodletting known as the Terror. Brig-sloop Commander Nathan Peake is on smuggler patrol off the Sussex coast and desperate for some real action. As revolutionary France declares war on England, he seizes his chance.

Peake is given a vital mission: to destroy the French economy by smuggling millions of French banknotes across the Channel and into the heart of Paris. His operation leads him from perilous seas to the Empire of the Dead – a labyrinth of catacombs under the French capital where bodies are buried, secrets hidden and plots hatched.

But as opposition to the Terror mounts, Peake is forced to leave Paris and join the storm-tossed British squadrons in the Atlantic in the first thunderous battle between the rival navies.

The Time of Terror is the first in a trilogy of novels featuring Nathan Peake, British naval officer and spy during the war with Revolutionary France, and is historical adventure fiction at its thrilling best.

978 0 7553 4714 8

headline
review

To Play The Fox

Frank Barnard

North Africa, 23 October 1942. The eve of El Alamein, the battle that turned the Second World War.

Two RAF fighter pilots will play their part: the Englishman Kit Curtis in an unarmed photo-reconnaissance Spitfire, and Ossie Wolf, American volunteer.

Since they flew together during the Siege of Malta, both men have taken different paths, Curtis following his conscience, shaken by the human cost of war, Wolf insouciant and headstrong, killer in the air, liability on the ground.

But Alamein unites them in a desperate struggle for survival as Curtis, downed by a Luftwaffe ace, finds Wolf on a mission that could change the course of war. And together they encounter the Desert Fox himself.

TO PLAY THE FOX is a heart-pounding thriller of non-stop action and suspense, a triumph of the unexpected twist, a tour de force that will leave you breathless.

Praise for Frank Barnard:

'A gripping fusion of thrills and historical plausibility . . . a fine balance of freshness and authenticity' *Daily Telegraph*

'A gritty story . . . the detail that he imparts gives this book an authentic feel. A jolly good read' *Sunday Express*

978 0 7553 3892 4

headline

ROBERT RYAN

Empire of Sand

The First World War rages in Europe, but intelligence officer Thomas Edward Lawrence has been consigned to the Map Room at GHQ in Cairo. Yet, spurred on by personal tragedy, he is about to unlock a secret that will alter the course of history.

Lawrence is convinced that an Arab revolt is the only way to remove the Ottoman presence and achieve a free Arabia. But through his network of spies, alarming reports reach him of a tribal uprising against the British, orchestrated by infamous German agent Wilhelm Wassmuss. Hostages have been taken and the War Office in London immediately despatch government assassin Captain Harold Quinn to Cairo on a deadly mission.

With a shared purpose, Quinn and Lawrence begin the hazardous journey to the deserts of Persia. They soon discover that their German nemesis is an experienced master of stealth and deception. But has he finally met his match when he confronts the shrewd and resourceful tactician, Lawrence of Arabia?

Praise for *EMPIRE OF SAND*:

'Plenty of action, sharp dialogue and swift characterisation. The whole is intelligently structured so that this is absorbing and thoughtful as well as tense and exciting' *Daily Telegraph*

978 0 7553 2926 7

headline
review

The Guns of El Kebir

John Wilcox

'Fonthill, if things go wrong, you are dispensable . . . To repeat, you will be on your own.'

1882. Lieutenant General Sir Garnet Wolseley is under pressure. News of an uprising against the British powers in Egypt has reached London, and he must react decisively and forcefully. But there is little time to assemble an army and, for his campaign to succeed, he needs someone on the ground to assess the movements and strength of the Egyptian rebels.

Fresh from a scouting mission in South Africa, former army captain Simon Fonthill is kicking his heels in Brecon. When the request from Wolseley comes, Fonthill and his servant, '352' Jenkins, accept the assignment, fully aware of the dangers they will face in hostile terrain without back up.

But they could never have foreseen the bloodshed that awaits them in the desert at Tel el Kebir . . .

Acclaim for John Wilcox's Simon Fonthill novels:

'Grown-up *Boy's Own* stuff, a pacy read' *Sunday Express*

'Full of action and brave deeds. If you are a fan of Simon Scarrow or Wilbur Smith, then this is for you' *Historical Novels Review*

'A hero to match Sharpe or Hornblower . . . Wilcox shows a genius for bringing to light the heat of battle' *Northern Echo*

978 0 7553 2721 8

headline

Now you can buy any of these other bestselling
Headline books from your bookshop
or *direct from the publisher.*